THE BEAR'S CLAWS

A NOVEL OF WORLD WAR III

ANDREW KNIGHTON
RUSSELL PHILLIPS

SHILKA PUBLISHING

CHARACTERS

1st Motor Rifle Company

Leontev, Captain Seraphim — commanding officer.
 Valeev, Lieutenant Filip — zampolit (political officer).
 Chugainov, Lieutenant — commander, 1st Platoon.
 Egorov, Lieutenant — commander, 2nd Platoon.

3rd Platoon

Tikhomirov, Lieutenant Padorin — commanding officer.
 Rakovich, Praporshchik Vladislav Ivanovich — deputy commander.

1st Section

Zimyatov, Sergeant Makar Alexandrovich — squad leader; close friend of Rakovich.
 Rebane, Markus — BMP gunner and assistant squad leader.
 Lobachov, Jaromir — BMP driver and mechanic.
 Niyazi, Elman — rifleman and medic.

2nd Section

Kholodov, Sergeant Pyotr — squad leader; former artist.
    Plakans, Raivo — BMP gunner and assistant squad leader.
    Akayev, Yajub — BMP driver and mechanic; Kyrgyzstani.
    Tammert, Oskar — machine gunner.
    Obolensky, Ilia — rifleman and medic.
    Khymka, Serhiy — rifleman.
    Beletsky, Radoslav — SAM gunner.

3rd Section

Zinoviev, Sergeant Leonid — squad leader.
    Dologodin, Fediv — BMP gunner and assistant squad leader.
    Shistyev, Cheslav — BMP driver and mechanic.
    Snegur, Turpal — rifleman.
    Szolkowski, Stasis — rifleman.

Civilians in Leningrad

Anna Ivanovna Rakovich — chemistry student, Vladislav's sister.
    Tatyana Orlova — chemistry student, Anna's best friend, Zimyatov's girlfriend.
    "Papa" Ivan Mikhailovich Rakovich — Anna and Valdislav's father.
    Vadim — cafe owner and veteran of the Afghan war.
    Pavel Semenov — union leader.
    Boris — factory worker, union member.
    Klara Ivanova — union organiser.
    Mikhail — print worker, union organiser.
    Maksim Pavlov — Anna's ex-boyfriend, son of a Communist Party official.

1

THE WILL OF THE PEOPLE

Vladislav Ivanovich Rakovich sat at the window of his small barracks room, looking out across the vehicle yard and the barbed wire fence to the forest beyond. He tapped his pen ever faster against his knee, a drum roll beating out the fruitless seconds. Anna would have known how to describe those woods, the way their shadows haunted and yet called to him. She would have been able to pick out the words that evoked this scene, to set this moment on paper before the unit was moved on to some other concrete shit hole in some other corner of the GDR, this sorry Soviet half of the once mighty German nation.

Of course, if his sister was here then he wouldn't be writing to her in Leningrad. Just thinking about it was a waste of time.

Movement down by the gate caught his eye. A command car sat outside the barrier, motor running. The driver was shouting at the sentry to let them through, but the sentry was some conscript from the backwoods of Siberia and they couldn't understand each other's accents. The driver gesticulated furiously and the sentry waved his rifle around. If they'd been in Rakovich's unit, he would have smacked their heads together for acting like such idiots, especially in front of senior officers. But then, his men didn't get to drive generals around.

He cast the pen aside and picked up a newspaper. It was from the capitalist half of Germany, contraband he'd confiscated off Szolkowski. The date read 4th of May 1982, making it weeks out of date, but Rakovich didn't care about that. The news would all be lies anyway, propaganda cooked up by the decadent western press. He'd kept it to practice his meagre German, not to learn about life beyond the Iron Curtain.

The main photo was of a warship, smoke billowing from a hole in its side. It was a melancholy sight, a mighty machine sinking into the depths. All around were men fleeing in lifeboats, while in the background towered a headland Rakovich had seen in some schoolbook years before, though he was fucked if he could remember where it was.

He picked up the hefty German dictionary he'd spent his spare money on and tried to make sense of the article. The ship was British, he understood that much. It had been attacked by Argentine saboteurs just off Gibraltar — that was the rock, wasn't it? Apparently the Argentinians had already taken some islands off the British, but now the Spanish were angry and NATO were getting involved.

Rakovich didn't know much about Argentina, but he hoped they kicked the shit out of the British, and the rest of NATO too while they were at it.

Someone knocked on the door. Rakovich hastily shoved the newspaper under his mattress, then went to answer.

An infantryman stood in the hallway, one of the men from Zimyatov's section. He saluted smartly.

"Praporshchik Rakovich," the infantryman said. "Lieutenant Valeev requests that you come to the main garage."

"On my way." Rakovich grabbed his jacket and strode down the corridor after the private. He shook his head as he went. He liked Filip Valeev, and that in itself was a problem. A company's political officer shouldn't be liked, he should be respected. The zampolit should order people like Rakovich around, not request their presence.

Rakovich had spent three years in the army, rising to become a praporshchik, that distinctive Soviet rank above NCOs and below commissioned officers. Three years of hard work and commitment, of learning obedience and how to get others to obey. That time had taught him a lesson he'd always secretly known, but that Valeev seemed immune to — that you got more done with fear and fists than with kind words.

When Rakovich reached the garage, it was echoing to the sound of excited chatter. Nearly the whole company was here, including the officers, none of whom had to listen to Valeev's talks on the forward march of international communism. Most of them kept well away from this place, with its smells of diesel and dry rot. Something big must be happening if they'd joined their men today.

Makar Alexandrovich Zimyatov was leaning against a wall at the side of the garage, watching proceedings with the same cynical smile he'd been wearing on the day they met. A sergeant's rank might have given him responsibilities, but nothing could force him to treat the world seriously.

"Any idea what this is, Vlad?" he asked.

Rakovich shook his head. "Hoped you'd know."

"It can't be anything good. Maybe they're rotating us out to Siberia."

"Why would they do that?"

"Those snowmen can't protect themselves."

"They're probably capitalists. Otherwise the warm glow of communist virtue would keep them warm."

Zimyatov laughed. "Because we're all so virtuous?"

"Heroes of the revolution, from our calloused feet to our retreating hairlines."

"I can't understand why you're not a general already, with inspiring words like that."

"And I can't see shit from back here. I'm going to find a better view."

Rakovich climbed onto one of the BMPs, the armoured vehicles that filled half the garage. It was a squat, ugly machine, and Rakovich liked that he and his transport had that much in common. With the tracks on its sides and a low turret on top carrying a cannon and missile launcher, it was the sort of vehicle that a younger Vladislav Ivanovich Rakovich would have pointed at eagerly during military parades as he tried to spot the tanks. But the BMP was something else, with lighter weaponry and seating in the back for a full squad of infantry. This flat-topped contraption, with its chipped green camouflage paint, was how the Red Army would ride to war.

Sitting on the edge of the BMP, Rakovich could see over the heads of his comrades, most of whom were taller than him. Across the crowd, Lieutenant Valeev was also climbing one of the BMPs. He looked out earnestly across the men, bright eyes shining while he waited for silence to fall.

"Comrades!" Valeev called out, his voice echoing from the concrete walls. "As I warned you yesterday, capitalist Germany has become more belligerent. Now our comrades in the intelligence services have discovered that they, with their NATO allies, are planning to attack us."

Rakovich watched the reactions of the crowd. In front of him, rifleman Szolkowski leaned toward Sergeant Zinoviev.

"At least someone here has some intelligence," Szolkowski hissed.

Rakovich leaned over and smacked Szolkowski across the back of the head. The rifleman looked around, snarling with anger, then hid his rage when he saw who his assailant was.

"Show some respect," growled Rakovich.

"Yes, Praporshchik," Szolkowski mumbled, turning his attention back to Valeev.

"We will soon be at war," Valeev said.

Several men gasped or cursed. One cheered.

Rakovich just stared. It didn't seem real. Germany was meant to be a safe posting, a country where everything was too valuable for either side to start a fight. The company was due to sit here menacing the border for a few months and then head home. However much the government talked about war with the West, the reality was too absurd.

And what about nuclear weapons? If they started fighting the Americans, wouldn't somebody fire the nukes? He thought of

Leningrad and of Anna, fervently hoping that those terrible weapons never flew.

"This was not our choice," Valeev continued. "But once again, the security of our homeland is threatened by the Germans. Our fathers and grandfathers defeated them in the Great Patriotic War. Now it is our turn to show them the ferocity of the Soviet bear."

More cheering this time. Szolkowski glanced around, grinned, and joined in. Zinoviev followed his lead.

Valeev waved them into silence. He was smiling now, even as he talked of war.

"This time, the Germans have new allies. We, comrades, will be fighting the British. Make no mistake, they are good soldiers, but we are better, and we will be fighting to protect our homeland, to protect our families. So make sure your weapons are cleaned and ready. Two days from now, we go to war."

As one last cheer went up, Rakovich looked around for his men. Lieutenant Tikhomirov, the platoon's commanding officer, wasn't here. In his absence, it fell to Rakovich to make sure the men were ready.

"Third Platoon!" he shouted, standing on the BMP so they couldn't miss him. "Gather round!"

As others dispersed, his men gathered around to listen to Rakovich. They were a motley band, a mix of conscripts and professionals from across the Soviet Union, bound together by no more than love of their homeland. But they were his motley band, and whatever they had to do tomorrow, they were going to do it well.

"Lobachov, Akayev, Shistyev," he said, starting with the drivers. "Make sure the BMPs are fuelled up and ready to roll. I don't want us stuck in a queue at the pumps while the war's starting."

Akayev gave him a blank stare, and Rakovich realised that he'd again hit the limits of the Kyrgyzstani mechanic's Russian. If he weren't so good with engines, Rakovich would have had him packed off months ago. But knowing Akayev, his machine was fuelled and ready to go already.

"The rest of you," Rakovich said. "Every weapon gets stripped down, cleaned, and tested. Check your ammunition. Check your rations. If you're short of anything, tell your sergeant. Anyone who isn't ready in two hours answers to my fists.

"Beletsky, make sure that missile of yours is ready. NATO like their helicopters, let's show them why a BMP is better."

The men cheered again, and now Rakovich was grinning, just like he'd seen Valeev do. The anticipation of action made his heart beat faster. At last he'd have a chance to lead in battle.

Since the moment he first donned his uniform, he'd dreamed of making a career in the army. To do that, he needed to prove himself and earn an officer's epaulettes. What better chance would he have than this?

The men moved off, discussing how real war would compare to training exercises. Watching them, Rakovich had his own thoughts. He'd never been to Afghanistan, unlike some of his peers. He knew men who had and he'd heard their stories, each one full of horror and loss. Surely this would be different? The British, the Germans, and the rest of NATO were capitalists, not religious fanatics like the mujahideen. They wouldn't shown the same brutal dedication to their cause.

Would they?

If Anna was here, he would have asked her. His sister was smart enough to go to university. She knew how the world worked. But Anna was in a safe place hundreds of miles from the front, and for that he was grateful.

He would just have to ask Valeev instead.

As he leapt down from the BMP, he noticed a pair of boots protruding from the rear doors. He stomped around to find Sergeant Kholodov sat in one of the seats that lined the middle of the troop compartment, facing out through a gun port in the side. His sleeves were rolled up, pencil and paper in hand.

At the sight of his superior, Kholodov thrust the paper away, not quite quick enough to hide a sketch of the forest beyond the fence.

"That doesn't look like weapons maintenance to me," Rakovich growled.

"No, sir." Kholodov bolted upright, banged his head against the ceiling, and smiled sheepishly. He was a pretty bastard, Rakovich would give him that, with his blond hair and his boyish looks. Probably had women all over him back home. But pretty looks didn't get a man anywhere in Rakovich's platoon. "I was just—"

"You were slacking off again." Rakovich stepped inside the vehicle, grabbed a fistful of that pretty blond hair, and hauled the sergeant up against the wall. There wasn't much space around the seats, nowhere for Kholodov to try to squirm into. "You might be an artist back home, Kholodov. You might be the finest talent in Moscow for all I care. But out here you're just one more soldier like the rest of us. And I'm not letting those other poor bastards die because of your laziness. So see to your guns, see to your transport, and see to your men."

He knocked Kholodov's head back against the wall one last time, then strode away.

"And next time tuck your fucking shirt in," he called back as he went.

RAKOVICH HAD SET up the private lounge on their first day on base. Trying to get the lay of the land, he'd noticed a door ajar and gone inside. There he'd found a dusty office half filled with abandoned furniture. A couple of hours of hauling out broken chairs and rearranging what remained had created a comfortable space to retreat to, as long as you ignored the slightly odd smells from a stained sofa and mismatched armchairs. The simple expedient of an "AUTHORISED PERSONNEL ONLY" sign kept out everyone except Rakovich and the people he liked, which amounted to Zimyatov and a couple of sergeants from third company. He had considered inviting some of the men from his platoon, like Akayev, the crazy Kyrgyzstani driver, or Obolensky, second section's medic. But inviting one of them in risked opening the floodgates to the rest. Besides, he was in a position of command now, and his socialising should reflect that.

Third company had shipped out ahead of the rest, to start

preparing positions along the front line, so this evening it was just him and Zimyatov in their hidden club house. A small black and white TV was on in one corner, showing a football match. Zimyatov, half an eye always on the game, poured them both tea and added a slug of vodka, while Rakovich dealt cards onto a coffee table.

"Are your boys ready?" Rakovich asked as he put the remains of the deck down.

"Ready as they'll ever be. Rebane's been bitching about not having enough ammunition for the cannon, but Niyazi has a contact in supplies who claims he can sort us out. How are the rest of them?"

"Kholodov thinks he's still at art school and Zinoviev's so dim he can barely hit the ground with his own arse. When I'm not forcing one of them to do his job I'm telling the other how to do his. But fuck it, they can point a gun, they're good enough to fight for Mother Russia."

"The mighty Red Army, the world's greatest fighting force."

"I assume all the capitalist soldiers are children and cardboard cutouts."

"That would make the firing range more realistic."

"It might even make our commanders look competent."

"Oh come on!" Zimyatov leapt from his seat and shouted at the TV. "That was clearly a foul!"

"Are you here to watch or to play?"

"A bit of both."

Zimyatov sat back down and took a good gulp of tea. Then they picked up their cards and started to play.

Outside the dirt-smeared window, a truck rolled past, laden down with parts and ammunition. Bit by bit, the whole base was emptying out, depositing its contents across what would soon be the fighting front. It seemed strange to Rakovich that they could still sit like this, their lives peaceful and normal, when death and destruction lay less than forty-eight hours away. But he supposed that this was how it had always been, from ancient Sparta through to the Great Patriotic War. Long stretches of quiet before the time of destruction came.

"I was talking with Tatyana yesterday," Zimyatov said, looking from his hand to the TV and back again. "She mentioned you and Anna."

Rakovich frowned. Even with his best friend, this wasn't a topic he knew how to talk about.

"My sister has no respect for what I do. She's happy to waste the life our mother gave her on parties and idle chatter."

"Sometimes idle chatter is good. Even you crack a joke from time to time."

"I'm the funniest fucker on this base. Just give me a clown nose and I could do children's parties. But there's a difference between enjoying life and dedicating it to your own pleasure."

"I can't imagine why she finds you judgemental and condescending."

"And I can't imagine why more people don't tell you what's on their mind."

"Oh, for fuck's sake!" Zimyatov shook a fist at the TV, then turned back to Rakovich. "Sorry, you're right. Guess we're not great listeners in my family."

He poured more vodka into his tea, but Rakovich held out a hand over the top of his cup.

"No more for me. And you should consider how much you drink — you're going to need a clear head."

Zimyatov snorted.

"This is nothing. I could have half the bottle and still be fine tomorrow."

"So could your father. Do you want to end up like him?"

Zimyatov froze, the bottle still inches above Rakovich's cup. They stared at each other and the corner of Zimyatov's eye twitched.

"I'm sorry," Rakovich said, looking away. "That was—"

"That was what I needed." Zimyatov put the stopper in the bottle and rolled it away into a corner of the room. "You're right, and sometimes I need you to be right even when I don't want to hear it."

Rakovich scooped up the cards and shuffled them, using another round to move the conversation on.

"You should make the most of this," he said. "It might be your last chance to win my money."

"Screw that. I'll have your back all the way across Germany, just so I can rob you blind at the end."

"And I'll have your back, because what else am I going to do with my money if not lose it?"

"Save it up and settle down?"

"I don't see myself with the quiet little house and the quiet little lady, do you?"

"No, I see you with a solid, red-faced matriarch who screams at you every time you breathe wrong."

"It is the Russian way. But so is death in the army, and I know which I choose."

They laughed again, while on the TV the half-time whistle blew. Outside, another transport truck rolled by, heading for war.

2

BEFORE THE WAR

R akovich stood in the corner of the briefing room, clutching his gurgling stomach. He didn't know if the cooks had been in a rush or if his nerves were keeping the food from settling, but his guts hadn't felt this bad in years. He half expected the sound to echo back from the bare concrete walls, announcing his indignity to the gathered officers and NCOs.

"What the hell is wrong with you, Rakovich?" Captain Leontev snarled.

"Sorry, sir," Rakovich said. "Something I ate."

"Well it had better be done by tomorrow," Leontev said, as if Rakovich could somehow control his digestion.

Lieutenant Tikhomirov gave Rakovich a sympathetic look. Rakovich knew from bitter experience that was all the support his superior would give him. Tikhomirov wasn't a bad man, but he lacked the nerve to stand up to their captain.

"It's started," Leontev said, gesturing at the map spread out on the table in front of them. Twenty men, the leaders of the First Motor Rifle Company, peered over each other's shoulders, trying to take it all in. "Our German allies have launched the first assault. So far, the British have stayed in their defensive positions and haven't had much time to reinforce. Our battalion will knock a hole in their line, then push through and hit the capitalist Germans in the flank. We'll be forming the second echelon of that attack."

"We're not at the front?" asked Rakovich, disappointed.

All afternoon, he'd been building this attack up in his head. He'd imagined charging into action at the head of a band of riflemen, guns blazing as they stormed the British foxholes. As the enemy fled, they would mount up and pursue, driving the capitalists back in disorder, a triumph to earn him his lieutenant's epaulettes.

But instead, they'd just be following along, mopping up stragglers and supervising prisoners.

"Don't be an idiot." Leontev, a veteran of Afghanistan, glared at him from beneath bushy eyebrows. "Everyone knows that the British are hard bastards, especially when they're defending. There'll be plenty of work for us."

"Will there be artillery support, sir?" Lieutenant Tikhomirov asked.

"Of course." The captain smiled. "A battalion of 122mm guns has been attached to us. They'll hit the British with smoke and high explosive as we start the attack. That should keep their anti-tank missiles out of action."

Just the mention of missiles turned everyone's expression grim. They'd all had the training. Some of them had even tried out the anti-tank weapons, firing them at old armoured vehicles on training courses. All it took to kill a BMP and its crew was one lucky hit.

"They'll be targeting the tanks, not us," Rakovich said, trying to lift their spirits. "And the T-80s have special armour that missiles can't penetrate."

"Perhaps you should take over the briefing," Leontev said. "Seeing as you're such an expert."

"Sorry, sir." Rakovich took a step back before his mouth could get him in any more trouble. He couldn't see over the others' shoulders, but he could always look at the map later. Right now, he just wanted to be out of Leontev's sight.

"The artillery won't help with helicopters, so make sure you keep watch for them," Leontev said. "We'll have anti-aircraft support, of course, but they'll be looking out for the whole battalion. Each platoon's missile man should be in the second section, along with the praporshchik. Make sure he's ready to use his missile as soon as you spot enemy aircraft.

"We will be observing radio silence until the attack begins to avoid giving them any warning. The artillery won't start until just before we launch the attack. With luck, we'll catch them drinking tea and just drive right through. If not, they'll find out what Russians are really made of."

They laughed, but it was the hollow, nervous sound of men looking for a reason to be happy.

"Captain Leontev?"

They all turned at the voice from the doorway. Lieutenant Valeev stood there, smiling uncertainly, a mug of tea in his hand.

"I'm conducting a briefing, lieutenant," Leontev said. "Can it wait?"

"I was hoping I might address your men."

Leontev hesitated. Rakovich and Tikhomirov exchanged a surprised look. Valeev might be the political officer, but he was only a lieutenant and so pushing his luck by interrupting like this.

Leontev looked down at the map, then back up at Valeev.

"Why not," he said, stepping back. "We're almost done here anyway. Might as well finish with one of your pretty little speeches."

The assembled officers and NCOs stepped back from the table so that they could all see Valeev as he talked. Only the captain showed a hint of scorn.

"Tomorrow, we go to war," Valeev said. "For the first time in nearly forty years, we have the chance to spread communism in Europe. To bring equality and brotherhood to those oppressed by the capitalist system.

"But this isn't just about us and our neighbours. On the far side of the world, Argentina and her allies are fighting to free the Falkland Islands from British imperialism, to throw back the tentacles of a monster that once spanned the world, bending the global proletariat to the interests of London's bankers and aristocrats. With NATO's attention divided, we and the Argentinians have a real chance to bring about change. To discard tyranny and bring freedom to people half a world away.

"We fight for our families. We fight for our homeland. We fight for this continent, divided by the capitalist tyrants. But we fight for more than that. We fight for a better future."

Rakovich stood tall and smiled at the words. This was the war he had been waiting to fight since he was a child, a chance for him to make the world a better place. His mother would have been proud.

Across from Rakovich, Sergeant Kholodov cleared his throat then began to sing. His voice was far deeper and richer than Rakovich had heard it before. The words of the State Anthem rolled out across the room, transforming a humble concrete box into a place of power and dignity. Rakovich's heart stirred, remembering how his mother had taught him the song when he was small. Around him, men straightened their backs, chests swelling with pride. Soon they all joined in, a chorus defined more by passion than by tunefulness, but which made Rakovich's heart soar.

"Long live the creation of the will of the people,

"The united, mighty Soviet Union!"

RAKOVICH STOOD with Lieutenant Tikhomirov in the doorway of the garage, watching the men load their equipment into the BMPs. The place was full of noise and bustle. They had to be on the road in forty-five minutes, and that meant everything had to happen right now, from fuelling the transports to packing spare socks. No amount of manoeuvres had prepared Rakovich for a base swarming into action on such short notice.

The Lieutenant scratched at his arm, where the end of a scar protruded from his sleeve, a souvenir of his service in Afghanistan.

"This could be an opportunity for you, Rakovich," Tikhomirov said.

"I'd had the same thought, sir," Rakovich said. "That there might be a chance for promotion."

"You're that eager to see me dead?"

Rakovich flushed with embarrassment. He opened his mouth to explain that he'd meant promotion into other units, or promotion in general, or just a chance to prove himself. But his tongue seemed to have swollen until no coherent words could escape past it.

Tikhomirov laughed.

"I get it, Praporshchik," he said. "And I'll be looking out for opportunities for you. You've earned your shot at an officer's epaulettes."

"Thank you, Lieutenant." Rakovich said. "I've really appreciated your help, teaching me how to fight, how to organise the men, how to lead them in battle. I promise, I won't let you down."

"You'd better not."

Tikhomirov turned to look at Rakovich, his expression serious.

"There's something else you'll need to do, though," he said. "And that's not piss off Leontev."

The mention of the Captain's name made Rakovich grimace.

"What's that guy's problem?" he growled. "He's had it in for me from the start."

"You've got a mind of your own, and Leontev doesn't like what he can't control. Learn to hold your tongue and to do what he says the moment he says it, no matter how stupid it seems. Otherwise he'll keep you where you are until he's got an excuse to court-martial you."

"Can he do that?"

"Should he? No. Can he? Yes. So try to behave yourself while we're in the field."

Rakovich stared at the ground. It felt childish to moan, even inside his head, about how unfair life was. He hadn't done anything to earn a captain like Leontev, or a lieutenant like Tikhomirov, who had enough skill to train him but not enough spine to stand up for him. He was trapped by pettiness and mediocrity, and the only person who could get him out was himself. The question was, did he have the discipline to do it?

"So no leaving a dog turd in the Captain's command seat?" he said at last.

"Not unless it's disguised as a medal."

"I'll see what I can sculpt."

THAT NIGHT, they slept in their vehicles, only a mile from the starting point for the next day's offensive. The sound of distant guns drifted sporadically over the treetops and jets streaked past through the star-scattered sky.

Rakovich couldn't sleep. His whole body was tense, his mind buzzing with possibilities.

By the light of a small electric torch, he walked away from the armoured vehicles and found a quiet place to sit beneath a gnarled old oak. He pulled a battered copy of the Communist Manifesto from his pocket, the same copy his mother had carried when she worked for the party. He spread his writing paper out on the well worn book and tried to write to his sister again.

The words came with difficulty. Or rather, hurtful words came too easily, urging him to pick up their old fight again. To make a point of his diligence and patriotism compared with her carefree ways. To urge her to be responsible in this hour of national need.

If he ever wanted to hear a reply then he needed to quash those words, to focus on the facts and on the moment at hand.

And so he began...

"DEAR ANNA,

"My time has come. I am going to war.

"I do not know what news will have reached you by now, but the Soviet Union has been attacked."

HE PAUSED. They had been attacked, hadn't they? Except that Valeev had talked about attacking NATO while its attention was divided. And if they were the defenders, why weren't the British coming to them?

He shrugged off the doubts. His mother had taught him that the world was not always simple. The only way to get through its complexities was to keep a goal in mind. The goal of equality. The goal of communism.

"I WILL BE JOINING the second wave of our advance," he continued. "I can't tell you more, but I can tell you that I am proud to be part of this war, to serve my country as I always swore I would.

"Don't worry about me. I will keep myself safe and come visit you when this is over. I know that you did not want me to stay in the army, but I'm sure you see now that I have done the right thing. I will protect our homeland for you and papa, and do right by mother's memory.

"This war will not be like the ones we have fought before. Everything has changed since last we faced the German menace. But I am ready. Russia will emerge victorious. We must, for all the world's sake.

"Your loving brother

"Vlad."

3

POLITICS AND PICKLES

Anna Ivanovna Rakovich stepped out of the chemistry department and into the bustle of Sredniy Prospekt. A tram rattled past, its overhead wires shaking, its tightly packed passengers staring out at rows of pale-fronted shops and apartments. A warm summer breeze blew away the worst of the traffic fumes and flapped Anna's skirts against her legs. She laughed as she walked down the steps to the pavement.

"It's like hanging out with a small child," her friend Tatyana said, smiling even as she shook her head. "What's got you grinning this time?"

"It was just tickling my legs," Anna said.

She removed a hand from the pile of books clutched to her chest, so that she could point at the offending piece of clothing. The books slid from her other arm, tumbling down the steps and into the street. Her heels clattered against the steps as she ran down after them, snatching at the papers. An ageing textbook exploded as it hit the pavement, scattering pages of essays and diagrams in every direction.

Anna darted between the passers by, trying to catch the escaping pages. She lunged between the legs of a stern man in a smart suit, who scowled at her over the top of his glasses.

"So sorry!" Anna waved the papers. "Don't want to let all this learning go to waste."

She tried to look serious. Anyone that well dressed was probably a party official, and it was never a good idea to upset people in positions of power. She managed to keep her composure just long enough for him to give a derisive snort and stride away, but by the time Tatyana caught up, Anna was bent double laughing.

"Did you see his face?" she asked, cramming pages back inside the broken book. "He's probably never had a girl that close to his you-know-what."

"He's a party man." Tatyana glared after him, her eyes tiny points of menace behind her spectacles. "I'm sure he has a whore for every day of the week."

"Tatya!" Anna grinned at the scandalous accusation. "I thought you were a good daughter of the motherland, not a filthy-mouthed purveyor of scandal."

"You think that's scandalous?" Tatyana said. "You should hear what they—"

"Excuse me." A young man approached them, holding out a handful of pages from the book. "Are these yours?"

He favoured Anna with a lopsided smile. With his tousled hair and slim figure, he looked like a gangling puppet from a child's entertainment, which made Anna laugh again. But he was at least a cute children's puppet.

"Um, I..." The young man blushed. "Did I say something funny?"

Tatyana rolled her eyes. "No, she's just hysterical. Think of it as a tiny breakdown and you'll be on the right track."

"Ignore her." Anna took the proffered papers. "And thank you. I wasn't laughing at you, I promise. It's just one of those days."

"A lot of your days involve destroying chemistry books and laughing hysterically?" He raised an eyebrow.

"The fumes in the department get to you after a while."

"Sounds like I chose the wrong subject. History is just old books full of old men."

"You don't seem all that old."

"Well I—"

"Excuse us." Tatyana took Anna by the elbow and started leading her away. "Nice meeting you, history man."

"Hey!" Anna protested half-heartedly as they made their down the street. "What was that about?"

"Remember what you said after Maksim?" Tatyana asked sternly.

"That I was going to concentrate on my studies." Anna sighed. "Fine, let's find a café we can go study in."

An hour later they sat huddled over tea and lecture notes amid the familiar noises and smells of Vadim's café. Vadim's wasn't much to look at from the outside — just one more concrete shop front in a street filled with simple, brutalist architecture. But inside, it was a place of warmth and comfort. Vadim had painted each chair using brightly coloured leftovers and sanded down the tables to hide their scars. There wasn't much food on offer, just like there wasn't much food in the shops. But he somehow seemed to have an unstoppable source of tea, and it was worth spending what little cash Anna could spare to sit here and enjoy a steaming cup, away from the realities of study and family.

She sighed and leaned back in her seat.

"One can concentrate too hard on learning," she declared. "We need variety or our minds will grow stagnant."

"You don't mean variety," Tatyana said, not looking up from her notes. "You mean boys and parties."

"No!" Anna said indignantly, tucking back a few strands of her long blonde hair. "I just mean something different. One cannot live by chemical equations alone."

"Actually, you could describe all of life in terms of—"

"You know what I mean!"

Tatyana leaned back in her seat, giving Anna an evaluative look. Then she glanced around the café, checking that no-one was nearby, before leaning forward.

"You want something different?" she asked quietly. "Come with me to the meeting tonight. There's a man from Poland speaking. He works with the Solidarity trade union, he's seen what's happening there. If you want something other than chemistry, how about learning to change the world?"

Anna leaned forward too, curling protectively over her cup of tea, as if the precious elixir might be tainted by the dangers of treasonous talk.

"Tatya, you know I don't like the system," she whispered. "The way the party treated my father after mother's death. All the shortages and the restrictions, while men in suits get lives of luxury. But just talking about these things can get you sent away."

"You're just worried about what your brother would say."

"You think I haven't said these things to him? Why do you think we barely talk any more?"

"I'm sorry." Tatyana looked away, embarrassed. "I shouldn't have mentioned him."

"It's sad, really," Anna said, surprised to hear the words tumbling out of her mouth. "He carries mother's old Manifesto around like it's the last living part of her. It doesn't matter what I say or what I show him. I think he sees criticism of the party as criticism of her."

She swallowed. Not crying in public was another promise she'd made after Maksim, and it looked like she was going to break this one too.

Tatyana's hand touched hers — a soft, brief gesture, but one that reminded her that she wasn't alone.

She forced a smile, then looked up as Vadim approached, a pot of tea in his hands.

"Ladies!" the café owner said, leaning over to refill their cups. "Always a pleasure."

This close, Anna could see every tiny detail of the scarring where his left eye had been. Vadim seldom wore a patch, preferring to let the world see what he had endured, a reminder that he would let it happen again if duty demanded.

"Your brother, he's in the GDR, isn't he?" he asked.

"Yes," Anna said, pausing to enjoy a sip of the tea. "He's a prapor-shchik now, second in command of a platoon."

"I was a praporshchik," Vadim said with pride. "It is good work. And he will be needed now, I think."

"What do you mean?" Tatyana raised an eyebrow.

"You have not heard? There is trouble on the German border. They said the damn British are stirring up war. Filthy capitalist pigs."

Vadim made as if to spit on the floor, then seemed to remember that he would be the one to clear it up. Instead, he cleared his throat.

"What I mean is," he said, "I am glad we have good men like your brother, out there to defend us."

Another customer came in, drawing him away before Anna could ask any questions about Germany. She felt like a great weight was pressing down on her chest, as heavy with dread as when she had heard her mother coughing in the night.

"I'm sure Vlad will be fine," Tatyana said, touching her hand again. "Your brother's as tough as Lenin's leathery corpse."

Anna squeezed her friend's hand.

"Makar will be fine too," she said. "He knows what he's doing."

Tatyana looked away, embarrassed. Unlike Anna, she didn't like talking about her love life. Anna wasn't even sure what had been happening since Vlad introduced Tatyana to Sergeant Makar Zimyatov, but Tatyana had been unusually busy the last time Vlad's unit was on leave, and that was surely a sign.

Reinvigorated by fresh tea, they got back to their studies. All the while, thoughts of war wormed away in the back of Anna's mind. She might feel like she hated Vlad some days, but she loved him really. She didn't want to see him end up like Vadim.

At last, Tatyana gathered up her notes. Anna swallowed the final mouthful of cold tea and got ready to go.

"Are you sure you won't come to the meeting this evening?" Tatyana asked.

Anna hesitated. Just because she couldn't get through to her brother didn't mean that she should accept the world as it was. If they could make the country more equal then maybe young men wouldn't be sent away to die in pointless wars, trying to prove that their way of life was best.

But she didn't want to upset Vlad or her father. And was there really any chance she could change anything? The possibility seemed so remote as to be unreal.

"No," she said, picking up her books. "But thank you for asking."

WHEN ANNA GOT HOME, her father was asleep in his armchair in the corner of the apartment. She kissed him gently on his greying head, put her books down on a corner table, and went to look in the kitchen.

The apartment wasn't large, but Anna had never minded that. It had enough space for her, Papa, and Vlad when he was home. They could fit in some friends and neighbours to help celebrate on special occasions, as long as not many people wanted to sit down, and who wanted to sit around at a party anyway? If anything, the apartment's size gave it a cosy atmosphere. Every inch was filled with memories of family life.

As she'd suspected, the cupboards were almost bare. It wasn't the first shortage she'd lived through, but they seemed to be getting worse. Did that have anything to do with the trouble in Germany? Were the capitalists really trying to strangle Russia's trade, as the newspapers claimed, and now the motherland was fighting back? Or was it all fuss and noise over nothing?

Here and now, it didn't matter. She wanted to make sure that there was food on the table when her father woke up.

She trudged down the stairs of the apartment building, past mould and stains and the smell of urine, crossed the street, and joined the queue for the nearest shop. By this time of day, she hadn't expected many people to be waiting. She'd hoped that she could just buy whatever had been left by those more organised than her. Instead, here she was, joining the little old ladies queueing for their husbands' dinners.

"There was a delivery truck an hour ago," said a woman in a black and blue shawl, treating this mundane event like some herald of great days.

"From the bakery," another added. "I swear, I smelled fresh bread."

Just the thought made Anna's stomach rumble. Maybe this would be worth it after all.

A murmur of excitement rippled down the line. The shoppers at the front seemed to be moving, causing a chain reaction of excited exclamations and people clutching at bags. A big man in a frayed sweater stood at the front of the queue, a stick in his hand, eyeing them with the wary tension of a shepherd watching for wolves.

The queue began to move. With slow, shuffling steps they made their way towards the hope of being fed. The line became more dense, each person pressing up against the one in front, moving those few extra inches closer to their desire.

After half an hour, Anna finally approached the door. Inside, she saw the assortment of assistants every shop was expected to recruit, as part of their patriotic duty to support full employment. One assistant to fetch items from the shelves for shoppers; another to weigh, wrap, and price; a third to make up the bill; a fourth to operate the till; a fifth checking that the purchases matched and then producing a receipt. And overseeing it all the manager, his jaw clenched and arms folded, watching his customers through narrowed eyes.

The manager's stance of eagle-eyed vigilance seemed out of all proportion to what was at stake. The shelves were almost bare already, meagre supplies stripped away by starving shoppers. If a swarm of locusts had arrived, they would have found themselves too late, their work done by the Soviets themselves.

This was the system that her brother defended. A system where ordinary people starved for lack of food. Where little old ladies had to queue in the street for hours. Where a shop couldn't run properly for fear of triggering a riot. No trust, no care, no support. Where was the communism her mother had spoken about, the one of equality and wealth for all? What had happened to the dream?

At last she reached the front. She took a deep breath and flashed the assistant a smile.

"Pickles, please," she said. Her father loved pickles. "And tinned beef, or pork if there's no beef. And bread, of course."

"No bread," the assistant said, handing her a large jar of pickles.

"No bread?" Anna glared at him. She'd queued for hours, and now there was no bread? This was even more ridiculous than usual. "What do you mean, there's no bread?"

"Just what I said," he replied with a shrug.

"But I saw a lady with—"

"There's no more," the assistant said impatiently. "Most of the deliveries aren't coming in, so there's less to go around."

"I heard that all the trucks have been sent to Germany," said an elderly woman two places behind Anna. "The newspapers say that the Germans are going to start another war."

"That's right," said the woman next to her, the one with a baby in her arms. "The army will need all the trucks it can get."

"The Germans would never attack us." An old man waved his walking stick in the air. "We beat them bloody in 1945. They're not stupid enough to try it again."

"But it's not really the Germans, is it?" the mother said. "It's the Americans, using them as puppets to destroy the Soviet Union."

"Americans?" The old man spat. "Americans couldn't fight their way out of a nursery. Why, when I was in Berlin—"

"It's not the same as it was in—"

"They're not the ones who really—"

Suddenly everyone was arguing over everyone else, voices raised and hands waving, faces screwed up or glowing red with anger. Everyone had an opinion and everyone seemed frustrated that the others couldn't understand why they were right.

The thug outside looked in at the fuss, glanced over at the manager, and raised his stick. The manager shook his head. Until his goods were at risk, he wouldn't care how loudly his customers argued.

"They should all just read a newspaper," the till assistant said, as Anna paid for her shopping. "Then they'd know what's going on."

She bit back a response. The newspapers said whatever the politburo wanted them to, regardless of reality, but only a fool would say that out loud.

As she made her way home, she couldn't help worrying about

Vlad. If only he'd left the army at the end of his compulsory service, he'd be back home now. The army was something you did because you had to, but her idiot brother had decided to make a career out of it.

She didn't doubt for a minute that he could become an officer. He might not be as smart as her, but he had always been brave and determined, the boy who kept getting up and getting punched rather than admitting that the bullies had won. But now it looked like there was going to be a war and he'd be right in the middle of it. Worse still, he probably still thought she was mad at him for his decision to stay a soldier, when really she'd just been worried.

She trudged up the stairs, past the stains and the smells. It was getting dark and she took the steps two at a time, not wanting to be caught out in the shadows. There were good people in this building but there were others too, men she wouldn't want to face alone. She bet women in America didn't have to worry about every strange man they passed. After all, Americans carried guns.

Women in Germany though, they were about to have a whole other set of problems. She didn't envy them.

Breathless, she bustled into the apartment and dumped the shopping bags onto the kitchen counter. Her father stirred in his chair, giving her a bleary smile.

"Hello, my little Anya," he said. "How are your studies?"

"Good, papa." She walked over and kissed him on the head. "We've started on quantum chemistry. It's fascinating."

"Quantum, eh?" He laughed. "I swear, these things didn't even exist when I was a boy."

"Did you do a lot of chemistry on the farm?"

He laughed again.

"Only the practical sort. How to dissolve solidified chicken shit, that sort of thing."

"So glamorous." Anna smiled. "No wonder mama fell in love."

"I was just dreaming of her." Papa walked into the kitchen and peered into the bags. "Such a lovely dream..."

His voice trailed off sadly.

"Look, pickles!" Anna said, by way of distraction. "Let's see what we have to go with them."

They spent a happy hour together, going through their familiar domestic routine. Papa chopped vegetables and fetched pans while Anna masterminded their dinner, eking out what flavour she could from bland ingredients. They ate at the table, its wonky leg made level with a few folded newspaper pages, while Papa told stories about his father and the potato growers' union. Anna had heard the stories a hundred times before but she still laughed, not because she felt she ought too, but because of the warmth and comfort they brought her.

At last, Papa got into his overalls, kissed her on the cheek, and headed off for the factory.

Left alone, Anna found her thoughts drifting back to her brother. She hated that they'd left things so badly between them. He might be overbearing and bossy, obsessively obedient in his attitude to the party, but he was still her brother, and she still loved him. What if he was out there, risking his life for the people he loved, still thinking she hated him? Worse yet, what if he died and she never had a chance to make things right?

Rummaging around in her study supplies, she found a pen and a few spare sheets of lined paper. By the light of a single electric bulb, she sat down at the table to write:

"DEAR VLAD."

SHE HESITATED. What could she say? She wouldn't apologise for saying things she thought were right, but the spectre of their argument hung over the page. Maybe if she just talked about her life, that would show him that she cared, that what they had in common was more important to her than what drove them apart.

But what could she say? The army censors would never let anything demoralising reach him. Anything about the shortages or the rumours of war, the things that had made her set pen to paper.

After that, what was left? What might mean something to him?

"I WENT to Vadim's café today. He asked after you, said how proud he was that you are out there defending us.

"Afterwards, I went to the shops and found pickles for papa. You should have seen the look on his face..."

4

THE FACE OF BATTLE

Rakovich woke to a crick in his neck and the smell of engine oil. The ground next to a BMP was a lousy place to sleep, but it was a damn sight better than on the back of the metal beast, and quieter than inside, where the snores of a whole infantry squad resounded like the roaring of a tractor factory. The next few nights, he'd be in there for protection, if he got to sleep at all. At least tonight he'd had some peace.

"Rakovich." Lieutenant Tikhomirov was crouching beside him, a blacker shadow against the night-dark grey of the forest beyond. "It's time."

Rakovich shook himself awake and got to his feet, eager for what was to come. It took a moment for his eyes to adjust, letting him make out the shapes of vehicles and the men sleeping on and around them. As Tikhomirov walked on, Rakovich approached the second section BMP, the one he would ride in.

"Halt," Akayev called out in heavily accented Russian. "Who go there?"

"Praporshchik Rakovich," he replied. "Come with champagne and hookers for everyone. Or perhaps just orders — they'll have to wake up to find out."

Beletsky lay sprawled across the engine housing, an army issue blanket pulled up over his face. Rakovich shook him roughly awake.

"Come on, you sons of whores," the praporshchik bellowed, moving on to the next victim. "Time to show the British that our Soviet bear has claws."

Cursing and grumbling, the men stirred into action. Anyone too slow got a kick from Rakovich or a more gentle nudge from Akayev, eager to help now he understood what was happening.

"Good man," Rakovich said to Akayev. "Next time we get to boil a kettle, the first tea's yours."

They might bitch and moan, but the men knew their jobs. Within minutes, they'd pissed, straightened their uniforms, and taken their seats in the vehicles — eight riflemen and two crewmen in each BMP. Some chewed on rations or had a last smoke before action. Others checked their weapons, counted bullets, or bowed their heads in contemplation of what was to come. Rakovich turned a blind eye as Rebane, first section's gunner, pulled out a cross and twisted it back and forth between calloused fingers. Let them have their comforts, their opiates of the bourgeois system, if that was what it took to get them through this. He could get Valeev to have a quiet word later.

At last, they were mounted and ready to move out. Engines rumbled like the groaning of caged beasts.

Rakovich climbed into the BMP, taking his place in the back beside the riflemen. Here he'd hung up a miniature Soviet flag, to remind him of what he fought for. It looked childish next to the vehicle's other decoration, a sketch of a naked woman drawn by Sergeant Kholodov and much leered over by his men. But while Kholodov's work was more refined and its subject more worldly, the pieces were two of a kind — reminders of the homeland, tokens of what they fought for.

Akayev snapped out something in Kyrgyz and hit a panel. When no-one responded, he took a deep breath and tried again in Russian.

"Red light," he said. "Not working."

Now it was Rakovich's turn to swear. Akayev must mean the infrared driving light. They hadn't even started the assault and already things were going wrong. Had Beletsky kicked the damn thing as he climbed off the engine? Had some forest creature been nibbling at the electrics? Had those bastards at the depot sent them shoddy bulbs again? Battle was coming, and his own squad was effectively blind.

He forced himself to take a deep breath. Lieutenant Tikhomirov had once told him that both fear and panic were contagious. It was his duty to prevent both.

The first platoon were heading out. He was meant to follow.

"Follow the lieutenant," he said, speaking slow and clear for Akayev. "It's starting to get light anyway."

Akayev grumbled and squinted dramatically, but he put the BMP into gear and set off.

The German countryside rolled past outside, the forest growing thinner as they approached the border. Every briefing Rakovich had attended had emphasised the flat German terrain, the opportunity for swift movement by vehicle-mounted troops. But it wasn't too flat to jolt him around as they picked up speed, racing towards their destiny.

The first artillery shells whistled past overhead. Rakovich looked at his watch. At least the artillery was on time.

A periscope fitted into the roof of the vehicle let him see the view ahead as the first shells hit. The horizon ahead was lit by explosions as bright as the sunrise to their rear. The sheer volume of fire was awe-inspiring, a mass of noise and light that seemed to tear the world in two, ripping it away from the quiet land that had been here. Could anything survive such an onslaught?

Calm settled over Rakovich as the platoon deployed into line, each BMP taking its place for the assault. This was it.

Kholodov climbed past him into the rear of the vehicle, sleeves rolled up, helmet askew, a pencil stuck behind his ear. His sloppy grin faded as he saw Rakovich watching him, but he still had a smile for his men as he made sure that they were ready, their rifles loaded and fitted in the firing slots. Rakovich wondered if they should have done these checks sooner, so they were ready before they reached the line. So many lessons to learn from this.

If they lived to learn them.

Ahead of them, a tank from the first echelon fired. As if in response, both sides let fly.

Now the thunder of battle wasn't just on the distant horizon. It was all around Rakovich, a roaring of tank guns and of enemy shells landing around them. A tree to his left exploded, splinters filling the air. Suddenly, it all felt real.

British vehicles crouched in the woods ahead. Angular shapes loomed amid the tangled shadows of branches and leaves. There were no main battle tanks, which was a mercy. Some had the boxy turrets and slender guns of Scorpion and Scimitar light tanks, but the rest had flatter outlines, personnel carriers or perhaps Striker missile vehicles. No surprises yet.

Missiles hit two tanks in the front echelon. Flame shot from one turret, a bright flash of death amid the fading grey of dawn. The other one simply stopped, as if the driver had braked hard. A man scrambled out and jumped to the floor, running for the rear.

Rakovich pulled out a notebook and jotted down what he'd seen. The new armour had been pierced as easily as paper. The Soviet tanks weren't as safe as the generals had claimed. Would that apply to his transport too?

He paused, pencil in hand. Half a dozen men had just died, burning up in the bellies of those tanks, and here he was, coldly analysing the consequences. Did that make him a better soldier, potential officer material? Or did it just make him a psychopath?

They kept rolling forward as the guns boomed around them and the roar of explosions shook the BMP. They passed the flaming wrecks of Soviet vehicles lost during the first echelon's attack. From the limited view through his periscope, Rakovich counted the charred shells of four BMPs and two tanks, the latter with their turrets hanging askew. He had wanted to be part of that first wave, but now he saw how it had gone, he felt relieved. His men would still be needed to complete the break through into the enemy's flanks and rear.

Captain Leontev's voice crackled out of the radio.

"The British are retreating. Stay mounted and pursue."

Then Lieutenant Tikhomirov, this time over the platoon channel.

"The woods are perfect for an ambush. Keep your eyes open, fire at anything that moves."

Rakovich repeated the orders to the men in the BMP.

Obolensky, the medic, let out a bitter laugh.

"Never mind them moving," he said. "How are we supposed to shoot straight when we're bouncing around like this?"

"You couldn't shoot straight on the firing range," Rakovich said. "What makes you think you'll do any better now?"

The men laughed. They'd all seen Obolensky make perfect scores in target practice.

"Just point your rifle and pull the trigger," Rakovich continued, staring at each man in turn. "Don't worry about whether you're causing casualties. Just keep their heads down so they can't aim the anti-tank missiles. If one of those hits, we're all as dead as Leontev's love life."

The Russian column raced through the woods, tanks crashing through the undergrowth, BMPs bouncing over thick roots and rutted ground. Every few minutes, one of the riflemen would fire out of his tiny window, though none of them ever claimed a hit. They were shooting shadows, while the rest of the company did the hard fighting. No-one even seemed to be firing at them.

Then they burst out of the woods into open farmland. Suddenly, the air was full of the roar of shells and the rattle of automatic weapons. They rushed towards a village little more than a mile away, accelerating at they went, Akayev whooping and yelling incomprehensibly.

Then Rakovich saw the shape he had dreaded, hovering like the shadow of death above the village. He froze for a moment, shoulders tensed, just staring at the sight.

"Helicopter!" he yelled. "Beletsky, missile, now!"

Before Beletsky could respond, the BMP skidded to a halt. Akayev opened his hatch and scrambled out, his wild whoops replaced by noises of alarm.

There wasn't time to find out what was wrong. They were sitting in the open, with nothing more than trampled cabbages for cover.

"Dismount!" Rakovich and Kholodov shouted at once.

The rear doors were thrown open and the men tumbled out, running back fifty yards to the edge of the woods. One man fell as he ran, tumbling into the dirt like a pile of rags. Two more picked him up and kept running.

Panic was contagious. Rakovich couldn't let it take hold. Though his heart hammered like the piston of a racing machine, he didn't run at full pace towards the woods. Instead he retreated at a crouch, weapon at the ready, looking out for British troops. There was a movement in a hedgerow and he opened fired, but the only thing that fell was a scarecrow, its shirt flapping in the wind as it tumbled to the ground.

At the edge of the woods, he mustered his men. While Obolensky saw to the wounded, humming to himself as he applied bandages and stitches, Khymka was set to watch their rear, in case any British soldiers remained.

At last, Rakovich had a chance to pause and assess their situation.

It was a terrible scene. BMPs and tanks littered the fields, several of them on fire. His own vehicle had lost a track. Akayev lay underneath it, wrench in hand, doing something to the wheels while bullets bounced off the armour above him. The rest of the survivors were running back to the shelter of the woods, pursued by bullets and anti-tank missiles.

Thirty feet from where Rakovich lay, the ground exploded as an artillery shell hit. Running men were hurled through the air, tumbling crumpled and broken in the freshly churned earth. Another shell hit, and another, as the disorderly retreat turned into a full-blown rout. Dirt rattled off his helmet. All he wanted to do was to cling to the shaking ground, desperate not to be hit by the jagged, hurtling blades of shrapnel.

That was no way for a praporshchik to act. He was responsible for the men around him. He had to be strong.

"You!" he shouted at a pair of running riflemen. "By that tree. Covering fire for the retreat."

He didn't know whose section they belonged to, but they responded to the command. They took shelter beneath the tree, their eyes bright and their expressions grim, firing at anything that looked like a target. Other men joined them in the tree line, responding to Rakovich's orders or just to the courage that came from being part of a mob. Something like a line was forming, and though he doubted they were touching the British, at least they weren't running any more.

Now he needed Lieutenant Tikhomirov, so that he could get some orders of his own.

"Zimyatov," he called out, relieved to see his friend among the gathering men. "Where's the lieutenant?"

Zimyatov stared at him for a moment, then pointed at the burning wreckage of a transport.

Rakovich stared, uncomprehending. Then realisation dawned. That had been Zimyatov's transport and the lieutenant had been with Zimyatov.

The lieutenant was dead. That left him in charge of the platoon.

"You!" He grabbed Tammert, who was crouched behind a fallen tree, staring at the carnage. "Find Captain Leontev. Tell him that Lieutenant Tikhomirov is dead, we're two BMPs down and taking heavy fire. Ask him what his orders are."

As Tammert ran off, Rakovich looked around. They were vulnerable here, trying to hold a handful of trees against a British armoured formation. And now that vulnerability was his to deal with. What was he supposed to do?

The surviving BMP sat just inside the wood, but none of the men from that section were visible. Rakovich stalked to the rear of the BMP and heaved open one of the doors.

"Get out here, you miserable swine!" he bellowed.

Men tumbled forth, clutching their helmets to their heads as if they might offer more protection that way. Rakovich shoved them into defensive positions along the edge of the wood, with the BMP in the centre. Two men faced back into the wood, just in case.

Tammert reappeared.

"Praporshchik," he said. "Captain says we're to dig in while you report to him."

As the men dug foxholes, Rakovich ran back the way Tammert had come. It took him a minute to realise that he didn't know where he was going. Units were jumbled together in among the trees, infantry lurking in the shelter behind tanks, medics tending to wounded men amid the roots and fallen branches. The blasts of war had shaken the summer leaves from the trees, so that green confetti fell around him, a mockery of a victory parade.

"Have you seen Captain Leontev?" he asked, grabbing a soldier by the arm. "First Motor Rifle Company."

The man pointed to his right.

"I saw a command vehicle over there," he said. "Could be him."

Rakovich strode through the trees until he emerged into a clearing. There he found Captain Leontev, Lieutenant Valeev, and the other two platoon commanders stood in a circle, Leontev's BMP behind them.

"At last." Leontev gave him a hard look. "As I was saying, we've pushed the British back, but with heavy losses. The regiment is throwing reserves in further north, where things went better. We're to dig in and hold the British in place. Rakovich, how many men have you lost?"

"Lieutenant Tikhomirov and four others dead, two wounded, sir." Rakovich tried not to think about the reality of what that meant — the charred bodies, the blood, the screams. "One BMP destroyed, one damaged."

"I didn't ask about the BMPs, Praporshchik. Don't bother me with crap that I don't care about."

"Yes, sir."

Leontev redirected his attention, taking in all three platoon commanders. "I want every man dug in and the BMPs camouflaged as best you can. Once that's done, get the men fed, but for fuck's sake stay alert. If a counter-attack comes, we won't get much help."

Rakovich nodded. It didn't sound like any of them had much

choice about what happened now, but at least they knew where they stood.

"What are you all waiting for?" Leontev snapped. "Get back out there."

They all turned to head back to their units.

Rakovich's mind raced as he registered the responsibility that had fallen on him, and the opportunity. He'd wanted to lead a unit for years. Now a British missile had given him his chance, and he was suddenly forced to face a dozen different details, from checking supplies to finding help for the wounded, while trying not to get shot by the enemy. It was a lot of pressure.

As he strode through a drift of prematurely fallen leaves, Rakovich was surprised to find Lieutenant Valeev walking alongside him.

"You did well this morning, Praporshchik Rakovich", the political officer said. "I'm afraid Captain Leontev reserves his patience for senior officers."

"Thank you, sir," Rakovich responded. "I thought the BMPs were relevant. With two down, we're vulnerable to British tanks."

"Remember that Captain Leontev has to consider the company's problems. The platoon's shortages are your responsibility now, Rakovich."

"Yes, sir." The pressure pulled down on Rakovich and his shoulders slumped.

"Don't worry." Valeev clapped Rakovich on the shoulder. "I've seen you in action. You're ready to play your part."

A STRANGE CALM hung over the edge of the woods, despite the wind howling through the treetops. The men stood guard in shifts, those not on duty eating their rations, cleaning their weapons, or sleeping as best they could in their muddy holes. Akayev, lured back from the broken BMP, sat muttering curses that no-one else could understand.

Rakovich sat in the back of the BMP, eating a ration bar and flicking through his Communist Manifesto. After the chaos of the morning, it was good to have a moment with something comforting and familiar. The smell of the book and the sight of its worn pages reminded him of his mother, bringing back memories of more innocent times. With some food inside him, he could finally relax for a few minutes.

The peace was shattered by the whistle of approaching shells, then the thud of their detonations. As the ground shook and men raced for cover, Rakovich scrambled forward to look out through the driver's periscope.

Smoke was billowing across the fields. The wind tore at it, creating a thin, patchy miasma through which the shapes of the approaching enemy could be seen. There were FV432 armoured personnel carriers, flat-sided boxes covered in camouflage paint with little feature beyond their tracks. Alongside them came a pair of Chieftain main battle tanks, few in number but deadly in potential, the long barrels of their guns directed toward the Soviet positions.

Rakovich grabbed the vehicle's radio.

"Zoryn 210, this is Zoryn 218, over."

Captain Leontev replied. "Zoryn 218, this is Zoryn 210. Go ahead."

"Sir, we're being attacked. I request artillery support. Over."

"The whole company is under attack." Leontev sounded even more impatient than usual. "There is no artillery support. You hold them with what you have. Out."

Rakovich switched the radio off and saw the vehicle's crew watching him expectantly. He looked up at the gunner.

"Dologodin, hold fire with the rocket," he said. "Wait until they're close enough for the gun as well."

"Yes, Praporshchik." The man peered out of his turret, resting a tattooed arm over the edge of the hatch, then looked back down in alarm. "Praporshchik, there are tanks. Should I fire a missile at them?"

Rakovich cursed and moved to the commander's seat, pulling on the helmet so that he could use the intercom. Through the sight, he saw more Chieftains lurking at the edge of the village, waiting to give long-range support to the infantry. The BMP's armour would be no protection against their guns, but its missile was the only hope of knocking one out.

"Hold fire," he said. "When the rest of the company fire their missiles, then you fire. Clear?"

"Yes, Praporshchik." Dologodin's voice wavered with fear and excitement.

"Shistyev." Rakovich turned to the driver. "When Dologodin tells you the missile's hit, move one hundred yards left. Not a moment before, understood?"

"Understood, praporschik."

"Every time you fire, you move. Once you're out of missiles, use the gun against the personnel carriers, then the machine gun against the infantry. Good luck, both of you."

He removed the helmet and moved back into the empty troop compartment, taking a deep breath to steel himself as he swung the rear door open. Then he dashed out into the maelstrom of noise and flying dirt.

"Hold your fire!" he shouted as he ran for his foxhole.

There was no need for the order. Everyone was down in their holes, more concentrated on survival than on killing. Only Szolkowski, further down the line, was peering out of cover, taking shots at the approaching enemy.

Rakovich jumped into a hole with some of his men. Together, they crouched in the dirt, waiting for the moment when the barrage would cease and the enemy would advance. Every few minutes, he risked a peek out over the edge to watch the British creep forward, judging how much longer this would last.

Missiles streaked out from positions to his right, their progress agonisingly slow. Smoke trailed behind them as they flew towards the British armour, deadly darts flying on wings of steel. As they hit their marks a pair of British vehicles exploded, chunks of armour flying away as smoke billowed from ruined engines.

Enemy tanks fired back at the BMPs. The roar of their guns joined the bellowing of artillery and the crash of exploding shells. Beneath Rakovich's feet, the earth trembled.

The personnel carriers were still approaching through the smoke, crawling forward like mechanical slugs. They would have to stop soon and let their troops out, or be left unprotected from infantry with anti-tank weapons. That was fine with Rakovich. His platoon had few weapons that could harm the personnel carriers, but it had plenty of rifles and machine guns.

A shape appeared over the distant houses.

"Helicopter!" Rakovich yelled at the top of his voice. "Beletsky, where the fuck are you?"

The answer came from Plakans, the weather-worn Latvian who operated second section's gun.

"He's two foxholes to the left, Praporshchik." Plakans pointed. "Under that oak."

Rakovich cursed and jumped out of the foxhole, just as a second, larger helicopter appeared. He ran at a crouch, his pulse pounding, trying not to expose himself as he made for the other foxhole. Bullets hissed past his head as he jumped in, almost landing on the unfortunate Beletsky, who was cowering in a corner.

He grabbed hold of the private and slapped him hard.

"You miserable little shit!" he said. "The British have got helicopters, and you're the one man in this platoon that can deal with them. Get your arse into action before I smash your teeth in."

Beletsky's blank stare gave way to something more focused. He picked up the surface to air missile from the floor of the foxhole and lifted it onto his shoulder, mechanically going through the arming sequence. Finally, he fired, then dropped back down into a crouch as he prepared a new firing tube.

Over the edge of the foxhole, Rakovich saw the missile streak away, just as the helicopters dropped below the level of the buildings. Not smart enough to realise where its prey had gone, the missile kept going in a straight line, disappearing into the distance.

At least the helicopters were out of the way.

Letting out a long held breath, Rakovich sank into a squat, his back against the side of the foxhole. Then he noticed the other figure sharing their space, sat at the far end from Beletsky. A rifleman, his arms draped across his knees, assault rifle lying limp. Rakovich thought it might be Khymka, but with half the man's face missing, it was impossible to be sure.

Rakovich recoiled, pressing himself against the wall.

"He only stuck his head up for a moment," Beletsky said in a flat voice. "Said he wanted to see what was happening."

Rakovich swallowed the bile rising in his throat.

"Never mind him," he said, dragging his eyes away from the ghastly sight. "There will be more helicopters and you need to be ready to take them down."

"Yes, Praporshchik," Beletsky nodded. "I only have one more missile, but I shall make it count."

More nervously than before, Rakovich lifted his head to see what was happening. The British vehicles had stopped and men were jumping out of the FV432s. If he didn't want to be overrun then he needed to get the platoon up and firing.

He ran to the next foxhole, trying to push the image of Khymka from his mind. Shrapnel and bullets hissed past, the air thick with the promise of death.

There were four survivors from first section in this hole. Sergeant Zimyatov was yelling at Bakhvalovich to get the machine gun up and firing. He turned to Rakovich at the Praporshchik jumped in.

"How are we doing, Vlad?" Zimyatov shouted above the noise of battle.

"Worse than one of your girlfriends," Rakovich replied. "I need your men to start fighting back."

"They're still too far away for the rifles," Zimyatov said. "And Leontev never gave me the missile I wanted for my birthday. But Bakhvalovich's machine gun will give them something to think about."

"Watch the flank," Rakovich said. "The BMP will be dealing with the tanks, but he'll be too busy for the infantry."

Then he was out in the open again, dashing back past Beletsky to the third foxhole. Here, Sergeant Kholodov and two riflemen crouched in the dirt. Their only movement was to look up as Rakovich appeared among them.

"What the fuck are you doing, Kholodov?" demanded Rakovich. "The British are advancing. Get up and get your men firing while the blood's still inside their bodies."

Kholodov's gaze flitted back and forth nervously and for a moment Rakovich thought he would have a serious problem. Then the sergeant slowly rose.

"You heard the man," he said. "Get up and get that machine gun working."

On down the line Rakovich went, darting from hole to hole, cajoling, encouraging, and berating. Even as he finished, the machine gun in Zinoviev's foxhole let rip.

The British were advancing through what remained of the smoke. One group would lie prone and fire while the others ran forward, then they would switch, a steady, systematic approach across the farmland. One of the tanks had lost its track, but the other was still coming.

His own weapon in hand, Rakovich waited for the infantry to come within rifle range. The machine guns were taking their toll, but it was not enough to stop the disciplined British. A few fell, but more kept coming.

Then they were in rifle range.

Rakovich opened fire and his men followed suit. The sound of guns grew like the chatter of an excited crowd. The British fired back and dirt sprayed his face as bullets struck around the foxhole. A shell shattered a tree to his left, filling the air with shrapnel and splinters. He remembered Khymka, but forced himself to stay steady.

Panic was contagious. He couldn't let it take hold.

At last, the weight of fire wore down the exposed British. A few started to back off, then a few more. Slowly at first, but with growing momentum, the advance turned into a retreat, then from a hesitant walk to a full run. Damaged personnel carriers lay abandoned as their crews ran. The Russians cheered as their enemies fled.

A rifleman jumped up from one of the foxholes. Rakovich shouted at him to get back down, but his words were lost in the noise of battle. A second man started to climb out, but stopped as machine gun fire burst from the retreating tank, ripped into the first man's stomach, and brought him down in a spray of blood.

Rakovich stiffened at the sight, then reddened in anger at the man's idiocy. What if more had followed him? Hadn't they lost enough?

The firing subsided as the British passed out of range. Rakovich let himself rest for a few seconds. His rifle was warm in his hand, cold metal heated by the fire of battle, and the air smelled of burnt propellant. Soon he would have to go down the line again, checking on ammunition and casualties. First though, a moment to breathe and to gather his thoughts, to come to terms with everything that had happened.

He had survived a British attack, and thanks to him so had his men. This was a moment he could be proud of.

5

A LONG NIGHT

Rakovich sat in the back of the BMP, waiting for the platoon's sergeants to arrive. His sergeants, for now at least. Here was the opportunity for command that he'd been wanting, and he was excited by the prospect, but it was hard to relish the moment when they might all be blown to hell at any second. Gunfire and explosions still sounded, somewhere in the distance. Though a sort of quiet had settled across this part of the line, he was under no illusion that it might last.

"How many missiles do you have left?" he called out to Dologodin, the gunner.

"None, Praporshchik," came the reply. "I used them all on the British tanks."

"Cannon rounds?"

"About three hundred left. I used the rest on their personnel carriers."

"You got any bricks to throw at them when that runs out?"

"I'll see what I can find, Praporshchik."

Rakovich considered where that left them. A few hundred rounds plus the machine gun, all the support his infantry could expect until... He didn't know when. That was part of the problem.

One by one, the sergeants appeared and took seats around him. Kholodov came first, looking as relaxed as any man could amid this carnage, sketching on a scrap of paper while they waited for the others. Zinoviev arrived bright and eager to take his seat. Last came Zimyatov.

"Praporshchik." He winked and threw Rakovich a salute. "Or should that be lieut—"

"Still Praporshchik," Rakovich said, cutting him off. Things were confused enough without muddling up ranks, even as a joke between friends. "I'm just running things until they send us a new lieutenant. And no saluting in the field — do you want me to get shot?"

"Sorry, Vlad," Zimyatov said, then looked at him wide-eyed, realising what he'd said. "I mean Praporshchik."

Rakovich waved him to a seat.

"Let's get this done before the British come back to beat us bloody," he said. "Casualties?"

Kholodov spoke first, his easy expression turning grim. "Khymka's dead."

"I saw." Rakovich nodded. "Zinoviev, one of your men got hit near the end, who was that?"

"Popov." Zinoviev frowned. "Sorry, Praporshchik. The idiot wanted to chase the British back. No other casualties in third section, though."

"Zimyatov? Any more losses?"

"No, Praporshchik."

Two down, plus the crew of one of the BMPs. Rakovich had feared far worse.

"Sounds like we did well," he said. "Tell your men that—"

"Praporshchik." Dologodin cut in over the intercom. "Captain Leontev is calling for you."

Rakovich moved to the commander's seat and switched to the company radio. "Zoryn 210, this is Zoryn 218, over."

"Zoryn 218," Leontev said, "give me a sit rep, over."

"Zoryn 210, we lost two men in the attack. One BMP remaining but no more anti-tank missiles. Over."

"Zoryn 218, understood. Zoryn 210 out."

Rakovich moved back to the rear troop compartment, considering the call. Was Leontev checking in on all his units, or was he keeping a special eye on Third Platoon? Support would be good, but having the captain peering over his shoulder could quickly become a ball-ache.

"Do you all have enough ammunition?" he asked, and the assembled sergeants nodded. "That's something, at least, but we'll need missiles. There should still be some on second section's BMP. Kholodov, when it gets dark, I want you and your men to go retrieve them."

Kholodov gestured in alarm toward the battleground.

"You want us out in the open?" he asked. "Can't we wait for supplies from battalion?"

"Are you questioning my orders?" Rakovich snapped. "We don't know what battalion's dealing with, and if we face a tank attack without those missiles then we might as well fuck ourselves with hand grenades. So yes, unless battalion send us supplies before nightfall, you're going out there."

Kholodov blanched, but at least this time he had the decency to keep his mouth shut.

"Perhaps my section could—" Zinoviev began, but Rakovich held up a hand.

"Second section's vehicle," he said. "Second section's job. And remember who's in charge here."

Was this how it was going to be, people challenging his orders from every direction? Would they just shut up and accept it if he was a lieutenant?

"The aim is to get the missiles without the British knowing you're there," he continued. "First and third sections will provide covering fire if you need it. If you come under attack, try to get the smoke launchers going. That'll help to cover your return. Clear?"

Kholodov nodded.

"We have two dead bodies," Rakovich continued. "I want them out of sight. Hide them back in the woods until battalion send a team to collect them. Once that's done, get the weapons cleaned and equipment checked, then set up rotas so the men can get some rest. Dismissed."

Kholodov and Zinoviev climbed out of the BMP and headed away, but Zimyatov hung back. He stood uncertainly in the doorway and Rakovich could see him caught between two worlds — one where they were friends, the other where they were praporshchik and sergeant.

"It's OK, Zim," Rakovich said quietly. "Just us now."

Zimyatov smiled. "I just wanted to say, you're doing a good job, Vlad. Everybody appreciates it, even if they can't say."

"Thanks." Now Rakovich was smiling too. "It's definitely going better than that exercise in January."

"You weren't to know that movement was pigs."

"First Platoon are ugly, but even they don't have snouts."

They laughed at the memory of the paint-spattered pigs and the farmer, his expression shifting from indignation to fear as he realised he was shouting at soldiers.

"How are you feeling after our first real battle?" Zimyatov asked.

"Glad to have come out with the same number of holes I went in with. And you?"

"Tired. Relieved. Excited for the next one. It changes every two seconds."

"That's adrenaline for you."

"Adrenaline and nearly getting shot."

Zimyatov pulled a hip flask from his pocket.

"You want to take the edge off it?"

"Just a taste. I've got a platoon to run."

Rakovich took a swig from the flask. It tasted like filth and burned all the way down.

"What the fuck kind of Russian drinks vodka that bad?" he spluttered.

"The kind on a sergeant's salary." Zimyatov grinned. "If you don't want it you can give it back."

"I should confiscate this for your own good."

Rakovich took another swig, grimaced for effect, and then handed the hip flask back.

"Have you written to Tatyana lately?" he asked.

Zimyatov shook his head.

Rakovich pulled a pen and paper from his pocket.

"For when you get a chance," he said. "Bad enough for the poor girl that she's fucking you — at least let her know that you're alive."

"Thanks, Vlad." Zimyatov hesitated a moment longer at the hatch of the BMP. "You think we're going to get out of this alive?"

"I might shoot you for killing morale with your morbid questions. But other than that, yeah, we'll be fine. We've trained for this. We're big damn heroes of the Soviet Union. What could possibly go wrong?"

RAKOVICH WAS RELIEVED NOT to be the last one arriving at Leontev's vehicle. He could do without more black marks from the captain.

Valeev was already there, leaning against the BMP with a steaming mug of tea in his hands. As a political officer attached to the company, he got to take part in command discussions, he just didn't have any authority over the outcome — unlike the platoon commanders, who had yet to arrive.

"Good evening, Praporshchik," Valeev said, greeting Rakovich with a smile. "How are your men?"

"Doing well, sir," Rakovich replied. "Keen to show the capitalists what we're made of."

"Good to hear."

Leontev emerged from his BMP, glaring all around.

"Where are your runners?" he demanded.

"My runners?" Rakovich asked.

"You're leading a platoon. You should have two men with you as bodyguards and messengers."

Rakovich flushed. He'd seldom seen an officer on their own in the field, yet somehow he hadn't realised why. This meeting was a chance to show his leadership skills and he'd failed before he even arrived.

"I'm sorry, Captain," he said. "I'll know for next time."

Leontev stepped up close to Rakovich, looking down at him.

"The behaviour of my officers reflects on me," he said. "That's why I like people who know what they're doing, not thick-necked upstarts from the factory districts. You're not smart enough to be an officer, Rakovich, but you're also too stupid to accept your place. Try not to get your whole platoon killed while I find it a proper leader."

Rakovich clenched his fists and stared stiffly past his commander's left ear. Leontev had judged him already, based on little more than where he came from. It was bullshit of the highest order, but this was an officer, so he wasn't allowed to answer back, never mind knock the man on his arse.

"Yes, Captain," he said though clenched teeth.

"Where are the others?" Leontev growled, looking around.

As if on cue, two figures emerged from the darkness, the lieutenants in charge of the other platoons. It was strange to see their reactions to war. Both men were senior in rank to Rakovich, trained and tested by the Soviet system. But while Chugainov looked implacable as ever, Egorov was pale and haggard, his eyes twitching nervously about. They gathered around their captain, Chugainov leaning casually against the BMP, Egorov puffing at a series of cigarettes.

"Ammunition and rations will arrive later this afternoon," Leontev said. "Replacements for the dead and wounded come this evening. Replacement BMPs too, and mechanics to repair Rakovich's damaged one."

"Will there be enough to bring us back to full strength?" Chugainov asked.

"That's the plan," replied Leontev. "At dawn tomorrow, we take that damned village. Single echelon attack with helicopter and mortar support. Remain mounted until you get to the village and right through it if you can. No-one dismounts without my orders."

Rakovich remembered the bursting of shells all around them, the destruction of one of his platoon's BMPs and the crippling of another. That charred and ruined vehicle had become Tikhomirov's tomb.

"There were tanks in the village today," he said. "They could destroy our BMPs before we get close."

"Not your concern," Leontev snapped. "Our tanks and helicopters will deal with the British armour, you concentrate on getting to the village. Once we're through there we cross the river and keep going until we reach Königslutter am Elm." He pointed on the map. "Any questions?"

Rakovich clenched his fists again, but this time he kept his mouth shut.

As DARKNESS DESCENDED, Rakovich crouched in a foxhole next to Kholodov. He'd been hoping that the promised supplies would include missiles, but the afternoon had passed without ammunition, rations or replacement troops. They were going to have to risk retrieving them from the disabled BMP.

"You can do this," Rakovich said, slapping Kholodov's shoulder with more confidence than he felt.

"I wish someone else would," Kholodov replied before crawling out of the foxhole, the rest of his section following him.

Rakovich watched them go, peering into the night for signs of British troops. His stomach tightened and he took long breaths to try to ease out the tension, to stop his own body becoming a distraction. All across the platoon, men stood in their foxholes, weapons at the ready, waiting for when their comrades needed them.

Second section scurried across the open ground. Some went at a crouch, keeping as low to the ground as they could. Others ran flat out, counting on speed to keep them safe. Their footfalls seemed to fill the quiet of the night.

Something moved in the darkness beyond the BMP. Rakovich snapped his rifle around, ready to open fire.

A tree swayed in the wind, then went still.

Clattering sounds followed, along with whispered Kyrgyz curses as

Akayev tried to detach something from his vehicle. Rakovich almost laughed at the absurdity of it. But the absurd could get a man killed on a night like this.

A booming noise announced low-flying warplanes overhead. Rakovich looked up in alarm, unable to make out any shapes in the darkness. Had the British committed fresh forces to this zone? Were they about to come under attack?

But there were no explosions, no sound of guns firing from above. The planes, whichever side they were on, vanished into the darkness.

Kholodov and his men came running back out of the night. Some of them paused along the way, looking back with assault rifles raised, covering the retreat. The others moved awkwardly, weighed down with their precious burden.

At last, they reached the trenches. Rakovich let out a breath he hadn't realised he was holding.

"What do we have?" he asked as Kholodov slid into the foxhole.

"Four missiles," Kholodov replied. "Plus the ground mount launcher. And Akeyev grabbed something, but who knows what our crazy Kyrgyz comrade is about."

"Good work," Rakovich said. "Send two of the missiles to the BMP, then set up the launcher on the left."

As Kholodov started giving orders, Zinoviev jumped down into the increasingly crowded hole.

"Praporshchik," he said. "Supply trucks have arrived."

"Beautiful," Kholodov groaned. "We hang our arses out in front of the British for a handful of missiles, and ten minutes later a truck-load of them appear."

"It's not just ammunition," Zinoviev said. "They've brought mail and rations, too."

Rakovich followed him out of the hole and back through the woods, to where the delivery truck was unloading. As promised, there were crates of ammunition and cartons of food, but that wasn't what interested Rakovich the most. He grabbed the mail bag and, by the light spilling out of the truck's cab, flicked through letters.

It was only when he got to the end, finding nothing for him, that he realised how much he'd wanted to hear from Anna. It hadn't been realistic to expect it. They didn't write to each other very often since he became a praporshchik and he was intensely aware of the distance that put between them. But out here, amid the mess and loss of war, he craved the comfort of a connection with home.

"Here." He thrust the bag at Zinoviev. "See these are delivered. Zimyatov can deal with the supplies."

He trudged back to the BMP, sank into a seat, and let the weariness of a long day overwhelm him.

"PRAPORSHCHIK."

Someone was shaking Rakovich's shoulder. Still half asleep, he batted their hand aside. Couldn't they see that he needed his rest? Parade couldn't be for hours yet.

"Praporshchik, replacements have arrived."

Reality caught up with Rakovich. He sat bolt upright in the BMP. He wasn't in barracks, he was out in a war zone, and there were soldiers who needed his attention.

He could just about make out the shape of Zimyatov in the darkness, and beyond him some other men.

"Did they bring a new BMP?" he asked, rising from his seat.

"Yes, Praporshchik," Zimyatov said. "And a recovery vehicle. It's heading out for Kholodov's BMP now."

"What about a new lieutenant?"

"Not unless he's invisible. You're still in charge."

Too tired to work out whether that was good news or bad, Rakovich forced himself into alertness and followed Zimyatov over to the newly arrived soldiers.

There were eight of them, standing stiffly to attention beside the BMP. To Rakovich, they looked like boys rather than men. Too clean, too innocent. Or did the rest of the platoon just look old and tired? It was amazing the difference a few years in the army could make. Or a few hours at war.

He had to keep everything under control until the new lieutenant arrived. That way the rest of his old, tired men might get through this alive.

"Which ones are the BMP crew, Zimyatov?" he asked.

One of the new men spoke. "Sir, I drove the replacement BMP, and—"

Rakovich rounded on him. "Is your name Zimyatov?"

"No, sir, it's—"

"I don't fucking care what your name is!" yelled Rakovich. "I was not talking to you, so shut the fuck up. And next time you call me sir, you'd better fucking well hope I've been promoted."

The new man fell silent. His chin quivered as he stared past Rakovich into the darkness.

"Listen to me, all of you," Rakovich said. "In the morning, we attack the British. For you lot, it'll be your first time in action, right?"

Heads nodded but no-one spoke.

"So do yourselves a favour," he continued. "Shut the fuck up, do as you're told, and don't get in anyone's way. If you do that, you might just live long enough to become something resembling Red Army soldiers. Understood?"

"Yes, Praporshchik!" they said in chorus.

"Good." Rakovich hoped the darkness hid the sudden sagging of his shoulders. It wasn't as if he hadn't balled men out like that before. Hell, it was the only way of keeping most recruits in line. But the outburst had come suddenly, as if from nowhere, and its passing left little inside to hold him up.

"Alright, Zimyatov," he said calmly. "Which one is the BMP gunner?"

He inspected the men, then gestured to the two crewmen and three of the infantry.

"You five are in first section. Go with Sergeant Zimyatov and do whatever he tells you. You other three, come with me."

He led them through the increasingly familiar mass of trees and fox holes, dropping one off with Zinoviev and the other two with Kholodov. Then he moved to the edge of the wood to watch the damaged BMP being towed back. Akayev stood with the repair team, eager to get to work.

"Can you get her ready for dawn?" he asked one of the mechanics.

"Probably," the man said. "If I've understood the damage correctly."

He glanced at Akayev, who grinned and waved a wrench.

"Fix good," he said. "Go fight British, yes? Save world."

"Exactly," Rakovich patted the pocket that held his battered old Communist Manifesto. "Time to save the world from the capitalist scum."

Something wasn't right, though. Something Akayev had said had lodged in his brain.

The British. They were still out there, watching as the mechanics retrieved the broken down BMP, sounds of engines and tools drifting across the fields. Men stood exposed in the open, retrieving valuable equipment that could help the Soviet cause. So why weren't the British doing anything to stop them? He would have at least set a sniper to work.

Whatever was going on, he couldn't work it out. The best he could do was set his sentries, get some rest, and hope to be ready when trouble came.

THIS TIME, Rakovich was ready when someone shook him awake. He climbed straight to his feet and looked around.

The deepest dark of night had passed and the sky was starting to gain a little grey. The time for action was near.

"Praporshchik," the lead mechanic said, "your BMP is repaired and ready."

"Thank you, Sergeant," Rakovich replied. "I don't suppose you installed a beer tap in there while you were about it?"

"Sorry, Praporshchik, that's only for generals and above."

"Then I'll find you again in ten promotions time. For now, you can get back to battalion."

The sergeant nodded and walked back to his vehicle, where his men were stowing their tools away. The engine started and they headed back through the woods, away from the front line and the danger.

Rakovich didn't envy them. He'd wanted to be a soldier. He'd wanted to do good. This fight was his chance.

Zimyatov was dozing in the back of his replacement BMP, using a half deflated football as a pillow. A field telephone sat next to him, wires trailing from it out the back of the vehicle and into the forest. The field engineers had had a busy night providing them with communications the British couldn't intercept, and they'd have a busy time gathering it all up again when they moved on.

Rakovich shook his sergeant awake.

"How are the replacements?" he asked quietly, not wanting to disturb the other men in the vehicle.

"And good morning to you, Praporshchik," Zimyatov replied, rubbing his eyes. "The new guys seem keen enough and the crew know their way around a BMP. The driver did a full check of the engine as soon as it was in position and the gunner did the same during the drive over. If you really want to know, though, ask me after the bullets start flying."

"So what do you think of our chances?"

Zimyatov looked around, checking that no-one else was awake and listening in.

"Honestly, Vlad?" he whispered. "If those tanks are still out there, it could be a massacre. We can't hit them while we're on the move, and they could destroy us before we're half-way to the village."

"You're not wrong." Rakovich sighed. "We're gonna stick our dick through a hole in a fence, and if those tanks are there, they'll bite the fucker right off."

Zimyatov sniggered and one of the men stirred in his sleep. At a gesture from Rakovich, the two of them stepped away from the BMP.

Around them, the trees rustled in a breeze from the east. Something scampered through the undergrowth, tiny paws pattering across splinters, fallen leaves, and churned dirt. The woods would have seemed idyllic if not for the shell holes and snoring soldiers.

"Leontev says our tanks and helicopters will deal with the British armour," he said, once they were safely out of earshot. "But if he's wrong, we're in a lot of trouble."

"Come on, Praporshchik." Zimyatov pulled a hip flask from his pocket and offered it to Rakovich. "This is what you signed up for, remember? Action, adventure, a chance to be shot to death for a few square feet of mud."

Rakovich took a swig of the vodka. It was still awful but at least it woke him up some more.

"This was all just theory before," he said, handing back the flask. "Now I have to face the reality. The reality of command and the reality of two corpses back there among the trees, men who died on my watch."

"You'll adjust. You're better at this than anyone I know. Most of us are going back to our normal lives once our time is served, off to marry our sweethearts and find work in the factories. But you, you were born for this."

"Do you really think you'll be able to go back to civilian life now? The only ones who'll understand you are the Afghan veterans and the old men who fought in the Great Patriotic War."

"Maybe we should just give up and be target practice for the British." Zimyatov turned his arms into a crude circle, like a target on the range.

Rakovich laughed.

"You do that, and I'll kick your corpse all the way home to Tatyana."

"Then you leave me no choice, Praporshchik. I shall fight like a lion to free the imperialist lackeys in the West."

They each took another swig from the flask, the spirits warming Rakovich's throat.

"Don't let Lieutenant Valeev hear you talk like that," he said. "He may not appreciate your humour the way I do."

"But I am deadly serious," Zimyatov said with a wink. "Always."

Above their heads, something fluttered through the trees. A bird let out a brief chirp, the first to herald the coming dawn.

Rakovich handed back the flask. "Let's go to war."

6

KEEP MOVING

The BMPs raced across the fields, engines roaring with power. Rakovich's body shook as they hurtled over bumpy ground and he clung tightly to the lip of the hatch in the vehicle's roof. He was exposed here. One good hit from a British tank and he was as dead as Tikhomirov. But he needed to be up here as long as he could, where he could see what was happening, where he could act like a real leader. He was going to get this right or die trying.

With every second that passed, he expected the British to open fire. They had fought hard to keep him and his men back yesterday, surely they would do the same now.

But the bullets didn't fly. There was no thunder of artillery or roar of shells exploding around him. Only the rumble of the Soviets' own vehicles, the thump of their mortars, and the whir of the supporting helicopters.

The lack of fire somehow made it worse. At least if he was being shot at he would know that he was in a fight. Instead, he felt like he was driving into a trap. But it was too late to change the plan. He just had to keep going and do the best he could with whatever he found.

The mortar barrage stopped as they got close to the village. The helicopters swooped in overhead.

At last, Rakovich's BMP reached the first of the buildings. Akayev barely slowed as they entered, avoiding a heap of rubble but clipping a civilian car as they hurtled through the narrow streets. His voice came over the intercom.

"Which way, Praporshchik?"

Rakovich glanced around. There was still no sign of where the enemy were hidden, but Akayev needed an answer.

"Left," Rakovich said, and held on to the edge of his hatch as the BMP turned.

A civilian car careened down the street towards them, swerving all over the road.

"Gunner," Rakovich snapped, "scare that fucker out of our way."

A high explosive round blasted the tarmac to the left of the car. Its panicked driver veered right, off the road and through a garden fence. Even as the sound of the gun died away, there was still no answering fire from the British.

The BMP turned a corner and suddenly they were out of the village, roaring across open country. Less than a mile away, two bridges straddled a river.

Rakovich grinned. The objective was wide open.

"Go left," he said into the intercom. "We need to get there before—"

A span of the closest bridge burst apart, stone blocks tumbling into the river below. A moment later, the rest of the bridge exploded, disappearing in a cloud of dust. Even as Rakovich turned his gaze toward the other bridge, it too disintegrated, chunks of concrete smashing into the bank and throwing up fountains of water.

Rakovich cursed. According to reconnaissance, those bridges were by far the best way across the river. Now they would have to do this the hard way.

He halted the BMP behind the cover of a ruined building and waited for the rest of the platoon to catch up. Smoke billowed around the far bank of the river as the battalion's mortars prepared the way for them.

There was a clatter from the driver's compartment as Akayev replaced his regular periscope with a taller one. He pulled a lever and the trim vane rose on the front of the vehicle, an extra section of metal to raise their prow and stop them becoming swamped.

"Gunners, keep firing as we go," Rakovich said into the radio. "Make them keep their heads down until we're across."

Then the BMP jumped forward and they were away again, the whole platoon racing through the smoke screen towards the river. Heavier weapons than they carried were already blazing away, tanks and helicopters hitting the British on the far side of the river.

Akayev zig-zagged the vehicle across the open ground, swerving back and forth at alarming speed. Just as they reached the riverbank he slammed on the brakes and their speed plummeted, but they still hit the water with a loud splash and a plume of spray.

In theory, the BMP was designed for this sort of action. In practice, Rakovich felt horribly vulnerable as they crossed the river at little more than a crawl, floating in a steel box. The angle of the bank put them out of sight of the waiting British, but that didn't mean they were safe from mortar bombs or aerial attacks.

Then there was a bump and growl as the tracks bit into the ground on the west bank. The BMP shot up and over the edge, coming back down hard. Rakovich was thrown about, his elbow collided with the wall, and he fought back a yelp of pain. The back of the vehicle filled with a chorus of curses.

He'd expected to land facing tough resistance, but instead he saw the British in retreat. Their tanks and infantry were pulling back, firing as they went, leaving ground scattered with craters and the burning shells of broken tanks.

Rakovich's platoon were the first across. What he did now could decide the outcome of this engagement.

His instinct was to keep moving and try to turn the British withdrawal into a rout. But until the engineers got a bridge across that river, the tanks couldn't cross. If he advanced fast, then he'd soon lose their support.

"Keep going, Akayev," he said. "But slow down. We need to give the others time to catch up."

He smiled at the sight of his platoon moving unprompted into formation around him, even as Lieutenant Chugainov's voice burst from the radio, cursing out his men as they failed to get into line.

His relief was cut short as British helicopters appeared above the retreating tanks, their rocket launchers pointing straight at him.

Beletsky stood upright in his BMP, trying to balance an Igla surface-to-air missile on his shoulder even as the vehicle swerved from side to side. Further back, engineers were bringing up MTU-72 vehicle-launched bridges, the ponderous vehicles rolling toward the river. Shilka anti-aircraft guns and Strela-10 missile vehicles lined up on the bank and started offering covering fire.

The air filled with metal, bullets and shrapnel scything through the blue. The first of the British aircraft fell, its front window shattered, smoke pouring from where the pilot should be. It seemed to take forever to hit the ground, tumbling around and around before crashing to earth.

Even through the clouds of covering smoke, Rakovich could see that the British tanks were all gone. The helicopters, exposed and under fire, followed them.

"Turn off the smoke generator," he ordered. "And head for that hill."

Cautiously, the platoon approached a nearby ridge, the other two BMPs forming line formation around Rakovich's vehicle. It all seemed too easy, the British melting away like snow on a city street. He held himself tense, waiting for the counter-attack that must surely come at any moment. As he crested the ridge, he expected to see them waiting there, British armour and infantry, lined up and ready to destroy him.

There was nothing. Just more countryside, with a farm maybe three miles west and a patch of woodland beyond that. If not for the smell of burning vehicles and the sound of fighting further down the line, he could almost have believed that this was just a quiet country day.

More woods were off to the north, to the right of the platoon's route of advance. A perfect place for an ambush, just as the farm was. He'd heard stories of Russian peasants in the Great Patriotic War resisting the German invaders. Would the Germans resist them in the same way? He was just a praporshchik, and these sorts of problems shouldn't be his concern, but men's lives were in his hands now.

Aircraft flew out of the west, low and fast. Suddenly the river behind him was the sight of frantic activity. One of the portable bridges exploded as a bomb hit, tipping a tank into the river. Anti-aircraft batteries fired and two of the planes plummeted from the sky, while a third trailed smoke as it twisted around and headed back the way it had come.

One more thing that wasn't his concern. One more thing that could kill him. He had to trust in the others to do their jobs. He had to get on with his.

At his signal, the platoon leaders dismounted from their vehicles and came to join him. Zinoviev was grinning, Kholodov looking around nervously, as if he expected the NATO fighters to reappear just to catch him in the open.

"We haven't got much time, so just listen," Rakovich called down to them from his BMP. "When the tanks catch up, we advance again. My main concern is that farm. The British might have left an ambush or the farmer might decide to be a hero. We can't get bogged down, so we keep rolling past, but keep your eyes on it. The slightest hint of trouble, blast the fucker with everything you've got. Clear?"

All three sergeants nodded.

"Good. We're heading for a town named Königslutter am Elm, on the far side of those woods. Try not to fuck up and die before we get there. Dismissed."

As they got back into their vehicles, tanks passed through the company and down the hill's western slope. Rakovich waited for the other platoons to take the lead, then led his off the hill.

"Gunner, keep an eye on that farm," he said. "If you see anything suspicious, shoot the crap out of it."

The ground was open, only flimsy fences obstructing their advance. The tanks tore through those and the BMPs followed, scattering broken posts and tangles of wire. Rakovich found his attention torn between checking their progress and watching the woods.

Nothing went this smoothly — last night had proved that. Surely something was coming.

"Praporshchik!" Yefrimov shouted, his voice too loud over the intercom. "I think I see someone in the farm."

"Then shoot," Rakovich replied. "Don't wait for them to shoot first, you idiot!"

Even as the gun roared, Rakovich felt a twinge of doubt. What if it had just been a farmer, sheltering in his farm because he had nowhere else to run?

No. That was bullshit. No civilian would stick around through this. He couldn't risk his men's lives for someone too stupid to exist.

A high explosive round hit the farmhouse square in the centre of the front wall. Wood and plaster crumpled at the force of the blast. Windows shattered. Seconds later, more HE shells and 5.45mm rounds spattered what remained, as the whole platoon joined in.

"Zoryn 217," Leontev said through the radio. "Situation report. Over."

"Zoryn 210, this is Zoryn 217," Rakovich replied. "Suspicious activity spotted in the farm house, we are engaging on the move. Over."

"Zoryn 217, have you taken any fire? Over."

"Zoryn 210, no sir. Over."

"Then stop wasting ammunition you bloody idiot. Over."

Rakovich scowled. They could have been in real danger. Leontev wasn't here. He didn't know.

He tried to keep the anger out of his voice as he responded.

"Zoryn 210, yes sir. Over." He switched to the platoon channel. "Cease fire, all of you. Apparently we have to let the enemy shoot us first."

As they approached the trees, there was still no resistance. The only signs of British activity were the track marks left by their retreat, the ground torn up by tanks and transports as they fled the battle front. Maybe the British really weren't as tough as everyone made out. Maybe they were too scared to face the might of the Red Army, the force that had brought down the German Reich.

Or maybe they were waiting in the woods. All it needed was a few men hiding behind a tree, rocket launcher at the ready, and Rakovich's whole platoon would be reduced to corpses in smouldering steel shells.

He wanted to dismount the men. They could sweep the woods, using the trees as cover, while the BMPs provided fire support. But the tanks were rushing on, the radio full of excited talk of keeping the British on the run, of pushing for Königslutter and then on to Bonn. They had to keep advancing, to make the most of the shock their attack had caused, to prevent the enemy from pausing and regrouping. And for that, the men had to stay in their vehicles.

His thoughts were interrupted by a call on the radio — Leontev again.

"Zoryn 217, this is Zoryn 210. Change of orders. Wheel left and head south. You are to take the village of Süpplingenburg. Over."

"Zoryn 210, this is Zoryn 217. Understood. Over."

He pulled out a map and scanned the local area, plotting out a route to their target. A moment later, he was on the radio to his section leaders, telling them the new plan.

He didn't know why this Süpplingenburg mattered. But then, he hadn't known much about Königslutter either. What mattered was that he had his orders and that they suited him better than rushing on into the teeth of whatever the enemy had planned.

He snapped an order into the intercom and they turned south.

7

RIVER CROSSING

This time, the British were parked behind a shallow river, with one flank anchored on a series of barns and the other on a small wood. Peering at them through a pair of binoculars, Rakovich saw that they were well dug in, with two lines of trenches and machine-gun emplacements several hundred meters apart. He didn't know how many men were there, but he wasn't worried. Only so many could fit into those two lines of defences, and his own men had shown their worth now. They could take on whatever the capitalists threw at them.

He lowered the binoculars and turned to his troops, who were spread out behind the BMPs.

"It's like looking at the world's worst beauty pageant," he said. "And I'm not even the winner."

"There are no winners in this contest," Zimyatov said.

Some of the men laughed. Others were still nervous, clutching their rifles and looking towards the river.

This was Rakovich's chance to make a mark with them, his moment of heroic leadership. He was in command now, and though that came with responsibilities, it was also a privilege he was ready to rise to.

"You can do this," he said. "You know how I know that? Because you've already done tougher stuff and lived to tell the tale. Think about it. Who fought off a British attack, with tanks?"

"We did," some of the men said.

"And who fought their way across a river, right in the face of the capitalist guns?"

"We did." More of them this time, and with some enthusiasm.

"And who punched straight through that first British line and kept on rolling, so now we're onto their second line?"

"We did!" It was practically a cheer, all of his men joining in.

"Right. That river's nothing compared with what we crossed before, and there aren't any tanks and helicopters around to back them up here. So let's get stuck in, you brilliant bastards."

This time they really did cheer. Then the engines of the BMPs started up and they began to advance, marching behind the cover of the transports.

The mortar fire started as they were approaching the river. There was a whistle, then a thud and a fountain of dirt.

"Faster!" Rakovich called out. "We want to get in there before they find their aim."

The cannons on the BMPs started firing, causing great gouts of dirt to spray from the ground around the British lines. Assault rifles let rip and bullets clanged off the fronts of the BMPs.

Clutching his gun tight, Rakovich hurried after the middle BMP. Despite the deadly bullets swarming through the air around him, he grinned and felt his heart lift. They were going to do this. They were going to make another breakthrough before the rest of the army even showed up. This was what heroes and officers were made of.

A mortar bomb landed behind them. Dirt showered Rakovich's back. A man bellowed in pain and sank to the ground, clutching his leg. Immediately, Obolensky was on him, medical kit out, wrapping the wound and delivering morphine.

The bullets seemed to fly faster as they approached the river. The men crowded in closer behind the BMPs, running hunched towards the peril ahead. But bunched up like this, a whole section would be vulnerable to a single well-placed mortar bomb.

"Rebane, Plakans, Dologodin!" Rakovich bellowed, hoping to be heard by the gunners above the roar of the engines. "Take that fucking mortar out!"

Maybe someone heard him or maybe they were just getting their eye in, but either way, the cannon fire zeroed in on where the mortar was firing from. It was hard to tell from this angle, but as he glanced out, Rakovich thought he saw a British soldier falling near the back of that trench.

They were getting close to the river. The BMPs slowed and headed down a muddy bank. There were splashes as they hit the water and kept going.

"After them!" Rakovich shouted, urging the men forward. A few had stopped at the edge of the water, leaving them exposed. A burst of gunfire caught one man and he went down, the blood from his side soaking into the mud. That was enough to get the others moving and firing as they went, trying to keep the enemy's heads down.

But Rakovich was starting to see the problem with their situation. The British positions were well located to strafe the water. Though his men could wade out behind the BMPs, they couldn't benefit from their cover much with the British on high ground. And though they could fire back, the British had the cover that they lacked.

He paused for a moment, assault rifle raised, surveying the British trenches. A man appeared, head and shoulders out, his own rifle raised and ready.

Rakovich fired first. It was a hastily aimed shot, but it was on the mark. The British soldier jerked and the rifle fell from his hands. For a moment he stood there, staring dumbly into the distance. Then he fell back into his trench.

One down. But how many more were there?

A mortar round burst in the shallows close to Rakovich. On instinct he threw himself to the ground. Except that it wasn't ground, it was water, and now he was completely submerged. An involuntary gasp filled his mouth with mud and left him choking. He pushed himself to his knees and emerged dripping from the river. He coughed and spat, his throat raw, then got back to his feet.

The BMPs had stopped halfway across the river. Their engines were roaring but none of them were moving. Rakovich strode angrily towards the nearest one, yanked open the rear door, and stuck his head inside.

"What the fuck are you doing?" he yelled.

"Obstacles in the river, Praproshchik!" Lobachov shouted back. "We're stuck on something."

"Then push harder!"

"I'm trying, but I don't think it'll get us through."

Water dribbled from Rakovich's hair into his eyes, blurring his vision. He wiped it away only for more water to spray in his face as bullets hit the river.

He crouched in the water to create as small a target as possible, then peered around the BMP. He couldn't see what was blocking the way, though he could see something poking out of the water up ahead.

"Snegur, Szolkowski!" he shouted. "Get over here, you useless wastes of breath."

The two riflemen ran over and crouched in the shallows beside Rakovich. Snegur's scars made his scowl fiercer, but both bore expressions of terrible determination.

"I'm going past the BMP to see what's getting in our way," Rakovich said. "If anyone seems to be shooting my way, you send so much lead at him he'll think he's in a pencil factory. Understood?"

"Yes, Praporshchik."

Rakovich flung his dripping rifle into the back of the BMP, then slid forward through the water, advancing at a crouch with only his head protruding. It was relatively still here, in the shadow of the BMP, but he could see the current swirling and foaming ahead. After a few moments, he reached those unsettled waters, took a deep breath, and plunged fully in.

The water was full of dirt churned up by the grinding of the BMP's tracks and Rakovich cursed himself for ordering Lobachov to push harder. But he couldn't just turn back — each time he advanced like this he increased the likelihood of being shot.

He crept forward, feeling his way with hands and feet. Something loomed out of the gloom ahead of him and a moment later he found himself holding onto an iron post.

He had been under long enough that he was feeling it in his lungs, that heavy, burning pressure that said he didn't have the oxygen his body wanted. Still, he ran a hand down the side of the post, trying to work out what was going on. He got far enough to feel that it was firmly wedged in the ground before his need for air forced him to surface.

He emerged gasping amid the swirling waters, next to one of the protrusions sticking out of the water. Bullets cracked off the BMP, then hit the water next to him. He snatched a lungful of air and pushed back down out of sight.

This time he clung to the post, running his hands down until he reached the bottom. He crouched next to it and peered through the water.

Somehow, the British had managed to wedge this post firmly in among the rocks and rubble of the river bed. There were even signs of concrete, messily laid down but tough enough to keep him from pulling out the post.

He pushed along the bottom to the next post over. The situation was the same there, and at the next one along. A row of metal rods like sturdy fence posts, driven in all along the crossing area, with barbed wire connecting them beneath the surface.

His lungs aching again, he rose to a crouch. As his head emerged from the water, he realised that he'd moved away from the shelter of the BMP. Bullets hit the surface all around him and spray lashed his face.

There was a rattle of fire from his own line and shouts from Snegur and Szolkowski, urging everyone else to join them in blasting the British positions. The hail of bullets around Rakovich subsided and he seized the moment, wading rapidly back through the water and in behind one of the BMPs.

Zimyatov and Zinoviev were there, the latter wide-eyed with eagerness, the former shaking his head in relief.

"Bloody hell, Vlad, you look like you've been shoved up a mermaid."

"And yet I still look better than you."

Rakovich grabbed his rifle, then raised his voice to be heard by his men.

"Cut the engines! The BMPs aren't going anywhere."

As the noise died away, he considered his options. They couldn't get through those posts and there was nowhere else nearby where they could readily cross the river, especially not with these British troops in position to flank them. They had to deal with this here or not at all.

Besides, weren't they Red Army soldiers? Desperate assaults were the stuff on which they had been raised.

"The vehicles can't get through," he said to the sergeants. "That means we go in without. Gunners can give us covering fire. We get close enough to use grenades against their trenches, then charge in behind."

"What about smoke?" Zimyatov asked quietly. "To cover our advance."

"Wind's the wrong way. All we'll do is blind ourselves for the first few steps. Now go tell your men, and Zimyatov, make sure Kholodov and his men know."

As the others moved away, Rakovich pointed his rifle at the British defences and squeezed the trigger. Despite it's dip in the river, the gun fired as well as it ever had. That was Soviet engineering for you — not fancy but reliable.

He looked around. The men were ready, crouching behind their vehicles with weapons in hand. Some stood tall, instinctively trying to avoid a soaking, while others crouched, preferring the certainty of cold and wet to the risk of bullets.

"Ready?" Rakovich bellowed. "Now!"

They ran out around the vehicles, rifles raised and firing. The cannons on the BMPs roared and dirt burst from the ground around the trenches. Bullets hissed back and forth. The soft thud of the mortar firing was followed by the thump of an explosion.

They reached the front of the BMPs and started trying to get across the barbed wire. But with the water in the way, it was hard to see where the wire lay. Men cursed as clothes tore and they got tangled in the barrier. Some pulled out cutters and felt around beneath the water, searching for strands of wire, but that meant there was less firepower directed against the enemy. One man screamed as a bullet struck his left arm.

"Grenades!" Rakovich shouted from where he was stuck behind one of the posts. "Let's make life miserable for those bastards."

The men pulled grenades from their pouches and flung them with enthusiasm. Rakovich himself pulled his arm back and threw with all his might, sending the deadly orb hurtling in a long, smooth arc.

But even before they landed, he could see that the grenades were falling short of the trenches. In his desperation to do something he had misjudged the distance and the effect of the slope the British held. The grenades hit the dirt and started rolling back, to explode along the bank and in the shallows. His own men ducked and covered their heads as mud, water, and shrapnel hurtled past.

Obolensky had reached the injured man and was bandaging his arm, a difficult job while they both stood in waist high water with bullets raining down around them. A mortar bomb landed, close enough to cause some flesh wounds to men on the left.

"Do we charge now?" Zinoviev cried out, one hand on a post, about to try to leap over the unseen barbed wire.

But Rakovich could see a lost cause when he was part of it. With a heavy heart, he called out the inevitable order.

"Pull back!"

ONCE RAKOVICH and his men were up the bank, the British ceased fire.

It felt like a moment of pity, though Rakovich suspected that their reasons were more pragmatic. Everybody had burned through a lot of ammunition in that fight. Soldiers with any sense would preserve what they had for the next assault.

He set his men to work digging foxholes in the field behind their bank. They needed somewhere to shelter while he worked out what to do next.

"Are you sure we can't get around?" Zimyatov asked as the two of them stared across the river.

"Look at the water. Anywhere the banks are suitable, they've put those damn posts in. Unless you fancy a night in the water with a pair of wire cutters, we're not going anywhere."

"So what do we do instead?"

"I don't know. Fly over like fairies. Make friends with the local moles and dig a tunnel underneath. Maybe sit here and hope they die of old age first."

"I'm not sure you're taking this seriously."

"I'm sure the British are."

A shout from one of the BMPs made them look around.

"Praporshchik!" Lobachov called out. "It's the Captain for you."

Rakovich gritted his teeth. This was bound to turn into another dressing down, but putting it off wouldn't change that. He reached the BMP, set aside a paperback Lobachov had left in his seat, and took the radio.

"Rakovich here."

"Why aren't you across that river yet?" Leontev snarled, his voice twisted by the crackle of the radio set.

"The British have set up anti-vehicle obstacles in the river. We couldn't get across."

"Couldn't you? Or weren't you willing to do what needed to be done?"

"My men tried their best."

"It's not your men I doubt."

"I'm working on a plan. We'll have another go at crossing in a couple of hours."

"Like hell you will. I'm not letting you waste time and resources on a task you're not up to. Head south through the woods, around the bend of the river. I'm going to give you coordinates for a village I want you to seize there. And Rakovich?"

"Yes, Captain?"

"You'd better not fuck it up this time."

8

HOUSE TO HOUSE

The three BMPs shot out of the wood at full speed, their tracks churning the fields as they tore toward the village. This time, Rakovich kept his head down. Any recklessness he'd felt when they set out had faded. They'd lost enough good men already, he didn't want to add himself to the pile.

They'd barely left the wood when flashes appeared just inside the village. Explosions filled the air to left and right. Debris clattered off the side of his vehicle.

Rakovich looked out from the commander's station in the turret, surveying the state of his unit. Kholodov's BMP was fine but Zinoviev's had taken a hit. The front right was a mangled mess of jagged metal. The vehicle had skidded to a halt sideways-on to the village, the wrecked remains of its track lying in the dirt.

"Fire at the smoke!" Rakovich yelled at his gunner. "We have to take out the anti-tank rockets."

He turned to shout at the men in the back of the BMP. "Enemy in the village. Fire at anything that moves."

To his amazement, men were stumbling out of the ruined vehicle, waving the smoke away as they emerged. The bark of rifle fire filled the air and the first man fell. The others flung themselves into the dirt, crawling for shelter behind the shell of their transport.

Rakovich stared at the village. It was the woods all over again — not knowing where an enemy might be hidden, ready to cripple them with a lucky shot.

He toggled his radio to the platoon command channel.

"Kholodov, you see that line of trees just before the village?"

"Yes, Praporshchik," the sergeant replied.

"Stop there and dismount. Leave your gunner to provide covering fire. We're going in on foot."

"On foot? But all that gunfire—"

"You want to go the same way as Lieutenant Tikhomirov?"

"No, Praporshchik!"

"Then get out at those fucking trees and use the cover to advance."

"Yes, Praporshchik."

Zimyatov was already passing on similar orders to Lobachov, their driver. The BMP came to a halt behind the frame of a half-built barn and the men tramped out, rifles raised and ready.

Rebane hit a button. Smoke grenades shot from the sides of the turret, landing in front of them. Within seconds half the buildings were hidden from view.

"Go, go, go!" Rakovich yelled, running out past his men.

The AK-74 was cold and hard in his hands, swinging back and forth as he ran. He kept his eyes on the buildings as they appeared through the billowing smoke, but he couldn't tell which shapes were soldiers in the windows and which were shadows.

Bullets hit the ground inches from his feet. He put on an extra burst of speed. His lungs burned and the smoke tickled his throat but he didn't care. Only when he reached a wall at the edge of the village did he let himself stop, ducking out of view.

Next to him, the soldiers of Number One Section flung themselves down behind the wall. Zimyatov was grinning, as was the man next to him. Others shook with nerves. One of them was staring in disbelief at the hole where a bullet had torn through the edge of his sleeve but somehow missed flesh and bone. Back behind the ruined barn, their

BMP was firing at the village, its gun giving the enemy infantry a reason to keep their own heads down.

A hundred yards to the east, Kholodov and his section were advancing through the cover of trees and bushes. But something was wrong with their BMP. The gun wasn't firing, the turret instead making jerky movements as it failed to draw a bead on the village. There was no sign of damage on the vehicle, and Rakovich cursed as he realised that his men had been endangered by a mechanical fault.

Someone would get a kicking for that later. Now, he had to focus on the task ahead of him.

"Zimyatov", he shouted, "we need to clear out those houses. You take the one with the red door, then move left. Kholodov will take the houses to the right."

"And you, Praporshchik?" Zimyatov asked.

"With Kholodov," Rakovich replied.

He wouldn't say it to the men, but he trusted Zimyatov to the ends of the earth, while he wouldn't trust Kholodov to the far side of the street. The man was no coward, but he had no discipline. This was what happened when you put an artist in charge of something that actually mattered.

Head down, Rakovich dashed across the open ground between the wall and the trees. Dirt spurted up around him as bullets hit and his heart hammered with every swift step. After seconds that felt like hours, he flung himself down next to Kholodov, his back against the trunk of a tall pine.

"When Zimyatov starts to move, we're taking that house with the blue door," he said. "Then we move right. I'll go first, leading your second fire team. You cover us. Then we alternate down the street."

"Sounds like so much fun," Kholodov said. "Beletsky, new guys. When the Praporshchik runs, you run with him."

The men joined them, crouching behind the tree with assault rifles in hand. One of the new recruits was pale as a ghost, his eyes wide. Beletsky, in contrast, already looked like a man well accustomed to war, grim visaged and ready to go.

On cue, Zimyatov rose and started running toward the village, half his section with him. Their BMP launched more smoke, the wind swirling it around the vehicle and across the fields.

"Now!"

Rakovich was on his feet, running as fast as he could towards the houses. Gunfire flashed from the windows, but Kholodov and his team opened fire, forcing the defenders to duck back inside.

Reaching the house, Rakovich pressed himself against the wall beside the front door.

"You." He nodded to one of the new men. "Grenade through the window. Beletsky, you follow me, then you two follow Beletsky."

The new man pulled the pin from his grenade and threw it through the shattered window. The explosion blew out the remaining glass, shards shining in the sunlight.

Rakovich kicked the door open and ran in, rifle raised. Bullets shattered the doorframe behind him. He moved left, returning fire at the flash amid the dust and shadows. A body fell to the floor.

Beletsky followed, firing at something to the right. A moment later, the two new men entered, looking at the body as if it were going to rise up and bite them.

"Come on," Rakovich said. "There are more upstairs."

He headed out of the room's only internal door, keeping his rifle facing forward, finger on the trigger.

As he passed the body, he couldn't help but look down. The man was older than he had expected, his face starting to sag into late middle age. He stared at the ceiling with a look of shock and disappointment.

Rakovich didn't know if this was the first man he had killed. Anything could have happened in the chaos facing the British earlier. But this was the first time he had been sure, the first time he had seen the results up close. The first time he had faced his own victim.

Should he have felt some guilt or grief? He almost wished that he did. It would have made him more human, at least by the standards that his family held. But all he felt was a deadened sense of curiosity, an idle wondering at what had brought this man here.

"Capitalist German territorials," Beletsky said, pointing at the uniform. "Maybe I'll get home to my wife after all."

"How did they mobilise to quickly?" Rakovich asked. "They weren't meant to be ready."

"So it's not a good sign?"

"Is it ever a good sign when some bastard shoots at you?"

As they approached the stairs, a burst of fire ripped holes in the wall next to them. Rakovich ducked back hurriedly. As he considered his options, an explosion sounded through the ceiling, followed by a scream.

There was no time to hesitate. He ran up the stairs, rifle forward, ready to face anyone who had survived.

There was no need. At the top of the stairs lay a body, the left arm and half the chest blown away. In one of the bedrooms another man lay screaming as blood streamed from his arm.

Ignoring the screams, Rakovich checked the rest of the rooms, but they were all empty. While Beletsky stemmed the bleeding from the injured German's arm, he descended the stairs, reaching the bottom just as Kholodov's fire team arrived. Obolensky, the section medic, was first through the door.

"There's a wounded man upstairs," Rakovich said. "Do what you can for him."

Kholodov looked around, counting off his men.

"Beletsky?" he asked sadly.

"He's fine. Just keeping the patient alive."

"So we're treating the British wounded, Praporshchik?"

"German. And yes, we are. I might be a bastard, but I'm not a murderer."

They moved out and down the street, hugging the wall as small arms fire crackled around them.

Reaching the next house, Rakovich burst straight in, rifle at the ready, to find no-one there. His fire team followed, working their way through the ground floor.

At the top of the stairs, one of the new men opened fire. Rakovich raced up after him, taking the steps two at a time, only to find that there was no-one else around.

"What were you firing at?" he asked.

The man blushed and replied with a heavy accent. "Thought I saw someone."

"Alright." Rakovich nodded. "Better to kill a few cupboards than to let the enemy shoot first."

The man smiled. "Yes, Praporshchik."

Beletsky interrupted. "Praporshchik, Sergeant Kholodov is about to move across the street."

Rakovich led the others back to the front of the house. "Beletsky, you take the door, we'll take the window. Any sign of British or Germans, shoot."

He crouched at one corner of the window, rifle covering the far side of the road. Any window could hold a man with a gun. He found his attention constantly shifting as he tried to watch it all, to keep his men safe.

Kholodov ran out of the house and was half-way across the street before someone fired. Rakovich and his men replied, bullets spraying the neighbouring windows. Broken glass and bullet casings rattled to the ground as the sound of shots echoed from the buildings.

Then Kholodov was at the door, bursting straight in and disappearing from sight.

"Cease fire," Rakovich shouted. "Now onto the next one. Beletsky, take the lead."

Beletsky ran out and to the next house. He threw his weight against the door, cursing as it failed to give way. Even as Rakovich emerged to follow him, he fired at the lock, then shoulder-charged it again. The door gave and he careened through it, disappearing from sight amid the sound of gunfire.

Rakovich swung around the doorframe, rifle raised, and almost tripped over Beletsky. He was lying on his side in the hallway amid a spreading pool of blood, groaning and clutching his chest.

"Obolensky!" Rakovich yelled.

He couldn't stop to help Beletsky. If the enemy were still in the house, they could kill him while his guard was down. He had to keep going and hope the medic came soon.

Through a doorway to the left was a reception room. An enemy soldier slumped in one of the chairs. If it wasn't for the red stain across his belly, Rakovich would have thought he was resting.

He followed the rest of his fire team through the house. The new men seemed more determined than before, their movements more certain. One fired a burst ahead of him as he advanced up the stairs, taking out a German before the man could aim. The other opened fire as he rounded a corner and a body thudded to the ground. They might be green conscripts, but these men had been trained by the Red Army, and now that the initial shock had passed their learning was coming back.

As soon as the house was clear, Rakovich ran back to the hallway. Beletsky was still breathing, but it was shallow. Blood was bubbling out of his chest. Rakovich ripped open a first-aid kit and pressed a bandage onto the wound.

"Obolensky!" he yelled again. "Get in here."

Guns were blazing somewhere else in the village. He heard other people shouting Obolensky's name. Were they calling him here or had someone else been shot? What if Obolensky himself was down? Anything could be happening out there. His men needed him but he couldn't bring himself to leave the wounded man.

"Stay with me, Radoslav," he said. "I don't want to replace you with another idiot fresh out of basic training."

"You've never called me Radoslav before, Praporshchik." Beletsky smiled sadly. "It must be bad."

"You should be so lucky." Rakovich pulled out another bandage. Nothing he did seemed enough to stop the flow of blood. "You won't be fucking off to some rear-area hospital to get sponge baths from the pretty nurses. We need you here, understand?"

"But I need to get home. Sasha's waiting."

Beletsky's expression changed. His formerly pained look became one of calm.

Footsteps approached and Obolensky ran into the house, clutching his medical kit.

"You're too late," Rakovich said. "The fucker just died on me."

Ignoring him, Obolensky knelt to examine Beletsky.

"Not quite, Praporshchik," he said.

He opened his bag, pulled out a dose of morphine, and jabbed Beletsky with it. Then he ripped open a bandage and set to work around Beletsky's chest, directing Rakovich to hold it in place while he worked.

"He needs to get back to the regimental aid station, fast." Obolensky tied off the bandage. "Can we get an ambulance here?"

"Not likely." Rakovich shouted out the doorway. "Get a BMP now! Beletsky needs medical evacuation."

Beletsky groaned, the first sound he'd made in minutes. Rakovich had never been so glad to see a man in pain and he almost laughed in relief. But then he heard gunfire, and the grim challenge of their situation came crashing back into his mind.

Gathering the two recruits who were the remains of his fire team, he headed out into the street again. He ran to the next house, barged open the door, and rushed straight in. The place was empty. No German soldiers. No-one he could give the same treatment Beletsky had received. His finger tensed uselessly on the trigger.

"Fucking shit!" he snarled as the new recruits returned from checking upstairs. "You took hours going up there. If there were Germans, they'd have shot you before you were up the first three steps."

He pointed at one of them.

"Next house, you lead."

As NIGHT FELL, Rakovich gathered his sergeants beside Kholodov's BMP. Nearby, a rifleman stood watching the few civilians who hadn't fled before the fighting. Two injured German soldiers lay on blankets next to them, waiting for retrieval to an aid station. Rakovich didn't fancy their chances of survival. After Beletsky, he didn't much care. He wanted the enemy to hurt. He wanted them to bleed out in each other's arms, to see the light dying in the eyes of men they called friends. He wanted them to suffer like his men did.

"Casualties?" he asked, looking around at the squad leaders.

"Two dead, two injured," Zinoviev said. "And the BMP's fucked."

"One dead, three injured," Zimyatov said. "One of them isn't too serious, but the others had to go back."

"Just Beletsky," Kholodov said. "They got him to the surgeon, but..."

They stood in silence. Akayev had said that Beletsky was screaming as he drove away from the medical station. That meant he had been alive still, but it didn't mean he was going to last the night.

"We won't be getting reinforcements any time soon," Rakovich said. "Or a new BMP. Zinoviev, your section can split up and take the seats of the others we've lost."

"Yes, Praporshchik," Zinoviev said. "We're still keen to do our part. You'll see."

"Grab some food, have a smoke, take a shit if you need to," Rakovich said. "I doubt we'll be here for long, so take the rest while you can. Just don't get caught with your dick in your hand if the enemy shows up. Dismissed."

As they turned to walk away, he grabbed Kholodov by the arm. The sergeant looked surprised as he was dragged into the darkness between the trees and the BMP.

"Your turret," Rakovich said, pointing up at the gun that had refused to turn. "When did you last test it?"

"I don't know," Kholodov said, looking away. "You'd have to check Akayev's log. He's the one who—"

Rakovich punched him in the gut. Kholodov doubled over, gasping for breath.

"You're the section sergeant, you lazy sack of shit," Rakovich growled. "You're the one who makes sure the equipment works. And if you'd done your job, we might not be wondering if Beletsky's wife is now a widow."

Kholodov grimaced as he forced himself to stand straight.

"Yes, Praporshchik," he wheezed. "Will there be anything else, Praporshchik?"

Rakovich looked him in the eye. The man was slack and decadent, but at least he'd shown nerve in leading his men.

"You fought bravely today," he said. "But that doesn't mean you can get away with your usual bullshit. It's life or death now, and I'll be watching to make sure you don't get us all killed. Is that clear, sergeant?"

"Yes, Praproshchik."

9

DISCIPLINE

The distant rumble of an engine jolted Rakovich awake. He grabbed his rifle with twitching hands and crouched at the house's broken window, staring out into what passed for a street. His eyes darted back and forth, looking for men, for movement, for any sign of trouble.

A vehicle was approaching out of the pre-dawn light, its headlights narrow slits. He could just make out the shape of a military transport truck, jolting up and down as it traversed the ill-kept road to the village. It was coming from the north-east, where the rest of the company were based, but he wasn't taking any chances. He raised his weapon just in case.

Akayev stepped out from behind a wall, rifle at the ready. The driver brought the truck to a stop but didn't turn off the engine. Instead, he leaned out of the window to talk with Akayev. A moment later, the sentry waved him on into the village.

Rakovich rose from his place of concealment and eyed up the sofa on which he had spent the night. He had men on guard and he should trust them to rouse him if trouble came. Now might be his best chance to get another hour of sleep.

But now that he had woken up, his nerves jangled with tension.

Soft cushions weren't enough to let him sleep, and if he was awake anyway then he might as well make himself useful.

He slung his rifle over his shoulder, picked up his helmet, and headed out the door.

The truck stood across the road from where he had been sleeping. Its engine was switched off and the driver stood by the lowered tailgate, peering around at the bullet-scarred buildings.

"Hey you!" he called out, then stiffened as Rakovich came closer. "Sorry, Praporshchik. I couldn't see your rank in the dark."

"What have you got?" Rakovich asked, looking at the crates in the back of the truck.

"Rations, bullets, a few rockets." The driver pointed at each heap in turn. "Oh, and post."

He walked around to the cab, took a satchel from the passenger seat, and pulled out a handful of envelopes which he handed to Rakovich.

"Can I get some help with the boxes?" he asked. "The sooner I'm unloaded here, the sooner I can load up and supply the next platoon."

"I've got just the man for you."

Rakovich headed through a door that had been knocked off its hinges, into what had once been a well-kept family home. The carpets were nicer than the ones back home and there were more pictures than he was used to seeing on the walls. He tramped up the stairs and into a bedroom. A uniformed figure lay sprawled across the double bed, boots still on, his rifle leaning up against the nightstand.

"Up." Rakovich smacked Kholodov across the back of the head, waking him with a start. "Get your lazy arse downstairs and help unload the supply truck."

Kholodov groaned as he rolled over.

"Can't one of the privates do it, Praporshchik?" he asked.

"Did one of the privates fail to maintain our BMP?" Rakovich snarled.

"No, Praporshchik."

"And do you want me to tell command about what happened with that BMP?"

"No, Praporshchik." Kholodov showed more energy now, grabbing his rifle and rising from the bed.

"Then get downstairs and get to work." Rakovich kicked the sergeant in the arse as he passed. He didn't want him under any illusions that a little work was the limit of his punishment.

As Kholodov slouched down the stairs, Rakovich saw Szolkowski peering out of another bedroom, a cigarette dangling from between his lips, a look of malicious glee on his face.

"You go help him, private," he said. "Show you're useful for more than drawing bullets away from better men."

With his hastily assembled work crew gone, Rakovich pulled out a small flashlight and looked through the mail. Several men had letters from back home, including Beletsky and one of the privates they'd lost on the first night. Now that he was in charge, was it his job to reply to letters like that, to tell the families that their sons would never reply? What the fuck would he even write? "Sorry, Mrs. Beletsky, your husband got unlucky. I wish they'd hit one of my other useless bastards instead." That was work for an officer, not a Praporshchik with dreams of promotion.

To his surprise, one of the letters was for him. Inside, he found a sheet of neatly folded paper covered front and back with Anna's flowing writing. He smiled at the sight, glad of any human contact from beyond the war zone. Rather than rush to read it now, he thrust it into his pocket for later, then headed down the stairs.

Outside, the truck had mostly been unloaded, the crates piled up in front of the house.

"You dozy bastards," Rakovich said. "Don't just pile them up in the open. What happens then if the British attack, huh?"

While his men unloaded the last boxes into a nearby house, Rakovich approached the driver.

"What do I do with the letters for dead men?" he asked, quietly enough to ensure that no-one heard his moment of doubt.

"I don't know," the driver said. "We haven't been briefed for that."

"Can you take them back?"

The man shook his head. "My orders were to deliver them to the units."

Rakovich clenched his fist, crumpling the letters.

"Can you at least take this one?" He extracted Beletsky's letter from the bundle. "He was evacuated to an aid station last night. It will do him good to hear from home."

The driver hesitated, looking from the letters he'd only just offloaded to the expression on Rakovich's face.

"Sure," he said, taking the envelope. "I mean, if there's somewhere else to deliver this to, that makes sense."

Woken by the noises in the street, more men of third platoon were emerging from the occupied houses. Some were chewing on rations, some enjoying the first smoke of the day, some peering warily out into the countryside, guns clutched tight in their hands. None were the same men they had been two days before. The lucky ones had relaxed into war like a cosy bathrobe, finding that the swings of violence and calm suited them. Others were living on a knife edge of tension and Rakovich hoped that those would get over it, but if there was a way to help them then he didn't know what it was.

"Mail call," he shouted.

The men gathered around and he handed out the letters, to looks of pleasure from those who were hearing from loved ones. Others lingered by him, as if hoping he might have more that he'd forgotten about.

"Quit moping," he said. "I didn't get one either and you don't see me pulling a face like a drowned rat. We'll all hear from home soon enough."

He felt no shame at the lie. His job wasn't to be honest with these men, it was to keep them alive.

By now, Zimyatov had appeared.

"Morning, Praporshchik," he said brightly.

"Morning, Zimyatov. You sleep well?"

"Like a baby."

"So you shit yourself and then woke up every two hours screaming to be fed?"

"I've done worse on nights when Dynamo lost their match."

Rakovich grinned and shook his head, remembering some of the nights out they'd had while on leave. Zimyatov had a knack for finding quiet little drinking holes that got a whole lot livelier late at night. It was a gift that was wasted in a warzone.

"I need you to distribute the supplies," Rakovich said. "I left my ration tin down the back of a sofa, need to retrieve it while I remember."

He headed back to the house where he had spent the night. As he went, he cursed himself internally for his weakness. A commander didn't have to explain himself to his men, but he didn't want them to realise what he was really about. Not even Zimyatov.

He settled back onto the sofa, pulled out his flashlight, and started reading the letter from Anna. It was only a couple of days old. The rush to supply front line troops must have brought their mail forward with it. He could think of better reasons to sort out the mess of the army postal service, but he wasn't going to complain.

Reading about the little details of home life, from his father's pickles to Vadim's café, brought a smile to Rakovich's face. Anna didn't talk about his job or what was going on with the army. Mercifully, she also kept away from politics and their previous conversations. For once, she said nothing that could piss him off, and that made the letter an unadulterated pleasure. It was good to have something other than war to think about.

Knocking snapped him out of his reverie. He hastily thrust the letter away into a pocket, beside his dog-eared Communist Manifesto.

Zimyatov stood in the doorway. Despite the concerned look on his face, it was better to see him than anyone else in the platoon. Rakovich sank back into the sofa, safe in the knowledge that his friend wouldn't tell anyone about the letter.

"What's the matter, Zim?" Rakovich asked.

"It's the men." Zimyatov settled into an armchair beside the sofa. "I overheard some of them grumbling about the way you're treating Kholodov."

"What the fuck have they got to bitch about?"

"Some of them were just saying that you're being a dick."

"Ha!"

"But Zinoviev was saying that it's no way to treat a sergeant, that it could undermine morale in the unit."

"Fuck Sergeant Zinoviev. Of course he doesn't want to be treated that way."

"But if he's talking like that in front of the men..."

"I'll deal with it."

Rakovich stood, all ready to storm out and give Zinoviev a discrete kicking. But he stopped himself before he reached the door, caught by a thought.

Even if the words had come out of Zinoviev's mouth, they hadn't come from his brain. Zinoviev wasn't smart enough or articulate enough to think of a thing like that. So who had suggested it?

"Who else was Zinoviev talking with out there?" he asked. "Before you overheard him?"

"A few people. Plakans. Akayev. Szolkowski, I think."

"Fucking Szolkowski." Now it made sense. A man with a few brain-cells knocking around inside his head and a chip on his shoulder. "I'm going to cut this bullshit off before it spreads."

He stomped out into the street. The sun was rising, birds singing in the trees. A summer breeze brought the smell of smoke into the village, along with the sweet blossom scent from a nearby orchard. Down the road from the northeast, a jeep was approaching, its soft top down, the only occupant the driver.

What now?

Rakovich walked to the edge of the village, reaching the sentries just as the jeep squealed to a halt.

"Praporshchik Rakovich?" the driver said, leaning around the windscreen.

"That's me."

"Captain Leontev says you're to come to him."

"What for?"

"Not my job to know." But whatever the reason, the driver's face said it couldn't be good.

Reluctantly, Rakovich climbed into the jeep and let himself be driven away.

IN THE CENTRE OF A CLEARING, Rakovich stood stiffly to attention, letting Leontev's wrath wash over him. Of course he was getting shit from the captain. He was always getting shit from the captain. Why should things have been different just because they had a real enemy to fight?

"What the hell were you thinking?" Leontev asked, pacing back and forth beside his BMP, red-faced and scowling. "Sending one of your vehicles back while the enemy were still in the area. You could have lost us that village, Praporshchik Rakovich."

Leontev stopped pacing and stood glaring at him.

"Well?" the captain demanded.

"Sir, Private Beletsky was badly wounded," Rakovich said. "I concluded that he needed urgent care."

"Because now you're a doctor too? Let's hope you're better at that than soldiering."

"Sir, I was advised by our unit's medic that—"

"I don't care what your medic thought. You weakened your tactical position for the sake of one man. Do you know how many more you could have lost? I'm told you were already down one BMP. What if the enemy had counterattacked?"

"Sir, if we had been attacked in force, I don't believe that a single BMP would have made the difference."

"So you don't need a full complement of BMPs?" Leontev took a step closer. He spoke more softly, but there was steel behind his words. "Is that what you're saying?"

"No, sir." Rakovich made sure not to catch his superior's eye. He had to keep his temper. He was just a praporshchik, and this was a company commander.

"No, sir." Leontev gave the words a mocking edge. "You're running a platoon now, Rakovich, and I know you want to be an officer one day. Let me tell you, if you act like this, that promotion will never happen.

"An officer has to make hard decisions. He has to accept that some men will die to keep the rest safe. Sometimes he has to order them to their deaths. That's the job you're trying to do now, Rakovich, and you're making a piss-poor showing of it."

Rakovich clenched and unclenched a fist at his side, doing what little he could to release the rage building inside him. This was stupid and it was unfair. He'd done a good job of taking that village and he'd made the right call saving Beletsky. They'd been fine without the BMP, and now a man might live because of it. Not just a man but a soldier who had risked his life for his country. Leontev hadn't been there. He didn't know what Rakovich had seen or why he had done what he had done. The captain was full of shit.

But he didn't say any of that. Because he did want to be an officer, and picking this fight would be the surest way to screw his chances.

"Yes, sir," he said instead through gritted teeth.

"I'm going to send Lieutenant Valeev to keep an eye on you," Leontev said. "Make sure there's no more of this bullshit."

"Yes, sir." Rakovich's cheeks reddened. He didn't have a problem with Valeev. The political officer was far more reasonable than the captain and might prove useful in a fight. But this would send out a signal to everyone that Rakovich wasn't trusted, that his commander felt a need to give him a babysitter. That was a hard thing to bear, one that wouldn't help in keeping his men in line.

"That will be all," Leontev said. "Dismissed."

He turned his back and stalked away.

Valeev approached.

"Come on, Praproshchik," he said, smiling kindly. "Let's get back to your unit. We've got a war to win."

The jeep was waiting at the edge of the clearing, where the driver sat reading a magazine, studiously not watching the confrontation between his superiors. In the back were two men from the platoon, Tammert and Snegur, the runners Leontev had said Rakovich should have with him. Tammert looked away, red-faced. Snegur, a scarred veteran of Afghanistan, kept his expression carefully neutral.

"It's really not that bad," Valeev whispered as they approached the vehicle. "The Captain is just passing on the stress he's getting from above. The company to our right were hit hard in the early fighting so the advance hasn't gone as far as anyone wanted. I'm sure we'll be on the move again soon, but people expect a lot from First Company."

"I'm sure we can deliver that, sir," Rakovich said. "The men fought well yesterday."

It was true. Even Kholodov had done him proud during the assault, making the man's failures all the more frustrating.

"I'm sure you're right."

Valeev climbed into the front passenger seat while Rakovich took a place between his men in the rear. The driver flung his magazine into the back, revved the engine, and took them out of the clearing in a cloud of diesel fumes, the jeep bumping over tree roots and broken ground.

Rakovich glanced at the magazine. It was a glossy German publication, something that must have been pillaged since they crossed the border. He recognised a few words but not the people who smiled inanely at him from the cover photos. Vapid and decadent as they looked, he found himself curious to know who they were and eager for a chance to practice his German.

He resisted picking up the magazine. It could too easily become more gossip among the troops, something else for Szolowski to twist against him. The commander of the unit relaxing and reading capitalist tracts while his men were on the front line. It could even become another weapon for Leontev to use against him. The captain had turned a blind eye to what the driver was doing, but he would never let any failing of Rakovich's go.

Two days in and already he was struggling with both superiors and subordinates. So much for the glory of war.

10

DISSIDENTS

A nna hurried down the street, clutching the newspaper and letters she'd grabbed on her way out of the apartment. She had meant to get up early and head to the café, to get some time to herself before Tatyana arrived. But after a long week of lectures and labs, the urge to roll over and fall back asleep had been too tempting.

Heads turned as she burst into Vadim's. The place was quieter than usual. People still talked, but in hushed whispers, hunching over their steaming pots of tea.

"Over there," Vadim said, his one eye flitting towards a corner table. "I will bring you tea."

Tatyana sat at the table, her hands curled around a cup, gazing out of the window. Her hair was dishevelled, her glasses halfway down her nose. It wasn't like her to become so lost to the world, but Anna supposed that everyone needed to rest their brain from time to time.

She dropped the newspaper onto the table and settled into the seat opposite. It was hard and uncomfortable, but it was good to be out of the house and have some company.

"How are you doing?" she asked, following her friend's gaze in case there was something of interest — a cute boy perhaps, or an argument between motorists. But all she saw was the usual Saturday morning traffic, mothers leading their children by the hand, fathers strolling along ahead of them, heading to the park or for a walk by the river. It made her a little melancholy, missing those long ago days of arguing with Vlad while their father shook his head in weary resignation. Sometimes even with their mother, when she wasn't too busy with the party's work.

"Fine, fine," Tatyana said, her gaze shifting to the newspaper. "May I?"

Anna nodded. Her father often picked up the early edition on his way home, so that he could read about the sports. He left it out for her, perhaps hoping that she would pick up his interests. She'd taken it more to make him happy than from any great desire to read.

But as Tatyana picked up the paper, the headline finally caught Anna's attention:

"WAR IN GERMANY."

So it was official. Rumours had been circulating through Leningrad for days, and now here was the announcement. What had they been waiting for, she wondered. Had the gossip got ahead of the reality, and the fighting had only just started? Or had the government been holding back, waiting to make sure that there was a good story to share?

She moved around the table so that she could read over Tatyana's shoulder, suddenly eager to know what was going on.

The newspaper said that the capitalist Germans had been driven back. All along the inner-German border, the Soviet army and its Warsaw Pact allies were advancing, liberating the country from NATO occupiers. Soon, the columnist predicted, the whole of Germany would be a socialist state.

There was so little detail, nothing about which units had been sent or what casualties they had suffered. How was she meant to work out what was happening to Vlad? He could be dead by now, or he could be halfway to France. What use was a newspaper when it told her almost nothing?

"Makar said there were a lot of woods near them," Tatyana said quietly. With one hand she spread the newspaper across the table, while the other rested on her belly. "Do you know where in Germany there are lots of woods?"

"I should have listened better in geography," Anna replied. "I just never imagined a moment like this."

"I was so used to the Cold War, with all its posturing. I never thought we would be mad enough to come to blows again, and now it's come, poor Makar's caught up in it."

Anna wrapped an arm around her friend.

"He'll be alright," she said. "Vlad will make sure of that."

"You're right." Tatyana smiled sadly and returned Anna's hug. "Your brother knows what he's doing. They'll get through this together."

Vadim appeared and placed a fresh pot of tea on the table, along with a second cup.

"On the house," he said. "For the sister of one of our brave fighting men."

Giving up on getting anything from the paper, Anna sat back down opposite Tatyana. She poured the tea and watched as Vadim prowled the room, delivering orders and talking loudly about the glory of the Soviet Union. He didn't care where the fighting was happening, only that the capitalists were taught a lesson in blood and bullets.

"This is stupid," Anna said. "Why won't they tell us more?"

"It's annoying," Tatyana admitted, still perusing the paper. "But maybe they're worried about spies. Wouldn't you rather that Vlad was safe, even if it means us not knowing?"

"I would rather they hadn't started this stupid war," Anna hissed, just quiet enough to avoid being overheard. "Years of peace without any trouble, then as soon as my brother's on the border they start this nonsense."

"I agree, it's idiocy," Tatyana said. "But it's also an opportunity."

She folded the paper up and slid it away from her, then leaned forward, lowering her voice even further.

"If there's a war, then the government will need the workers more than ever," she said. "I was at a meeting last night. Unions are forming, like the ones in Poland. They're going to use this chance to demand rights from the government. I don't want soldiers fighting and dying, but if they're going to, at least something good can come from it."

Anna stared, shocked by her friend's callous words.

"Would you risk Makar's life for that?" she asked.

Tatyana looked away, frowning, and Anna felt a pang of guilt. But when Tatyana replied, her voice was as steady as it had always been.

"Makar's life isn't mine to risk," she said. "I'll just have to change the things that I can."

An awkward silence fell between them. Uncertain what she could say, Anna turned to her letters. The first was in an official university envelope, probably information about next year's courses, and she opened it eagerly, keen to consider what she might learn next. Then the handwriting on the other envelope caught her attention and studies were forgotten.

She tore the envelope open. Inside was a single sheet, four brief paragraphs in her brother's handwriting. It was dated only a few days before, when tension had not yet tipped over into war.

She devoured the contents, hoping for any hint of where he was, any detail that she could compare with the news. But Vlad was as cautious as ever, saying nothing specific about army life. He managed a whole paragraph about some trees outside the barracks and another about the lousy food, but though she scoured it until her gaze almost burned through the pages, Anna couldn't find anything that might connect to the places in the paper. The only hint he gave came in the last paragraph, when he said that they were preparing for action.

That told her something at least. The fighting had not just started yesterday. The party had been waiting for its moment to break the news. During that time, her brother had been laying his life on the line.

Her fingers tightened, crumpling the paper, as she read his words again. How proud he was to serve his country, to protect her and Papa, to honour their mother's memory. The words felt twisted, as though she was looking at the world through a distorting lens. She was in no danger and neither was Papa. Did Vlad really swallow the propaganda so easily?

Despite that, she felt a stirring of sympathy for her brother. This was the most emotion she had read in his letters in a long time. That he was proud of his work, that he thought of his family as he headed to the fight, these were sentiments she could understand.

She hoped that the next letter would come soon.

"Anna, could I ask you a favour?" It was a strangely tentative phrase for Tatyana, who usually barrelled straight into whatever was on her mind.

"Of course." Anna put the letter in her pocket and looked across the table. Her friend seemed to have shrunk into herself. One hand still rested on her belly, while the other toyed with her empty teacup. "What's the matter?"

"There's a meeting tonight," Tatyana said. "Will you come with me?"

"Urgh, no," Anna replied. "All those grumpy men taking themselves terribly seriously? I'd rather spend all night cleaning up my department's toxic crud."

"Can't you give it a go?" Tatyana asked. "Just this once?"

"Papa has enough to worry about with Vlad," Anna replied. "I'm not going to get myself arrested."

"It'll be safe. I just need—"

"No!" Anna snatched up her other letter. "I won't turn this war into politics while my brother's fighting it."

As she stood, she saw tears glinting at the corners of Tatyana's eyes. Her glasses trembled near the tip of her nose and her cup clattered against its saucer.

The anger that had driven Anna to her feet evaporated. She slid into a seat next to her friend and wrapped an arm around her shoulders.

"Whatever is the matter?" she asked.

"I don't want to go alone," Tatyana said. "In case something happens with... with... with my baby."

Anna's mouth hung open. A hundred questions rocketed through her mind. How had Tatyana let this happen? What did it mean for her future? Was Makar the father?

She held them all back. Only one thing mattered now.

"Of course I'll come with you," she said, hugging Tatyana tight. "Whatever you need."

ANNA FOLLOWED Tatyana down a corridor in an ageing factory, past leaking pipes and groaning ventilators. Other people were here too, some of them wearing stained overalls, others clearly outsiders like them. All were heading in the same direction, towards a simple, anonymous doorway with a sign above it reading "Break Room".

The room beyond was as run down and poorly lit as the rest of the factory. Black mould and flaking paint marred walls that had once been green but were now stained by years of spillages and tobacco smoke. The close air made Anna feel nauseous and she found herself hunching down, trying to hide from the grim-faced people around her.

She dragged Tatyana over to one side, trying to find a safe, quiet space for them, but Tatyana kept pulling away. Every second person seemed to be someone she knew, leading to hugs, handshakes, and greetings that were too loud for such a confined space. It was only when she withdrew to a seat by the wall that Anna again saw the worry that had plagued her earlier, eyes downcast and hands clasped protectively over her belly.

As the room filled, Anna fought to defend her little corner, to ensure a safe space for Tatyana. A man like a great bearded bear pressed in from the left, so she thrust out an elbow and gave him an angry glare. It might not be cosy, this little corner of a factory break room, but it was hers.

"There are still people trying to come in," the man said, giving her an accusing look.

"And there are people here who still need breathing room," she replied. "Or do you want us climbing onto your shoulders so we don't get crushed?"

The man seemed to consider her for a moment. Then he laughed, and suddenly she had a friend who could really protect Tatyana's space.

"I am Boris," he said, offering a hand.

"Anna," she replied. "What do you—"

She was cut off by someone banging a can against a radiator. The clanging spread through the pipes that ran exposed across the ceiling, filling the air with a harsh, angry note. By the time the sound subsided, a man was standing on a desk, facing the assembled throng. They watched him expectantly, faces filled with respect. Behind him, a tall woman with long, dark hair leaned against the wall, watching proceedings with no hint of pleasure.

"For those who don't know me, I am Pavel Semenov." The man on the desk was short and lightly built, with features that would have looked youthful if not for the bags beneath his eyes. His cheap suit had a pale stain on the shoulder. "I've been working for a decade to get us more rights, and now our chance has come."

Cheering bounced around the crowded room, the sound almost deafening. Near Anna, a man in overalls and a green cap whistled and stamped his feet. Others shouted at the tops of their voices.

Semenov gave them a minute, then waved them into silence.

"You're right to be excited," he said, grinning. "But remember, secrecy is still our friend, because the state isn't.

"The Soviet ideal has become corrupted. The workers were meant to control the means of production, and instead we are being controlled. But we can change that.

"Some of you have heard the radio transmissions from abroad. They confirm what we already knew — that this war will not be as easy as the party claims. It will be long. It will be bitter. It will take great resources. And so the government will need us more than ever, to produce the materials for their war machine.

"Now is the time for us to plan, to spread the word, to formulate our demands. When the pressure is on, then we can strike. For better conditions. For better pay. For a voice in the way that our factories and our lives are run."

The cheering started up again, and this time Semenov didn't try to silence it. He let the wave of noise rise, a tide that lifted the hearts of his audience like a fleet ready to sail.

Anna felt none of their adulation. This was dangerous talk. If the police heard the noise then they could all end up under arrest, locked up in jail cells or sent off to Siberia. Semenov talked a good talk, full of concern for the people, but he was putting them in peril just by speaking. And what about the men at the war front, the ones who would be relying upon them for supplies? Men like her brother. Men like the father of Tatyana's baby.

"Many of you will have concerns," Semenov said. He looked around the room, catching the gaze of one doubter after another. As he locked eyes with Anna, she saw something deeper within him. A depth of sorrow that had not been there for the cheering crowd. A moment of openness that made her feel, absurd as it was, that he was sharing a part of himself only with her. "You are right to have doubts. This is dangerous work, not just for us, but for the people we love."

He rolled up his sleeve, revealing a scar that ran from wrist to elbow. A ragged line of raised flesh.

"I know what it is to fight for our country," he said. "To suffer because the supplies you need aren't there.

"But I also know that people suffer away from the front. Labourers struggling to feed their families. Widows and orphans left desolate by accidents on the factory floor. Every day in our country is a fresh tragedy.

"Our fight isn't against those men on the fighting line. It is for them. We fight to create a nation worth coming home to. One where those veterans will find jobs deserving of their sacrifice. One worthy of the blood spilt in its name."

Again, the cheering. Again, Anna felt detached from it all.

Would Vlad really appreciate what was being done here in his name? He had never appreciated anyone challenging the system before. Using his image to advance their cause would surely only make it worse.

But then, that was Vlad's problem, wasn't it? He refused to see the problems in the system. He just wanted to serve it as their mother had done. Never mind the weeks where they had barely seen her because she was doing party work. Never mind that, when she died, the system had moved on as if she had never been there.

Semenov was right. Something had to change. Men like Vlad could save the Soviet Union from outside threats, but they couldn't save it from the rot within. Now was Anna's chance to play her part.

She found herself cheering along with the rest. To her left, big Boris bellowed his approval. To her right, Tatyana clapped and stamped her feet. They weren't just celebrating Semenov's words. They were joining together in supplication, calling out for justice from a world so long indifferent to their lives.

When the cheering died down again, it was time for practicalities. Semenov pointed out men and women who would gather information, who would lead recruitment, who would collect funds. Trusted men and women who were already part of the struggle alongside him.

"I need team leaders too," he said. "To coordinate printing and putting up posters around the city. Any volunteers?"

Anna's hand shot up even before she had thought it through. Semenov smiled as he pointed her out and she found herself smiling in return.

She was part of something now. Something bigger than her. Something more important than drinking tea and watching boys go by outside the window.

"I thought you didn't want to be part of this?" Tatyana whispered.

"What can I say?" Anna replied. "You're a good influence."

A POT of stew sat on the stove. It was still warm, left there by Papa when he headed out for work. Anna spooned some into a bowl, took it to the kitchen table, and ate it while reading Vlad's letter again. Then she got out a pen and paper and began a reply.

She wanted to be honest with him, to let him know that she also faced a struggle, that he could take pride in her. But even if she had thought he would understand, she knew better than to write any of it down. The slightest hint of what they did could doom the people she had met today. Semenov, with his stained suit and his tired smile. Boris, full of laughter and determination. Tatyana, with a baby resting in her belly. The people who had flocked to Anna when the meeting was over, eager to join her poster team.

Besides, what would Vlad think if he heard what she was up to? He believed in the Party and the cause, as he'd made loudly clear any time she even asked a question about politics. That wasn't going to change just because she'd started making friends with dissidents. This had to stay her secret, both from Papa and from Vlad.

Her hand tensed around the pen. Just as Vlad had started opening up to her, she was closing herself off to him. But what choice did she have? She was building a better nation for them both. One day he would understand.

At last, she wrung the words from herself and began to write:

"DEAR VLAD,

"Your letter arrived today, along with news of the war. I wish that I knew more about what was happening where you are. I understand better than ever that you cannot tell me. I only hope that you are safe, and that one day I will be able to hear the stories you cannot share now.

"There is little to tell you about at home. A letter arrived from the university today, all about next year's courses..."

11

DEATH FROM ABOVE

A mortar bomb exploded a dozen yards to Rakovich's left. He ducked and kept running as dirt rained down around him and bullets spattered the road up ahead, some of them clanging off the front of the lead BMP. His heart raced and he clung tight to his rifle as the breath came harsh and ragged in his chest. He had to keep moving. That was how he would survive.

A jet roared past, cannon blazing as it swept low over the battlefield, strafing the Soviet advance. No-one even tried to fire back. They had other targets, ones they stood a chance of hurting.

Niyazi, one of Rakovich's riflemen, stood frozen behind a signpost, his rifle clutched to his chest. His eyes were wide as he stared back at the bodies of the men lost in the last attack.

Those men were from another company. They weren't Rakovich's responsibility and he didn't have time to stop and worry about them. Niyazi, on the other hand, was one of his.

"Get a fucking grip," Rakovich yelled, slapping the rifleman across the face. "You think a post can protect you from this shit? The only safe place is that village. We take that place or we die out here!"

Grabbing a fistful of Niyazi's jacket, he swung him around into the road. Something seemed to click in the man. He scurried forwards, weaving from side to side across the road, heading for the next piece of cover and then the next one after that, advancing with the rest of the platoon.

Rakovich ran after him. He was shorter than Niyazi but more confident. He passed him at the edge of a ditch, then jumped in as bullets smacked into the tarmac only a foot in front of them.

"Get into cover!" he yelled, as Niyazi stood dumbly in the road.

He grabbed the man's ankle and dragged him down. Niyazi fell like a bag of cement, landing on Rakovich and pinning him in the stagnant water.

"Get off of me, you dozy bastard." When Niyazi didn't move, Rakovich heaved him off, flinging him against the muddy bank. It was only then that he saw the blood pouring from his chest and the slack, lifeless look in his eyes.

Blood swirled in the swampy water, the sight making Rakovich feel sick. Men who couldn't face battle shouldn't be out here at all, never mind being dragged around by their platoon leaders. Dragging Niyazi forward had been the right thing to do. Without the courage to face the enemy, the unit would never make it out alive. It wasn't Rakovich's fault that one of them had taken that bullet.

He slammed a fist into the bank and used it to drag himself up, so that he could see what was happening all around. The rest of the company were pinned down in fields to his right, caught by fire from mortars and heavy machine-guns in prepared positions outside the village. To the left, one of his own BMPs was crawling across the fields, the men of the third section crouching as they advanced behind it.

"Zinoviev!" He waved to the sergeant.

Zinoviev looked up. He said something to his men, then came dashing toward Rakovich. Instead of using cover, he headed straight for the bewildered Rakovich, surviving by luck rather than judgement as bullets flew past him. As he slid down into the mud, he wore an excited grin.

"We're getting there, Praporshchik," he said, nodding toward the town.

"I need you to get there quicker," Rakovich replied. "First platoon are getting murdered in the open, and you're our best shot of reaching the British positions. Pick up the pace and you can take that machine-gun on the end before they even know you're coming. While they're reeling from that, the rest of the platoon moves in. Clear?"

"Yes, Praporshchik." Zinoviev rose.

"And for fuck's sake, go along the ditch!"

"Yes, Praporshchik."

While Zinoviev made his way back to his section, Rakovich signalled the other squad leaders. They would need to move in quickly after that first BMP and the men behind it. Otherwise, Zinoviev's section would soon be overwhelmed by the enemy's numbers.

He looked around and his jaw fell open as he saw what was happening. Instead of speeding up the advance of his BMP, Zinoviev had emerged from behind the vehicle, the rest of his men with him. While the BMP picked up speed, they dashed across the open ground, exposed to any armed enemy looking in the right direction.

"Not like that, you moron!"

Rakovich almost leapt to his feet, but common sense held him back. His sudden appearance would only draw attention this way and probably get him killed in the process. Instead, he raised his rifle and started firing at the front of the enemy position. He wouldn't hit anyone through the sandbags, but maybe he could keep their heads down and their attention away from what was happening to his left.

He fired frantically as the men advanced. By the time Zinoviev was halfway there, Rakovich's magazine was empty. He yanked it out, thrust a new one in, and looked up.

Zinoviev and his men were almost upon the British, but someone had seen what was coming. The machine-gun had disappeared from the front of the position.

Rakovich fired, trying to hit the soldiers repositioning their gun, but heaps of sandbags sheltered them for all but the briefest of moments. He aimed and squeezed the trigger, once, twice, three times, even as the British hurried to raise the gun.

Some brave soul had emerged from the front of Zinoviev's group, putting on an extra burst of speed. As he pulled away from the rest, Rakovich was amazed to realise that it was Szolkowski, firing from the hip as he charged.

The Russians were forty yards from the British position and closing when the barrel of the machine-gun emerged. Fear squeezed Rakovich's chest, fear not for himself but for the men serving under him.

Szolkowski's arm swung around, a grenade arcing through the air.

The machine-gun fired, taking out the legs of one of the advancing men.

The grenade exploded in the British dugout. The machine-gun stopped firing, though there was still a bark of small arms.

Szolkowski leapt up onto the side of the position, firing down. Zinoviev's section poured in after him and the British guns fell silent.

As the rest of the platoon advanced, Rakovich scrambled out of the ditch and ran to join them.

THIS VILLAGE WAS LARGER than the last one they'd taken. It was also less empty. The inhabitants, whether out of choice or some misfortune of war, hadn't got out before the Soviets arrived. It was Rakovich's first chance to meet the people he was liberating and he was determined to get it right.

"Tell them they're all safe now," he said. "But we need them to follow our orders for the sake of their own safety."

Kholodov raised the loudhailer and talked in German to the people assembled in the village square. Rakovich wondered if Captain Leontev had sent him here because he had a German speaker in his unit, or if he'd just wanted to give him the awkward job. The answer could so easily be either, or both.

This could have been Rakovich's chance to practice his German, but he knew his limits, and just because he could count to a hundred didn't mean that he could deal with this. While Kholodov answered the questions of the anxious-looking crowd, Rakovich scrutinised their clothes, their faces, the way they watched the soldiers around them. If he was in charge of these people, whether for hours or for weeks, then he needed to know who they were.

Their clothes were similar to the ones he'd seen in the GDR, but subtly different. They fitted better, had more variety of colours and styles, and few had the faded shabbiness that came with years of endless wearing and washing.

It was the same with the houses. They weren't all that different from those in the east, but they were better kept. The paint on most was relatively new. None of the window frames were rotting. Most of the recent additions were pleasantly designed to fit in with the place. Only a few garage extensions showed the sort of concrete architecture he'd got so used to.

It wasn't that these people took more pride in their homes. He knew just how much care people back home took of their houses, even when all they had to maintain them was a few rubles and a spare hour of labour. But these people had more wealth. They must be part of the privileged class that capitalism kept above the rest. The real Germans would be further down the road.

"I think they've got the message, Praporshchik," Kholodov said, lowering the loudhailer. "And they know to come to you or me if they have questions."

Rakovich nodded. He would struggle to answer any question of more than four words, but at least he could try. He was in command here, so the people should have access to him.

"Go check on your men," he said. "I want a status report in an hour."

"Yes, Praporshchik."

As the crowd dispersed, Rakovich walked through the village, taking in the layout of streets, working out where he should station men if an attack came. Everywhere he looked, his attention was drawn to the cars. Like the people and the buildings, they were better than most of those he was used to. Larger, more slickly shaped, more boldly coloured. True, some looked like they had years of wear on them, but none had tyres worn bald or windscreen wipers falling off and windows drifting down of their own will, like the old banger Zimyatov drove back home.

Clearly, there was a need to spread the wealth of this decadent nation. Who knew what poverty the workers lived in to support this.

The rest of the riflemen seemed less concerned with deep reflection. Outside a pair of shops on the main street, a small cluster of them stood laughing and chatting, pointing at the buildings, smoking cigarettes and chewing chocolate bars.

As he approached, they stood to attention.

"At ease," Rakovich said. "You've earned a moment's rest, especially you, Szolkowski."

The rifleman grinned and took a drag on his cigarette. "Thank you, Praporshchik."

"It took a lot of guts to do what you did today," Rakovich said. "And brains not to get yourself killed in the process. The rest of you could learn from him."

Szolkowski puffed out his chest.

"Thank you, Praporshchik," he said again.

A bell rang and Zinoviev emerged from one of the shops, carrying two bulging plastic bags.

"Look what I found!" he said, then stopped short as he saw Rakovich.

"What?" Rakovich glared at him. What sort of shitty example was the sergeant setting now?

"Just a few things to take home, Praporshchik," Zinoviev said. "For my family."

"Show me."

Zinoviev opened one of the bags. Inside were t-shirts, trousers, a jigsaw, and a cuddly rabbit the size of an artillery shell.

"I said you could take food and essentials," Rakovich said. "Nothing else."

"But cigarettes aren't essentials," Zinoviev said, looking at the other men. "And I just thought—"

"Cigarettes?" Rakovich snatched a packet from one man's hand. Sure enough, they were American cigarettes. He'd secretly expected small infractions like this and been ready to overlook them. But he couldn't have his men carrying away whole armfuls of loot. Zinoviev was forcing him to draw the line.

"Szolkowski said that stuff about not looting was just something you had to say," Zinoviev said. "That it wouldn't matter if we just—"

Rakovich smacked the cigarette from between Szolkowski's lips.

"My orders are my orders," he snarled. "You don't get to reinterpret them to suit your desires."

"Sorry, Praporshchik." Zinoviev dropped his bags and sprang to attention. Beside him, Szolkowski stiffened as he stared into the distance, eyes glittering with anger above his reddened cheeks.

"If you can't eat it, drink it, or wipe your arse with it, you put it back now," Rakovich said. "And be glad we're too busy fighting a war for me to report you to the captain."

It didn't feel like enough, but what more could he do? Lock them up for stealing a soft toy and some smokes? He needed the men more than that. And if he reported them to Leontev, he'd probably be the one to get grief for not keeping them on a tighter leash. It was a half-arsed solution to a ridiculous situation, but what else could he do?

He flung the half-smoked packet of cigarettes on the ground and strode away, back toward the centre of the village. There, a BMP was parked at the intersection, watching over the people as they passed. Kholodov sat on its roof singing a gentle folk song, a sketchbook open across his knees, his helmet sat beside him.

"More looting?" Rakovich snatched the sketchbook and tossed it on the ground.

"I brought that with me!" Kholodov said, leaping down to fetch his drawings from the mud.

"I told you to check on your men, not sit staring at the flowers."

"I did check on them."

"And to give me a status report."

"You said in an hour, and I—"

Rakovich grabbed Kholodov's helmet and stared at the bright shapes scattered along the side. Stickers of cartoon mice stared back at him.

"What the fuck is this?" he demanded, shoving the helmet in Kholodov's face.

"I found them in a shop," Kholodov said. "I just thought—"

"You paid for them?"

"No praporshchik. The woman said to just—"

"And you think this is the way to treat military equipment? To stick ridiculous little capitalist symbols on the side? To put a brightly coloured 'shoot here' sign right by your temple?"

"I'm sorry, Praporshchik."

"Yes, you are. Everyone around here is sorry, but no-one's thinking about their orders or about—"

"Incoming!" The shout echoed around the square.

Rakovich turned, expecting to see tanks and troops approaching along the road. Instead, a pair of jets were streaking through the sky out of the west.

"Are those ours?" Rakovich asked.

"Harriers." Kholodov made a sweeping gesture with his hands. "Shape of the wings."

"Take cover!"

This time, everybody followed Rakovich's order. Up and down the street, men flung themselves behind vehicles or through doorways, out of sight of the approaching planes. Rakovich ducked behind a small yellow car and swung his rifle off his shoulder. He couldn't do much against a jet, but this might be the start of something more. If all he could do was ready his rifle then he would damn well ready his rifle.

A rocket hit the ground right next to the BMP, sending chunks of dirt and concrete flying. A paving slab slammed into the side of the car next to Rakovich, crumpling the door. He shook at the thought of how close it had come to flattening him.

As the smoke and debris cleared, he was relieved to see that the BMP was still intact.

"They're coming around again," Kholodov shouted from the doorway of a grocery.

"Where are our anti-air missiles?" Rakovich shouted back.

"I don't know. Who took over from Beletsky?"

Rakovich cursed under his breath. He hadn't picked a new rocket man. If they even had any anti-air missiles left, he didn't have anyone with responsibility for using them. With so much going on, he was missing important details, and now they were defenceless.

Rounds burst against the surface of the road as one of the Harriers swept past, strafing their position with its cannon. Most of the shots missed, but one round punched through the roof of the vehicle and out the side, leaving behind two holes and a blast mark. Rakovich sighed in relief that no-one had been inside to take the hit.

As the other plane approached, he was horribly aware of the missiles slung under its wing. He could be blown apart at any moment and there was nothing he could do about it.

Four more planes were approaching. Rakovich crawled around the car, putting its bulk between himself and the target of the attacks. At least if they hit the BMP this might protect him from the shrapnel, though if the shot came any closer then he would be blown to bits.

Hatred rose inside him. Hatred for all those pilots, bringing death from the safety of the skies. Hatred for those too scared to come and face them on the ground. Hatred for the west, which had forced his people to this.

Then Kholodov cheered.

"Sukhois!" he shouted. "The cavalry are here."

Rakovich peered out to see the new planes approaching the Harriers as they circled for another strike. The British clearly sensed the danger, as they turned and headed west, away from the village, with the Soviet planes on their tail.

As the roar of jet engines faded into the distance, Rakovich stepped cautiously out into the street and approached the BMP.

A moment later, Akayev was beside him, running his hands over the damaged areas. The mechanic sighed and shared a look of deep relief.

"Is all good," he said in his broken Russian. "Is just... What is word for..."

He made a scooping motion, then repeated it against the damaged area.

"Dented?" Rakovich asked.

"Yes! Dented!" Akayev grinned. "I get hammer."

Letting out his own sigh of relief, Rakovich walked over to the doorway where Kholodov sat, his rifle across his knees. He had an open jar in one hand and was eating a pickle. As the praporshchik approached he froze, looking nervously from the jar to the stickers on his helmet to his approaching commander.

Rakovich sat down beside him and reached into the jar. He fought to keep his hand from trembling as he drew out a pickle.

"Taking food's allowed," he said. "We have to fucking eat, don't we?"

He bit into the pickle. It was crisp and tasty, better than the ones he and his father shared back home. Everything here was better than what his men were used to, it was only fair that they should have a taste of it.

Maybe he would let them have their American cigarettes. What harm could it do?

12

PROFESSOR HOFMANN

"I want you to stay put." Even as he delivered welcome news, Leontev's tone showed his disdain. There was a snarl to his voice that said he would rather be sending Rakovich straight into the storm of war, but had been held back against his own better judgement.

Rakovich couldn't say that he didn't care. His career had long been in this man's hands, but now it was more than that. His life, and those of the men he was responsible for, depended upon Leontev's decisions. It was a harsh fate that had thrown him together with a man who so thoroughly detested him.

Despite that resentment, the words lifted his spirits. His men needed a rest and so did he. He'd take that rest now it was offered, even if he wasn't sure why it had been offered.

"Might I ask why we're staying, sir?" He stood stiffly to attention beside the captain's vehicle, trying to work out whether this meant that he'd done well or if it was just the prelude to some fresh punishment.

"The company has been pushed hard for three days," Leontev said. "Now we're being rested while others advance. I've pulled the other platoons back, but someone needs to hold this place, so this is where you rest."

"Thank you, sir," Rakovich said. "I'm sure the men will appreciate it."

"I'm sure they will."

Leontev's eyes slid to where Kholodov lay singing in the sunshine on top of his BMP, sketchbook open beside him.

Rakovich gritted his teeth. It didn't matter if Kholodov was off watch. That was no way for a sergeant to behave while their captain was around. Worse, it set the wrong tone for Rakovich's next request.

"Sir, could you arrange fresh supplies and reinforcements?" he asked. "If we're going to make another push soon, then—"

"I'm not an idiot," Leontev snapped. "I have your casualty list and I've put in requests for fresh ammunition."

"And the lost BMP?"

"I'm not having my company going in ill-prepared." Leontev looked again at Kholodov and then back at Rakovich, a different sort of intensity in his expression now. "If that vehicle isn't here by the morning, contact me. The colonel has promised he'll put a boot to whatever arses need it."

"Thank you, sir."

The captain climbed back into his BMP, which turned and headed towards the woods.

Rakovich grinned as he made his way around the village, briefing the men and organising sentry shifts for the next twenty-four hours. It wasn't just Leontev's departure that had affected his mood. The sunshine, the prospect of a rest, even the news that the battle lines were moving on without them, all of it combined to lift his spirits. He relished the prospect of pushing on and smashing the capitalists, but it would be easier to do that once they had more bullets, vehicles, and troops.

The men — his men — responded with confusion and then delight as he told them about the break from combat. Even Szolkowski managed to spare his Praporshchik a smile. Some of them pulled a table out into the street and started playing cards. Others went in search of beds and a chance for real sleep.

The locals were mostly staying indoors. That suited Rakovich. It made life easier for his sentries, who watched warily for any sign of movement. The fewer unfamiliar bodies on the move, the easier it was to avoid some twitchy conscript blowing away the wrong person.

He'd told the villagers that they could go about their business during daylight. After all, he was a liberator, not a conqueror, and he didn't want to keep them all locked up. This was his chance to prove that the Red Army really was here to help. Lieutenant Valeev had even given him a box of pamphlets to hand out, explaining how communism would make everybody's lives better. Neither Rakovich nor Valeev was fool enough to think that these people would believe it straight away, after years of American indoctrination. But given time, the message would eventually sink in. Their lives really were changing for the better.

Zimyatov was in the main street when Rakovich returned, kicking a football around with Tammert. They were watched by a short, plump woman with grey hair, wearing an old-fashioned woollen dress. As Rakovich approached, Zimyatov set the ball aside and waved the woman closer while Tammert wandered off to pet a nearby cat.

"This is Professor Hofmann," Zimyatov announced. "She says she wants to help."

"Pleased to meet you, Professor." Rakovich shook the professor's small, wrinkled hand. She had a surprisingly firm grip.

"And you, Praporshchik," she said. "Thank you for meeting with me."

Rakovich blinked in surprise. Not only was the woman's Russian flawless, with barely even a hint of a German accent, but she had got his rank right. He knew plenty of people back home who couldn't manage that.

"It's good to meet someone who appreciates our presence," Rakovich said. "I feared we wouldn't meet a welcome reception until we reached the big cities."

Hofmann peered at him over the top of her half-moon glasses. She reminded him of one of his primary school teachers, a woman who had repeatedly beaten him for disobedience. That teacher had helped keep him on a path of discipline, and he had fond memories of her despite the pain.

"I thought that you might appreciate a translator," she said. "I wish to avoid anyone being injured due to a misunderstanding or poorly rendered turn of phrase. And I can help you to find the right people to talk to."

"Is anyone in charge in this village?"

She bobbed her head from side to side. "In a way. We have a small local council. Would you like to meet them?"

An hour later, they were sat at a row of tables in the village's only café, along with half a dozen locals and Lieutenant Valeev. The political officer had been delighted to hear that Rakovich had arranged the meeting, and rushed over to be part of it. The locals looked less enthusiastic, exchanging nervous glances with each other or staring tensely at the top of the table. Everyone had a cup of tea or coffee in front of them, but most were untouched.

Hofmann translated as Rakovich explained that he and his men meant no harm. When that didn't elicit a response from the villagers, he explained it again, and again, searching for new ways to get the message across. How hard could it be for them to grasp simple facts?

"They understand what you're saying," Hofmann said. "But you have to understand, this a peaceful, out of the way village. Half the residents retired here for a quiet life. Now there are soldiers in their streets, even in their homes. It is making them exceedingly worried."

"We've liberated them," Valeev said, spooning sugar into his third cup of tea. "Tell them that they'll soon be enjoying the benefits of communism. Equality, prosperity, security. Their lives will be better."

As Hofmann translated, the expression of one of the councillors lifted into a bitter sneer. He spat a few angry words before the man next to him grabbed his arm and urged him back into silence.

By the tone alone, Rakovich could tell that the second man's words were an apology, and that it came from a place of fear.

"This is absurd," Valeev said. "Perhaps I can find some better pamphlets, or deliver a talk on the benefits of a communist system."

Hofmann's eyes darted back and forth between the two Russians.

"Might I say something on my own behalf?" she asked.

"Please do," Valeev replied, smiling benignly.

"You cannot make people agree with you through pure reason," Hofmann said. "Trust me, as an academic I have been trying for my whole career. Emotions get in the way of logic, and the emotion we are all feeling here is fear.

"Many of us are old enough to remember the last war. Some fled west before the end because we heard such terrible things about your army."

"You shouldn't believe those stories," Valeev said, shifting uncomfortably in his seat. "I'm sure it's just lies that were put about by Hitler and his cronies."

"Of course. But it is hard to break out of that belief. If you want to convince people of your good intentions, the best that you can do is to treat them well. That will win them around better than any fine words, if you just give it time."

Rakovich felt like a fool for not seeing it himself. Actions always spoke louder than words — that was why he sometimes had to use his fists to get through to the men. And if action was what it took, then these people would soon see the benefits of the Soviet system first hand. As long as they didn't actively resist, he could wait for that to happen.

But could Valeev?

As they left the meeting, the political officer had a thoughtful look on his face.

"I should go back to the regiment and consult with my superiors," he said. "Professor Hofmann is right about the lies spread during the last war and those spread by the Americans since. We need to think about how best to tackle them." He smiled ruefully. "I might be out of my depth here."

"Surely not, Lieutenant," Rakovich said. "The party has trained you for this role."

"The party's goals may be perfect, but my abilities are not. I need to refresh my own learning before I talk with these people again."

Rakovich watched, shaken, as Valeev headed for his jeep. He had always imagined Valeev as a little like his own mother, ready with political answers whenever they were needed. It was unsettling to see him lose his edge so quickly and completely.

But then, they weren't dealing with ordinary citizens. The state of the village showed that these were wealthy people, and the wealthy had a vested interest in maintaining the hegemony of capital. To bring equality, you had to take from the privileged few, and these people could see their time coming. They cowered in fear at losing what others could barely dream of. They disgusted Rakovich.

"Praporshchik." Professor Hofmann waved to him as she emerged from the café. "Would you care to join my husband and I for dinner tonight? I imagine a home cooked meal will be most welcome after days in the field."

"I..."

Caught by surprise, Rakovich struggled for what to say. The simple gesture of welcome was so at odds with the picture he had been spinning in his head, it left him scrabbling to regroup. But one thing was certain — he was tired of eating ration packs.

"Thank you," he said. "That would be nice."

"ARE YOU ALLOWED A GLASS OF WINE?" Professor Hofmann took three glasses down and drew a bottle from a rack. Across the kitchen, her husband Wolfgang was busy at the gleaming chrome stove. Their kitchen was to Rakovich's as an assault rifle was to a musket. But then, their apartment was better than his family home in so many ways, big and small. From the condition of the paintwork to the quality of the furniture to the art and the crowded bookshelves along the walls, it was in every way superior. Even the television in the corner of the spacious living room, with its large screen and a remote control to save the viewer from standing up, was a reminder of how much better off his hosts were.

Rakovich held himself a little taller just to prevent it from intimidating him.

He hesitated over the question of the drink. He should keep his senses about him. But if the wine was as good as everything else about this place...

"Just a small glass, perhaps?" the Professor suggested.

"That would be good," Rakovich said. "Thank you."

She led him into the dining room, where they settled into plushly upholstered chairs.

"Wolfgang prefers to be left alone while he's cooking." Hofmann gave a small shake of the head. "Such a prima donna. This is what comes from marrying gifted young graduate students. You end up with a spoilt middle-aged husband."

Rakovich struggled for something to say. He wasn't used to formal dinners and polite conversation with professors. Everyone he knew worked in factories or the army. Only Anna had a fraction of this woman's education, or an inkling of how to behave in places like this, and his sister was hundreds of miles away.

"How did you learn such good Russian?" he asked, settling on what seemed like a safe subject.

"The war," Hofmann replied, peering into her glass. "Or rather, the last war. As a specialist in eastern European history, I already knew your language. The army employed me to help translate conversations with prisoners."

"Conversations?" Rakovich felt a flash of anger. He had heard about how the Nazis treated prisoners from the east.

"I'm not proud of what I was a part of," Hofmann said, looking up sadly. "Many of us carry a weight of regret we can never shake. Some let that regret eat them away. I use it as a reminder that, no matter what you are told you must do, there is always a better way of dealing with the world."

"Easy to say when you live in luxury." Rakovich gestured at the room around him.

"Luxury?" Hofmann looked surprised for only a moment, then let out a sigh. Realisation transformed her expression to one of soft sympathy. "Of course, I had not considered what your own home must be like. Please, forgive me if I appear to be using this to intimidate you. I only wanted to make you feel comfortable."

"Of course you did." Rakovich knocked back his wine and reached for the bottle. "After all, it's more convenient for the capitalist elite if the proletariat are appeased, isn't it?"

"The elite?" She shook her head. "Praporshchik Rakovich, my husband and I are humble academics, getting by on the salary of public servants. Look at the other homes in this village. You will find that they are much like this one."

"Of course they are. You've probably all fled the cities, leaving the poor behind. You live in luxury while they labour. But change is coming, believe me."

He swallowed the second glass of wine in one gulp. It was good stuff, as he had expected. He poured himself a third.

Wolfgang appeared at the kitchen door, peering nervously in. He said something softly in German, and his wife waved him irritably away.

"Praporshchik, you have us all wrong. You will find it is the same in the cities. This is simply how we live in the Federal Republic."

"So this is why you brought me here," he snarled. "To butter me up and convince me of your propaganda. To try to turn me against my own people. Did they teach you that during the last war as well?"

"Don't be absurd. I just—" She stopped abruptly, then gave an embarrassed laugh. "Forgive me. I am doing exactly what your Lieutenant Valeev did, trying to use logic when it is all about feelings."

"You think this is funny?" Rakovich stood, letting the chair fall behind him. "I could have you shot as a spy."

"You could," she agreed. "But I don't think you're that sort of man, are you?"

"That is a dangerous assumption for you to make."

In Rakovich's hand, the glass cracked beneath his tightening fingers.

Hofmann bowed her head.

"I'm sorry," she said. Then she straightened her back and addressed him in a flatter tone. "Will you still eat with us?"

"No."

"Will you at least let us give you dinner to take away?"

The smells from the kitchen were delicious, better even than the pickles Kholodov had found in the village store. The smell of beef stew made Rakovich's mouth water. He was loath to give any ground to her false kindness, but he was suddenly very hungry.

"Yes," he said. "I will take it now."

Hofmann went into the kitchen and exchanged a few words in German with her husband. Their voices were quiet, and Rakovich couldn't make out more than a few words. There were clattering and slopping sounds for a few minutes. Then Hofmann emerged carrying a plastic bag full of neat plastic tubs.

"Wolfgang always over caters," she said, setting the bag down on the table and adding cutlery to its contents. "That should be more than enough for you and your sergeants."

As Rakovich picked up the bag, he caught another waft of the delicious smell.

"Might I give you one more thing?" she asked. "By way of an apology."

Rakovich didn't answer. He knew that she was an enemy set on tricking him, but it was hard to match that idea with the kindly old woman handing him a pile of glossy magazines.

"To help you practise your German," she said. "If you would like more, please ask."

He tossed the magazines in with the food. Bag in hand, he strode into the kitchen and pulled another bottle of wine from the rack. By the stove, Wolfgang stood staring at him, his face a mask of terror.

Good. Let them fear him. Let all the decadent capitalists fear the future that was coming for them.

Wine in one hand and food in the other, Rakovich stormed out of the house.

A BMP WAS APPROACHING as Rakovich stepped into the street, still seething from his encounter with the Hofmanns. The vehicle's paint-work was pristine, not scarred by bullets and shrapnel. It pulled up in front of him and the gunner thrust his head out of the turret.

"Praporshchik Rakovich?" he asked.

Rakovich nodded.

"Reinforcements and supplies for your platoon, Praporshchik."

Fierce pride filled Rakovich. Of course he couldn't trust the locals, but at least he could rely upon the Red Army to come through for him. Men, ammunition, even a new BMP — everything he needed for the battle ahead.

A rifleman emerged from the rear doors, leaving them open for Rakovich to see inside. There were several young men wearing uniforms and the new soldier's mixture of nerves and pride. Between them were stacked the ammunition crates. Not as many as he had hoped for, but maybe more would be on their way.

"Where are the rockets?" he asked, looking over the labels.

"What rockets, Praporshchik?" the rifleman asked.

"The anti-aircraft rockets, of course. Without those, the first NATO helicopter we meet will fuck us all in the arse."

"We weren't given any rockets, Praporshchik."

The young man trembled at the ferocity of Rakovich's glare.

"Take it to that BMP," he said, pointing up the street. "I'll distribute it in the morning. And if you see any sergeants there, tell them to come find me."

The table the First Section had been playing cards at was still sat out in the street, deserted now except for an abandoned mug. Rakovich put his bag down on it, pulled up a seat, and set to eating the stew with gusto.

Determined not to waste the time he had, he flicked through one of the magazines, looking for a page without too many words. It was full of bright pictures of life in the west, with celebrities living the sort of decadent lifestyles he had imagined.

Those lives were nothing like what he had seen at the Hofmanns'.

Had the Professor been telling the truth? Was her home really so ordinary by the standards of this country?

Kholodov strolled up, Zinoviev not far behind him.

"Here." Rakovich held out a fork. "Eat."

"What are you reading?" Kholodov asked, opening a tub of stew.

"Nothing." Rakovich closed the magazine and dropped it in the dirt. "Let's talk about tomorrow."

13

BAD FAITH

T he rain was nothing more than a drizzle, dampening Rakovich's hair and darkening his uniform. But it was enough to send his men indoors, hunkering down in living rooms and kitchens more comfortable and well-stocked than any they had known back home. The residents of these houses hid in their bedrooms or stood watching tensely while their cupboards were emptied by the voracious appetites of soldiers. He'd seen the same pattern all over the village this morning. Sentries stood in doorways, trying to stay dry while they watched out for enemy forces supposedly still miles away. Everywhere else, clusters of soldiers sprawled across couches and armchairs, their muddy boots staining once proudly kept carpets, listening to the radio or watching television.

He was fine with that. The Hofmanns had shown him what people around here thought of him and his men — laughing at them, looking down on them, trying to fool them with their obvious lies. He had no time for them and their superior attitude. His men had earned a chance to be comfortable, and if it meant that a bunch of bourgeoisie Germans had to do an honest day's cleaning afterwards, so much the better.

He stamped his boots briefly on a doormat and then trudged

inside. This should be the last house he needed to visit. Only three members of his platoon were unaccounted for and others had told him that they were here.

Sure enough, he heard the sound of a television and of Kholodov talking over it. He followed the sound down a wood-floored hallway lined with prints of old engravings.

A tabby cat watched him from the stairs. It reminded him of old Mrs Romanova, who had an apartment in the same block he'd grown up in and who had filled her life with cats. One of her tabbies had followed him around the neighbourhood when he was younger, keeping him company while he built dens in the local park and fought wars against imaginary Nazis. When that cat died, he'd helped Mrs Romanova bury it, placing one of his own toy soldiers as a parting gift inside the shoe box coffin. He'd been there with the old lady for every cat funeral that followed, his way of honouring his furry friend.

"Here, kitty." Rakovich pulled a packet of beef jerky from his pocket, tore off a strip, and offered it to the cat. It was only a small sacrifice, and he was sure he could find more for himself when they advanced again.

The cat sniffed suspiciously at Rakovich's fingers, then snatched the meat between its teeth and scampered away up the stairs. Rakovich laughed as he watched it go.

"See, kitty?" he called out. "Even you benefit under communism."

He carried on into a neatly kept living room where a colour TV flashed brightly in one corner. Kholodov and Akayev sat watching from the hugely padded sofa, while Shistyev, the driver from Third Section, dozed in a matching armchair.

On the screen, cartoon figures were standing around in some sort of control room. They wore bright, skintight outfits with matching cloaks and helmets that made them look a little like birds. Suddenly the view shifted to show a spaceship floating against a background of stars. All the while, Kholodov kept up his commentary, translating and explaining for Akayev. Though with the translation being into Russian, Rakovich wasn't sure it would help the Kyrgyzstani much.

"What the balls is this?" Rakovich asked. "It looks like a twelve-year-old took magic mushrooms and then told them what to draw."

"They are war for planet, yes?" Akayev said, grinning. "Much action. Very fun."

"That's no way to dress for war." Rakovich settled onto the arm of the sofa, his gaze drawn to the TV. "Those uniforms are as fit for purpose as a clown suit in a strip club."

"You want coffee?" Kholodov asked. "These people have good coffee."

"Why not."

As Kholodov disappeared into the kitchen, Shistyev opened his eyes.

"We moving out, Praporshchik?" he asked eagerly.

Rakovich shook his head. Shistyev wasn't the first to ask that question, and the reason was becoming increasingly clear. The men were already getting used to the fine things they'd found in this village, and those things had got them excited for what else Germany might hold. To many, this seemed like a taster now, and they felt as though they were missing out while other companies rushed ahead.

It was easy for them to see it that way. They didn't hear about the casualties at the front. But though Rakovich was also eager to keep moving, it was his job to hold them back.

"Soon," he said.

"Here, Praporshchik." Kholodov handed him a mug of coffee. It smelled as good as promised. "Let me explain what's happening in the show..."

Five minutes later, Rakovich was still staring at the screen, still as confused by the brightly coloured mayhem and German dialogue, when a knock on the front door brought him back into the real world. None of his men would knock, which meant it was a local. But if the house's inhabitants were in then they were hiding away.

Coffee in hand, he went to the door.

"Praporshchik Rakovich," Professor Hofmann said, pushing a lock of damp grey hair back across her forehead. "Please, please will you come with me? Something terrible is happening."

Rakovich considered her for a moment, first with disdain, then with growing unease. He was the leader of an invading force that had occupied this woman's village. Terrible to her and terrible to him were not the same thing. But the tightness of her voice stirred a flicker of dread inside him.

He stepped back into the living room, put down the coffee, and picked up his rifle from where it leaned against the sofa. As he stepped outside, he checked the chamber of his gun.

"Show me," he said.

A RIFLEMAN STOOD at the corner of the street, keeping watch along the road to the north. As Rakovich and Professor Hofmann passed, the man glanced in their direction, then fixed his gaze on the distance. His back was stiff, not like a soldier stood to attention, but like a teenager caught misbehaving by his parents.

To Rakovich's surprise, Hofmann didn't take him toward the guilty looking soldier, but on down the street. There stood one of the BMPs, its flanks spattered with mud, one track on the pavement and the other in the road. The vehicle was facing them, the main gun pointing at Rakovich above the sloped front.

From around the back of the vehicle, a woman's voice emerged, shouting in protest.

In Rakovich's mind, the pieces fell into place. He strode with renewed determination, leaving Hofmann behind as he rounded the rear of the BMP.

Szolkowski sat on a folding chair just behind the BMP, a grin on his face and a cigarette in his hand. The grin vanished as he looked up to see Rakovich. He jerked to his feet and the chair folded in as it fell with a clatter into the street.

Rakovich put his hand on the cold metal of the BMP, just above an open rear door. Fingers tightened as he leaned down to look inside.

The first thing he saw was the back of a rifleman, his trousers around his ankles and his arse on display. The man stooped as he stood in the confines of the BMP, looming over a woman he had trapped in the corner. Though she had been forced back against the wall and her denim skirt had been torn away, she was still fighting back against him, long-nailed fingers raised like claws. She bared her teeth as she shouted for help.

"What the fuck is this?" Rakovich growled.

The soldier turned. It was Snegur, one of the platoon's few real veterans. The scar on his left cheek, which he claimed came from a tribesman's knife in Afghanistan, gave his leer an extra feral menace.

"Praporshchik," he said. "Come to join in?"

With Snegur distracted, the woman drew her foot back ready for a kick.

"Stop." Rakovich pointed his rifle at her.

The young woman froze, the anger on her face replaced by fear.

"Stupid bitch." Snegur laughed.

"Out." Rakovich gestured with his rifle.

"But Praporshchik," Snegur protested, both his smile and his erection drooping. "I'm not done."

"Both of you," Rakovich snapped. "Out. Now."

Hofmann had caught up with him. She repeated his words in German. The younger woman hastily pulled up her torn skirt and barged out past Snegur. After a moment's hesitation, the veteran pulled his trousers up and followed.

As Snegur emerged, Rakovich slammed his rifle into the man's stomach. Snegur doubled over, the air bursting out of him in a single grunt of pain. When he straightened up again, he stood to attention, and his trousers fell back down. He stared past Rakovich's right ear as if something of terrible fascination had caught his eye.

Rakovich stood inches from him, looking up into that scarred face.

"What did I say about the women, Snegur?" Rakovich asked.

"You said not to touch them, Praporshchik."

"That looked like a lot more than just touching."

"Yes, Praporshchik."

"So what made you think that you could get away with disobeying my orders?"

"Cigarettes, Praporshchik."

"Cigarettes?"

"When we got here, you said that we couldn't touch the women or take the cigarettes. But then you changed your mind about the cigarettes. So we thought..."

"We? Who's we?"

Snegur's eye's flicked to the side, pointing for a moment at Szolkowski, then came back to the centre.

"Just me, Praporshchik," Snegur said.

"You thought that, just because I let you have a few cigarettes, I was going to let you rape the people we're liberating?"

"In Afghanistan—"

"I don't care about Afghanistan. I don't care what a tough bastard you were out there. I don't care if you've got a collection of fucking mujahideen ears that you wank off over as you cry yourself to sleep at night. You're under my command now, and I won't tolerate rapists. Understand?"

"Yes, Praporshchik." Snegur looked him in the eye at last. He looked defiant. "Whatever you say, Praporshchik."

"I know what you're thinking," Rakovich said, staring back at him. "You're thinking there won't be time for a court martial out here. That the command won't bother punishing you for getting your dick wet.

"But it's not command you have to worry about."

Rakovich grabbed Snegur's exposed junk in a vice-like grip. The rifleman gasped in pain.

"You do this again, I'll cut off your dick and feed it to the crows," Rakovich whispered. "And every fucking man in the platoon will back up my story that you did it to yourself. Because I'm the Praporshchik, and you're just a rapist piece of scum. Understand?"

"Yes, Praporshchik," Snegur croaked.

"Good."

As Rakovich let go and took a step back, Snegur curled over, clutching his balls.

The women still stood watching, waiting. Hofmann had her arm around the younger woman, who looked like her grin might turn to tears at any moment.

"Professor, you take her home," Rakovich said. "Make sure she understands that this ends here."

"Thank you, Praporshchik." Hofmann led the woman away.

At last, Rakovich turned his attention to Szolkowski. He wanted to punch the arrogant, manipulative little shit right in the face. But there was no blame he could pin to him here, and without that, Szolkowski would find some way to use it against him, to undermine his position, just like he'd done with the cigarettes.

"Seems like some of you need a reminder of what's at stake here," Rakovich said. "I think it's time we went out on patrol."

RAKOVICH TOOK the patrol on foot. He wanted to move around without the noise and attention the BMPs brought, to see things that he might otherwise miss. More that that, he wanted to march the men hard and blow off some steam.

He'd picked some of the patrol from among the trouble-makers he needed to deal with. Szolkowski and Snegur were ones he wanted to teach a lesson. He'd brought Akayev and Dologodin because he needed men he could rely on to have his back and who wouldn't be easily led by Szolkoski. Zinoviev, always eager to please, had come as a volunteer.

It had been tempting to bring Zimyatov too. If there was one man in the platoon Rakovich could really trust, it was Zim. But that was why he'd had to leave him behind, so there was someone with an ounce of sense in charge of the village. The alternative was Kholodov, with his coloured stickers and his airy artist's dreams — no way to run a creche, never mind a freshly liberated community full of doubts and fears.

They found the farmhouse an hour out of the village. It stood beside the road at the bottom of a hillside, with a barn to the left and a small orchard to the right. There were no signs of life, but that didn't mean much. As they'd seen in the village, locals learnt to keep their heads down when soldiers were coming.

Rakovich split them into pairs — Szolkowski and Zinoviev; Snegur and Akayev; Dologodin with him. Then they split up and approached the farm.

If he was going to lead the men into hazardous situations, Rakovich had to prove that he was willing to take risks himself. The farmhouse was the most obvious place to hide ambushers, so he and Dologodin went straight towards it, with the other pairs to left and right. He kept his rifle raised as he walked warily towards the building, eyes peeled for any sign of movement.

The farmhouse was old, shaped by years of renovation and rebuilding. Bricks filled the spaces in the timber frame, some of them plastered over and whitewashed, others left exposed. To the left of the front door was a chopping block, its wood battered and stained, an axe buried in the top. Blood red roses ran on barbed stems around the closed door and sun-bleached window frames.

A car was parked outside the farmhouse. Rakovich stopped and crouched behind it, surveying the windows of the house, trying to get an idea of its layout before he went inside. Sheltered behind the vehicle, he took a moment to check the progress of his other teams.

To the right, Snegur and Akayev were advancing slowly through the orchard, using the trees for cover as they worked their way around the side of the house.

To the left, Szolkowski and Zinoviev were by the barn. They exchanged a few words, then Zinoviev headed into the building. Framed by the open doors, Rakovich saw him lower his rifle and reach for something. He held up a can, waving it for Szolkowski to see.

Beyond him, a hay bale moved.

"Zinoviev!" Rakovich yelled. "Get down!"

Zinoviev flung himself to the ground.

The hay bale fell, revealing two men in civilian clothes, both pointing hunting rifles.

Before they had a chance to aim, Rakovich opened fire, a hasty spray of bullets that blew great chunks of straw into the air. Both his targets took cover, giving Zinoviev a chance to scramble clear.

Even as Rakovich's attention was taken, there was a crash of shattering glass and a bark of gunfire. Beside him, Dologodin groaned and slid down the side of the car, blood pumping from the shattered mess that had been his shoulder.

Rakovich ducked. Bullets thudded into the car, one bursting through the window above his head. Shards of glass tumbled across him, one slicing the back of his hand.

He froze for a moment, caught between two urgent needs — to save Dologodin and to deal with the threat.

"Akayev, Snegur, covering fire!" he shouted.

As bullets sprayed the farmhouse, the firing at his position stopped.

He fumbled with a bandage, tearing off the wrapping and trying to bind it around Dologodin's wound. Protruding bone tore the cloth and he had to pull out another bandage, trying to fix something, anything in place. Blood coated his hands, soaked his sleeves, sprayed his face with a fine mist. No matter what he did, however he tried to bind the wound, the blood kept flowing.

Dologodin let out one final gasp and fell limp.

"Fuck." Rakovich flung the useless bandages down and took up his rifle again. To the left, Zinoviev and Szolkowksi were pinned down by the barn doors, exchanging fire with the men inside. Those fuckheads could deal with their own problems. He had to tackle the farmhouse.

"Akayev!" He waved to the men in the orchard. "Covering fire. Snegur, you're with me."

Pulling a grenade from his pouch, Rakovich ran at a crouch around the front of the car, heading towards the house. A bullet clanged off the engine block to his left. Another bit the dirt inches from his foot. He ignored them, running straight towards the shattered window ahead. Winding his arm around, he flung the grenade through the window and then hit the ground below, just as the blast filled the air with glass and shrapnel.

Then he was up again, leaping through the window with his rifle raised. Snegur was a second behind him.

A body lay by the window of a living room. A teenage girl, no more than sixteen, with a hunting rifle in her hands, her face full of shrapnel.

Moving quickly and quietly, Rakovich and Snegur made their way across the room and through the adjoining kitchen. At the bottom of the stairs they paused.

Rakovich looked at Snegur, a man he'd threatened to castrate only hours before. It would be easy, with the two of them alone in here, for Snegur to take his revenge. Easy for a Praporshchik to wind up dead in an ambush. There would be no forensic teams sweeping the battle site for evidence. No-one would check which bullets had hit who.

He gestured up the stairs. Snegur, his steps slow with reluctance, led the way.

Whatever his faults, Snegur was a professional. As they reached the top, he pulled a grenade from his pouch and flung it around the corner. As soon as the blast cleared, he followed, rifle at the ready.

Rakovich followed. As he rounded the corner, he saw a man and a woman, both grey-haired and both blood-soaked, lying on the floor. There was a shotgun in her hands and an open box of shells beside him.

Snegur advanced past one doorway, surveying the room as he went. There was another doorway at the end of the landing. He looked briefly inside, then turned.

A shudder ran through Rakovich as he realised that Snegur's rifle was pointing at him, the barrel level with his gut. His hands tensed around his own weapon, but he held perfectly still. Was this deliberate, an act of vengeance because of what had happened earlier? A rapist could so easily be a murderer too. Or was it just chance, the way the rifle happened to point as Snegur turned to his commander with habitual hostility?

In the end, it didn't matter.

There was a roar as a shotgun went off, the blast catching Snegur in the face. He was flung back, the front of his head a red ruin.

The blood-soaked old woman on the floor tried to shift the gun again. But she was badly hurt and had lost the element of surprise. Rakovich shot her twice through the chest and the shotgun fell to the floor.

Outside, the last sounds of gunfire died away.

Rakovich slumped against the wall, fighting back the urge to puke. Horror and relief swirled like oil and water inside him as he stared at the pulped mess that had been Snegur's face.

HALF THE PLATOON came out to stare as the farm truck drove into the village, Akayev at the wheel. By the time Rakovich stepped grim-faced out of the passenger side, villagers were watching too, peering in curiosity from the upper windows of their houses.

Riflemen helped the four survivors unload the bodies of Dologodin and Snegur. Each of the dead men was lifted up with more delicacy than his companions had ever shown for him in life, the coldness of flesh drawing out the hidden warmth of their hearts. They were laid out in a roadside flower bed, sheets draped reverently across them, red soaking through the white.

Rakovich watched it all as if from a distance, his mind narrowing in on practicalities in preference to anything else. He would have to call Captain Leontev about retrieval or whether they should bury them here. But other things came first.

Rakovich climbed up onto the back of the truck.

"Hofmann!" he shouted.

The professor threaded her way through the small crowd of soldiers. When she saw what he was standing on, she stopped, mouth gaping in horror.

"You know them?" Rakovich asked, pointing at the bodies of the civilians who had attacked his patrol.

"The Franks," she said in a small voice. "They have a farm over towards—"

"I know where their farm is," Rakovich said. "Now raise your voice and translate. I need your neighbours to understand what I'm saying."

He kicked the first body off the back of the truck. The girl's arms and legs flopped as she fell into the street, a limp, broken thing, her flesh pale against the black of the tarmac. The villagers, who had started to gather around the soldiers, let out a collective gasp. Someone groaned.

Rakovich ignored them. Any empathy he might have felt for these people had been smashed by the bullets flying from the farmhouse. As he talked, he kept rolling bodies to the edge of the truck and kicking them out, letting them fall crumpled into the street.

"We are not cruel," he bellowed, then paused while Hofmann translated, her words broken as she kept staring at the bodies. "We are not here to hurt you. But if you attack Soviet soldiers, if you sabotage our equipment, if you even start stirring trouble against us, then this will be you."

The last body hit the ground with a thud. The old woman stared up at him with dead eyes, and for a moment pity seized him.

Only for a moment.

"Tonight's curfew starts now," he shouted. "Don't let me see any of you before dawn."

He jumped down and looked at the hesitating Hofmann.

"That includes you, professor," he said. "Get the fuck home."

She scurried away, leaving him with his men. Their expressions were grim. One spat on the bodies of their attackers. Others followed suit.

"These bodies go on display," Rakovich said. "Remind these people not to mess with us. Zimyatov, you get our casualties stowed until I've talked with the captain."

"Yes, Praporshchik."

"Szolkowski, a word."

As the others dealt with the bodies, Rakovich led the rifleman away down the street. Both of them were covered in blood. Both held their rifles close.

"Zinoviev says you saved his life," Rakovich said once they were out of earshot of their comrades.

"Yes, Praproshchik," Szolkowski said, the beginning of a smile breaking through his grim expression. "Had to get up close and personal, but I dealt with both men in the barn."

"That's good work," Rakovich said. He looked the rifleman in the eye. Szolkowski was smart enough for his smile to disappear when he caught that look. "But you're the one who got Zinoviev distracted and vulnerable. You're the one who let them get the jump on us.

"I'm not going to punish you after you saved one of my sergeants. The men need to see some kind of win in today's shit show. But every time there's bullshit to deal with in my platoon, you're mixed up in it somehow. Sooner or later, rifleman, that bullshit is going to land on you. And unless you shape up, I'm going to make sure it hurts."

14

RUNNING FROM TROUBLE

Anna drew back into the darkness of a doorway, sheltering in the shadows as a car drove past. Just her luck to run into one of the few drivers allowed out after curfew. At least the half-masked headlamps limited the light it produced. She doubted the driver had even seen the poster half-glued to the side of the shop, never mind her standing there, clutching a paintbrush and a bucket of paste.

A shiver ran up her spine, not from the cold but from the thrill of coming so close to capture. She felt like one of the heroes from the stories her mother had told her as a child, revolutionaries daring to challenge a broken system. Back then, she had preferred her father's stories, filled with powerful witches and terrifying monsters. Now, she preferred something closer to her life.

Once the engine noise was gone, she crept out of the doorway and around the building. Boris was crouched between the bins behind a restaurant, which did little to hide him from view. As she approached, he peered out, looking like a bear emerging from its cave at the start of spring.

"Is it safe?" he asked as quietly as his deep boom would allow.

"As safe as it will ever be." Anna took another poster from the roll in his hands. "Come on. I want to get some of these up around the subway entrances, so commuters will see them."

The two of them had developed a comfortable rhythm for these nights. They talked quietly as they walked, discussing their friends and family, her studies, his work. Boris worked in a factory making tins for food, but since the war started there had been changes. A technician from the government was trying to convert their machines to make shell casings and the whole process fascinated Boris. While he worked longer shifts to prepare rations for the army, he watched the engineers at work, and then told Anna about it later. It wasn't the most thrilling conversation, but his enthusiasm was uplifting, as was his trust in her judgement.

"But can it be done?" he asked as he slapped a paste-covered poster onto a wall. "Changing the machines from cans to shell casings?"

"I don't know," Anna said. "I study chemistry, not engineering."

"Oh." He looked around. "Where next?"

"The underpass."

It turned out that one of the other teams had been there before them. Anna smiled at the sight. She was the one who had given them their posters and paste. She was making a difference here.

"Why is there a curfew?" Boris asked.

"In case of bombers," Anna said, leading him on through the night.

"But there aren't any bombers." Boris pointed at the sky.

That gave her pause for thought. The government had been clear that only authorised workers would be allowed out past eight in the evening, to keep the streets dark and people safe from NATO bomber attacks. But there had been no planes in the skies above Leningrad, no sight or sound of bombs.

"Perhaps it's to save electricity," she said, though a darker possibility was crossing her mind. "Or perhaps it's to keep us under control."

There was a creaking noise from up the street. Anna froze. Beside her, Boris breathed slow and heavy as he eased his way towards an alley mouth.

A door to a stationery shop had opened. Two men emerged in a pool of neon light. One wore the uniform of a police captain. The other had his overall-clad back to her and his hair was hidden by a green cap, but there was something familiar about the way he stood.

The two men talked in hushed tones, their words too distant and muffled for Anna to hear. She didn't dare move a muscle. In this darkness, she was invisible to the policeman, just one more indistinct shape. But if she moved, if she drew his attention, that could change in an instant.

Her pulse raced. Paste dripped from her brush onto the baggy trousers she had borrowed from Vlad's room. What had seemed daring and heroic moments ago now seemed dangerous to the point of terrifying.

And the man in the overalls seemed so familiar. Where had she seen him before?

The mewling of cats burst out of the alley Boris had been creeping towards. Bins fell with a clang and tiny footfalls came racing into the street. Two hissing shapes shot past Anna.

The police captain looked up, his hand going for the baton at his side. Anna stood frozen in the darkness, hardly daring to breathe. His gaze swept across the street, squinting into the near-perfect darkness. For one long, terrible moment it seemed to settle on where she stood, then moved on past, following the fighting cats up the street.

She sagged in relief.

A lump of paste fell from the brush, spattering the street. The pale mix of flour, water, and cheap glue seemed shockingly pale against the darkness.

The policeman stared straight at her.

"Who's there?" he called out. "Show yourself."

Anna stayed perfectly still. Maybe he hadn't really seen her. Maybe he was just responding to movements in the dark. Maybe he'd think it was more cats.

He drew his baton but didn't come any closer.

The other man, his back still to them, hurried away, whistling as he walked off into the deserted night.

Anna held her breath.

The policeman squinted uncertainly into the darkness.

Suddenly, a gust of wind blew down the street. It snatched one of the posters from the pile in Boris's arms, sending it flapping to the ground.

The policeman grabbed a radio from his belt, bringing it to his mouth even as he strode towards them.

"Run!" Anna shouted.

She was first into the alley mouth, Boris lumbering after her as she raced into almost total blackness. She crashed into a bin, bruising her thigh, shoved it aside and ran on past. Its clatter was followed by another as Boris also ran into the unseen obstructions.

Light blazed after them — the beam of a torch.

"Stop!" the policeman shouted.

Boris caught up with her, his longer legs making up for his extra weight. They burst out of the alley mouth and into a street. A car was heading towards them, police lights flashing on the top.

"This way." Boris beckoned her across the street and into another alley. Anna followed, flinging aside her bucket and brush. She could get new ones. These wouldn't do her any good in a jail cell.

This alley was shorter. They darted out of the far end just as the police car was screeching to a halt behind them, the captain shouting at the driver as he caught up.

"Left," Boris panted.

They ran on, down side streets and pedestrian paths, across the strangely quiet streets of a city under curfew. The sounds of footsteps kept following them. Sirens were blaring in the distance.

A public park appeared up ahead. Boris headed straight for it.

"What are you doing?" Anna asked. "They'll see us running across!"

"Trust me."

Boris vaulted the low gate, Anna hot on his heels. There was a small stand of trees to one side. Boris ran in among them and stopped in front of a bush.

"We can't hide in there," Anna said. "They'll see us."

He lifted up some branches, then reached down and pulled at something underneath. A hatch opened.

"Down," he hissed. "Quick."

Anna scrambled down a set of concrete stairs into darkness. Boris followed, lowering the hatch over them. He rummaged around in the darkness, then a lighter clicked, illuminating them with its small flame.

"What is this?" Anna whispered, looking around the rubble-strewn space. It seemed like a cellar, except that there was no building above it.

"Originally?" Boris shrugged. "I don't know. These days, it's just a secret place kids come to get high."

"How did you know about it?"

"I was a kid once."

He let the lighter go out. They sat together in the dark, waiting for the danger to pass.

ANNA SAT at the kitchen table, staring at the scarred wood.

She ought to get going. People were expecting her at the meeting. She had a fresh batch of posters to distribute and more volunteers to coordinate.

Before last night, she had been excited for any sort of union activity. Now the thought of stepping foot outside the door made her legs feel like lead.

It didn't make sense. She had chosen this. She wanted to do it. She yearned for the freedom and equality the union offered. And there was no rational reason why the danger should be any greater than it had been before.

Yet she struggled to move.

"Are you alright?" Papa stood by the front door, his cap in his hands. "You're not sick, are you?"

"No, Papa."

"It's not that Maksim, is it? If he's broken my little girl's heart again, then I'll—"

"It's not Maksim, Papa. I haven't seen him in weeks." She looked up, forcing a smile. "I just... I was meant to be going out tonight. I was looking forward to it. But now the time's come, I'm not sure I want to any more."

"That's probably for the best," Papa said, coming to lay a hand on her shoulder. "There is a curfew, after all."

"But people are expecting me. They're counting on me." That should have motivated her to move, but instead the thought made everything so much harder.

"Will it do any harm to miss this?" Papa asked. "Do you really need one more university party?"

"It's not like that."

"Oh, so you would be studying?" He raised an eyebrow. "At eight on a Friday night? I have my doubts."

He gave her shoulder a gentle squeeze, then put his hat on and headed for the door. In one hand he clutched a paper pass, his permit to travel from home to the factory after curfew.

"Do you think that's all my life is about?" she asked, voice trembling. "That all that matters to me is having fun?"

"Of course not, sweetness. But you are only young once. It is not bad that you make the most of it. Leave the serious work to your brother. Your time will come."

The door clicked shut behind him.

Anna glared at the table. Of course people would want her to leave things to Vlad. He was the serious one, the capable one, the mature one. She was just some little girl.

But she understood the world better than her brother did. She had seen and heard things he hadn't. Not everything could be left to men like Vlad — they were too afraid of change. Someone needed to make a better world, like the revolutionaries had done in her mother's stories.

She got up from the table, pulled a bag of posters out from under her chair, and went to the door. She could almost hear the footsteps of the police pursuing her, the heaviness of Boris's breath as they cowered in their hiding place, hoping not to be caught.

If only she had papers like Papa, she could go out safely. But there were no papers for revolutionaries.

She took a deep breath and turned the door handle.

THE PEOPLE RUNNING the union had found a larger venue this time, a hall in a run-down sports centre just out of site of one of the canals. A podium for medal ceremonies had been dusted off and brought to the front, so that Pavel Semenov and the other speakers could be seen. Their audience was bigger this time, and the sound of their excitement echoed around the cavernous room.

"How are you feeling?" Anna asked, leaning in close to Tatyana. They had seats near the front row, an honour accorded them because of Tatyana's work with the union committee. But now that she had a chance to catch up with her friend, other issues came to the top of Anna's mind.

"I'm OK," Tatyana said. "A little bit moody, but who isn't right now?" She paused to pat her belly. "I guess things will be different once it starts to show."

"Will you have to give this up?"

"No way! Pavel has a baby and he's leading us. Besides, look at how much this has grown in just a few days. By the time the kid comes along, our work might be done."

That thought lifted Anna's spirits. If the union movement was gaining momentum, if change was in the air, then maybe she wouldn't have to worry about running from the police for long. It was sad that it had taken a war to bring them to this, but maybe the tipping point had been coming. Maybe she'd be back to studying and partying before Vlad even got back from the front.

If he came back, said a sad, dark voice inside her. But she shut that thought away, forcing herself to focus on the here and now.

Cheers broke out as Semenov took his place on the podium. He looked even more exhausted than at the previous meeting, but he was grinning triumphantly, as if the energy of the crowd was giving him new life.

Around the podium, senior members of the union stood watching the crowd. Many of them were unknown to Anna, but she recognised Klara Ivanova, the tall, dark-haired head of street teams. Behind her, a middle-aged man in an ink-stained apron leaned against the wall, his gaze downcast. Others were more alert, cheering on their leader with as much enthusiasm as anybody in the room.

Semenov waved his hands and the room went quiet.

"Comrades, thank you," he said. "Thank you for your work. Thank you for your passion. Thank you for making our country a better place."

Cheers again, even louder this time. And again, at Semenov's signal they fell quiet. Anna didn't understand how he managed it, this small man in his rumpled suit, but every man and woman here was his to command.

"Things have moved fast in the past few days," Semenov continued. "But there's no time for complacency. We have bold plans for what comes next. And to explain them, I'd like to introduce the youngest and brightest member of the committee."

He looked down, and for a moment Anna thought he was gazing at her. Her heart skipped a beat.

"Tatyana, come on up."

Anna gaped as her friend rose from her seat. Tatyana glanced at her just long enough to give an apologetic shrug, then started making her way towards the podium. Some people moved respectfully out of the way to let her through. Others touched her shoulder or shook her hand, as if they were star-struck fans desperate for a brush with celebrity.

What had Tatyana been doing while Anna was putting up posters?

As Tatyana approached the stage, a man moved a chair so that she could use it to climb up. He was wearing overalls and a green cap. As he turned away, a terrible sense of familiarity hit Anna.

"Tatyana!" She shouted. "Tatyana, wait!"

The cheers were rising and she couldn't be heard over them.

She grabbed Boris and shook him by the arm.

"Police," she said urgently. "There's a police agent here."

Tatyana was climbing up onto the stage. Semenov reached out a hand to welcome her.

"What's that?" Boris leaned in closer. "What are you talking about?"

"Police!" Anna shouted. "There are police. We have to warn the leadership."

Boris frowned.

"Say that again. I could have sworn you—"

There was a bang as the doors burst open. People at the sides of the crowd screamed and began to run. Police poured in, batons raised, some carrying riot shields.

Anna tried to push through to Tatyana. But the man in overalls had pulled out a police badge and a gun, as had half a dozen others, and they were storming the stage. Two of them grabbed hold of Semenov while another snatched at Tatyana.

"Run!" Semenov bellowed, his voice carrying over the chaos. "Keep the movement alive!"

The back of the room had turned into a messy brawl, a tangle of policemen and protesters. Others were streaming through the fire exits, trying to get out before it was too late.

Anna looked one last time at Tatyana, being dragged from the stage. Her heart sank and she wished she had the courage to go to her. But what could she do against armed police?

She joined the wave of people surging for the doors. It was like being a boat caught up in a storm, tossed around by forces beyond her control. The best that she could do was to ride it out and hope to reach safety.

Someone slammed into her, almost knocking her to the floor. She stumbled, was pushed, regained her balance, and kept moving, squeezed tightly in with others as they neared the edge of the room.

In desperation, she looked around for Boris. He was built like an ox. He could keep her safe. But she had lost him amid the madness of the moment. Boris was nowhere to be seen.

Held up by the people crammed around her, she was carried out through the doors and into the street. Suddenly the crowd loosened and she almost fell again, just getting her feet underneath her. There were mobs of police to left and right, but up ahead someone had broken through the fence onto waste ground and the union members were fleeing that way. Anna ran with them, legs pounding, arms flying, breath burning in her chest. She could hear cries of pain and of panic but felt powerless to affect them. All she could do was save herself.

At last, she found the shelter of an abandoned brick-built factory, far beyond the sounds of struggle and the eyes of the police. She leaned against a wall, lungs heaving, trying to drag in enough oxygen so that she could run again.

Others had stopped here too. Some had collapsed, panting, on the ground. Others sank to their knees in despair.

"What now?" a young man asked.

He looked around, longing in his eyes, searching for an answer in each face in turn. When he reached Anna, all she could do was look away. She was no-one here.

She wished that Tatyana was with her. Boris even. Anyone she knew. Anyone who could give her the strength to help these people. But she was just one more ragged dissident in a broken revolution.

As the sound of sirens approached, she started running again.

15

BREAKTHROUGH

The BMPs sat in a row outside the village, engines running. Behind them, the men were lined up with full packs and rifles at the ready.

As he walked along the line, Rakovich inspected each man in turn. He was glad of this chance to assert order and of the action that would soon follow. He'd felt things slowly slipping out of his control while they waited in the German village. Insubordination from his men. Resistance from the locals. Men killed in a fire fight that did nothing to move the war on. Getting back into action would let him take control and make a difference to the war again.

Days sitting idle had robbed his men of the edge they'd had on entering the war, that sense of urgency and tension. Details were slipping. That had been fine while they were sitting here guarding a bunch of scared civilians and an irrelevant road junction. It couldn't continue now.

"We're being sent to exploit a breakthrough," he said as he peered at rifles, boots, and ammo pouches. "It's a more independent role than they'd normally trust us with, but the regiment's all strung out, so they're using whatever they've got. Try to think of it as a compliment rather than a chance to get ourselves killed.

"We won't just be facing front line troops. There should be some easy targets. Transport staff. Artillery. Emergency reserves. Remember, they're still the enemy. You won't feel any less dead just because you were shot by a mechanic."

He took Rebane's rifle, looked down the barrel, and handed it back.

"Clean that properly," he said more quietly. "Once we're on the move."

He took a step back and raised his voice again.

"You've had a lovely few days sitting on your fat arses, watching TV and eating candy like a bunch of kids. But it turns out there's no genie among these capitalist toys and so we can't wish the war away. Now it's time to be real soldiers again."

The men headed for the BMPs, taking up their familiar seats. Rakovich took one last moment to make sure they hadn't left any of their ammunition or supplies behind.

As he looked around, a soldier came running out of the village towards him — a sergeant from the reserve platoon sent to relieve them. He didn't carry himself with the authority of a sergeant and Rakovich doubted he'd learnt to use his rifle properly, never mind fired it in anger.

"Praporshchik," the sergeant said, holding out an envelope. "Post just arrived. This is for you."

Rakovich took the letter. The sight of Anna's handwriting made him smile and the sergeant returned the expression.

"From your girlfriend, Praporshchik?" he asked, a glint in his eye.

Rakovich barked a laugh. "Fuck, no. It's my sister."

He stuffed the envelope into his pocket, alongside the other one and his battered Communist Manifesto. Looking back up the street, he saw Professor Hofmann standing in the road, watching him with a steady gaze. She was somebody else's problem now.

Stooping to get through the rear door, he climbed into his BMP.

"Let's go," he shouted.

The doors closed behind him. One by one, the BMPs started driving away.

ONCE FULL OF beet fields and pig farms, the valley was now littered with broken bodies and the wreckage of battle. The charred shells of tanks, both Soviet and Western, lay behind every barn, hedgerow, or rise in the ground. Twisted corpses of jets lay strewn across valley sides or buried in deep gouges in the earth, where the planes had torn the ground as they came crashing down.

There were survivors too. Tanks protecting hard won vantage points. Injured men queueing outside medical tents, clutching their bandaged bodies and leaning on each other for support. Orderlies burning severed limbs on a bonfire, fending off a mangy, emaciated dog as it snatched at the charred remains. The smell of burning flesh filled the air. Behind Rakovich, Rebane groaned, leaned out of his gunner's seat, and puked into the back of the BMP. Bakhvalovich cursed as vomit spattered his legs.

"Sorry," Rebane said, wiping his mouth with his sleeve. "God save us from such a fate."

The BMPs bumped over uneven ground and shell-shattered roads, heading for a bridge and then the broader road on the far side. Men and mobile guns guarded the crossing. Beyond, tanks sat along the roadside. Some sat sentinel, but others were firing.

"This is it," Rakovich tensed as he spoke into the radio. "Hold on tight, it's going to get ugly."

Leontev had put them at the front of the company, making Rakovich's vehicle the first into the gap. He wished he was in the familiar second section BMP, with Akayev at the wheel. But the leader of the platoon was meant to be in number one section, so here he was.

Shells hit the ground to either side of the road, hurling up fountains of dirt and debris. Guns roared to right and left as Soviet armour fought to widen the breach, while the British and Germans sought to seal it. Overhead, planes filled the air with contrails and explosions. Somewhere, artillery was thundering away. It seemed that the war was all around them, but there was nothing they could do. Fighting wasn't their mission. Not yet.

The noise grew as they raced forward, Lobachov squeezing all the speed he could from the BMP. Bullets rattled off the side and shrapnel thudded against the roof. The thunder of explosions grew into a discordant symphony, a maelstrom of noise that filled the cabin and shook Rakovich to the bone. It seemed that the whole world was exploding around them.

Then they were through, the sounds of battle fading as they raced down an unbroken road into the Allied rear.

"Fuck yes!" Zinoviev shouted over the radio. Someone else whooped.

Rakovich clung grimly to his seat and watched the countryside roll by, alert for signs of trouble.

This had barely begun.

STALKING through the trees with his rifle in hand, Rakovich heard the British soldiers before he saw them. He held his fist up, then gestured to the other men, showing them where the danger lay and what he expected.

Together, they advanced.

Step by step, they crept towards the edge of the woods. The mulch of old pine needles gave way beneath their feet, releasing the soft scent of decay. To Rakovich's left, the remains of some long-dead bird lay spread at the foot of a tree, one last half-rotten feather protruding from a wing tip. Ahead came the sounds of nervous laughter and the thud of equipment being moved around. The sounds of the enemy.

He took a deep breath and then another, keeping his breath steady, keeping his ears open for trouble. He had this.

Rifles raised, eyes darting around for signs of danger, the Soviets advanced to the edge of the tree line.

Beyond, a transport helicopter sat near the top of a hill. A dozen soldiers in berets and camouflage jackets stood guard or sat waiting on boxes of supplies. At the rear of the helicopter, a hatch was open, engine parts scattered gleaming across the ground next to it. A man in a flight suit stood swearing and waving a wrench, his face knotted in frustration.

"Wait for it," Rakovich whispered as, beside him, Zinoviev started to rise. "Not yet."

One of the British soldiers looked around, towards a narrow road from the east. Others joined him, weapons pointed towards the growing sound of BMP engines, away from Rakovich and his team. Some took cover behind heaps of supply crates. Others crouched or lay on the grass, rifles pointed towards whatever might be coming.

It would do them little good.

A BMP's 30mm cannon barked, sending shells whistling through the air. They hit the hillside fifty yards from the nearest soldier, exploding in a harmless cloud of dirt.

The British returned fire.

Rakovich grinned. That was it. Let them waste their bullets on the armour of the transports. Let them pass through these first moments when they were fresh, focused, at their best. Let their attention get drawn more and more onto that one area, while Rakovich and his men crept towards them through the undergrowth. And then...

"Now," he said.

The Soviet patrol opened fire. There weren't as many of them as there were British soldiers, but they had the advantage of surprise. Even as the British turned their attention to the woods, the first of them fell, one man flung back by a sudden spray of lead, another falling as his legs were blown away. The engineer made a dash for the helicopter's cabin, only to go down in a spray of blood. Beside him, a man grabbed a grenade from his pouch, which then dropped from lifeless fingers, taking out his nearest comrade.

Rakovich crouched behind the trunk of a tree, elbow steadied on his knee, rifle blazing. One of his targets went down, blood pumping from a shattered shoulder, but Rakovich couldn't tell if he had scored the hit.

It didn't matter. All that mattered was that they won.

Two of the BMPs sped towards the helicopter, then skidded to a halt just before the British lines. The main guns fired and the rear doors opened, men leaping out with rifles firing.

To their credit, the British didn't turn and run. The last few retreated along a hedgerow that ran down the hill, making the most of what cover they could. One man would dash back a dozen yards while another gave covering fire, then they would switch, leap-frogging past each other. One lucky shot hit Bakhvalovich, who sank to the ground calling out for help.

But it didn't do the British any good. The third BMP raced down the hillside, cutting off their retreat. Guns blazing, the British tried to race past. The BMP tore through the hedge, crushing one of them beneath its tracks. The others went down to the bullets of Kholodov's section, shooting from the safety of their vehicle's firing ports.

The wounded British were still screaming as Rakovich emerged from the bushes. He ignored them. He didn't have the time or resources to look after anyone but his own. NATO troops would respond to the sounds of fighting and he didn't want his men here when they arrived.

He pulled the pin from a grenade and thrust it into the open workings of the helicopter, just to make sure it didn't fly again. Then he strode back towards his BMP.

"Mount up!" he shouted. "We've got more chaos to sow."

There was a roar as the grenade tore up the helicopter's engine. Rakovich grinned.

ZIMYATOV LEANED out of the passenger compartment, looking up at Rakovich in the command seat.

"Bakhvalovich's in a bad way," he said. "Can we stop to treat him properly?"

It wasn't a surprise. They'd got off lightly for the carnage they'd wrought, but Bakhvalovich had been hit in the hip, and the sounds of his pain had filled the BMP the whole way down the hill. The sound was starting to get to Rakovich. Each scream or groan made him imagine what pain had caused that noise, and those imaginings made his skin crawl.

He looked again at his map. There was some sort of building by the side of the road a mile away. That would give them some shelter while Obolensky did what he could for the wounded man. For the sake of everyone in the vehicle, they needed to stop.

He spoke sharply into the intercom, giving instructions to Lobachov in the driver's seat.

"Five minutes," he said to Zimyatov. "Tell Bakhvalovich to hang in there. If he dies, I'm coming back to kick his arse."

"Yes, Praporshchik," Zimyatov said with a grin.

The road was clear, local forces drawn into fighting further east, and they soon reached their destination. The building turned out to be a café at a roadside layby, clean but cheaply maintained, with paint peeling from the window frames. Rakovich suspected it hadn't seen many visitors even before the war broke out. A few trucks sat in the parking lot, but there was no sign of any drivers.

The three BMPs drew up outside the café. There was no movement inside, no sign of life closer than the thud of guns beyond the nearby hills.

"Zimyatov, get Bakhvalovich inside and have Obolensky see to him," Rakovich said. "I need to radio command."

As Bakhvalovich's comrades carried him groaning and shaking into the café, Rakovich wished there was more they could do. The platoon's medics had basic training in emergency medicine, not the skills and experience for battlefield surgery. Normally, he would have sent Bakhvalovich to an aid station, but they weren't in the line anymore, and there was no-one to send him to. Not until the whole division got through the gap.

He flicked the radio onto the command channel and called Leontev.

"What do you want?" the Captain barked. "I thought your instructions were clear enough."

"They are, sir," Rakovich replied, trying to keep the bitterness from his voice. He didn't have a problem with the instructions, but it seemed that Leontev still had a problem with him. "I wanted to know if the breakthrough's complete yet. I've got a man who needs a doctor."

"I see." Even over the radio, Rakovich could hear Leontev taking a deep breath. "First Platoon has taken casualties too, but there's nothing we can do about it yet. Stabilise your man and stay on mission. Our best chance is to mess up the enemy's rear and buy the others time to widen the breach. Understood?"

"Yes, Captain," Rakovich said. "Zoryn 217 out."

This was always how they were going to win the war — get through a gap, smash up the soft elements in the enemy's rear, and create a chance for the rest to catch up. He'd been excited to make that happen. But now he was here, he saw the downside for the first men through. No supplies or support, no way of knowing what they might meet as they roamed away from the main combat zone. He couldn't plan properly, couldn't use the resources that had been assumed in his training. Whoever had come up with this plan hadn't thought this far ahead, or perhaps hadn't cared, and now one of his men was suffering the consequences.

A scream emerged from inside the café. Rakovich hoped that meant they were digging the bullet out, and not just that Bakhvalovich's condition was getting worse. He barely knew the man, but he was one of his, and that mattered. All of these men were Rakovich's responsibility now.

He looked around the truck stop, just a stretch of packed dirt covered with tyre tracks. Half his men crowded around the trucks, looking for keys in the cabs or trying to force open the rear doors.

"Kholodov!" he shouted.

The sergeant looked up from where he sat on the hood of one of the cabs, sketchbook in hand.

"Praporshchik," he said. "How can I help?"

"How do you fucking think?" Rakovich said. "Set some people to keep watch."

He frowned, his gaze drawn to the tracks in the dirt. There were a lot of them, and they bothered him, which made no sense. There were bound to be lots of tyre tracks at a truck stop. Worrying about them was just paranoia.

Still, he kept looking, something prickling in the back of his mind. Some of the trails matched the trucks parked here, but those weren't the most recent ones. Broader marks, some of them left by tracks rather than wheels, criss-crossed in the dirt. There had been a lot of activity since their owners abandoned those trucks.

If they had abandoned them.

He looked up and down the road. In one direction stood a small cluster of houses, enough to hide a couple of vehicles or a platoon of infantry. In the other, trees and drainage ditches lined the fields, perfect cover if it was needed.

But needed for what?

"Look what I found!" One of the riflemen had got into the nearest truck. He stood with his back to the interior and his rifle hanging by his side, holding up a large TV. "There's enough for everyone!"

The men cheered in excitement and more scrambled into the truck.

The shutters of the other two vehicles rolled open. Rakovich's eyes went wide in alarm.

"Ambush!" He raised his rifle and strafed one of the trucks. He couldn't see who or what was inside, but that didn't matter. It wasn't his men.

His wasn't the only gun firing. The leading looter fell from the back of the truck, his prized TV crashing to the ground, blood running down his side. Another man fell back, clutching his arm. A third, too close to the truck for comfort, dived underneath while the rest of the platoon fell back.

Rakovich sprinted towards his men. As he ran, he tugged a grenade from his pouch.

German soldiers had appeared in the backs of all three trucks, firing from behind the cover of heaps of boxes. The Soviets, caught unprepared and in the open, descended into a mass of panic. Some swung their rifles around. Some ran. Some stood bewildered, their reactions a fraction too slow.

Rakovich flung the grenade into the back of one of the trucks. Men and bodies went flying. The Germans in the other trucks ducked into cover.

"To the BMPs," Rakovich barked. "Now!"

Up the road, a pair of armoured vehicles had appeared from behind the houses and were accelerating towards the truck stop. In the other direction, infantry were scrambling out of a drainage ditch. Two of them set up a mortar, while others opened fire with automatic rifles.

As Rakovich herded his men towards their vehicles, Zimyatov appeared in the doorway to the café. He clutched the door frame, his expression grim.

"Bakhvalovich's bleeding like a pig," he shouted. "We can't move him yet."

A mortar bomb exploded to the rear of the café. The Germans' aim was wildly off, but that wouldn't last.

Szolkowski was urging the slower men back towards the BMPs. Even as he shouted at them to get to safety, Germans climbed out of the nearest truck. He brought his rifle up and shot one, forcing the others to duck into cover.

Rakovich pressed himself against the wall of the café, with the corner sheltering him from the soldiers in the trucks. His men were firing back but it was erratic and disorganised, brief shots taken between the more urgent business of finding shelter.

He looked from those trucks to his men to the enemy closing in. If he got them into their transports now, most of the platoon might survive, but that meant dooming Bakhvalovich.

If he gave up on one man, what did that say to the rest?

"First section," he shouted, "into the café. Second and third, hold the BMPs."

As his men took up firing positions, Rakovich ran for the rear of the lead BMP. Bullets sprayed around his feet and a mortar bomb whined through the air. He dived into the vehicle just as the ground burst open, showering the BMP with shrapnel.

Inside, Rakovich reached for the radio.

They were going to need help.

16

BACKUP

Bullets clanged against the side of the BMP, making a sound like a city's worth of tuneless church bells. Inside the steel shell of the vehicle, Rakovich climbed into the commander's seat and grabbed the radio. His heart raced and his hand shook as he pressed the button.

"Zoryn 210, this is Zoryn 217," he barked into the microphone. "Do you read me, over?"

Static was the only reply. Outside, there was a thud, followed by the crash of shrapnel against the BMPs.

"This is Zoryn 217, can anyone hear me?"

Still clutching the handset, Rakovich peered out of his periscope. His men had laid down enough covering fire to pin the nearest German troops, and the armoured vehicles had stopped two hundred meters up the road. Still, the pressure was growing, mortar and gunfire filling the air with noise and flying death.

"This is Zoryn 217," he said again. "Some bastard had better answer me right fucking now."

Zinoviev ran into the vehicle, a couple of his riflemen behind him.

"We were too exposed out there," he said, looking nervously at Rakovich.

When the praporshchik didn't respond, Zinoviev went to one of the firing ports and started shooting out across the car park. His men did the same. There was a scream and some foreign cursing. That was something at least, to know that the capitalist bastards were hurting as much as they were.

"Zoryn 217, this is Zoryn 211." Lieutenant Chugainov's voice came through the radio. That distant, tinny sound made Rakovich's spirit soar. "I have sight of Zoryn 210, but there are hostiles in the area. Can it wait?"

Rakovich bit back a curse. Chugainov had no way of knowing what he was going through.

"My platoon is exposed and under heavy fire," he said as calmly as he could. "We are pinned down and have taken casualties. Need assistance as soon as possible."

"Understood," Chugainov said. "I'll get the Captain."

The radio went silent just as gunfire sprayed across the BMP's side. Rakovich hoped like hell that Chugainov had switched off at that exact moment, and that the radio hadn't just been fucked up. He didn't dare test it, for fear of missing the call back from Leontev. Instead he crouched against the wall, knocking his fist impatiently against the side, the receiver clutched tight in his other hand.

Zinoviev ducked away from his firing port while he changed the magazine in his rifle. He looked at Rakovich with a mixture of embarrassment and puppy dog eagerness to impress.

"I'm sorry, Praporshchik," he said. "I should have kept the men away from the trucks. I just didn't think about—"

"Later," Rakovich growled. "We can deal with how you fucked up later. For now, let's focus on surviving."

"Yes, Praporshchik." Zinoviev took a deep breath, then spoke again. "I was wondering if we should counter-attack. I volunteer to—"

"Did you manage to shit your brain out when you were a child?" Rakovich asked. "Because I can't think of any other reason you'd have such a crushingly stupid idea. We're outnumbered, we're surrounded, and there's open ground between us and them. The only reason to attack is if we have no other options, or if you want to get yourself shot. And if it's that last one, then you can wait until it's not my fucking problem."

"Yes, Praporshchik," Zinoviev said.

He turned to firing again.

"Zoryn 217, this is Zoryn 210." Leontev's voice emerged from the radio at last. "What do you want now, Rakovich?"

"Captain, we need help," Rakovich said. "We're surrounded by German troops and have at least two men down. Request immediate backup."

"What is your location?" Leontev asked.

"We're at a truck stop west of the breakthrough point."

"A truck stop?" Leontev's voice dripped with disdain. "You got surrounded in the open by the side of the road?"

There was no time to explain, and Rakovich doubted it would have made a difference.

"Yes, Captain. And now we need your help."

"Lots of people need my help. I don't know if you're exaggerating, bullshitting, or so stupid that you deserve to be shot, but I'm not sending good men to save a screw-up. Zoryn 210 out."

Rakovich pressed the button on the side of the radio.

"Zoryn 210, this is Zoryn 217," he said. "You need to understand, they came out of nowhere. We're surrounded and we need help."

"Zoryn 217, this is Zoryn 211," Chugainov replied. "The Captain's gone, Rakovich. Give it up."

"But we're fucking surrounded!"

"Just try not to get everyone killed. Zoryn 211 out."

Rakovich's fingers tightened around the silent radio. Something cracked beneath the pressure.

He flung the handset away. It clattered against the wall then lay dangling from its cable.

A string of expletives poured unbidden from his mouth, frustration bursting forth as unstoppable as a bomb blast. Then he remembered the other soldiers in the BMP, all of whom had turned to look at him in shock.

He took a deep breath, forcing his anger back down. It could be a fuel, a way to get them through this. It had to be, because help wasn't coming.

"None of you breathes of word of this to the others," he said with cold menace. "If you do, I'll fuck you up worse than we're going to fuck up the Germans. Understand?"

They nodded.

"Now get back to fighting, while you still can."

As he watched them turn their attention to the battle, guilt knotted itself around his stomach. He was the one that Leontev hated, the reason they would get no help. This was his fault.

Except that the fight with Leontev wasn't his doing. He hadn't done anything wrong, hadn't argued back, hadn't even questioned the meaning of the Captain's commands. For some reason, Leontev had decided to make him miserable, and he was powerless to stop that destroying him.

No. Never powerless. There were always options, whether he was facing Leontev or a German fighting unit. He just had to work out what those options were.

"Zinoviev, I need covering fire," he said.

"Yes, Praporshchik!"

The sergeant shot a wild spray of bullets through the firing port. As the others joined in, Rakovich ran out of the back of the BMP and across the few meters to the café. Bullets whistled through the air, but none came close enough to hit him.

He slammed into the door, which flew back against the wall. Glass fell from its already ruined window.

The soldiers of First Section were scattered around the café, positioned at windows covering every approach. At least he could count on Zimyatov to do things right.

Bakhvalovich lay on the counter at the side of the room. His shirt had been cut open and there were bandages across his chest. His face was pale, eyes closed, breathing steady but shallow. Obolensky stood over him, syringe in hand, humming softly to himself.

"How bad is it?" Rakovich asked.

Obolensky cast away the empty syringe and pulled a drip feed bag from his pouch.

"Could go either way," he said. "Wish we could get him to a proper aid station."

He connected the tube from the bag to a large needle, which he thrust into Bakhvalovich's vein.

"Can we move him?" Rakovich asked.

"Is that a real question?" Obolensky asked. "Or a way of telling me that you're about to do it?"

"Sounds like they handed out brains along with those medical kits. Whatever you can do to get him ready, you do it."

A burst of gunfire made Rakovich turn towards the windows facing away from the road. Half a dozen German soldiers were rushing towards them, guns blazing.

He swung his own rifle around and, barely taking time to aim, returned fire. The café filled with broken glass and the roar of gunfire. Bullets splintered tables and burst open padded seats, but brick walls protected the Russian riflemen as they returned fire. Soon three of the Germans were down and another stuck behind the cover of a half-demolished wall. The other two were retreating across the fields, back to the rest of their unit.

Rakovich looked around at the devastation. This place was a ruin. If the Germans had got close enough to use grenades, they'd all have been blown to bits.

He had to get them out now.

He approached the doorway at a crouch and peered outside. A plan was starting to form in his mind but he needed to know if it could work.

"Akayev," he called out. "Where are you?"

"Praporshchik!" The reply came from behind one of the BMPs.

"Covering fire!" Rakovich yelled.

On cue, there was a burst of shooting from inside the café. He dashed to the BMP, then pressed himself against its side, next to the Kyrgyzstani driver.

"I know your Russian's shit," he said, "but I really need you to understand me now."

"Yes, Praporshchik." Akayev nodded.

"What would happen if we rammed their vehicles with ours?" Rakovich asked, pointing up the road at the Germans.

"Ram?" Akayev asked.

"Ram." Rakovich used his hands to mime one vehicle knocking another aside.

"Ah!" Akayev nodded, then shook his head. "Not good. They are solid like us, yes? Much armour. We..."

He imitated Rakovich's mime, but this time the moving vehicle stopped as it hit, then Akayev splayed his fingers in a display of destruction.

"So we go that way." Rakovich pointed up the road in the other direction.

Again, Akayev shook his head.

"I watch," he said. "They lay mines."

"Could we go across the road and out?"

"Big ditch."

"Fuck."

A nearby mortar blast interrupted Rakovich's train of thought.

"Zimyatov!" he shouted. "How are you doing in there?"

"Like shit, Praporshchik," Zimyatov replied. "All the stories about lazy western workmen are true. This place is falling to bits around our ears."

Rakovich looked at the café, then back at Akayev. An idea had come to him, and it was either the greatest or the stupidest idea he'd ever had.

"What if we drive a BMP through there?" he asked, pointing at the café.

Akayev looked from the brick walls to his vehicle, then back to the walls again.

"Is weak," he said, grinning. "As long as roof not fall down, we go straight through."

"Alright then." A wild, desperate laugh burst out of Rakovich. They could stay here, waiting for the Germans to find reinforcements, or they could take their lives into their own hands.

The fire raining down against them had dropped off. Past the other German vehicles, a pair of Leopard tanks had appeared, steel harbingers of death rolling steadily towards them. It was now or never.

Rakovich raised his voice.

"You ready, Obolensky?" he called out.

"As ready as I can be," the medic replied.

"On my mark, drivers and gunners to your vehicles," Rakovich shouted, hoping that none of the Germans understood Russian. "Everyone else, covering fire.

"Ready? Go!"

Gunfire burst from the BMPs and the café, accompanied by a mad dash of movement. Akayev left Rakovich's side and ran to his vehicle.

The Germans made little effort to hit the running men. The mortar didn't even fire, apparently waiting for their tanks to come and do the job.

"On my mark, drivers start your engines," Rakovich shouted. "Gunners provide covering fire. Anyone else, into your BMPs.

"Ready?"

He gripped his rifle tight.

"Go!"

By now, the Germans realised that something was happening. As the riflemen ran for the BMPs, two of them carrying the injured Bakhvalovich, mortar bombs and machine-gun bullets flew. Tammert yelped as a bullet clipped his arm and blood ran down the side of another man's face.

Rakovich was among them, darting around the nearest BMP and through its rear doors. He shoved Kholodov aside, scrambled into the command position, and grabbed the radio.

"Drivers, lay down some smoke," he ordered. "Gunners, fire at will."

Guns roared, knocking holes in the trucks where the German infantrymen hid. Smoke billowed from the front of the BMPs, obscuring the view of the approaching tanks.

"Sections one and three, follow Akayev," he said into the radio. Then he switched to the intercom and addressed the driver. "Let's go."

The engine roared and the BMP rolled into the road, picking up speed as it turned in a tight arc. Rakovich's stomach lurched as they accelerated towards the wall of the café, but it was too late to turn back now. Something bounced off the hull and exploded to their left, but he ignored it, clinging on tight.

The building rushed towards them.

Akayev yelled in Kyrgyz.

Then they hit the wall with an almighty crash.

The BMP shuddered and slowed. Its front rose as they mounted a pile of rubble. For a moment Rakovich feared they weren't going to make it.

Then they were heading down again, crashing through the rear wall in a shower of broken bricks and splintered window frame. He caught a glimpse of a German soldier leaping from cover and sprinting away.

"Go right," Rakovich said into the intercom. "Past their transports and back onto the road."

He looked back as they cleared the building. The second vehicle was following close behind, crushing rubble beneath its tracks as it emerged into the field.

On the road, the German vehicles were trying to turn, but there wasn't space for both to do it at once. As they shuffled around, infantry ran to find new firing positions, taking the mortar with them.

"Gunner!" Rakovich snapped. "Get that mortar team."

"On it," Plakans replied, opening fire.

The third BMP was coming through the café now. As Rakovich looked back, the ceiling above it gave way.

He remembered what Akayev had said about this stunt. They could do it as long as the roof didn't fall.

"Fuck," he muttered, gripping his seat tight, watching timber and tiles fall across the front of the vehicle.

It kept going, flinging them aside, jolting over the broken walls, and emerging in a cloud of dust.

"Yes!" Rakovich yelled, and his men joined in. "That's Sovet engineering!"

166 ANDREW KNIGHTON & RUSSELL PHILLIPS

The German transports had almost turned and the tanks were accelerating to join the fray. But it was too late. The BMPs bumped up onto the road, picked up speed on the smooth tarmac, and roared away.

The tanks fired a few desultory shells after them, blowing craters from the road and the surrounding fields. But Rakovich and his men were clear.

He sank back in his seat and let out a huge breath of relief. In the back of the BMP, men cheered.

THEY FOUND the rest of the company in what had once been a small NATO base, the bodies of a score of German infantry now lying in a ditch out front. There were no signs of bullet marks or blood, only faces contorted in their final painful spasms.

"What happens them?" Akayev asked as they drove past.

"Chemical weapons," Rakovich replied. He knew the theory, but he'd never seen its horrible reality before — the bulging eyes, the foam crusted on their lips, those frozen looks of abject horror. "Fast dissipating ones, so that our troops could come in after."

Better them than him, or than anyone on his side. But still, it looked a monstrous way to go.

Inside the base, he found Leontev meeting with his officers and praporshchiks. Most of them seemed relieved to see the Third Platoon alive, and his chest swelled as he was greeted with handshakes and slaps on the back.

But not by Leontev.

"So much for your desperate situation," the Captain said. "Only five wounded, I'm told, and only one seriously."

"My men did their country proud, sir," Rakovich said, not meeting his commander's gaze. "Akayev and Obolensky deserve credit for their work."

Leontev snorted.

"If your men did so well, how did you get surrounded?" he asked.

Reluctantly, Rakovich began telling him about the trucks, the men's excitement at their contents, and the distraction it had caused.

"I've had the same problem," Lieutenant Egorov said as he flicked ash from his cigarette. "Every village we drive through, my men want to stop and go hunting for jeans."

"Then you both need to sort your men out," Leontev said. "There are no such problems in First Platoon, are there Chugainov?"

The normally unflappable Lieutenant Chugainov grimaced.

"Sorry, Captain," he said, "but I've been through the same shit. We're in the land of Marlborough and Nike, and now our men want what they can't have."

"The problem isn't going away, Captain," Rakovich said, emboldened by the officers' support. "For my men, or for anyone else's. They are like small boys in a toy shop, surrounded by wonderful distractions."

"Small boys indeed." Leontev snorted again. "They are soldiers of the Red Army and they should know better."

"Perhaps this is something I could help with?" Lieutenant Valeev said, treating the Captain to a warm smile. "After all, I am here to keep us on the true path."

"Fine," Leontev said. "Go do your thing. And Rakovich?"

"Sir?"

"From now on, keep a proper leash on your men."

Rakovich bit back an angry response. They'd just said the problem wasn't just his men, yet here he was, being singled out. He wanted to argue back, but there was no point. This wasn't about what was fair, for him or the soldiers in his platoon. It was about getting through this.

"Yes, sir," he said.

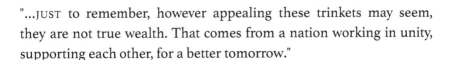

"...JUST to remember, however appealing these trinkets may seem, they are not true wealth. That comes from a nation working in unity, supporting each other, for a better tomorrow."

His speech finished, Valeev stepped down from the roof of the BMP. The men clapped politely, but there was no passion in their eyes. Rakovich wasn't surprised. After all they had seen, the political officer's words rang hollow even to him. He needed time to gather his thoughts.

Someone had left a plastic chair outside the end of a barracks block, a litter of cigarette butts on the ground around it. Rakovich sat down and pulled out his battered old Communist Manifesto. Here, in the words his mother had left him, he would find something to restore his faith.

As he opened it up, he saw an envelope inside. The latest letter from Anna, which he hadn't had time to read.

He opened the envelope and looked over the letter. At first it made him smile. She talked about the dangers he must be going through, how she was thinking of him, and how both she and Papa knew he could make it through. It filled him with a warm glow, knowing that his family understood and supported him.

But somehow, she couldn't resist digging up old moans. Mentioning the breadlines on the streets, the problems in the city, the lack of real information in the government news. She stepped around it carefully, never so blatant that the censors would have stopped it reaching him, but he could sense the old arguments between them.

His faced flushed. Why did she have to do this? To snipe away at the nation that nurtured them? To bitch and moan while others did the hard work?

He pulled paper and a pencil from his pocket. Resting on the back of his book, he began angrily scribbling:

"ANNA,

"You talk about bread lines and ignorance, but you know nothing of the reality we face. My men are dying out here every day, so that you can live in comfort.

"Today, I saw a man shot in the hip, his blood seeping out as his comrades struggled to keep him alive..."

17

CAPTAIN HARE

D arkness carried Rakovich through the forest like a trusted comrade. Thickening clouds drifted out of the east, blocking most of the moonlight, and what little made it through was swallowed by the branches overhead. He could barely make out the shapes of the trees and of the men advancing with him.

They walked as silent as shadows, their tread muffled by a thick carpet of old pine needles. Not a word had passed between them in the past hour. He had chosen his men well and soon those choices would earn him his reward. They would prove their worth again and prove how absurd Leontev's accusations of incompetence were.

Rakovich froze at the sound of an engine overhead. A British helicopter, making another of their night-time sweeps. It had been like this for days, as NATO gained control of the skies. The Soviets would advance, their footsteps bloodied by the enemy's fighting retreat. Then night would come and NATO would bring out their fancy toys. By morning, they would have identified the Soviet positions, ready to greet the dawn with a barrage of rockets and artillery shells. The Soviets would fall back, regroup, and start their advances again. Ground was being gained, but it came blood-soaked and littered with the bodies of good fighting men.

It was typical of NATO. They didn't have the superior strength of the Soviet soldier, their spirits weakened by their decadent lifestyle. Instead they relied on fancy toys to see them through, toys they only had thanks to the injustices of their imperialist system.

But their toys could not save them forever.

Ahead, voices drifted through the trees. Rakovich didn't recognise any of the words. That meant British troops rather than Germans. Their intelligence was correct.

As he crept forward, the night was broken by the yellow glow of a small electric lamp and the flickering of a campfire, brief fragments at first, but more with each step he advanced. He smelled woodsmoke, coffee, and roasting chicken.

To his left, a twig snapped.

Rakovich froze, silently cursing whoever had made the sound.

The British kept talking. No-one even turned to look into the woods.

Rakovich sighed in relief. Any one of them could have trodden on a twig in the darkness, and these woods must have animals to make noises too. As long as the British weren't expecting trouble, they would be fine.

He advanced again, the others following his lead. He could make out shapes around the fire. Half a dozen men, some silhouetted, others illuminated on the far side. They smiled as they drank from tin mugs and watched a wooden spit turn over the flames. Behind them was some sort of transport vehicle, antennae protruding from its roof.

Close enough. Rakovich crouched, then waited while his men fanned out among the trees. A little light reached them, just enough to highlight fragments of faces or the shape of a limb. Szolkowski's grin, his teeth exposed as he tasted the night air. Plakans' shoulders shifting as he took aim. One of the new men, eyes twitching back and forth as he watched their prey. Together they waited, watching Rakovich as he raised his fist.

Rakovich brought the fist down, raised his rifle, and counted to three.

They opened fire.

Rakovich shot one of the silhouettes first. The man fell into the fire, casting ashes and embers across the ground. Flames caught his hair and his jacket, illuminating Rakovich's next target more brightly. The man was opening the door of their vehicle, but Rakovich's bullet hit him before he could get inside. He sank against the door, clutching a limply dangling arm.

With a shout, Rakovich charged into the clearing. More British soldiers had appeared around the transport, joining those who had survived the initial shooting. It would have been safer to fire at them from the forest, but his blood was up and he had a mission. Better to risk the enemy's bullets than to risk them getting away. Death or glory for the motherland.

An officer drew a pistol. Rakovich reached him before he could raise it. The praporshchik slammed the butt of his rifle into the man's face and he fell stunned, the pistol firing a single useless shot into the undergrowth.

A bullet clipped a tree to Rakovich's left. He turned to see a British soldier, rifle raised, aiming at him. Then Plakans slammed into the man, smashing him against the side of the transport. There was a crunch of breaking ribs and the rifle slid from the British soldier's grasp.

Rakovich raised his rifle, surveying the scene by the light of the fire and the overturned lamp. Nine British soldiers lay scattered like so many rag dolls. Only his men were still standing.

FOUR OF THE British were dead already, and the man who fell in the fire was on his way. Nothing they had out here could deal with his burns or the bullet hole through his lung. He lay groaning and shaking while the Russians dealt with the other four. The stink of his singed flesh made Rakovich want to puke.

Plakans had all the outdoor skills that came from growing up in a Latvian logging community. Szolkowski also seemed to know his way around a knot, though Rakovich doubted that came from anywhere so wholesome. Together, they bound their captives.

Two of the prisoners took careful handling, thanks to fractured ribs and a shattered humerus. A third was concussed and lay gazing groggily into the distance.

That left the officer.

"My name is Captain David Hare," he said. "Serial number—"

"You speak Russian?" Rakovich looked at him in surprise. He had known that this was a signals unit, and they were being captured because of the intelligence they might have gathered. It hadn't occurred to him until now that, to gather intelligence on the Russians, the British would have to use Russian speakers.

"If I didn't, the question would be a little redundant." Hare's tone was steady, but Rakovich sensed mockery behind his words.

"You're a prisoner," he snapped. "Don't fuck with me."

"Wouldn't dream of it," Hare replied.

"Do you all speak Russian?"

"Rowe does." Hare nodded to the burned man. "Or did, by the looks of him. Lucas too."

This time he indicated one of the corpses.

Rowe's groaning grew louder and more high pitched. He tried to roll over, then shrieked as his burned face pressed against his shoulder.

Rakovich tightened his grip on his rifle. Perhaps he should just put the man out of his misery. His survival was unlikely, and the sound of his screams might bring trouble.

"I don't mean to be a bother," Hare said, "but could I give him morphine?"

Rakovich hesitated. If there was morphine here then it could be saved for his own injured men.

But what if one of them had been in British hands?

"Do it," he said.

Hare fumbled at a pouch on his belt, his movements made awkward by the rope binding his hands. Having drawn out a small syringe, he walked over to Rowe and crouched beside him. He yanked the man's trousers down and pressed the syringe against his thigh.

Moments later, Rowe fell silent and still.

"Thank you," Hare said.

There was a softness in his voice that caught Rakovich by surprise. He had been taught that the British lived between two extremes — violent thuggery and a cold, unsmiling superiority. Hare's concern fitted neither expectation, nor the image of the West as a land of decadent, self-interested capitalists. It showed a humanity that he should have expected from any other person, and yet hadn't thought to see in his opponents.

He looked away uncomfortably as Hare laid a hand on his comrade's shoulder and said something quietly to him in English.

The sound of an engine approached through the trees. Everyone stiffened and Rakovich instinctively brought his rifle to bear.

"Looks like our rescue is here," Hare said, his calm confidence returning.

"I don't think so," Rakovich replied.

A BMP appeared along a track from the north, the driver steering by infrared rather than draw attention with his headlights. It halted by the British vehicle and Akayev poked his head out.

"Bus is here, yes?" he said. "Take you home now."

Two men emerged from the back of the vehicle, rifles out just in case. There had always been a risk that this would go wrong, that they would be rescuing Rakovich's team instead of transporting captives for interrogation. If he'd learnt one thing over these past weeks, it was the stupidity of assuming that you would always win.

Other assumptions could cause problems too. He had assumed that the British would mostly die in the firefight, leaving only a captive or two. A single BMP couldn't take all the men he'd captured.

He looked over the prisoners. Hare, an officer with linguistic skills, was clearly the most valuable, and the one command would want to see. Sending him first would be the smart move. But Rakovich was intrigued by this encounter with the British and loath to let go of it so soon.

"Take the injured in the BMP," he said. "Get them to a medical station first — Leontev will have our heads if they don't survive. This one can come with us."

"We have to walk back?" Szolkowski protested. "But we already tramped through half the night."

"Yes, we walk back," Rakovich said, abandoning thoughts of calling for another transport. "You have a problem with that?"

He glared at Szolkowski and for a moment the rifleman returned the look. Then he lowered his head.

"No, Praporshchik," he muttered. "No problem at all."

THE SHORT SUMMER night was already fading as they set out through the woods — four Russians and their single prisoner. Without the need to stay silent and hidden, they made faster progress this time. Even Hare accepted the need for a swift march, not slowing them down in hopes of escape.

"You did my men a kindness back there," he said. "You made sure they got the care they need, and the least I can do is to cooperate."

"It was not kindness," Rakovich said. "Just practicality."

"Of course," Hare said. "My mistake."

But he still kept moving.

"Is it true that you hunt foxes in England?" Plakans asked as they emerged onto the road. "Not like normal people hunt, but in blood red jackets and riding war horses?"

Hare laughed. "Not all of us, no. My wife doesn't even eat meat."

"You don't look poor," Szolkowski said, looking the man up and down.

"It's not a matter of money," Hare replied. "She doesn't think people should kill animals."

"But you're a soldier," Plakans said, looking confused. "You kill people. She's good with that?"

"The heart wants what the heart wants," Hare said with a shrug.

They walked on a little longer, Rakovich mulling over the man's words. His mother had said the same when he asked how she and his father had found each other. The heart wants what the heart wants.

"What about televisions?" Plakans asked. "Do you all have colour televisions?"

"Most of us," Hare said.

"Big ones?" Szolkowski asked.

"How big is big?"

Szokowski held out his hands, showing the size of the TVs they'd seen in capitalist German homes.

"Yes," Hare said. "Most of us have televisions at least that big."

"This is the capitalist way," Rakovich said. "Cheap entertainment to hide the oppression of the people."

"I'm not sure they're terribly oppressed," Hare said. "If they were, they couldn't afford those televisions."

This time the laughter in his voice was unmistakable. The arrogance of it set Rakovich's teeth on edge.

"What do you give up for your televisions?" he asked. "Instead of a nation that cares for you, it is every man for himself. What kind of life is that?"

"I suppose you're right," Hare said. "I mean, apart from national health care, pensions for the elderly, support for the disabled and the unemployed, free education, a few other odds and ends. Honestly, it's brutal."

"This isn't how capitalism works," Rakovich snapped. "You're lying."

Hare pulled up his shirt.

"See this?" he said, pointing at a scar. "That's where they whipped out my appendix. Didn't cost me a thing. Capitalism lets us raise the taxes that paid for that."

"That's not capitalism!"

"Then what are you fighting against?"

Rakovich clenched his fist, fingernails digging into the palm of his hand. This man was wrong. He was lying. Beneath all this calmness and charm, there lay the soul of a viper.

He glared at Hare, who smiled and shrugged. Beyond him, Szolkowski hid a smirk by lighting a cigarette.

"When we liberate the West, you will see how miserable you have been," Rakovich said through gritted teeth.

"You're not exactly winning me around." Hare turned to Szolkowski. "Could I possibly have one of those?"

Szolkowski's gaze flicked briefly to Rakovich, then he held out the pack. Hare took one while Szolkowski raised his lighter and thumbed the wheel. The two men stopped, huddled over the small flame.

"Keep walking!" Rakovich snapped.

"Yes, Praporshchik," Szolkoski said. "Of course, Praporshchik."

Dawn rose across the fields and trees. Oblivious to the violence humanity was inflicting upon itself, birds filled the air with the beauty of their song. Rakovich wished they would shut the fuck up and let him think. Maybe then he could find a way to prove Hare wrong.

Tanks and BMPs appeared in the road ahead. Whatever advance was planned for today, they hadn't waited for Rakovich to complete his mission. Troops would begin pouring towards the nearest NATO positions, hoping to achieve the next great breakthrough.

Rakovich and his small band stepped off the road, onto a narrow stretch of grass between the tarmac and a drainage ditch. Behind them, birds fluttered above a beet field, bobbing and weaving in an elaborate acrobatic display. As the armoured vehicles approached, Szolkowski lit himself another cigarette and passed one to Hare.

Out of the west came a sound like a door slamming, followed by a whistling.

"Artillery!" Rakovich shouted. "Take cover!"

He flung himself into the ditch, moments before a shell struck the road. The blast shook him and made his ears ring. He pressed himself down against the side of the ditch, muttering curses against NATO, against field guns, against farmers and rotten, stinking ditches.

Outside the ditch, the sound of artillery mingled with that of the Soviet armoured column. The ground shook and the air filled with a roar like a thousand subway trains. A door, blown off a shattered vehicle, crashed down into the ditch next to Rakovich, barely missing

Plakans' head. Szolkowski was pressed flat in the mud, while the new rifleman lay curled in a ball against the bank, clutching his helmet to his head, eyes squeezed shut.

As the roaring receded to sporadic shell bursts, Rakovich realised that Hare wasn't with them. He cursed his own idiocy. He'd kept his most precious captive out of misguided curiosity, and now the man was dead. Captain Leontev would give him so much shit for this, he would wish he'd just stood up and let the shells take him instead.

He pushed himself up the bank and peered out across the road. The tarmac was a mess of shell holes, surrounded by twisted metal, shattered glass, and mangled bodies in pools of blood. The armoured column, its way blocked by a pair of ruined tanks, had scattered into the fields. Enemy fire pursued it as it retreated, and though few shells found their mark, they still fell all across the area. The frustration and helplessness of his situation knotted Rakovich's guts. What could an infantryman do when faced with this?

"Praporshchik," a voice said from behind him.

He turned to see Hare standing in a field, still smoking his cigarette as he watched the shells fall. One landed across the field behind the Englishman, the blast wave blowing his hair around.

"Are you insane?" Rakovich shouted. "Get into cover!"

"Like that will do any good," Hare said. He pointed along the ditch. "It didn't save him."

Rakovich's stomach sank as he looked at the rifleman beside him. He still lay curled up in the bottom of the ditch. His helmet had fallen off and his hands were pressed to his head in a futile attempt at protection. A shard of shrapnel had buried itself in his head, pinning those hands in place.

"Fuck," Rakovich hissed. The worst part was that he couldn't even remember the young man's name. Something Ukrainian, wasn't it? Something with a B? Something that didn't matter because now he was dead, like too many of them.

The rifleman's head fell forward, blood and brains falling from a hole in the back. Plakans stared in horror at the sight, then muttered some Latvian curse. Rakovich struggled not to throw up.

He looked again at Hare. If the English officer had died, at least he would have done it with dignity. There was a courage there that he couldn't help admiring. If Hare could face the ugly truths of his life, maybe Rakovich could too.

BY THE TIME they reached the company, it was too late to try another advance. Rakovich passed Hare to his superiors, checked in on his platoon, and then went to wash his filthy clothes in the bathtub of a bombed out farmhouse. While he sat on shattered bathroom tiles, waiting for his trousers to dry, a thousand thoughts flowed through his mind, battering at his consciousness until his head seemed ready to explode.

He needed to get these ideas out.

Beside him sat pencil and paper, taken from his jacket before he washed it. He spread the paper out on his knee and started to write:

"DEAR ANNA,

"By now you will have read my last letter. I hope you understand why I had to write so harshly. We suffer and die here for you and for what is right. It is a heavy burden, and one that gets no lighter as the days pass. I cannot say that I am sorry for what I said, but I am sorry if it seemed that all I have for you is hate. If I die, it is important that you remember me for more than that.

"Today, I met a British officer for the first time. He was not like I had expected from the stories we are told..."

18

KEEPING HOPE ALIVE

A tap dripped in the kitchen of the flat. Drops fell irregularly, a broken rhythm drumming against the plates in the sink. Anna had tried to fix it three times already, but it needed a new washer, and she couldn't even find one in the shops, never mind afford it. Nothing that might go into a machine of war would be spared for the people of Leningrad.

It was for the best, she supposed, looking down at the letter from Vlad. Her brother's anger at her burned in every word, but she still loved him, wanted him to have everything he needed. If not to save their broken homeland, then at least to live through this.

A newspaper lay next to the letter on the kitchen table. The state could find the resources to tell people how good their lives were and how terrible the enemy was. The paper was flimsy and uneven, the print illegible in places, but there was no keeping the party's words from the people.

With trembling hands, she picked the newspaper up and forced herself to read the article again. Like the letter from her brother, the words were over a week old, but that did nothing to lessen their pain.

"SABOTEURS ARRESTED IN LATE NIGHT RAID," the head-line said, each heavy set letter like a boot pounding on her heart.

Underneath was an account of the police action at the union meeting, including the arrest of Pavel Semonov and dozens of other dissidents. All were being questioned by the Ministry of Internal Affairs.

She imagined Tatyana in a cold concrete cell, desperately trying to protect the baby inside her. Pavel Semenov, torn away from his newborn child, being tortured by agents of the state. Boris, chained and beaten, blood running through his beard. However hard she tried to push the images away, they came back worse than ever.

The union was broken. There would be no reform. Shamed as she was to admit it, she felt lucky just to be alive.

The knocking on the door turned to a steady pounding, finally registering on Anna's mind.

"Papa?" she said, wondering why he hadn't answered. Then she noticed the darkness outside the window. Night had fallen while she sat here. Her father must be at work.

The pounding on the door came again.

"Anna?" called a rumbling voice.

Was this it, she wondered. Had someone mentioned her name to their interrogators? Was the Ministry finally here for her?

"Anna, I know you're in there."

She drew herself to her feet. If she didn't let them in then they would break down the door, and then Papa would have to find the money to replace it. She could do this right, at least.

The latch was cold to the touch. She turned it, hesitated for one last moment, and then opened the door.

"Anna!" A huge figure grabbed hold of her and she almost screamed. Then she saw his face and felt his beard against her cheek as he swept her up in a hug.

"Boris?" she mumbled. "But I thought..."

"Inside," he said, glancing over his shoulder as he pushed past and closed the door behind him. "I've stood out here too long already. We can't make your neighbours suspicious."

"Boris!" As her wits returned to her, she returned his hug. "I thought they had you."

"It was close," he said. "I think they might know my face, so I've been hiding out in my cousin's basement."

She took a step back and smiled hopefully at him.

"Have you heard anything about Tatyana?" she asked.

"Sorry," Boris said, his face falling. "She's on the list."

"The list?"

"The list Klara Ivanova got from a friend in the Ministry. It's all the people they arrested that night."

"Oh."

"Don't you know about the list?"

"I haven't seen anyone from the movement all week. I didn't want to put them in danger, if the Ministry was watching me."

"So considerate." Boris shook his head. "I never even thought of such a thing."

Anna blushed.

"Let me make us some tea," she said, picking up the kettle. "You can tell me what's been happening."

"I can do better than that." Boris grinned. "There is a meeting tonight. I came to take you there."

Anna stopped with her hand on the tap.

"But the police," she said. "The Ministry."

"A smaller meeting this time. A core group to plan, then to spread the word."

"So why me?"

"You led the poster teams. You're an important part of the movement."

"All I did was give people posters and glue. I'm really not sure that counts as important."

"You did more than most of us, and you're smart, too. We need you now."

"But shouldn't I—"

"Come on! We have to go."

Anna looked from Boris to the world outside the window. Her grip tightened on the handle of the kettle. She remembered crouching in the darkness of the ruined factory, desperate for breath, surrounded by the terrified survivors of the police raid. And then running through the night, fearing the unknown authorities ahead of her as much as those snapping at her heels.

"The curfew," she said. "We can't be out on the streets."

"Yes we can." Boris flourished two sheets of paper, neatly printed with official state logos. "We have passes."

"How?"

"Advantages of working on your poster team — I now know some very clever printers."

Fear kept Anna rooted to the spot. Fear of the night. Fear of the authorities. Fear not just for herself but for those around her.

But she remembered the thrill that came with putting up those posters, the confidence that came with believing she was making a better world.

She put down the kettle and went to fetch her coat.

THE MEETING PLACE was a run-down flat on the southern side of the city. Mismatched chairs sat in a circle around an otherwise empty room, heavy blankets acting as curtains to hide them from the world. A single bare electric bulb cast familiar faces into stark visages of bright light and deep shade. Some looked grim, some restless, some utterly drained.

Anna had seen them all in passing and talked with a few at meetings. But this was the first time they had sat together like this, and she realised how little she knew about her comrades. They must be driven, to risk meeting after everything that had happened. What motivated them and what sort of lives they were laying on the line, those were mysteries. A score of virtual strangers had to find a way to work together without bringing disaster upon themselves again.

"Let's get this shit started." At the far side of the circle, Klara Ivanova rose from her seat and looked around. She was a tall woman, pale-faced and dark-haired, without a trace of joy about her. "Who's seen the latest edict from the Ministry?"

A few of them nodded. Most, including Anna and Boris, shook their heads and looked to Klara to tell them more.

"I'll let you read the details for yourselves," Klara said, passing a sheet of paper to the man to her left. "Short version is that it's everything you'd expect from those bastards. Tighter curfew, travel restrictions, more rationing, a lot of forced recruitment into the factories and armed forces. And of course a clamp down on any sort of dissent."

She looked around the circle again, watching each of their reactions. Nobody flinched.

"What now?" a man asked. "I don't want to give up, but they hit us hard."

"So we hit back harder," Klara said, smacking a fist into the palm of her hand. "We start a strike."

Anna gasped. She wasn't the only one. They could all be arrested just for listening to these words.

"But the war..." someone said.

"The war makes this the perfect time," Klara said. "They need the munitions. That means they need the workers. That means we have more power than ever. Strike now and they'll have to listen to us."

Murmurs of agreement rippled around the room. Women and men grinned at each other, energised by the thought of action, of influence, of making a change. A minority looked less convinced, and like them Anna sat uncertainly, chewing on her lower lip. She couldn't help thinking about the way the police had clamped down on their meeting. What would stop them doing the same to striking factory workers?

In her mind's eye there were riot shields and truncheons, men like her father being beaten into the dirt and dragged away.

She looked around the circle, waiting expectantly for someone to speak up. But everyone who wasn't agreeing with Klara was doing like Anna, waiting for someone else to take the lead.

Klara sat back in her seat and looked around, arms folded across her chest. The anger in her eyes was enough to leave Anna cowering in her seat.

"Well?" Klara said. "Are we agreed?"

Many nodded and voiced their assent. Anna didn't want to defy them, but she didn't want to let this moment pass, to let them take the wrong road because she lacked courage.

Reluctantly, she raised her hand. All eyes turned to her, some questioning, some challenging, some relieved.

"Isn't there another option?" she asked. "A strike is a huge risk. People might lose their jobs, their freedom, even their lives."

"There is no progress without risk," Klara said. "Would you have the workers accept their oppression like a beaten dog?"

"Of course not!" Anna said. "I'm here, aren't I?"

"So what should we do instead?" Klara asked.

"I don't know. More of what we were doing before, for now at least. Posters, recruitment, building momentum. Trying to draw attention without putting people in danger."

"We're already in danger. And what point is there in recruiting if we don't use the people we have?"

"Something else then. There must be other options beside striking."

"Where did you think all this was going? We're building a fucking union. That means the workers united, standing up against the government, using the only power we have — our labour. That means strikes."

"But with a war on—"

"Ha! I fucking knew it."

Klara rose to her feet and the tension in the room tightened another notch. She pointed across the circle at Anna.

"You're brother's in the army, isn't he?" she said.

Anna nodded. "Lots of us have relatives who—"

"Not just a soldier. A praporshchik. A man who gives orders. A part of the system."

"I... Vlad's a praporshchik, yes, but so what?"

"We all know how it works. Men with just a little power are the ones who cling to it the tightest. They never want to rock the boat, for fear of falling into the river with the rest of us. And where a man leads, the women around him follow."

"I'm not following my brother!"

"Then why bring up the war?"

"Because I don't want him to die!"

Even as the words escaped her lips, Anna knew that she had made a mistake. It was true, she didn't want Vlad to die, but that had nothing to do with what she was doing here. Except that now the others would think it was all she cared about.

A hint of a smile lifted Klara's lips. She shook her head. She wasn't the only one.

"It's not just about Vlad," Anna said, trying to find a way back, some timber she could cling to amid the wreckage of her position. "It's all our fighting men, and the freedom of our homeland. Strikes would put that at risk."

"It's sad, but understandable," Klara said, her voice softer than before. "To put concerns about relatives at the front ahead of our comrades here. But other people are risking their lives too. People like Pavel, who's now rotting in a cell, waiting for the day when they take him out and shoot him. If we want to save those people, comrades who risked their lives to see the change we want, then we have to act."

"She has a point though," someone else said. "About defending the homeland."

"The excuse of imperialists throughout history," Klara said. "Look at where the fighting is. Our homeland was never at risk. The best thing we can do for it is to seize this moment, to make our nation a fairer, stronger place. Once we've liberated ourselves, then we can get back to liberating the world."

All eyes turned to Anna, waiting to hear her response. She felt as though she was shrinking beneath the weight of expectation, crushed by the pressure of the moment. Breathing came hard and sweat ran down the back of her neck despite the chill of a draught blowing in from the next room.

This was why she didn't speak up. She didn't have the wisdom or the eloquence for which her mother had been famed, or the strength of will Vlad showed every time he faced a challenge.

All she wanted now was a way out.

"We should vote," she said. "Before we act."

"On that we can agree," Klara said. "If we're to build a more democratic society, we have to start with ourselves. So, all those in favour of a strike?"

Of the twenty present, fifteen raised their hands.

"Those against?" Klara asked.

Anna forced herself to vote. Boris's hand rose loyally beside hers. Two others joined them.

"What about you, Mikhail?" Klara asked, turning to the one man who hadn't voted. "Don't you care to join in our democracy?"

"You've got your win," Mikhail said. "Now let's deal with the consequences."

THE PRINTERS' workshop was filled with the clatter of presses and the roar of machines. The air smelled of old paper and fresh ink, at once both sharp and musty. Sitting quietly in the corner, Anna watched men hurry past pushing trolleys or carrying heavy piles of off-white sheets, ready to be filled with tomorrow's news.

How many of these people would come out on strike, when the call went out? Anna hoped it was all of them. If this was going to work then they needed everyone they could get. It this was going to fail... Well, it seemed best not to think about that.

"I didn't expect them to send you," Mikhail said, setting down two heavy bags beside her. Behind him, the door to his managerial office hung open. "Not after you spoke out against this plan."

Anna looked at the bags. It was going to be a long walk home.

"This isn't what I wanted," she admitted. "But maybe I was wrong. The movement is more important than my hurt feelings."

Mikhail raised an eyebrow.

"Not many people could say that out loud," he said. "You're tougher than you look."

"Hardly," Anna replied. "I've barely slept since they took my friend. Every time my brother writes from the front I fall to pieces. The only reason I wasn't arrested was because I ran at the first sign of trouble. That's no show of strength."

"It takes a lot of strength to speak up when you're in the minority." Mikhail laid a hand on her shoulder. "More strength than I had."

"It doesn't matter now, anyway. We're going on strike. It's time for me to accept my place and go back to sticking up posters, not trying to shape our path."

"You can do both."

Mikhail whistled. Two people emerged from the office and came to join them. Anna recognised both from the meeting. They were the ones who had voted with her.

"We were hoping to speak with you later," Mikhail said. "But now is as good a time as any."

Anna frowned. This was more than a little confusing.

"You did well," Mikhail continued, "standing up to Klara like that. The movement needs someone like you, if we're not to end up like the rest of the country, giving in to whoever shouts the loudest."

"But I lost," Anna said, her throat tight.

"Everybody loses sometimes. What matters is that you try."

"We have some ideas," said the woman beside him. "Ways of reducing the risks and helping people get through the strike alive."

"We need someone to speak for us," her companion added. "We were hoping that might be you."

Anna looked at them in bewilderment.

"Why me?" she asked.

"Because you'll do the right thing no matter what," Mikhail said. "With you to give us voice, maybe we can too."

19

THE MINEFIELD

T he sign couldn't have been more than a few days old, but it looked like it had been there forever, its post filthy and starting to fade. The board itself stood out an angry red against the green of the field beyond, just like the dozens of others stretching off in either direction. The day was still, not even a hint of wind disturbing the long grass or the trees among which the platoon were parked. Yet in the presence of those signs, Rakovich felt his nerves dance electric with tension.

"ACHTUNG," the signs read above their skull and crossbones symbol. And then underneath, "MINEN."

Mines.

They'd been sent out here on a flanking manoeuvre, allegedly in response to intelligence from the Britons he'd captured. But if Captain Hare was anything to go by, those men wouldn't have given up anything of use, at least not yet. Rakovich suspected, not for the first time, that he had been given little more than busy work.

"I guess this means we're not going any further," Kholodov said, sounding relieved as he tapped a finger on the sign.

"Can we go around?" Zinoviev asked.

"Didn't you get the minefield training?" Zimyatov asked. "If there are mines here then there will be soldiers to either side. The minefield isn't meant to kill us — it's meant to force us into their fire zones."

"If it won't kill us," Zinoviev said, "can't we go straight across?"

Zimyatov rolled his eyes.

"Fuck's sake," he said. "How did you ever make sergeant?"

"My uncle got me it," Zinoviev admitted. "Wanted me to do proud by my dad. What's that got to do with anything?"

Kholodov pointed across the field. The remains of a cow lay scattered across the ground, flies crawling across strings of intestines. It had been torn in half by a blast, leaving both sides of the carcass a ragged mess. Exposed to the still summer air, rot had set in quickly, and the stink of it reached them at the edge of the woods.

"It's not that the mines can't kill us," Kholodov said. "That poor creature has painted a picture of what can happen. But the Germans are assuming that we're smarter than livestock, so won't just walk out across a field full of mines."

Rakovich could spot a conversation that wasn't going to be any use to him. Leaving his sergeants to it, he returned to the lead BMP, leaned in, and took the radio.

"Zoryn 210, this is Zoryn 217," he said. "Do you receive?"

"Zoryn 217, this is Zoryn 210," Leontev replied after a second's pause. "What is it this time Rakovich?"

"Captain, we've hit a minefield."

"Shit. What have you lost?"

"Nothing yet. We've stopped at the edge. Requesting instructions on how to proceed."

He pulled out a map and gave his coordinates to his commander. Then, while he waited for Leontev to consider, he pulled the German dictionary from under his seat and flicked through, looking up words relating to minefields. If they met a local, that might come in useful.

The radio crackled. "Zoryn 217, this is Zoryn 210."

"Zoryn 217 receiving," Rakovich replied.

"You are to clear a path through the minefield," Leontev said. "Then advance north to assault German troops holding up first platoon."

Rakovich suppressed a weary sigh. This was why he hadn't wanted to get on the radio.

"Captain, we don't have specialist mine clearance equipment or personnel," he said.

"You got basic minefield training, didn't you?" Leontev snapped. "Just like everybody else."

"Yes, captain."

"Then you clear a path through that minefield and you get first platoon the support I ordered. Understand?"

"Yes, Captain."

Rakovich signed off, set down the handset, and walked back towards the sergeants. Out of the corner of his eye, he noticed a house among the trees. If they were here for a while then he should reconnoitre that position. It might conceal enemy soldiers or partisans, waiting to spring out and catch them by surprise. If it turned out to hold a comfy chair and some coffee instead, well, he could hardly be blamed for making the most of it.

"What are your orders, Praporshchik?" Zinoviev asked.

"We're to clear the minefield," he said.

They all groaned.

"Not my choice," Rakovich continued. "Getting my hands blown off doesn't sound fun to me, but Captain Leontev has strange taste in entertainment. This is our job, so we don't bitch like a bunch of Americans, we get on with it. Find out who's had the training, find them sticks and bayonets, and get to work. Zinoviev, you organise the rest of the men. They'll need to provide cover."

"But there's no enemy—"

"Some days I think you've got cabbage instead of brain cells," Rakovich said, tapping the sergeant on his forehead. "Nobody just drops a minefield and fucks off. Somewhere out there are shooters, waiting to pick our men off while they're vulnerable. You'd better be ready to fire back, or I'll throw you out there and clear some mines the easy way."

∾

THE TINY COTTAGE seemed to have become stuck in time, making no progress in the past twenty years. There were none of the fancy gadgets that Rakovich had seen in other German houses, not even a radio, never mind a TV.

Despite this, the place had clearly been occupied until only a day before. There were crumbs on the sideboard, cold fresh ashes in the hearth, and a recent German newspaper on the kitchen table. Had the cottage's owner stuck around as the fighting advanced, or had NATO soldiers been using it while they laid the mines?

"Check the other rooms," Rakovich said to Plakans and Akayev, the entirety of his small reconnaissance force. As they ducked through a low doorway, he picked up the paper and tried to read.

The first few pages were all filled with reports on the war. He couldn't make sense of half the words, but there were pictures and diagrams that made more sense. One showed Soviet movements through Scandinavia. It looked like Norway was falling faster than expected. That was a good sign. The more defeats NATO faced, the sooner they would accept the inevitable and give in.

He folded up the newspaper and stowed it in a pouch on his belt. It could provide valuable intelligence, maybe even win him some favour with Leontev. Sooner or later, something had to get his commander off his back.

Laughter and ripping sounded from the next room. Rakovich frowned, wondering what bullshit his men were up to now. He strode through the doorway to see.

He found himself in a small living room, with a dresser to one side and a pair of armchairs facing a bay window. It would have been idyllic if Plakans and Akayev weren't tearing open the padding of the chairs.

"What the fuck are you two doing?" Rakovich snarled. "You're meant to be checking for the enemy."

"Already done, Praporshchik," Plakans said, stepping away from the chair. "There's no-one upstairs either."

"So you thought you'd kill this deadly menace?" Rakovich kicked the chair.

"We were just..." Plakans hesitated, then looked away embarrassed. "Everyone else has found stuff worth taking in western houses, but we've missed out. We were hoping we might find something."

"FM radio," Akayev said with a small, stupid grin. "I get FM radio, take home, hear music, yes?"

"You think Germans listen to the radio through their arses?" Rakovich pointed at the torn up chair seat.

"We thought they might have hidden—" Plakans began.

"Enough!" Rakovich snapped. "Back to the platoon."

Walking out of the house, both riflemen hung their heads. As they stepped out into the small fenced garden, with its rose beds and herb plot, Akayev looked at his commander.

"Sorry, Praporshchik," he said. "Not know why we do it. This place, is not like I expect, yes?"

Rakovich shook his head.

"It's not like any of us expected."

"WHAT THE SHIT ARE YOU DOING?" Rakovich growled as he strode into the space between the parked BMPs.

Men leapt up from the ground, casting aside cigarettes and brightly coloured magazines. A radio lay by Zinoviev's feet, western music emerging from its tinny speaker. No-one looked Rakovich in the eye.

He strode up to Zinoviev and stood staring into his face.

"I told you to guard the others," he said, raising a fist. "Do I need to start punching orders straight into your skull?"

"No, Praporshchik," Zinoviev said. "Of course not, Praporshchik."

"Then get guarding!"

Rakovich stormed away through the trees. Soon he was next to the red sign again, amid the mine clearing crew. They all held sticks or bayonets and were peering intently out across the field. But the smell of hastily extinguished cigarettes put the lie to their pretence of diligence. A trail of smoke still drifted up from next to Kholodov's boot and his sketch book lay abandoned in the undergrowth. Only two men, Zimyatov and one of the recent recruits, lay in the field, carefully raising a spine-topped metal orb from the dirt.

"How many mines have you cleared?" Rakovich asked Kholodov.

"None, Praporshchik," Kholodov admitted.

"And you?" Rakovich asked.

"None," the next soldier admitted.

"And you?" Rakovich asked, then cut the man off before he could reply. "Never mind, I can guess. If any of you don't have a better answer in half an hour, I'll start counting how many boots I can shove up your arses."

"Praporshchik." Szolkowski had emerged from the woods, the hint of a smile at the corner of his mouth. "Captain Leontev's on the radio. He wants to know how far we've got."

A KNOCKING on the door of the BMP drew Rakovich out his reverie. Zimyatov was looking in at him, his expression as uncomfortable as Rakovich had ever seen it.

"Hello, Makar," Rakovich said, setting the radio handset down in its cradle. "I suppose you want to hear what he said."

"Thought you might want to talk with someone," Zimyatov said.

Feelings hardened like concrete in Rakovich's chest. Feelings he knew he shouldn't have — shame, guilt, sadness. Feelings he damn certain wasn't going to acknowledge out loud.

"Bastard's talking about disciplining me," he hissed. "As if he's not the one who puts me in these fucking stupid situations. He'd send me to buy stripy paint and then put me on a charge for not finding it."

Zimyatov perched on a seat and pulled out a packet of cigarettes. He offered one to Rakovich, who waved it away. Then he pulled out a lighter made of glittery blue plastic and lit a cigarette for himself.

"You're right," Zimyatov said at last. "Captain's got it in for you. But I don't see what you can do, except to do the job well and hope he gets tired of fighting."

"Are you saying I'm not doing well?" Rakovich's hand tightened into a fist.

"Fuck no!" Zimyatov said. "But the men, they're another matter. Maybe you could be stricter on discipline."

"Fine." Rakovich cupped the fist in his other hand. "Some of them are long overdue a kicking."

"Don't take this wrong, Vlad, but I don't think that's enough."

Rakovich stared at his friend. "What?"

"Use discipline procedures. Write them up. Send them for a bollocking by the Captain or Valeev. Then it's something that'll last, not just a few bruises."

"If I do that, Leontev will have proof that I can't control them on my own."

"Nobody does anything on their own, Vlad. Surely the past month proves that."

Rakovich shifted in his seat. He wasn't like Papa, falling apart after Mama died, retreating into his bed until friends came to coax him back into the world. He could look after himself. He could prove it.

"I have heads to knock together," he said, climbing stiffly out of the BMP. "You should go clear mines."

"Yes, Praporshchik," Zimyatov said.

Rakovich looked around. He could hear tinny western music again, away through the trees. Anger became a cold fire burning in his chest. Not a fierce flash that would burst free and then be gone, but something that flowed through his veins, that pushed him on as he strode silently across the sun-dappled ground towards that decadent, capitalist sound.

Three men stood at the edge of the wood — Kholodov, Zinoviev, Szolkowsi. They were smoking and chatting. Szolkowski held a rifle idly in his hand. Zinoviev had his slung over his shoulder. Kholodov was twirling a bayonet in his hand. At their feet, Zinoviev's radio blared.

"Sergeants." Rakovich said the word with all the disdain he might have said "scum". All three men snapped to attention.

Rakovich kept walking until he was right in front of them. The two sergeants were sweating but Szolkowski looked cool as ever, any fear hidden behind his usual restraint.

Rakovich stamped down hard on the radio. Pieces of plastic and electronics scattered across the grass and the speaker fell silent. Zinoviev opened his mouth as if to protest, but stifled whatever words were about to emerge.

"Squad leaders in the Red Army," Rakovich said. "Standing around like idle children, playing with your plastic toys and listening to your juvenile music. Is this what the motherland deserves from her soldiers?"

"No, Praporshchik," the sergeants replied in unison.

"I could smash you both as badly as I smashed that radio. Do you think anyone would protest?"

"No, Praporshchik."

Rakovich raised his fist, but Zimyatov's words had hooked into his mind. He thought of all the threats and beatings he'd used before and how little difference they had made.

He lowered the fist. Both men sagged in relief.

"I'll be reporting your behaviour today," Rakovich said. "That report will go on both your files."

"What do you mean, Praporshchik?" Zinoviev asked, confused.

"I mean that command will hear how you slacked off when that minefield needed clearing," Rakovich said. "How you put men's lives at risk, here and in First Platoon. How you disobeyed direct orders. Any time someone looks at your file, whether it's for a promotion, a disciplinary proceeding, or just Zinoviev's uncle nosing through state secrets, they'll see what you did. And the consequences are on you."

The two men looked at each other in confusion and alarm.

"Can't we have a warning this time?" Kholodov asked. "I mean, this is the first time that you've—"

"Enough warnings," Rakovich said. "It's time for some proper fucking discipline around here."

Off to one side, Szolkowski sniggered. Rakovich rounded on him. Szolkowski was straight-faced, his moment of mirth entirely hidden.

"Think you're so smart?" Rakovich said. "I'm watching you, Private

Szolkowski. You're sharper than these bastards. You don't cross the line, you push at it to see how far how it will bend. But it's my line, and if I see you push it one more time, you'll be explaining yourself to the military police.

"Now all of you, get to work."

THE ENEMY DIDN'T ACT until the mine disposal team were halfway across. Maybe they had been waiting for the Soviets' attention to wane. Maybe they had wanted them well out in the open. Maybe they had just been as lazy as Rakovich's own men. Whatever it was, he was ready for them.

Two shots rang out. Dirt sprayed from near Zimyatov's elbow. Akayev yelped as the other bullet grazed his shin.

The breath caught in Rakovich's throat. That first bullet had damn near killed his best friend, but the best response wasn't panic or anger. It was getting the job done.

"Eleven o'clock," he called out, pointing to where he'd seen a flash of light. "Under the oak tree. All sections fire."

Along the edge of the woodland, Soviet troops opened fire. The guns of the BMPs roared and one side of the tree exploded, while the ground erupted in front of it.

Two men, small figures at this distance, leapt from their positions and tried to run. One fell immediately, caught in a hail of gunfire. The other made it away down the far slope of the hill.

Rakovich grinned. That should do it.

A long period of quiet followed, the mine clearance team inching their way across the field. As long as they moved slowly, it was easy enough to find the mines, which had been hastily laid. The nerve-wracking part was lifting them out, carefully avoiding the trigger mechanisms, hoping that they didn't have secondary detonators. One wrong move and a man might be blown to bits. Time and again, Rakovich realised that he was holding his breath and had to force himself to let it out.

The day dragged on. Men switched in and out on the minefield, giving them all a chance to stretch their legs and hydrate. The sun blazed down but no-one removed their helmets. Any eyes not on the mines were on the ridge beyond.

After the first shots, Akayev was switched out to have his leg seen to. It was pure dumb luck that he was out there again when the next shots came.

It was just one shot first, burying itself in the dirt in front of Akayev. From his vantage point on top of a BMP, Rakovich saw a mine fall from the engineer's hands. For a second he stood frozen, expecting it to blow Akayev apart. Instead, another bullet hit the ground, only inches from the first.

"Where's the shooter?" Rakovich shouted, scanning the scenery.

Another crack of a rifle. Akayev shouted something in Kyrgyz as blood ran down his shoulder.

"One o'clock!" Szolkowski shouted. "Behind the rocks."

"All sections fire," Rakovich shouted.

Again, the BMPs' guns roared. Again, the rifles opened fire. As Akayev scurried back, clutching a freely bleeding wound, the platoon smashed one small patch of ground with everything they had.

"Cease fire," Rakovich shouted. "Did we get him?"

They only found out after Zimyatov, dripping with sweat and trembling with tension, lifted the last mine in their way. The BMPs trundled through the narrow corridor they'd cleared, riflemen following with weapons raised. At last, they saw who had been standing in their way.

Amid a heap of shrapnel-scarred rocks lay the body of a young man in a German uniform. The BMPs' shells had torn off one of his arms and ripped open his chest. He looked so innocent, little more than a boy. Rakovich hoped it had been quick.

As the men mounted up, ready to ride on, he emptied the young sniper's pockets. There were no orders, no maps, nothing of use. Just a hand-written letter, half finished, to the man's mother. It was in German, one more document Rakovich could have used to practice his reading, but the thought repulsed him. As he slid the letter back into the boy's pocket, he imagined an older woman sitting at home alone, waiting for a letter filled with love, instead receiving an official telegram that brought only grief. Would she respond as Papa had, retreating into herself, needing to be rescued from a pit of sorrow?

He pressed a finger to his eye, hoping the others would think he was just clearing his vision. Then he turned back to his men.

All of his sergeants stood smartly to attention by their vehicles, pictures of discipline for a moment at least.

"Let's ride," Rakovich said. "First platoon are waiting for us."

20

AROUND DUSK

The engine filled the BMP with a thundering cacophony as they hurtled along the road. Rakovich peered out through his periscope, watching for any sign of NATO forces. They had to be here, between his platoon and the rest of the company. Every flicker of movement made him cling tight to his seat, expecting the vehicle to be shaken by the blast of a rocket or shell. But that blast never seemed to come.

The road was modern and well kept, the ride strangely smooth after so many journeys over broken ground. The vehicles raced along it like athletes on a track, nothing and no-one standing in their way. The tension of crossing the minefield still lay inside Rakovich like a coiled spring. Soon they would be at the battle lines. Soon he would have his release.

A roar from the sky above made Rakovich look up, then feel like a damn fool, trying to look through a metal hatch. He grabbed hold of his rifle, ready to scramble out if they were hit, and peered through a periscope at the outside world.

A moment later, dark shapes flashed past, and he recognised a pair of Su-25s. Rockets shot from beneath the wings of the Soviet planes and then they turned, heading back the way they had come. Even as explosions sounded ahead, they disappeared from sight.

"Nearly there!" Lobachov said through the intercom from his place in the driver's seat. "You want me to stop yet, Praporshchik?"

Rakovich peered along the road. Half a mile ahead, the road entered a small town. He could see the smoke and dust of fighting to the right, on the east side of the town. That must be where the rest of the company were engaged. Somehow, NATO troops still hadn't seen him coming, but that couldn't last.

As if summoned by that thought, a Lynx helicopter appeared above the nearest rooftops, turning to face them along the road.

"Stop!" Rakovich shouted, his throat constricted and his voice high. He repeated the order into the radio.

The BMP halted, fragments of tarmac flying as its tracks tore up the road.

"Dismount!" Rakovich shouted.

He followed his men as they emerged from the vehicle's rear doors, rifles at the ready. The other BMPs drew up beside them, forming a formidable wall of steel behind which the riflemen crouched.

A missile shot from beneath the helicopter, trailing white smoke. It hit the ground mere yards in front of the BMPs and Rakovich felt the blast wave as it exploded, dirt and shrapnel glancing off the front armour of the transports.

He gave a signal and the BMPs began advancing again. This time they kept to a walking pace, letting the men keep up behind them. Rakovich remembered the first time he had practised this tactic and how stupid it had sounded. Why should they dismount when they could stay inside the vehicle, moving safer and faster towards their target? Then he'd been shown footage of what happened when an artillery shell hit a BMP, footage that had turned his stomach. Once the enemy were close, it was best not to keep everyone in a single target.

The helicopter fired again. This time, its missile hit near the front of the left-hand BMP. Armoured plates buckled and the vehicle turned, shedding a mangled track as it ground to a halt.

Akayev leapt out, clutching his toolbox, then ducked back into cover as the helicopter approached, guns blazing.

"Gunners!" Rakovich yelled. "Get rid of that flying arse before it shits all over us."

One of the BMPs opened fire with its cannon, but the gunner's aim was off. The helicopter rose and then opened fire again from a steeper angle. Rakovich ducked as bullets sprayed the ground beside him.

A riflemen rose from a crouch, an Igla missile launcher balanced on his shoulder. Before he could pull the trigger, blood sprayed from his leg and he fell screaming to the ground.

Rakovich dashed over at a crouch, bullets still hammering the road around him. They had left the broken BMP behind to keep up the advance and now the men were crammed into a smaller space for protection. He needed to deal with that helicopter before any other enemies arrived.

He grabbed the missile, swung it onto his shoulder, and rose to his full height. The helicopter seemed to stare at him with dark, insectile eyes. He forced himself to pause and take a deep breath, properly sighting the weapon, despite the screams of the man who had tried to do the same. The bullets crept closer, clanging off the armour of the BMP, some whistling by so close he could almost feel them.

Seconds felt like years as he aimed at the helicopter. Then he squeezed the trigger.

The launcher rocked on his shoulder as the missile streaked away. There was a small flash of flame, then a larger one. The helicopter fell, trailing smoke as it crashed to the ground.

Rakovich grinned and took a moment to enjoy the sight. So much for NATO's superior weaponry. Sometimes what you needed was a good shot and some solid Soviet rocketry.

"Double time!" he shouted.

Men and transports picked up pace as they headed for the outskirts of the town. They rushed around sheds and across fences as NATO troops arrived to oppose them. Bullets flew and the low thud of a mortar echoed off the houses. Screams and shouts cut through the rattle of guns and the smell of cordite. Cries of pain that would have made Rakovich cringe a month before now meant nothing to him, as long as they came from the other side.

The BMPs opened fire, their guns tearing through the enemy's fragile defences. Rakovich leaned around to open up with his rifle, gunning down a German soldier as he tried to retreat. He watched the man twitch and then lie still, then kept watching him a moment longer, in case it was a bluff.

Now they were in among the houses, flinging grenades through shattered windows, kicking in doors and rushing rooms as they tried to clear buildings before they passed.

Rakovich followed Zimyatov into a kitchen, its work surfaces scattered with broken glass. The sun was sinking in the west and those clear shards caught its light, gleaming blood red. He stood for a moment, entranced by the surreal beauty amid the carnage.

Then he heard a door open and turned to see a German bearing down on him, bayonet raised. Rakovich lurched to the side and the strike caught the outside of his upper arm. Cloth ripped, pain flashed, and blood streamed hot from the wound. He swung his rifle into the man's face, causing a crunch of smashed cartilage and broken teeth. The German staggered back and Zimyatov shot him in the chest.

Rakovich looked down at the body without pity. Someone had to die in war and he wasn't going to let it be him.

They kept moving, out of that house and into the next, on down the street.

Ahead, the Germans were retreating, falling back north and west through the town. Smoke covered their withdrawal, thick clouds that spewed from launchers and sat clogging the streets.

The platoon advanced more cautiously now. After their day's work, they were horribly aware of the perils of mines and of hidden enemies. Between the smoke and the twilight, it had become near impossible to see what was happening, including who or what might lie ahead.

A shape emerged through the smoke, its angular edges those of a tank or transport. Rakovich took cover behind a postbox while Zimy-atov ducked into a doorway. They raised their rifles, ready to fire.

Then the smoke parted, revealing a familiar shape.

"Praporshchik Rakovich?" someone shouted from inside the BMP. "Captain Leontev is looking for you."

Rakovich groaned. He would rather have faced a whole night of this fighting than have heard those words.

AN ASSORTMENT of vehicles were parked on the east side of the town, with more arriving every few minutes. Tanks, transports, supply vehicles, they clustered outside a warehouse just off the main road. Inside, surgeons were dealing with the most urgent casualties, their aprons covered in blood as they dug inside barely sedated men, clamping severed blood vessels and trying to save damaged organs. Meanwhile, the walking wounded waited, patiently or exhaustedly, for their turn. Rakovich recognised a few of the men, few enough for him to know that many came from other companies.

At the end of the warehouse was an office. Through its windows, Rakovich could see a cluster of officers, Leontev among them. He was one of the more junior there and his usually dominant pose was more subdued. Though his words were blocked by the glass, Rakovich could see him nodding his head obediently and see how seldom he spoke. It was immensely satisfying to see him put in his place.

Clearly, Rakovich's own encounter with Leontev would have to wait. For a moment, he felt relieved, but the feeling vanished as he realised that he was just postponing the inevitable.

"Can I help you, Praporshchik?" a medical orderly asked, looking not at his face but at his arm.

Blood was still seeping from the wound there. In the heat of battle, Rakovich had forgotten about it, but as the orderly tugged frayed cloth from between flaps of sliced flesh, pain fried his nerves.

"Yes," he growled. "Please."

"We're low on morphine," the orderly said as he led Rakovich to a seat. "All I can offer you is brandy."

Rakovich grinned. "Brandy sounds good."

It was nowhere near good enough. Much as he enjoyed the taste of the looted German spirits and the warm sensation in his belly, it did little to deaden the pain. As the orderly started sewing up the wound, Rakovich gritted his teeth to keep from groaning.

Here he was, back in the supportive embrace of the Red Army. What could more perfectly sum up that support than an operation without anaesthetic? Hard work, pain, and only hope to see him through.

No, that was the booze talking. The orderly was doing what he could. It wasn't the army's fault that NATO had forced them to this, as the Western capitalists kept the proletariat down.

"All done," the orderly said as he finished tying on a dressing.

"Thanks." Rakovich held out the bottle. "You want this back?"

"You take another swig first," the orderly said with a wink. "You've earned it."

Rakovich enjoyed one last fiery swallow, then put the bottle down and left the man to his work. The officers' meeting had broken up, and Leontev was striding across the warehouse, heading for the way out. Rakovich hurried to intercept him.

"Captain Leontev," he said. "You wanted to see me, sir?"

Leontev scowled, his bushy eyebrows descending.

"You're late," he snapped.

"Sorry, Captain," Rakovich said. "We had some trouble with—"

"You don't have runners."

"The men are busy with—"

"Have you been drinking?" Leontev leaned in close and took a deep, dramatic breath.

"Anaesthetic," Rakovich said, gesturing towards his wound.

"I'll deal with you tomorrow," Leontev said. "When you're sober."

Without even dismissing Rakovich, he walked away.

More resigned than worried, Rakovich waited until his captain was out of sight, then followed him to the exit. Outside, a transport helicopter was landing in the road. With the blades still turning, Spetsnaz troops leapt out and started unloading. As the special forces pulled out bags and crates, it finally occurred to Rakovich that something significant was going on here, something far more substantial than a few rifle companies chasing the Germans out of town.

As the Spetsnaz strode away, a new group approached the helicopter. Two men in suits led a group of soldiers, each of whom held a civilian at gunpoint. Despite their protests, the civilians were loaded into the helicopter.

"Enjoying the circus?" The orderly who had treated Rakovich's arm stood beside him, holding a packet of cigarettes. He offered one to Rakovich. His head spinning with more than just alcohol and blood loss, Rakovich accepted.

He'd never been a smoker. Sure he'd tried a few when he was a teenager. Who didn't? But he'd never enjoyed it. Now though, anything that hid the lingering smell of his own blood was good, and if it gave him a brief, energising buzz, then all the better.

He took a deep drag and kept it down despite the scratching in his throat.

"If this is the circus then who are the clowns?" he asked as more civilians were marched up.

"Just locals," the orderly said. "Being taken for questioning."

"Those three are just kids," Rakovich said, pointing to a group of teenagers hauled one by one into the helicopter.

"Maybe they joined in the fighting. More likely the general just wants to question different sorts of people, learn as much as he can."

"It doesn't seem fair." Rakovich watched a teenage girl wrap an arm around a sobbing elder. "Seems cruel."

"Are you kidding? After what our boys went through today, that lot are better off out of town. It's the ones left behind I pity." The orderly ground his cigarette butt out in the dirt by the road. "Better get back to work. Goodnight, Praporshchik."

Rakovich stood watching the helicopter as it lifted off into the darkness. The image of that crying woman haunted him. What could she possibly have done to deserve this, a woman who responded like that?

He cast aside his burned out cigarette and walked away.

THERE WERE plenty of beds in the town. Half the platoon were making the most of them, sleeping in houses near where they had fought. But Rakovich couldn't bring himself to step inside those homes. What if he found a crying woman in there, or worse yet a crying man? He couldn't face their distress, whether it was his doing or not.

Instead, he sat in the command seat of his BMP, a blanket wrapped around him and a field telephone by his feet. Even without the sounds of Akayev hammering at twisted metal and cursing in Kyrgyz, he couldn't have slept. Every time he tried, he imagined people he knew back home being marched out of their homes and into helicopters. These things were necessary of course, for international communism and the good of all. But somehow, the images wouldn't go away.

At last, he gave up. Switching on a flashlight, he pulled out his battered copy of the Communist Manifesto. Surely here he would find the comfort he needed, something to reassure him that they were doing right.

The book fell open to his mother's favourite section, the chapter on proletarians and Communists.

"The Communists do not form a separate party opposed to other working-class parties," Marx and Engels declared, their words resonating down the years. "They have no interests separate and apart from those of the proletariat as a whole."

The flashlight flickered. Rakovich frowned and tapped it against the wall. The light grew steady again and he turned it back to the book, flicking on a few pages. Now Marx and Engels were talking about how communism did not deprive man of his own power, only of the power to subjugate others.

How did what he had seen fit with those words? Had teenage girls been seeking to subjugate others, that they deserved to be dragged from their homes and away? Had that old woman?

Had Professor Hofmann and her fellow villagers? Whatever crimes Hofmann had committed back in the last war, most of those around her were too young to be complicit. What subjugation had he saved anyone from when he threatened them?

No. They had fought back, had sheltered others who killed his men. That was just war. That was nothing to do with right and wrong.

But if the war was not about right and wrong, why was he fighting it?

He needed to stretch his legs. That would clear his head, chase away these doubts. Flinging aside the blanket and pocketing his book, he climbed out of the BMP.

With swift strides, he followed a track around the outside of town, back towards the medical station and supply point. Sentries raised their rifles to challenge him as he approached, then turned away when they saw his uniform and his grim visage.

The proletarians against the bourgeoisie. That was the struggle communism faced. That was the fight that his mother had raised him for. Sure, not all these Germans were soldiers, but that didn't make them innocent. The bourgeoisie kept the masses enslaved not through violence but through the tyranny of capital, through insidious inequalities to which the workers bowed. This war would change that for the Germans.

There was a helicopter outside the warehouse again, whether the same one or different he didn't know. The rotors weren't turning, but German civilians were gathered there in the headlights of a pair of BTR-70 armoured personnel carriers. Rakovich stood in the shadows, studying them.

At first, the sight was reassuring. He saw two men in well-cut suits, the sort who ordered working men around, who profited off their toil. There was a woman in a blue dress, with a haughty expression and high heeled shoes. The bourgeoisie, wrenched from the comfortable lives they didn't deserve.

Then he looked past them. There were men and women in

working clothes — overalls, worn jeans, heavy boots. One had his sleeves rolled up, revealing tattoos smudged by age. Another was missing two fingers off her left hand.

Wasn't this what the proletariat looked like? Surely, in the infamously decadent west, the bourgeois oppressors didn't dress in such lowly style.

Good Communists were meant to liberate people like this, not lock them up. Maybe there was a reason for treating them this way, but no-one had explained it to Rakovich. Even if they had done, there was a difference between a reason and a good reason.

A pilot climbed into the helicopter. The rotors started to turn. Soldiers shoved the civilians towards the aircraft.

Rakovich shook his head. The fuzz left by the brandy was starting to fade, leaving a deep weariness that he hoped might drag him down into sleep. His legs feeling like lead, he turned and walked away.

21

LITTLE THINGS

"Everybody up! Inspection in two minutes!"

Rakovich hammered his rifle butt against the side of a BMP. The clanging drew curses from the men sleeping inside, then grumbling from those nearby. They scrambled out of vehicles or hauled themselves from beneath improvised shelters. A window in one of the nearby houses opened and Zinoviev poked his head out.

"I'll wake the men in the houses, Praporshchik," he called out.

"If you're awake then they will be too, you dozy fuck," Rakovich replied.

"Oh." Zinoviev blushed. "Well, I'll make sure they come out quickly."

"You do that, sergeant."

Rakovich stood in front of the BMP, watch in hand, as the men assembled. Leontev thought that he was no good, that he was lax and indisciplined. He would show him. He'd get his unit into the sort of shape special forces would be proud of. It just might take some time to do it.

Each section formed its own line, with the sergeant at one end, the driver at the other, and all the others at attention in between. Some men were still buttoning their jackets or straightening their belts. Others arrived panting for breath, probably regretting having found a real bed, given the price they paid now.

He liked to think that he'd expected better of them. After all, they were his men, his comrades in arms even before they'd been his responsibility. But the truth was that if he had expected better then he wouldn't have done this. He needed something good he could report to fend off Leontev's latest round of bitching. If the best he could report was that he'd tried to beat some sense into his men, at least that might get the old bastard off his back for a few hours.

As the seconds ticked by, Rakovich counted off the men, noting who arrived late, who arrived orderly, who kicked up a fuss. Kholodov might have his sleeves rolled up, but at least he managed to look presentable in every other way. Akayev's grease stains were excusable for a man who spent half his time maintaining machines. Elsewhere, jackets hung half open, helmets were missing, and one soldier seemed to have left his rifle behind.

"Time," Rakovich said.

Everybody snapped to attention. Zinoviev, who had ushered the last of his men out mere seconds before, grinned proudly at having reached his position. If he was still grinning by the end of the inspection, then Rakovich was doing this wrong.

The Praporshchik approached the first section and started walking down the line. As he reached each man, he checked the condition of his rifle, his boots, and his grenade pouch — all the things they most needed to win the war.

"Are you feeling pleased with yourselves?" he called out.

"Yes, Praporshchik," some of the men replied uncertainly. Others had the good sense to stay quiet.

"Of course you fucking are," Rakovich replied. "You've got all the good sense of my left bollock."

He pulled the magazine from Rebane's rifle and held it up in front of its sweating owner.

"Empty," he said, banging the magazine against the man's helmet. "You going to shoot the capitalists with thin air?"

"No, Praporshchik," Rebane replied.

"I should fucking hope not. After inspection, you go fetch ammunition for the whole squad, make sure you remember next time."

"Yes, Praporshchik."

He went on down the line, raising his voice for the whole platoon again.

"When you start feeling pleased with yourself, you get complacent," he said. "You get lazy. You don't keep your rifle to hand."

He stood in front of Lobachov.

"Where's your rifle, soldier?" he snarled.

"Left it in the cab, Praporshchik," Lobachov said, staring resolutely past Rakovich's left ear.

Rakovich smacked the driver around the head, sending him staggering back out of the line.

"This is a fucking war zone," Rakovich shouted. "Yesterday, this place was crawling with NATO soldiers. Who knows what today will bring? But if you're not ready for it, and the man next to you takes a bullet for your fuck up, then that's on you, understand?"

"Yes, Praporshchik," Lobachov said, taking his place again. As he straightened his jacket, a paperback book fell out.

"You brought that and not your rifle?" Rakovich glared. "You can join Mister Empty over here on the ammo run, and I want enough for every man and every vehicle, understand?"

"Yes, Praporshchik."

Rakovich moved onto the other sections, critiquing poorly kept equipment, yelling at men who had come out unprepared. It was terrifying to see what a shower of incompetents he was lumbered with, men who his own life depended upon. At least the sergeants had managed to keep themselves professional, even Zinoviev turning up with all his gear. And Szolkowski, for all his faults, was the smartest one in the line — uniform neat, rifle oiled and loaded, boots polished. Rakovich realised that he'd been looking forward to screaming the man down, maybe venting some rage by using his fists. But today, the biggest trouble maker had shown his reliable side.

As he ended his inspection, he noticed Lieutenant Valeev standing nearby, watching them. The political officer gave a small smile and gestured for Rakovich to continue.

"Alright, you all know your duties," Rakovich growled. "Time to get on with them. Dismissed."

The men scattered like leaves before a winter wind.

"Good to see you keeping the men in order, Praporshchik Rakovich," Valeev said. "Dedication and discipline, these are the qualities that set the Soviet soldier above his opponents."

"Thank you, lieutenant," Rakovich said. "Can I help you with something?"

It wasn't that he was unhappy to see Valeev, but he couldn't help suspecting that his presence meant trouble. First an awkward conversation with the captain, now the political officer coming to check on him. Wheels were turning and he didn't like to think where they might take him.

He had thought that he wanted to go to war. Now he was in the thick of it, he found his life slipping out of control.

"I offered to fetch you for Captain Leontev," Valeev said, the words making Rakovich clench his fist. "But there's no rush, you have time for breakfast first if you need it."

"Thank you, Lieutenant." Rakovich felt an urge to repay the kindness, but how? He wanted to be able to offer Valeev coffee at least, but the men he'd put in charge of cooking were only just lighting a portable stove.

"Is something the matter?" Valeev asked.

"No, Lieutenant," Rakovich replied on instinct. But a moment's thought showed him a better answer. "It's just that the men are agitated. With so many troops gathering here, we're clearly part of something big, but no-one has told us what."

"And you're hoping I might tell you?" Valeev asked.

"If you can, Lieutenant."

"I wish I could." Valeev shook his head. "But don't worry, you'll be briefed soon enough."

So that was why Leontev had summoned him — to tell him about their objective. Rakovich's shoulders sagged with relief.

Then raised voices emerged from behind one of the BMPs and all the tension returned.

Rakovich stormed around the vehicle. Zimyatov and Akayev stood there, each of them pulling on the arm of a large stuffed toy. The cuddly bear's stitched expression was frozen in a smile, oblivious to the tug of war it was taking part in.

"What the fuck is this?" Rakovich snapped.

"My bear," Akayev said. "I find, send home to daughter."

"I was the one who found it," Zimyatov said. "It's for Tatyana. You know she'll like it, Vlad."

"That's Praporshchik to you right now," Rakovich said, glaring at his friend. He grabbed hold of the toy and the two men reluctantly let go. "I expect better of both of you. What sort of soldiers fight over a toy?"

"Is easy Russian say this," Akayev said, his brow furrowing. "In Leningrad, you have fine thing. Many toy. Book. TV even. Not where I from. My daughter, she never have bear. Now she not have father for year. She... she..."

He snatched at the air with his fingers, as if he might find the word he was missing.

"Deserves," Zimyatov said quietly. "Your daughter deserves this."

"Yes," Akayev nodded. "Deserves bear."

"I just..." Zimyatov's faltering didn't come from a lack of words, but from the shame written across his face. "I miss Tatyana. And there are so many things here we don't have back home. I thought it would be nice to send her something."

Rakovich's grip tightened on the bear. There was a soft thud of popping seams and a cloud of white filling burst from its back.

"This is capitalist bullshit," he said, waving the toy in their faces. "Nonsense to distract idiots from suffering and inequality."

He drew his arm back and flung the toy with all his strength. It spun through the air, trailing its cotton wool guts, and landed in a muddy puddle by the side of the road. Akayev and Zimyatov stared sadly at the sight.

"I will not tolerate this behaviour," Rakovich raised his fist. "Not even from you two. If I see anything like this again, from anyone, then I'll..." He looked at the fist, then back at Zimyatov, remembering the guidance his friend had given him the previous day. Taking a deep breath, he lowered his hand and unclenched his fingers. "Then I will put everyone involved on a charge. Now both of you, get back to your duties."

As the two men slunk away, Rakovich felt a hand on his shoulder. He had forgotten all about Valeev.

"Well done, Praporshchik," the political officer said. "It is hard to stand fast when circumstances become complicated, but others need the certainty good leaders provide."

"My mother used to say something similar, about how the Party provides stability."

"She worked for the Party, didn't she?"

"All her adult life."

"Then I'm sure she would be proud of how you're conducting yourself out here."

"Really?"

"Of course. What greater challenge is there to our faith than all the temptations offered to the capitalist bourgeoisie? You are a shining example to your men.

"Now, let's go get some breakfast and perhaps a cup of tea. You'll need it before facing the captain."

Together, they walked away from the platoon and its BMPs, past the sad remains of a torn teddy bear.

CAPTAIN LEONTEV HAD FOUND a study in one of the houses and was using it as his office. He looked very pleased with himself, sat up straight in a high backed chair with rows of German books arrayed behind him. Rakovich wondered if he could read any of them or if the one left open on the table was just for show. He pictured Leontev stroking his chin while he stared seriously at words he couldn't understand, and the thought almost made him laugh out loud.

In a corner, Valeev sat in the room's other chair, smiling beatifically.

"I see that you've written up two of your sergeants," Leontev said, peering down at a pair of crumpled forms. His thick eyebrows drew together as he squinted at Rakovich's handwriting. "Kholodov and Zinoviev."

"Yes, sir," Rakovich replied, standing stiffly across the desk from his commander.

"But not Zimyatov. Not your friend." Leontev looked up, one of those eyebrows raised.

"I caught Sergeants Kolodov and Zinoviev neglecting their duties. Not Sergeant Zimyatov."

"Of course you did."

Rakovich's eyes narrowed. Here it came again. Another streaming river of bullshit whose sole purpose was to drown him.

Leontev dropped the papers and steepled his fingers. The room shook as planes shot past overhead, then peace returned.

"You were late crossing that minefield," Leontev said. "Not the first time that you've failed to obey my orders."

"I'm sorry, Captain," Rakovich said. "It took longer than expected."

"A meaningless platitude. While you were idling, the rest of my company was facing the enemy without the support they deserved."

"I'm sorry, Captain."

"You certainly are. Do you even have an excuse?"

"Problems with discipline, sir. As set out on those forms."

"And whose responsibility is it to keep discipline in your platoon?"

"Mine, Captain." A sinking feeling came over Rakovich. This wasn't just one more petty bollocking.

"Damn right it's you." Leontev leaned back in his seat, eyes narrowed, his self-satisfaction barely contained. "You shouldn't be a praporshchik, never mind leading a platoon. But new lieutenants are hard to find right now so I've been tolerating your presence."

If this was Leontev's tolerance, Rakovich dreaded to think what the alternative felt like. He kept staring ahead, past his commander, fighting to keep his anger in check. The injustice of it made his blood boil. He'd worked hard, alone and without support, to lead the unit, though he had never had that duty before. He was serving his country as best he could, and all he got for it was this.

"This brings my tolerance to an end," Leontev said, picking up the disciplinary forms. "You fail to keep your platoon in line, then you try to pass the blame for the unit's failures onto them. In the aftermath, I find you drunk and halfway incoherent, stumbling around a medical facility."

"I wasn't—"

"I've heard enough of what you were and weren't doing." Leontev rose to his feet, hands planted on the desk, and leaned forward to glare at Rakovich. "Now shut up and take your discipline like a real soldier."

Rakovich's cheeks burned. He clenched and unclenched his fist, fighting the urge to slam it into the captain's face.

"I'm writing you up on a charge, Rakovich," Leontev said. "Dereliction of duty. You'll be sent back to barracks for a court martial to deal with."

"My men..." Rakovich began, then immediately shut up. Truth didn't matter. Justice didn't matter. This was all just about Leontev showing how tough he was. Rakovich's fate simply wasn't his own.

He had longed for a chance to prove himself, fighting for the motherland. This war had seemed to be that opportunity, as he led his platoon to glory against the capitalists. The prospect of a lieutenancy had seemed within reach.

Now it was all being snatched away. While the likes of Zinoviev fought on, he would be sent home in disgrace, his career and his reputation ruined, when all he'd tried to do was the right thing.

He fought to keep the quivering of his body concealed, to fight back the rising urge to scream.

"Excuse me, Captain Leontev," Valeev said softly. "Might I make a suggestion?"

Leontev turned his glare upon Valeev. The tide of hatred that had battered Rakovich into submission simply flowed around the political officer, who sat with a placid look upon his face.

"What?" Leontev asked, spittle flying.

"I'm sure that you're right to report on Praporshchik Rakovich's failings," Valeev said. "It's important that the Red Army understands the weaknesses of its men. But is now really the time to send him away?"

"What?" Leontev's frown grew even deeper.

"We're about to start the big push towards Bielefeld," Valeev said. "The Colonel has instructed us to put every last ounce of effort into that attack. Losing a single praporshchik might seem like a small thing, compared with the size of a company, but I'm told that the Colonel will be looking out for the small things. He prides himself on his eye for detail."

"Maybe he'll appreciate the detail of my enforcing discipline in my company."

"If your case stands up to scrutiny, then I'm sure he will. But you should make sure before you send a man away from the lines."

Leontev looked at Valeev through narrowed eyes. More planes roared past overhead, followed by the heavy whir of a transport helicopter. In the distance, artillery boomed.

"It is always good to have the advice of a zampolit," Leontev said at last. "Where would I be without astute political guidance?"

"Just doing my small part," Valeev said.

Leontev picked up another form off the desk. Rakovich's name was in a box near the top. The Captain pulled a pen from his pocket and crossed through two lines of writing near the end.

Again, Rakovich had to force himself to hold back his feelings. This time it was relief and not anger that swelled in his chest.

"Don't look too pleased, Praporshchik," Leontev growled. "This is still going on your record. And you may regret being on the front line soon enough."

He frowned bitterly as he closed the lid on the pen and then looked back at Rakovich.

"I already briefed the other platoon leaders, so here's the idiot version for you. The day after tomorrow, we're starting a big new push. An advance west to take the city of Bielefeld. There's a British barracks there, and their corps headquarters, the centre for their operations across Germany. If we crack that open, then we can split the British army, smash through the gap, and drive all the way across the country. But you can bet the British are going to fight us for every inch of ground.

"Things are about to get very bloody."

VALEEV WALKED BACK to the platoon with Rakovich.

"I want to see how the men are doing," he explained. "Do what I can to invigorate their spirits."

They were halfway there before Rakovich could muster the words he was after, even in some blunt and fumbling form.

"You saved my arse back there," he said. "Thank you."

"Just doing my job," Valeev said. "You're a good Communist, a good leader, and above all a good man. Far better to have you here than sitting idle back home."

"I..." Rakovich felt like he was choking on his own words. "Thank you."

"It's your own work that saved you, really," Valeev said. "You remember that English officer you brought in?"

"Captain Hare?" Rakovich pictured the strange Englishman standing in a field, smoking a cigarette while shells rained down around him.

"That's right, Captain Hare. Well, he shared some invaluable information on his people's dispositions. It helped the generals to identify our best approach to breaking the British. If someone started paying attention to Leontev's charge against you, they might ask why he was disciplining a man who's helping us win the war. And if he'd taken that man off the front line, that wouldn't look good, even if it was the right thing to do."

"You'd make them notice that?"

"I'm sure somebody would." Again, Valeev smiled his peaceful smile.

"I'm surprised that Captain Hare talked," Rakovich said. "He seemed very loyal to his side, full of misguided ideas about capitalism."

"Our interrogators have ways of making even the most loyal man talk," Valeev said.

An ugly image crossed Rakovich's mind. Captain Hare, that strangely admirable foe, lying bleeding and battered in a cell, while his interrogators questioned him with fists and boots. It sent a shudder up Rakovich's spine, thinking that the truth might be even worse.

But it was for the best. For the country. For the world. For the Communist cause.

Wasn't it?

As they approached his platoon's BMPs, he heard voices raised in anger. Rounding the corner, he saw two soldiers grappling over a looted tape player. Cassettes lay scattered across the ground, the boxes cracking beneath their boots as they pushed and pulled. The nearest man took one hand off the tape player and formed a fist.

Rakovich stormed towards them, Captain Hare forgotten as he bellowed at his men.

They had enough trouble ahead without fighting over these little things.

22

ENEMIES OF THE STATE

Anna tried hard not to stare at Maksim, just to keep her eyes on the table. But even after all the disappointments and the arguments, even after the months since they broke up, there was still something magnetic about him. Maybe it was his eyes, as blue and clear as an ocean in an oil painting. Maybe it was his hair, so perfectly tousled. Maybe, she admitted, it was just that body, with his shirt drawn tight across a perfectly sculpted chest. Whatever it was, she struggled to keep her thoughts and her hands to herself.

The two of them sat in awkward silence while Vadim poured tea into a pair of red cups. He'd acquired a lot of brightly coloured second hand crockery from somewhere, adding to the air of lively clutter in his café. In better circumstances, it would have made Anna smile.

"There," Vadim said, setting down the second cup. He glared at Maksim, then turned a softer look upon Anna. "You need anything, you just ask. Anything at all, you understand?"

Another meaningful glance at Maksim, Vadim's one eye skewering him with a look of pure malice.

"Thank you, Vadim," Anna said.

The café owner headed off to serve his next customer. At last, Maksim looked up and caught Anna's gaze.

"That's why I don't come here anymore," he said, his tone self-pity-ing. "Or anywhere we used to go. Too many grudges."

Anna forced herself not to respond. Now wasn't the time to remind him why her friends looked at him that way. She needed his help, not another screaming row.

"Did you find anything?" she asked.

"Must you be so businesslike?" Maksim asked. "We used to have fun, once upon a time."

"Please, Maksim," Anna said, taking hold of his hand and trying to keep from trembling as she looked into those eyes. "Don't play games. You know how much Tatyana means to me. I thought she meant something to you too."

Maksim snorted.

"That stuck up bitch never liked me," he said. Anna flinched and he looked away, his tone softening. "Maybe she was right."

He drew his hand away from Anna's and took a sip of his tea.

"She's out of high security," he said at last. "According to father's contacts at the Ministry, she's in a special facility for female prisoners in need of medical care."

Anna gasped.

"Have they..."

"She's pregnant," Maksim said. "Even the Ministry don't want to have to explain a miscarriage in a prison cell, so she gets a softer bed and better food. Did you know?"

"About the pregnancy?" Anna slumped as some of the tension left her. "Yes."

"The father?"

"Doesn't know. Please don't tell anyone."

"Like I'm going to tell people that I've been checking up on polit-ical prisoners. It was hard enough getting father to help with this, pretending that she's an ex I still care about. He thought it was my baby, threatened to take away my allowance until I persuaded him otherwise. If he hears that I've talked about this with anyone then I can kiss my car goodbye."

"What a hard life you lead," Anna said, with no effort to conceal her disdain.

"Hey, I did you a favour. The least you can do is lend a sympathetic ear. No-one else understands me like you do."

A month before, she would have melted at his sad expression and yearning tone.

A month before, she hadn't been a dissident with friends in jail.

"Is that why you stuck your dick in half the women's soccer team?" she asked. "To fuck them into understanding you?"

Maksim's eyes narrowed.

"You sound like your brother," he said. "Something in you has changed."

"Yes it has. And it didn't take a dick to do it."

She took a few coins from her purse and placed them on the table.

"For the bill," she said, getting up to go. "I wouldn't want to eat into your precious allowance."

"Anna," Maksim said, reaching for her hand. "Can't we just—"

"No." She shook him off and headed for the door, her heels clacking sharply against the tiled floor.

Vadim raised an eyebrow as she passed. She replied with a smile and a shake of her head. Then she was gone, leaving behind her regrets and a steaming cup of tea.

THERE WERE police all around as Anna stepped out of the subway car and into the bustle of the station. The press of bodies added to the summer heat and her blouse was fast becoming sticky with sweat.

Commuters barged past, showing even less consideration than usual as they steered clear of the uniformed officers. As she made her way up towards the street, she spotted men in casual suits standing too indifferently at intersections and kiosks, not really reading their newspapers. It seemed that the plain clothes agents were out in force too, or perhaps she was just more aware of them than she had been.

As she climbed the steps towards the entrance, chanting drifted down. The chatter of conversation died and travellers stiffened, readying themselves for trouble as they stepped into the street.

Out in the sunshine, she finally saw the strikers.

Marching past the newspaper offices was part of Klara's big plan, a way to ensure that the strike got the publicity it deserved. Anna wondered about the logic of it. Would the journalists who had ignored them for two days pay more attention just because they were on their doorstep? Or would the presence of half the Leningrad police department put them off?

Not just the police. There were other uniforms too, the familiar green-brown trousers and jackets she had seen on her brother and his friends. The soldiers stood in a line between the strikers and the station, helmets perched on their heads despite the heat, guns gleaming in their hands.

Anna stood stunned at the sight.

"Hey!" someone said, shoving her shoulder. "Get out of the way. Some of us have jobs to get to."

Anna advanced cautiously across the pavement and out into the street. There was no traffic, just the rows of soldiers and policemen, then beyond them the strikers with their placards, their banners, and their dreams. Joining them might be difficult with all the soldiers in the way.

Surely these men had better things to do. There was a war in the west. They were meant to be out there, defending the motherland.

The strike committee had been counting on it.

A junior officer, his face so smooth she wondered if he even had to shave, stood behind the line. She forced herself to approach him, then stood hesitantly, hand held out an inch from his back.

She could just walk away. It would be safer. Then she could find a way around to the strikers, or join up with them later in the march.

But this was a chance to find out more. To learn what the soldiers thought about the strike. Maybe to find out how many were in the city. She had to take it.

A deep breath in, a deep breath out, and then she tapped the officer on the shoulder.

He turned to her, his frown vanishing as his gaze swept up and down her body, as subtle as a horny teenager.

"How can I help you, miss?" he asked.

"I was just wondering..." She took another deep breath. "I thought most of the soldiers were at the front. Are there many of you here in the city?"

The officer's eyes narrowed.

"That's an odd question to be asking," he said.

"My brother's in the army," Anna said hastily. "At the front. I was hoping they might send him back."

"Sorry, but that's not likely," the officer said. "They're bringing more units here, and to Volgograd as well, but they're all reserves. It won't take proper soldiers to put down a few traitors."

He jerked a thumb in the direction of the strikers, who were still marching past in a vast, noisy column. Anna's pride at the sight was reduced by a growing fear.

"Wouldn't it be better if you were at the front?" she asked. "Fighting the enemy instead of our people."

"Enemies at home are just as bad as those abroad. They threaten our strength and unity. Your brother could tell you the same."

She heard the fiery tone Vlad took on when someone challenged the Communist dream. She could so easily picture him standing where this man was now, holding back the reformers with a sneer and a gun.

"It's a good thing you're here," she said, trying to make her smile convincing. "To protect us from this."

"Don't worry, you're safe," the officer said. "And we'll be dealing with this scum soon enough."

He patted his holster and gave her a wink.

Anna shuddered at the implication.

"Perhaps when this is over—" the officer began.

But Anna was backing away, losing herself in the commuter crowd.

They had made plans to keep the protesters safe, her and Mikhail and the other moderates. Pamphlets providing legal advice in case of arrest. Explanations of how to prevent a situation turning violent. They had even made a list of lawyers who might help.

None of that would matter. Not if the army was here.

She had to find the others. She had to find them fast.

It took an hour to find a way through the crowds and past the soldiers. In the end, Anna ran through a hairdressers, to the confusion of the staff, out the back door, down a series of twisting alleys, and finally through a bakery. The baker was sitting at the counter, watching the march go by with her front door locked. Anna spun a story about saving her cousin from this madness and the baker reluctantly unlocked her door, shoved Anna out into the street, and slammed the door firmly shut again.

Now she was among the protesters. They strode purposefully through the streets, fists and voices raised. Beyond them, the soldiers stood ready, guns against their chests.

She grabbed the first familiar person who walked past, an older man in a shabby jacket.

"Miss Rakovich!" the man said. "You're here at last. Klara said that you—"

"Where's Klara?" Anna snapped. "Or any of the committee? I need to talk with them right now."

"By that corner," he said, pointing back along the street. "They stopped to talk about what route we take after the park."

It was hard to fight the flow of the crowd, but there was no time to waste. The sun was blazing down on soldiers and protesters alike. People would get tired, dehydrated, angry. Tempers would flare, if there wasn't already a plan in place to make that happen.

She threaded her way through the marching masses. Some people smiled and encouraged her to join in the chanting. Others looked confused to see her going back the way they had come. Nimble as she was, it was hard to find a path through. As she twisted and turned, her ankle gave way with a jolt of pain. She staggered, leaned against a wall for balance, and massaged the tender flesh.

There wasn't time for this. With every passing moment she was more certain of it. She took off her shoes, these ridiculous, flimsy things with their high heels, and started barging her way through the mob. She pushed and shoved, desperation giving her a strength she normally lacked. Still, progress was torturously slow.

At last she saw a familiar figure, long dark hair tied back from a pale face.

"Klara!" she shouted, waving her shoes in the air. "Klara!"

Her voice was lost amid the melody of a workers' song. Anna kept pushing and twisting her way through the crowd, towards the cluster of men and women gathered beneath a lamppost.

"Klara!" At last she reached them. The committee turned to look at her.

"You're here at last," Klara said.

"We have to stop this," Anna said. "Find another way."

"It's the best route we could find," someone said. "Unless we go along—"

"Not a different route," Anna said. "A different way of protesting. This is going to get people killed."

Klara rolled her eyes.

"You lost the vote," she said. "Deal with it."

"We voted before we knew about the soldiers." Anna pointed at the nearest riflemen, their collars darkening with sweat. "The government won't want to keep them here. They'll put us down now so they can get them to the war."

"You can tell you're new to the struggle," Klara said. "There are always soldiers around, always guns on display for unrest. It's a show of force and if we give in to it then we lose."

"Was it a show of force when they broke up the meeting and arrested Pavel?"

"There were only a couple of hundred there. This is thousands, not just here but in cities across Russia. They can't crush that."

"That's not what they think. I was talking to an officer just now, and—"

"For fuck's sake." Klara held up a hand. "Enough. I know this is all thrilling to you, taking time off from your degree to help out the poor working man. But some of us have been building to this moment for years. We've watched the authorities. We've studied class struggle. We know how this works."

A few of the others looked away but most nodded along with Klara's words.

"How can you be so sure?" Boris asked.

"The same way you know how to set up the can making machines," Klara said. "Experience."

Expectant expressions turned on Anna. She felt like she was seven years old again, a little girl making too much noise at a funeral. An embarrassment to herself and those around her.

"I'm sorry," she said, looking down at her bare feet. "I... We should keep marching."

"Yes we should." Klara raised her fist and her voice. "Onward, comrades!"

The committee joined the stream of people heading up the street. Only Boris stayed, sheltering Anna from the flow of bodies.

"She's right," Anna said, certainty drifting in ragged tatters from her mind. "I don't know what I'm talking about. I should leave the committee."

"But you're so smart," Boris said. "You have good ideas."

"I don't have any experience."

"Who really has experience of this?" Boris waved a hand at the crowd. People kept marching past, thousands of them, cheering, chanting, waving placards, a spectacle Anna had only seen in history books.

"That's sweet of you to say," she said, laying a hand on her friend's arm. "But what do I really know?"

"You're brother's a soldier. That means you know soldiers."

"And if my brother was here he'd be in that line, just like the rest."

Bitterness joined the sadness in her voice. "He'd be as ready to stop this protest as any of them. If I can't change his mind then how—"

A noise caught her attention. Shouting, but not the rhythmic chants that had come before. A voice raised in sharp command.

The soldiers hefted their rifles and took a step forward, then another. The strikers were squeezed in closer together, the flow of their march broken. They turned to face the soldiers, fists and placards raised.

"This is an illegal gathering." A voice rang out through speakers set on poles along the street. The soldiers advanced again, pressing back the seething crowd. "Disperse now or face the consequences."

Anna's heart hammered. Boris seized her by the shoulders and pulled back towards a shop doorway.

"Fuck your consequences!" someone shouted. Others took up the cry.

"You have been warned," the voice of authority snarled. "Soldiers of the motherland, break up this mob."

"No!" Anna screamed.

It was too late.

The soldiers advanced. A woman tried to stand against them, but was clubbed down with a rifle butt. As others rushed to her aid, they too were knocked aside. Someone tried to fight back, used a placard as an improvised club. Blood flew as he was beaten to the ground.

Screams filled the air. Beyond the soldiers, shoppers and commuters were running for their lives.

The soldiers didn't care. They had their targets and they were going to take them. Their faces were filled with the fiery determination that Anna had seen on Vladislav when he talked of war. They charged into the crowd, not even trying to arrest anyone, just laying about them with their weapons.

"We have to get out of here." The words came out of Anna's mouth, but they barely felt like her own. She seemed to be seeing the whole world from a distance, watching her movements through another's eyes. Even as she grabbed Boris's arm and dragged him down the street, it wasn't her hand at work, but that of some stranger, someone more decisive than she could ever be.

There were screams of pain and of rage, the thud of rushing feet and colliding fists. Anna's view was filled with bodies rushing back and forth.

Then a gunshot. And another. And another. The screams intensified.

She was back at the bakery door but the baker was nowhere to be seen. The screams and shouts were closing in. Anna swung back her high heeled shoes, then slammed them into the glass of the door. It shattered, shards cascading across the floor.

"Come on!" she shouted, pulling Boris in behind her. Blood trailed from a gash in her arm and the glass cut her feet as she ran across the room.

She reached the back door and flung it open, peering out into the alley beyond.

"It's safe," she said, looking back to Boris.

He lay in the doorway, the back of his head bloody. A soldier stood over him, gun raised. He looked just like Vlad.

Tears running down her face, Anna ran.

23

AMID THE DEAD

R akovich crouched behind the command BMP, clutching his helmet to his head and wishing he was in better cover. The roar of engines and artillery hammered at his ears, making it hard to follow what was being said, and dust came to him on every breath, filling his mouth with the taste of dirt and ashes. Fumes from the blazing remains of a tank, blown about by a stiff breeze, made his eyes sting until they watered.

"This is our target," Leontev yelled over the sound of jet engines. He pointed at a spot on the map, a cluster of buildings two miles down the road. "The 21st Air Assault Brigade were dropped in to seize a bridge ahead of the main advance. They've taken the south side of the village, but the British still hold the crossing. Our orders are to break through to the airborne and provide whatever support they need to take that bridge."

He looked around expectantly at his command group.

Rakovich kept his focus on the map, not catching his superior's gaze. This man's wrath could lose him his career, his life even if a court martial went bad. Only Valeev had stood between him and disaster before. He wasn't going to do anything that might look like a challenge.

"What are we facing?" Lieutenant Chugainov asked.

"That's not clear," Leontev said. "We've hit the British so hard in the past two days, most of what we had on their dispositions is out of date. Without aerial or comms superiority, we're struggling to get more information."

"There are a lot of them, that's for sure," Lieutenant Egorov said, his pale face crumpled in a frown.

"The closer we get to Bielefeld, the more troops they throw at us," Leontev said. "Shows they're getting desperate."

Or that they're getting their act together, Rakovich thought, but there was no point in saying it out loud. It was exactly the sort of dissent Leontev could use to crucify him.

"Advances by our comrades in Norway have slowed down." It was the first thing Valeev had said since the meeting began, and a surprising revelation from a political officer. He was trusting them with news that others might have concealed, and it made Rakovich trust him all the more.

All eyes turned to the zampolit.

"Setbacks on other fronts make our role here all the more crucial," Valeev continued. "If we take Bielefeld, the British line unravels and their support for the Norwegians collapses. The war will be won or lost in Germany."

A house across the road exploded, its walls shattered by an artillery shell. The ground shook. Chunks of masonry crashed into the road.

"We leave in three minutes," Leontev said. "Lieutenant Valeev, you ride with Rakovich. Everybody dismissed."

Rakovich didn't need telling twice. He ran down the street to where his platoon were parked, smoke billowing from garbage fires in front of their BMPs, adding to the cover granted by a shelled-out row of shops. Number three BMP was closest, so Rakovich swung open a rear door and scrambled inside. Valeev followed, slamming the door shut behind them.

Zinoviev climbed out of the command seat to make room for Rakovich. The attention of the squad wasn't on them, it was on the political officer taking a seat left empty by a string of casualties. Some of the riflemen looked nervous at Valeev's presence, others curious. Szolkowski smirked, caught another soldier's eye, and shot a glance from Valeev to Rakovich. Now he wasn't the only one smirking.

"Something the matter, Szolkowski?" Rakovich growled, halfway to his seat.

"No, Praporshchik," Szolkowski said. "Why would you think there is?"

Just asking the question put the answer in everyone's minds. Word had got around that Rakovich had been dressed down by Leontev. Now the Captain had sent a political officer to keep an eye on him. Trouble hung in the air like a bad smell.

Saying nothing about Valeev's presence would lead them to speculate. Drawing more attention to it would only make matters worse. Rakovich bit back a response and took his seat in the turret.

Five minutes later, all the smirking and the politics were forgotten. They were on their way to battle.

"RAKOVICH!" Leontev's voice was thick with static. "Where are you?"

"We're just outside the graveyard," Rakovich replied, peering out through his periscope. "A couple of hundred yards short of the church."

"I need you to take that church. Second platoon just lost two BMPs to rocket fire from up there."

"We're taking heavy fire too, Captain. I don't think we can get close."

"It wasn't a request. Take that damn church."

Rakovich yanked off his headset and looked around at the men sat in the BMP, their expressions grim. Only Valeev and Szolkowski had an air of calm about them, one serenely straight-faced, the other with the cold stillness of a man with killing in mind.

"We're taking that church," Rakovich snapped. "Riflemen

dismount. Shistyev, hold position for now, get your gunner to give us covering fire."

He passed the same orders to the commanders of the other BMPs, then followed his men out the rear doors. They crouched behind a stone wall at the edge of a minor road. Behind them were bullet-riddled houses abandoned during the British retreat. Ahead was a graveyard and, beyond it, a church on a small hill. Its steeple still stretched untouched towards the heavens, despite a gaping hole in the roof of the nave.

As Rakovich assessed their position, there was a whistle and then the thud of a mortar round. It burst between the houses behind him, blowing out windows and sending a burst of shrapnel into the air. Another followed, landing closer this time. The third hit the road and men flinched from the blast.

"Into the graveyard," he shouted. "Take cover behind the graves."

The riflemen followed his lead, scrambling over the wall and into the field beyond. As they did so, there was a burst of fire from the church. One man slumped back into the road, clutching his bleeding arm. Another's helmet went flying from his head, but he kept moving, miraculously untouched, until he reached the shelter of a stone cross and lay there gasping for breath.

The BMPs opened fire with their cannons, blowing in windows and gouging chunks from the side of the church. The mortar and machine-gun barrage slackened, but sporadic fire continued, joined by the sharp retort of a sniper rifle.

Rakovich looked out from the cover of a lichen-stained grave stone, his rifle at the ready. He caught a brief moment of movement through one of the shattered windows, but not enough for him to find a target. He ducked back down behind the gravestone and whistled for attention.

"Advance by sections, in order," he shouted. "There are a dozen rows of gravestones between us and our target. Advance less than two rows and I'll shove your cover right up your arse. On my mark..."

He glanced around the gravestone again. Bullets were still flying from the church. Then the BMPs let rip and there was a moment of quiet as the enemy sought cover.

"First section, go!"

Eight men ran forward while their comrades fired above their heads, filling the air with enough lead to give the British pause. Rakovich joined in the shooting. He couldn't see a target worth hitting, but if they could force the British to keep their heads down, that was enough.

"Second section, go!" he yelled.

Again, men rushed forward under covering fire. This time, mortar bombs and machine-gun blasts flew their way. Despite Rakovich's exhortations, two men took cover before they'd completed their advance. Another fell, blood spraying from his neck across a pale headstone.

"Third section, go!"

This time he was running with them, out between the stones and across the graveyard. Bullets zipped past him and chips of stone flew. Grunts of pain and shouts of relief marked bullets finding bodies or men finding shelter.

He flung himself down behind a gravestone. His heart was pounding, the blood rushing through his veins. He'd never felt more alive.

He looked around. Tammert lay behind the next stone over. His sleeve had been torn off and a thin trickle of blood ran down his arm. His face was pale. Broad arms wrapped themselves around his knees while he stared wide-eyed back the way he had come.

"Are you hurt?" Rakovich called out to him.

Tammert just rocked back and forth.

"Answer me, you pale streak of shit," Rakovich shouted over the bang of the BMP guns. "Are you injured?"

"That was nearly my arm." Tammert pointed with a trembling finger. The ragged remains of his sleeve were draped across the gravestone opposite. "That was nearly my arm."

"Pull yourself together, man. We have to keep moving."

Tammert stared at Rakovich, wide-eyed.

"I can't," he said. "Not again. I can't."

"Yes you fucking can. I've seen you do this before, I'll see you do it again."

"I can't," Tammert said, tears streaming down his face. He pressed himself against the stone behind him, as if he could fall back into it and be sheltered forever from the storm of shells. "Don't make me go on. I can't."

"Praporshchik," said a voice from Rakovich's other side. Valeev crouched there, behind a flowering bush. "Leave him for now. We have to push on."

A rumbling sound made them both look up. To the left of the church, a pair of British Chieftain tanks had appeared. One was mounting the hill, while the other headed straight down the road that ran past the graveyard. A scattering of infantry advanced with them — fewer than Rakovich had come to expect, but enough to keep the tanks from becoming isolated and exposed.

"Fuck," Rakovich hissed under his breath. They'd struggled to advance before. Now they were well and truly screwed.

The tanks opened fire with their main guns. One shot landed in the graveyard, sending Russian soldiers and German headstones flying. The other landed in the road beyond them, its blast ripping the rocket launcher and a chunk of armour off the nearest BMP. Then their machine guns opened fire, and the infantry with them, spraying the graveyard with bullets.

He ought to pull the men back. They'd be leaving the airborne troops to their fate, but surely that was better than dying alongside them.

Then he thought about how Leontev would respond. He'd ordered them to take the church. If Rakovich turned back then he would label him a coward or worse. His career would be ruined.

But if he moved forward, if he could take that church with the odds so far against them, that would be a very different story. Then, Leontev would have to cut him some slack.

He looked around the gravestone again. The tanks, having made their presence felt, had stopped firing while they found better positions. This was his chance.

"Hold here!" he shouted.

Then he leapt to his feet and ran back across the field. Bullets plastered the wall of the graveyard as he vaulted over it and dashed into the damaged BMP.

"Radio still good?" he asked.

"Yes, Praporshchik," Lobachov replied.

Rakovich grabbed the receiver and switched to the platoon command channel.

"All drivers," he said. "Head through that wall and across the graveyard. Keep moving until you reach the church. Gunners, keep shooting. I don't care if you're bumping up and down too much to aim. I want noise and destruction."

"But Praporshchik," Lobachov said. "Those are solid stones out there. If we try to drive through—"

"Just do it."

Engines growled into action. Rakovich ran out of the BMP, jumped the wall, and dashed over to a nervous trooper clutching a rocket launcher. Around them, the bullets flew.

"Mikhailovich, isn't it?" Rakovich asked.

"Yes, Praporshchik," the young man replied.

"You're coming with me, Mikhailovich."

The trooper nodded earnestly and rose into a crouch, a pack of rockets across his back, the launcher cradled in his arms.

There was a crash as the first BMP hit the wall, knocking down the upper stones and riding over the rest.

The tank on the road fired. A shell whistled past the BMP and blew a hole in a house.

Rakovich ran in a low crouch, Mikhailovich trailing behind, bullets zipping past them to dig holes in the packed turf. He stopped behind a cluster of overgrown headstones, opposite an open gateway at the side of the graveyard. One of the Chieftains had almost reached that gap.

At Rakovich's signal, Mikhailovich raised the rocket launcher and took aim.

"Wait for it," Rakovich said.

Infantry on the hill were spraying the graveyard, forcing the riflemen to keep their heads down. Rakovich and Mikhailovich would be easy targets. If they were spotted...

"Wait for it," Rakovich said.

The tanks fired. Part of the rear wall was blown apart. First section's BMP jolted to one side and stopped moving.

"Wait for it," Rakovich said.

The tank reached the gateway, revealing its whole side. The machine gun on its command cupola turned.

"Now!" Rakovich said.

Mikhailovich fired.

The rocket shot out of the launcher, trailing smoke. A second later it hit the Chieftain. There was a roar. Smoke billowed from the tank and its crew came tumbling out.

The Russians whooped and cheered, firing at the tankers as they ran.

"Forward!" Rakovich shouted.

The two mobile BMPs advanced, leaving behind them a trail of toppled gravestones. Men joined them, running from cover to cover. They fired as they went, forcing the British infantry into cover.

Nearly all the fire from the church was now focused on the vehicles. But with terrible certainty, the main gun of the remaining Chieftain turned Rakovich's way.

"Come on!" he shouted, hauling Mikhailovich after him. They sprinted down a line of gravestones, heading for the cover of one of the BMPs.

The Chieftain fired. Its shell landed somewhere behind Rakovich, but the blast was close enough to catch him in the back and send him stumbling. Pain lanced through his shoulder and he felt blood run down his side. As he turned to look back, he saw Mikhailovich lying on the grass, a smoking hole where his chest had been.

There was no time for regrets, no time for loss. He grabbed the satchel of rockets by its torn and bloody strap, fumbled one out with shaking hands, and slid it into the fallen launcher.

The Chieftain's turret tilted, just a little lower, barrel pointing straight at him.

In one swift movement, Rakovich shouldered the launcher, aimed, and fired.

For an all too long moment, the rocket streaked away on a trail of smoke. Then it hit.

Fire burst from the front of the Chieftain. Armoured plates pinwheeled through the air. Crewmen scrambled out, only to be gunned down by the advancing Russians.

Rakovich cast the rocket launcher aside.

"Charge!" he shouted. "Kick the fuckers while they're down!"

He ran across the graveyard, his rifle now in his hands. As he went, others emerged from behind the gravestones. Valeev. Zimyatov. Zinoviev. Szolkowski. Beside them, the BMPs thundered forward, wobbling like toddlers as they crossed ground littered with gravestones and shell holes, their guns blazing wildly towards the church.

Then they were past the gravestones and heading up the hill.

As Rakovich approached the church, a British soldier appeared from behind the ruined tank. He aimed at Rakovich, but Rakovich was faster, gunning him down in a single sharp burst.

The church's doors of ancient oak stood ajar, like the jaws of a trap waiting for its prey. As Rakovich approached, a soldier burst out, charging at him with a bayonet. Rakovich parried with his own rifle, knocking the blow aside, and kicked the man in the crotch. As the soldier doubled over, Rakovich slammed his rifle butt into the back of his head, knocking him out cold.

The last of the British were retreating down the hill. Despite the struggle, Rakovich couldn't help but admire their courage. They pulled back in good order, providing covering fire for each other all the way to the bridge.

"Keep moving," Rakovich shouted to his men. "This isn't over yet."

Ahead and to the right, a pair of vehicles emerged from between two riverside houses. For a moment, Rakovich wished he still had the rocket launcher. Then he recognised the shapes.

BMDs, the smaller cousin of his own BMPs. This was the airborne infantry they had been sent to help.

"Who's in charge here?" he asked, approaching the nearest airborne troopers.

"I am," a man with a bandaged arm said. "Praporshchik Ivanovich, 21st Air Assault. And you are?"

"Praporshchik Rakovich. Motor rifles."

"Thanks for the rescue," Ivanovich said. "This whole area's swarming with NATO troops. It was insane of the generals to send us here."

"They say war is madness."

"Too true. Now let's get out."

"What?" Rakovich looked at the other man in confusion. They were winning. Why the fuck would they leave?

"Didn't you hear me?" Ivanovich said. "Swarming with NATO. We need to pull back to somewhere safer."

"What about the bridge?"

"Fuck the bridge."

"Fuck you." Rakovich raised a hand, still stained with Mikhailovich's blood, and pointed accusingly at Ivanovich. "You want me to punch your fucking teeth out?"

"No, but—"

"Fear spreads. Right now, it's among the British. Do you want to turn tail and let it take our men?"

"No, but—"

"Pull your soldiers together. We're finishing your mission."

A BMP pulled up and Lieutenant Valeev leaned out of the rear doors.

"Excellent work so far, Praporshchik," he said. "What now?"

Rakovich looked at Ivanovich and the handful of men behind him. Most were bandaged and bloodstained. Their grenade pouches were empty. Every one of them had a hollow-eyed look, inches away from imitating Tammert's graveyard breakdown.

"We're going to take the bridge," he said. "Praporshchik Ivanovich and his men are heading back for some well-earned rest. Please radio command and let them know that we'll need reinforcements."

"Thank you, Praporshchik," Ivanovich said.

"Just doing my job."

Rakovich thrust a fresh magazine into his rifle and followed the BMP.

24

HEROES

The bridge was draped in smoke, its stone sides dotted with bullet scars. British infantry were retreating back across it in twos and threes, covered by fire from the far bank, where a mortar and machine gun sat behind sandbags flanking the road. But they weren't the ones Rakovich was worried about. What he worried about were the packages strapped beneath each of the bridge's three spans, the wires trailing from them to the far side, and the men who must be at the end of those wires. He couldn't seize a bridge if some bastard had blown it up first.

Second Section's BMP rolled up to him, Kholodov and his men following at a crouch. Every few seconds one of them would lean out and fire, forcing the British troops back a few more feet. Beyond them, the rest of the platoon were doing the same, some men darting from cover to cover through ruined gardens, others following a BMP.

Rakovich ran from cover to Second Section. Familiar faces turned expectantly as he arrived.

"Everybody in," he shouted, flinging open the BMP's rear door. "Get ready to go swimming."

"Do we really need to?" Kholodov asked. "We'll have the bridge soon, and then—"

"Get in." Rakovich put his boot to Kholodov's arse, shoving him through the open door. The rest of the riflemen didn't need telling twice. As Rakovich leapt on board, they followed him in. The doors clanged shut behind them.

Rakovich shoved aside the miserable-looking Kholodov and took the commander's seat.

"Akayev," he said into the intercom. "Straight into the river and across, fast as you can."

"Banks are steep," Akayev replied. "You still want?"

"Of course I still fucking want. I'm getting across that river if I have to turn you into a canoe to do it."

"What is canoe?"

Akayev was already hitting the accelerator, sending them jolting through a fence, across a road, and down the riverbank. With a splash and a jolt that knocked a rifleman from his seat, they hit the water. The sound of the BMP's engines changed as its wheels went from driving tracks to dragging them through the river.

Rakovich peered out through his periscope, following the trail of wires to a pile of sandbags beside the British machine gun post. The machine gun flashed and bullets clanged off the front of the BMP.

Swaying with the movement of the vehicle, Rakovich climbed out of his seat and into the troop compartment. He crouched, rifle in hand, looking at the men there. Two men were missing, including Tammert. That left him five plus the vehicle's crew.

"We're the only people who can stop those bastards blowing the bridge," he said. "As soon as we hit the bank, I need you all out. Plakans, you let rip with the cannon, stop them from sending rein-forcements. The rest of you, grenades first, then charge. No time for fucking about. The whole Red Army's counting on you right now. Understand?"

They nodded.

"Kholodov, you lead two men right, take out the engineers," he continued. "I'll deal with the machine gun."

"Yes, Praporshchik." The petulant scowl was gone from Kholodov's face, replaced by something that might even pass for determination.

There was a crunch and another jolt that almost knocked Rakovich over. The BMP reared up, its engine noise changing again.

Rakovich stalked down the sloping floor and flung the doors open. "Out!"

He leapt into the shallows of the river. Machine gun fire tore up the bank beside him and clanged off the side of the BMP.

"Grenades!" he yelled, taking one from his own belt pouch. He pulled out the pin, risked a quick glance over the door, and then flung it at the machine gun nest. Others followed, tumbling towards the British line.

There was a shout of alarm in English, followed by the crack of the grenades going off. The machine gun fell silent.

"Go, go, go!"

Rakovich ran around the side of the BMP. The machine gun nest was only thirty yards away, but the gun was still pointing down the hill. Thirty yards was a long way to run straight into the teeth of death.

He felt as though some great red beast had taken hold of him, something angry and urgent, far beyond any instinct he had ever known before. Nothing mattered except the battle, the chance to master his enemies or die trying.

Rakovich was nearly at the sandbags when the machine gun jerked, someone taking control and swinging it toward him. Bullets whistled past his head and battered the ground, but the gunner's aim was off, too panicked to take his time. Rakovich screamed in rage and his men joined in, opening fire on the gap in the sandbags.

Then he was at the barrier, the momentum of his run still carrying him. With one hand, he pushed off the top sandbag and vaulted over. With the other he swung his rifle around, spraying anything in front of him.

A British soldier fell back, blood streaming from his chest, his rifle falling to the ground. Another, his hands still on the machine gun, looked up at Rakovich in shock. It was the last thing he saw before Rakovich's rifle smashed into his head, knocking him out cold.

There were other soldiers here too, their bodies torn by the grenade blasts. One was still alive, clutching his guts and groaning in agony.

Rakovich ran across them and out the back of the sandbag nest. He barely noticed his men coming up, firing past him as he went. What he saw was Kholodov and his group, stalled in front of the emplacement, exchanging fire with the men inside.

This time it was easy. Rakovich rounded the back of the sandbags, his rifle at his hip. Even as the British soldiers turned, he was gunning them down. One reached for the box with the wires trailing, but Rakovich was on him, breaking his outstretched arm with a swift blow. Even as he grunted in pain, the man tried to pull a pistol. Rakovich emptied his rifle straight into his chest.

The man fell still, his blood pouring out across the detonator. Rakovich reached out for that vital device, tugged the wires from the back, and cast it aside. Over the top of the sandbags, Kholodov starred at him wide-eyed.

"Come on, you heroes of the revolution," Rakovich said, grinning with exhilaration. "The war's not over yet."

THAT EVENING, Rakovich let the men loot. He knew that the people who lived here hadn't been the ones fighting, that on a surface level they were innocent. But in the aftermath of battle, his heart had still pounded with unsated rage. In the houses and the streets of this broken village, he saw the stubborn, destructive resistance of the Western capitalists, willing to spill the blood of half the world if it kept them on top. He wanted to see this place punished, and his men had earned the right to do it.

He dragged a pew out of the church and sat on it outside the great, gaping doors, looking down the hill towards the river. Soviet tanks and transports rolled across the bridge, ready to reinforce the bridge-head on the far side, and he smiled. It had been a good day's work.

"Praporshchik!" Zinoviev and Akayev walked up the hill, each carrying a large box in his arms.

"Sergeant. Rifleman." Rakovich gave them a weary wave. "How goes the harvest?"

Zinoviev set his box down on the pew and pulled out a bottle.

"Scotch whisky," he said, taking a swig and then passing it to Rakovich. "Try it."

The contents tasted as strong as any vodka, but smoother than most Rakovich had tried. It tasted of dirt, but in a soft, comforting way.

"That's weird," he said, passing the bottle back. "Not bad weird, but weird."

"See this." Akayev pulled out a soft pink unicorn. "For daughter. She like horses. Will very like this."

"I'm sure she will." Rakovich smiled. "Well done."

"Can I ask you something, Praporshchik?" Zinoviev asked, sitting down next to him. The young man looked a little nervous as he sipped at his bottle. "Something political."

Rakovich looked at him in surprise. This wasn't the sort of thing he expected from Zinoviev. The boy — it was hard to think of him as a grown man — was hardly a deep thinker.

"Go ahead," he said. "Ask."

"Why do they have all these good things in the West?" Zinoviev asked, pulling a pair of denim jeans out of his box, and then another, and then another. "I mean, is this what you get from capitalism?"

Akayev settled quietly on the grass, watching them both.

Rakovich frowned.

"What makes you ask that?"

"We're fighting because our way is better, right?" Zinoviev said. "But if that's so, why do they have all these nice things?"

Rakovich turned to look directly at Zinoviev. The sergeant flinched away, as if expecting to be hit, but still he looked to his praporshchik for an answer.

"I want to be a good communist," Zinoviev said. "But if you need capitalism to have things like this, that doesn't seem fair."

Scratching his own head, Rakovich searched for an answer. If his mother had been here, she would have been able to set them straight. But he wasn't his mother. He wasn't that strong of mind.

Yet a memory surfaced, something else he knew about the West.

"The Westerners aren't just capitalists," he said. "They're imperialists. In their greed, they stole wealth from half the world, and they're still profiting from that. You're right to say that something is unfair here. It's unfair that they're living off the profits of empire and no-one has ever brought them to justice."

"So what happens once we defeat them?" Zinoviev held up his jeans. "Will no-one have this?"

"One day, everyone will have this," Rakovich said. He grabbed the whisky bottle and took a swig. "This too. One day, international communism will let us all share the wealth a greedy few have hoarded."

"So I can be good and still have Levis?" Zinoviev asked, smiling now.

"Yes," Rakovich said, trying not to laugh. If it hadn't been such a good day, he might have found Zinoviev's childishness annoying, but today he enjoyed the innocence. "You can have it all."

Zinoviev stood and picked up his box. Akayev followed his lead.

"I'm going to wrap these so I can send them home," Zinoviev said. "Thank you, Praporshchik. I feel much better now."

The two men ambled off down the hill. As he watched them go, Rakovich wondered what the army post masters would think of their parcels. Were they really letting men send all this shit home? Better that than have it cluttering up the BMP, but still...

"That was good work." Valeev appeared from the shadowy interior of the church, a mug in his hand. "And not your first today."

"Thank you." Rakovich blinked in surprise. How long had the political officer been in there? Surely longer than he'd been sitting out here. "I didn't think you were the sort of man to pray."

Valeev laughed.

"I may not believe in God, but I believe in stones," he said. "Before my military service, I studied architecture. I wanted to design grand buildings for the nation and the party, churches of a more rational faith."

The bench creaked as he sat down. Rakovich, realising that he still had the bottle of whisky, offered it to him.

"Thank you." Valeev added a good glug of whisky to his tea. "You know, some people believe that to experience awe at a building like this is to experience God. I disagree. I believe that it is to experience our shared humanity, to recognise how much we can achieve when we work together. God is a mystification. Churches are man's work, and all the more spectacular for it."

"Will you go back to architecture?" Rakovich asked. "After the war is done and your service is complete?"

"No. I've found a higher calling. Architecture is my pleasure. Inspiring men, that is my duty. Speaking of which, your work in taking that bridge today was exemplary."

"Thank you, Lieutenant."

"Not only did you save the advance, but you have become an inspiration to your men. Kholodov has done nothing but sing your praises all evening."

"Kholodov? What does that decadent slacker care for inspiration?"

"He's an artist, inspiration is everything to him. He's filled a sketchbook with roughs for a painting of your assault. Now he's looting houses in search of more paper."

Rakovich's mouth hung open. In all his years, it had never crossed his mind that anyone might paint him.

"All I did was attack," he said. "We do that every day."

"No, Praporshchik Rakovich. Today you didn't just attack. You stormed a machine gun nest, at no small risk to yourself. In doing so, you saved our advance and countless lives. And you did so without a single loss among the men you took with you. You're the talk of the regiment."

Rakovich beamed with pride.

"Thank you, Lieutenant," he said, surprised at how much the words affected him. Was it just the drink again, or was this the proudest moment of his life?

"That's why I've put your name forward for the Order of Glory."

Now Rakovich truly was lost for words. The Order of Glory went to brave heroes of the motherland. Was he truly one of them now? His father would be so proud. Maybe even Anna, whatever she thought of his place in the war.

And what would this do for his career? Perhaps there was real hope of becoming an officer, of keeping his platoon, maybe someday running a company, or more.

A glorious future played out in the imagination of Praporshchik Rakovich, Soviet hero.

"Oh, look," Valeev said, snapping Rakovich out of his trance. The lieutenant's voice had lost a little of its lightness. "The Captain is here."

A BMP had parked at the bottom of the hill, one more armoured vehicle among the many streaming through the town. Out of it emerged Captain Leontev. He stomped across the churchyard and up the slope towards them, an aide scurrying along behind him.

"What is this bullshit?" Leontev bellowed as he reached them. For once, Rakovich wasn't the target of his rage. Instead, his red-faced fury was turned upon Valeev.

"Bullshit?" Valeev asked, setting his mug aside and rising to his feet. "I'm afraid I don't know what you mean, Captain Leontev."

"Yes you do, you weasel." Leontev pointed at Rakovich. "You put this sham of a soldier up for a medal. This man I'm an inch away from having in front of a court martial."

Rakovich was on his feet now too, standing to attention amid a whirlwind of emotions. The pride he had felt a moment before was ripped into shreds, cast about by Leontev's fury. That it was now directed at Valeev only made the matter worse. Had he become so toxic than those around him would suffer too?

"Praporshchik Rakovich fought valiantly today," Valeev said. "As political officer, it is my duty to draw attention to such feats."

"Your duty?" Leontev snarled. "You're in my company. You know the trouble I've had with this platoon. Your duty is to do as I tell you."

The dreams that had lifted Rakovich's heart faded away. For one glorious moment, he had thought that he really could be a hero. That anybody could. But that wasn't the way the world worked. The honours would go to the men who sucked up to their commanders, who took no risks and had no voice of their own.

"Respectfully, Captain, I disagree," Valeev said

"You what?" Leontev's dense eyebrows rose and spittle flew from his lips.

"As a political officer, I also report to other authorities. General Chaykovsky is looking for examples to inspire the other men. I saw an opportunity and—"

"You saw an opportunity to protect your little pet, but I'm not having any of it. This bullshit will not stand!"

Men had appeared on the hillside, drawn by Leontev's voice. Some were strangers, soldiers Rakovich had never seen before, come to witness his humiliation. Others were from their company, even from his own platoon. He could see their admiration crumbling before the captain's verbal assault.

Then another BMP appeared, one that had no unit identification or weapons but that bristled with the aerials of long range communications gear. It pulled to a stop at the bottom of the hill. The doors at the rear opened and a pair of military policemen emerged.

Rakovich hadn't thought that his spirits could sink lower. Now the prospect of arrest and court martial loomed before him like a void, dark and terrible.

A man stepped out and started walking up the hill. He wore a simple uniform, topped off with a general's distinctive cap. The MPs marched beside him, while a cluster of aides and officers trailed in his wake. One of the aides had a folder open and was pointing up the hill towards the church.

Every man on the hillside snapped to attention. Only the flitting of their eyes spoke to their unquenchable curiosity.

The general glanced at a photo his aide was holding out, then back up to where Rakovich stood.

"Lieutenant Valeev?" he boomed as he strode across grass torn up by tank tracks.

"General Chaykovsky." Valeev said.

Rakovich stifled the urge to salute and saw Leontev repress the same instinctive twitch. They both came to attention, eyes fixed on some imagined distant spot.

"Yes, yes, yes," Chaykovsky said. "At ease, the lot of you. This is a combat zone, not a parade."

Rakovich obeyed, but his back remained ramrod stiff.

"And is this Captain Leontev?" Chaykovsky asked. "You must be very proud."

"Yes, sir," Leontev said. "Our mission to liberate Europe stirs pride in all our hearts."

"Not just our mission, Captain," Chaykovsky said. "But your company's exemplary performance today. You and your men have done your country proud."

"Thank you, sir," Leontev replied.

"Now, where can I find this Praporshchik Rakovich?"

All eyes turned towards Rakovich. A photographer appeared from the crowd around the general.

"That would be me, sir," Rakovich managed despite the dryness of his throat. The general was a head taller than him and built like a bull, his physique amplifying his vast personal presence.

"You're Rakovich, eh?" Chaykovsky held out a hand and Rakovich, stunned, shook it. The photographer danced around, his camera clicking as fast as a machine gun. "I should have known, solid looking fellow like yourself."

The aide was at the general's side again, holding out a small box.

"I'm sorry I can't do the full ceremony," Chaykovsky said. "That will have to wait for later. But our country can't wait to have more heroes, and you are undoubtedly one of them."

He reached out and pinned a medal to Rakovich's chest.

"Praporshchik Vladislav Rakovich," the general continued. "It is my great honour to bestow upon you the Order of Glory, Third Class. Your bravery in the face of the enemy today saved our advance. It is an example to all true patriots, one that will burn brightly for all to see."

He flung an arm around Rakovich's shoulder and turned him to face the camera. It flashed and clicked a dozen times, then the photographer nodded and Chaykovsky let go.

"Good work, all of you," he called out to the crowd of onlookers. "You've done your country proud."

A spattering of applause turned into wild cheering as he strode off down the hill. Somewhere in the tumult, Rakovich heard men shouting his name.

He stared in amazement at his own chest.

"What the fuck just happened?" he murmured.

"Your heroism is what just happened," Valeev said. "That and a public relations need."

Rakovich's platoon were all around him now, shaking his hand, slapping him on the back, peering at his medal. Others crowded behind them, wanting to get up close with the hero of the hour.

His heart soared as they lifted him on their shoulders and carried him down the hill.

Looking back, he saw Leontev and Valeev, alone by the church doors. The Captain was red-faced with fury, but for once, Rakovich didn't care.

25

OUT OF THE WOODS

The woods were strangely still. Not silent — the distant sounds of artillery and aircraft saw to that. But quieter than they had any right to be, with the Battle of Bielefeld raging only a few miles up the road.

Rakovich had seen traces of that battle as they circled to the south and then raced northwest, aiming to cut off the British retreat. Rows of burned out wrecks by the side of the road, steel chassis painted black with ash. Columns of walking wounded, some of them on crutches, others missing arms or walking blind, their heads swathed in bandages. Farmers' fields were planted with rows of raised dirt six feet long, helmets and rifles resting at their heads.

He'd met a wounded man at an aid station, a grey-haired Ukrainian who had lost both feet to a shell blast on the outskirts of Bielefeld. He said that the fighting was as ugly as anything from the Great Patriotic War. The town had become a fortress, the streets littered with rubble and land mines, the British garrison and local militia fighting for every inch of ground. Forty years before, the Germans had destroyed Russian cities. Now the tables had been turned.

Victory was in the air. Rakovich could smell it as surely as leaf litter, tree sap, and cordite. The West was falling. The triumph of the people was nearly in sight. He and his men would help to ensure that. They'd won a glorious victory at the bridge, and they would win more before the war was over. Perhaps he would even win another medal. That would be a hell of a thing to take home to Anna and his father.

To either side, his men were spread out through the woods. They advanced carefully, moving from tree to tree, rifles at the ready. No-one spoke. Even their footfalls were muted by the soft ground beneath their boots.

Ahead, the trees thinned out and then gave way to open space. The only signs of British forces were the tracks they had left as they fled the main road. Somewhere out here, the remnants of their column would be trying to regroup. They couldn't be given the chance.

Zinoviev had taken the lead. He reached the treeline, his squad following close behind, and stopped. A moment later, he waved to Rakovich.

Having signalled the rest to hold, Rakovich strode over. He had expected to see another cluster of suburban houses, like the one where they had left the BMPs. Instead, he stood on a rough road, staring through a wire fence into an open paddock, with more woods on the far side.

"What is this place, Praporshchik?" Zinoviev asked, his voice a little too loud.

"I'm not sure." Rakovich looked around. To the left, the clearing ended and the road split, heading into the trees. To the right, it led to another open space and brief glimpses of buildings. He wished he had a map to tell him where they were, but there had been a fuck up somewhere in the supply lines. Soon, Leontev had said, intelligence officers would provide them with detailed maps of this region. Until then, they should just be grateful that they got food and ammunition.

He turned and signalled. His other sergeants hurried over, Zimyatov warily watching the way ahead, Kholodov looking at the trees with a dopey smile. Lieutenant Valeev, the platoon's constant companion since the bridge, came with them.

"Zinoviev, you take your men left," Rakovich said. "Hold the junction and check for signs of whether they went that way. Zimyatov, Kholodov, we're going to see what this place is."

The answer, it turned out, was some sort of zoo. Past that first paddock, they found a cluster of smaller enclosures and pools, most of them empty. He wondered if the animals had been rescued before the fighting arrived or if they were just hiding, frightened by the distant thunder of war. Maybe the westerners had killed them rather than let them fall into Soviet hands. He hoped not, but fanatics did strange things.

"Is that an otter?" Kholodov asked, pointing into the water. "See the grace with which it—"

Rakovich thumped him across the back of the helmet.

"Pay attention," he snarled. "This is a fucking war zone."

"Sorry, Praporshchik," Kholodov said, red-faced.

"That's odd," Valeev said as they advanced warily between the enclosures. "That's the third section of broken fencing I've seen."

"They must have let the animals out," Rakovich said, peering down his rifle at a café. Was it his imagination, or had something moved there? "Explains why we haven't seen them."

"But why?" Valeev asked. "We wall things in for a reason. We let them out for reasons too."

The conversation was cut short by a dull thump.

"Mortar!" Rakovich shouted, diving for cover behind a concrete animal hut.

Suddenly, the air was full of gunfire. Bullets cracked off trees and buildings. A shell exploded, flinging a soldier sideways in a spray of blood. Another landed in one of the pools, causing a fountain of water and weeds.

Rakovich took a deep breath and leaned out from behind cover. He took a fraction of a second to aim, then sprayed the window of the café with bullets. He was rewarded with the sound of someone screaming in pain.

"Kholodov!" he shouted. "Take your squad through the edge of the woods. Find those mortars and fuck them up."

"Yes, Praporshchik!"

"Zimyatov, we—"

More gunfire came from back the way they had come. A British soldier appeared in the tree line and took aim at Valeev, but Rakovich shot him before he had the chance. More figures were behind him in the undergrowth. The air was thick with the rattle of guns and the zip of bullets.

Beyond the British soldiers, someone was shouting for help.

"They've got between us," Zimyatov called out from behind a nearby tree. "Cut off Zinoviev."

Valeev, crouching behind a bullet-riddled ice cream cart, flung a grenade into the undergrowth, forcing the British to take cover.

In the three seconds of calm that followed, Rakovich considered his options. He could trust the most enthusiastically useless leader in his platoon, or he could go rescue those men.

Two minutes later he was in among the trees, Valeev to his left, two of Zimyatov's riflemen to his right. They moved in pairs, one group advancing while the other provided covering fire. The woods weren't dense and the undergrowth was thin, but there had been enough cover for the British to get behind them, and that meant there was enough to conceal them now. He had to be careful.

He rushed forward a dozen yards and then crouched behind a tree. A moment later the riflemen rushed past him. A British soldier appeared, rifle raised, but Valeev shot him before he could open fire. Then he was on his feet again, rushing on.

An enemy emerged from behind a tree, bayonet lunging at Rakovich. He parried the strike with his rifle and started raising his leg, but the other man was faster. The butt of his rifle hit Rakovich in the face, knocking him to the ground. Blood ran down his face as the man leapt on top of him, pulling a knife from his belt.

The world spun as Rakovich grabbed the man's arm and tried to wrestle the knife out of his hand. Around him, he heard shouts and shooting, but he didn't have time to make sense of any of it. There was a hand around his throat, knees pressed against his chest, what little breath he had being squeezed from his body. The strength in his arm faltered and the knife inched towards his face.

He tried swinging a leg up, but the English soldier was too far forward to kick. Instead, Rakovich slammed his feet into the ground and jerked his body up.

The movement dislodged the Englishman, but he still had a grip on Rakovich. They went tumbling amid the leaf mould, rolling over and over, punching and gouging at each other while the knife wavered between their faces.

Rakovich could breathe now. He found his strength returning. As they rolled to a stop, the Englishman on top, Rakovich slammed a knee up into his groin. The man groaned and his knife hand shook. He tried to bring his other hand around, to put his whole weight behind the blade, but Rakovich had hold of it. He brought his knee up again, and this time the man yelped in pain, the knife falling from his hand.

Rakovich pulled his arms suddenly apart, bringing the soldier down on top of him. As his opponent tried to work out what had happened, Rakovich snatched up the knife and slammed it into his side. There was a moment of resistance and then a gush of blood. Rakovich twisted, pulled the knife out, and rammed it in again, higher this time. The soldier gasped, jerked, and flopped lifeless across him.

Flinging the corpse aside, Rakovich rose to a crouch. He'd lost his rifle and apparently his comrades. He couldn't have got far from where he'd started, but his head was fuzzy and it was impossible to tell where sounds were coming from. The battle was all around him, yet it was nowhere to be seen.

Behind him, someone crept out of a bush. He spun around and almost stabbed Valeev before he realised who it was.

"We couldn't see the British shooting at us," Valeev whispered. "The others retreated."

Not Valeev though. Never the implacable political officer, the embodiment of the Soviet spirit.

"We'll go around quietly," Rakovich whispered. "There can't be many more of them than us, or we would have spotted them on the way in. If we can get Zinoviev organised, this is ours to win."

The world was coming back into order now. There was still shooting, but more sporadic than at the start. As both sides found cover, the ambush had descended into a drawn-out firefight.

It crossed Rakovich's mind that they might be able to wait this out. The rest of the company weren't far away. Eventually, they'd drive the British away. But every minute wasted was time the other NATO troops had to regroup, to organise their retreat or the relief of Bielefeld. And while he waited, Zinoviev's isolated squad risked being overwhelmed.

He had to take the initiative. There were no Orders of Glory for men who waited to be rescued.

With Valeev in tow, he crept through the woods, moving swiftly and silently from one tree to the next, knife in his blood-stained hand.

His footsteps carried him deeper into the woods and then around, towards the junction where he had sent Zinoviev. There were more sounds of firing here than in the heart of the park.

That was how it would have been if he had been in the British position. Piling on pressure to the weaker Soviet group, trying to break them first.

As he approached the firefight, he saw bodies between the trees. One lay on the ground, blood staining the dirt. Three others knelt behind trees, their backs to him as they fired.

To his left, a thick stand of bushes rustled. Rakovich shot it an alarmed glance, but no bullets flew his way, and a moment later the rustling stopped.

He signalled to Valeev to cover the forward two British soldiers. Then he raised his knife and crept towards the nearest one.

He was only four feet from the man when the bushes rustled again, more violently this time.

The British soldier turned at the sound, eyes going wide. He opened his mouth, but Rakovich got in first, clamping a hand over his face and pressing him back against the tree. The man struggled, but already Rakovich was sliding the knife in between his ribs, feeling flesh yield to the blade, steel sliding across bone, blood pulsing hot and wet across his fingers. He felt the man's last breath on his fingers and watched the light fade from eyes just like his own.

"I'm sorry," he whispered despite himself.

To his left, the bushes burst apart. A bear strode out, roaring and raising its arms.

Everyone turned and stared — Rakovich, Valeev, the British soldiers. Even the dying man cast his eyes towards the extraordinary sound, so that his last vision on Earth was a mass of fur and fury striding towards Valeev.

Surprised as they were to see the bear, the British were equally alarmed to see Rakovich. He dived behind a tree, leaving the knife buried in the body, as the air filled with bullets.

The bear roared again as it advanced on Valeev, a mad gleam in its eyes. The political officer raised his rifle and fired, emptying his whole magazine into its chest. The beast kept coming as he discarded the magazine and grabbed for a spare that he had already used up. Desperate, he flung aside the rifle and pulled out a pistol while the creature came growling towards him, blood-flecked drool running from its lips.

But the bear's steps were slowing. It wobbled, stumbled, and crashed to the ground.

For a moment, Valeev just stood, staring in bewilderment at the bear.

"Get into cover!" Rakovich yelled, flinging one of his last two grenades around the tree. The blast bought Valeev a vital moment before the British came to their senses, and he flung himself over the bear, taking cover behind its vast carcass.

Rakovich's eye fell on the soldier he had killed. The man's rifle lay beside him. It might not be a model Rakovich was used to, but it was a gun, and that would do.

He reached out. A bullet hit the ground an inch from his hand and he flinched back. Steeling himself, he reached out again, faster this time, snatching the rifle before the British could hit him.

The same exhilaration he'd felt crossing the river swept over him now. This was his chance to master more than just his own men. It was the moment when he could bend enemies to his will, could turn the tide of battle for his army and for his nation. This was his chance to be a big damn hero.

He flung his last grenade and heard the British soldiers dive for cover. As the blast went off he rose and strode towards them. One was rising, but Rakovich shot him in the chest before he could get up. The other lay groaning, a chunk of shrapnel in his side. That one Rakovich ignored.

There was still fighting nearby. He was close to it now, close enough to make sense of the noises and flickers of movement, to distinguish between the sounds of different guns. Could he have done that a month ago? War was making a real soldier of him, as he had always hoped.

Ahead and to his right were the British, to his left the Russians.

"Zinoviev?" he shouted.

"Praporshchik?" came the reply through the trees. "Thank fuck!"

"On my mark, grenades and then charge," Rakovich said. "Valeev and I will take them in the flank."

The political officer was by his side, lifting grenades and a rifle from their fallen enemies.

"Won't they know the plan now?" Zinoviev shouted back.

"Do any of us speak English?" Rakovich said.

"No, Praporshchik!"

"Then what are the odds these random bastards, left behind as chew toys for bears, speak the first pissing word of Russian?

"Now on my mark. Three, two, one, go!"

Even through the foliage, he saw one of the grenades fly. There were shouts and scuffling, then the bangs of explosions.

Rakovich charged, Valeev beside him, both letting out blood-curdling screams. His heart pounded and he felt a strength that was more than his own.

Others took up the scream, Zinoviev and his men following Rakovich's lead. Rifles roared, men cried out, and enemies fell before them. Rakovich howled in triumph as their opponents turned to run, heading straight towards the rest of Third Platoon. This was the real Order of Glory, the moment true soldiers lived for. This was victory, for him and for his men. These were the moments in which they proved to all the Leontevs of the world that they were not men to be trifled with.

He turned to share the moment of triumph with Valeev.

The lieutenant lay in the dirt, blood running into the ground beneath him.

A great weight of dread bore down inside Rakovich. With slow steps he approached the lieutenant, fumbling for a bandage at his belt as he went.

Valeev had no use for bandages, or for anything else that Rakovich might offer. Blood ran from a bullet hole where his eye had been.

Rakovich stared in horror at the body of a man who had saved his life.

LEONTEV ARRIVED at the same time as the men with body bags. He followed them over to where Rakovich stood by the bodies, looking as happy in his work as they did.

"What are you doing here?" Leontev snapped.

"I wanted to make sure my men were properly taken care of," Rakovich replied, gesturing at Valeev and the four more bodies beside him. Another three injured men lay nearby, waiting for medical support.

It wasn't a bad reason, but in his heart he knew it was just an excuse. The truth was that he hadn't had the strength to continue. When he saw Valeev's body, something had drained out of him. The furious fighting spirit faded, leaving a weariness so heavy he could barely stand.

"You're a platoon leader," Leontev said. "You're meant to be probing the enemy's movements, not crying for your friends."

"Zimyatov has it under control," Rakovich replied. "Found their main assembly point an hour ago. Didn't you get my message?"

Leontev's silence told Rakovich that his message had gone unheard.

He looked down at the bodies. Three of them had been new recruits, fresh-faced youths he'd barely even met. Another had been with them since the second day of the war. But Valeev he'd known for over a year.

More than that, Valeev had been a friend, someone who had helped him through his troubles. A good man. A good communist too, for whatever that was worth.

Rakovich remembered the tears he'd shed after his mother's death. Grown men did not cry.

"The political corps loved him and now he's dead under my command," Leontev said as unfamiliar soldiers lifted Valeev into a body bag. "I'm going to get so much shit for this."

Rakovich should have felt fury at the captain's callous words, should have been fighting down the urge to swing a punch. But everything seemed to reach him through a haze, his other emotions deadened by the numbing shroud of shock and grief.

One of the soldiers wrestled with the zipper on the body bag, trying to get it to close. It had got stuck halfway up, leaving Valeev looking half dressed, arms and face protruding from his black cocoon. The soldier tugged at the fastening and Valeev's body flopped about, like a broken toy being shaken by a frustrated child.

"Stop." Rakovich gently pushed the man aside. He undid the zipper a little, carefully blew away the leaf mould that had clogged it, and then finished closing the bag. In the last moment, his fingers trailed over Valeev's cold face, and a shiver ran through him.

"There's no-one to protect you from your fuck ups now, Rakovich," Leontev said. "It won't matter how many Orders of Glory you've earned. The next time you set a foot wrong, I'm going to bury you."

So many times, Rakovich had felt fury at Leontev's barbs. Today he barely noticed them. He was too spent to feel anything for his own plight.

He picked up one end of the body bag and helped the soldiers carry it to their truck. Then he walked away, towards where his men waited for him in the woods.

As he went, he wished his friend one last goodbye.

26

WORTH DYING FOR

In the darkness of the BMP, Rakovich stared at the backs of his fingers. He recalled the brief, cold touch of Valeev's skin against them. Was that why he kept reliving that last glimpse of the political officer's face? Because the bodies he had dealt with so far had still been warm to the touch, but the passing hours had turned his friend into a slab of meat? Without that touch, his mind would have been able to move on, as it had after all the other deaths he had seen. He would be focused, alert, preparing himself for the dawn that would soon appear outside the cramped space of his BMP.

He rubbed his eyes. The biggest battle of his career was coming and he needed to get some sleep. Instead, he was sitting in his command seat, staring at the darkness. Damn his men and their snoring for keeping him awake. Of all the nights for them to get so loud, why did it have to be this one?

He leaned back and rested his hands against his chest. His Communist Manifesto pressed through the cloth of his jacket, a familiar and comforting shape. He drew it out and held it in his lap. There was no light to read by but he didn't need it. The words of that book were etched across his heart, as surely as the memory of the day his father had passed it to him.

"Your mother would have wanted you to have this," Papa had said. "To remember her by."

And remember her he had, as he lay awake night after night, reading the words that had meant so much to her. The spine had cracked, the pages grown yellow, their corners become ragged with wear. Still he had kept reading, absorbing a cause by which to live.

A cause which elevated men like Leontev while others struggled and died. A cause which made his men's lives better, yet somehow left them poorer than people in the West. A cause which, according to Marx and Engels, would triumph through the natural work of history, but which they were still fighting to impose a century later.

"A spectre is haunting Europe," the introduction said. "The spectre of Communism."

Rakovich knew all about spectres. They danced around him in the dark, ghosts woven not from the fabric of the supernatural but from the threads of memory. Dologodin, Snegur, Mikhailovich, and so many more. Men from his unit who he had led to death for a higher cause, a cause Valeev had committed his life to.

He ruffled the pages of the book. At the front were irregular, loose sheets, not pages of the Manifesto but letters from Anna. Letters that told about her life back in the Soviet Union and of the ordinary people around her. Valeev could have been building monuments for those people, buildings that would have added beauty to cities for centuries to come. Instead, he had abandoned his dream to further the Communist cause.

What if that cause was just one more spectre, a ghost of a dream that had failed, leaving behind an impoverished society and a corrupted system? What if Anna was right?

What if Valeev had wasted his life on a broken cause?

The thought chilled Rakovich. This was his cause as well. It was everything he had fought for, everything he had believed in since he was a child. Valeev's belief in that cause had reinforced his own faith, papered over the cracks his adult mind had started to see in the system. With the political officer around, there had been some balance against the pettiness and corruption of men like Leontev, some possibility that, over the long arc of history, communism really was dragging the world toward justice. But if the cause relied on one man to make it good, was it a good cause? Or had he been kidding himself this whole time?

No, that couldn't be. Rakovich's mother had spent her life in service to communism. So had Valeev. If the cause was not just then their years of commitment had been in vain. All the evenings when his mother had been too busy to play. The holidays cancelled to make time for a rally or a district meeting. The hurried meals and the hasty departures, with only a fleeting moment to squeeze him tight and let him know that he was safe, that his mother was making the world better for him. That had to be worth something, just like Valeev's death had to be worth something.

Didn't it?

Rakovich stared at the shadowy shapes of his fingers and remembered the touch of cold skin.

A burst of static snapped him out of his reverie. A light blinked on the radio.

He slid the book into his jacket and put on his headset.

"Zoryn 218, this is Zoryn 210," Leontev's voice said, sharp beneath the crackle of crowded airwaves. "Do you receive me, over?"

"Zoryn 210, this is Zoryn 218," Rakovich replied. "Receiving, over."

"Zoryn 218, we are thirty minutes to go," Leontev said. "Get your platoon ready."

This was it, the big push they had been promised. A massive assault to rip the heart out of the British lines and split the survivors in two. If they succeeded, then NATO would be forced into a full retreat. If they failed... Well, it was best not to think about that.

Outside, the sky was turning from the black of night to a ghostly pre-dawn grey. Rakovich switched radio channels and called the sergeants in his platoon's other BMPs. By the time he had finished, the men in his vehicle were stirring into action. He heard the crackle of ration packs being opened, the click of magazines slotting in and out of rifles, quiet murmurs of conversation.

Suddenly, the world outside filled with a thunderous roar. Above the trees ahead of him, the sky flashed with a thousand fires as artillery thundered down on the British lines. Aircraft roared past overhead.

He was very glad not to be on the other side of the lines.

He slid from his seat and went back to join his men. The interior of the BMP was lit by a pair of flashlights taped to the ceiling. Three seats were empty, as there had been no time to reinforce after the park. Kholodov, still dozing despite the racket outside, had slumped halfway across one of the spare seats.

"Wake up, sergeant," Rakovich said, gently shaking his shoulder.

"Five more minutes," Kholodov mumbled, waving him away.

Rakovich tightened his grip on the shoulder. He leaned in close, until his face was right by the sergeant's ear.

"Wake the fuck up, you lazy bastard," he hissed. "Or once we've killed the British army, I'll use your arse as a burial ground."

Kholodov's head shot up and he looked straight at Rakovich.

"Sorry, Praporshchik," he said. "I wasn't really awake, had forgotten where I was, I would never..."

His voice trailed off as the other soldiers looked over, some looked amused, others disdainful.

Kholodov hesitated for a moment, then his chest swelled as he took a deep breath.

"Praporshchik Rakovich, may I say something before we go into battle?" he asked.

Rakovich narrowed his eyes. What was this?

"Go ahead, Sergeant," he said warily.

"I wasn't much of a soldier before this war," Kholodov said. "I don't think I'm alone in saying that. But you've shown me what a proper soldier can be. That day at the bridge, you showed us all."

Others voiced their agreement. Rakovich smiled despite himself.

"We're all proud to serve under you, Praporshchik," Kholodov continued. He pulled a few sheets of paper from his pocket. "If I live through my failings, I'm going to finish this properly, turn it into one of those grand historical paintings. That's what you deserve. But for now, in case I don't make it through, I wanted you to see."

He peeled off one of the sheets and handed it to Rakovich.

By the yellow glow of the flashlights, Rakovich saw a detailed pencil drawing. It showed a bridge over a river, soldiers storming up the bank, the ground erupting with shell bursts all around them. At the front, posed like a hero out of legend, he saw himself.

"You really are an artist," Rakovich said, smiling. He turned the picture so the others could see. "You've managed to make me look handsome."

The men laughed.

A voice crackled through Rakovich's headset.

"All units, this is Zoryn 210," Leontev said. "Fifteen minutes to go. Take your positions."

"Thank you for your faith in me, boys," Rakovich said, his heart swelling with pride. "I believe in you too. Now let's go win this war."

He carefully folded the picture and slid it into his pocket alongside his medal, then returned to the command seat. A moment later, the engine growled and the turret turned as Akayev and Plakans tested their equipment.

Rakovich counted his bullets and grenades. Not as many as he would have liked for any battle, never mind this one. But it would have to do.

Outside, a storm of shells continued to pound the British. There were explosions in the sky as jets fought for supremacy above the lines. A smattering of artillery fell somewhere to the left, and through his periscope he caught a glimpse of a burning Soviet tank. Even before the battle, death had arrived.

Engines roared. Tanks advanced. As the sun rose over the eastern horizon, a thousand shadows stirred and began to roll north.

"All units," Leontev announced. "We are go."

THE BMP SKIDDED down a rubble-strewn slope and hit the street with a jolt that almost threw Rakovich from his seat. Behind them, there was a boom as an anti-tank missile hit the vantage point where they had been parked moments before. Machine-gun rounds rattled off the sides of the vehicle and dust swirled through the rear doors as men leapt in, seeking shelter from the firefight outside.

MiGs shot past overhead. The world filled with noise as missiles rained down on the streets ahead.

"Akayev!" Rakovich shouted. "Forward to the next corner."

The engines growled and the walls shuddered as the vehicle heaved itself across the rubble that had come down with it. Peering out through a periscope, Rakovich saw first section's BMP appear down the road to the left, its front battered and blasted but still intact. Then came the third BMP, accelerating as it emerged from a ruined house.

"Zoryn 217, Zoryn 219, hold here," Rakovich said into the radio. He didn't like to sit still, not with so much firepower in the area, but he needed a moment to assess the situation.

Ahead of them, a Chieftain tank appeared from behind a bullet-riddled shop, smoke and brick dust billowing around it.

"Missiles!" Rakovich yelled.

The Chieftain's turret turned, its long gun swivelling towards them with deadly intent. Missiles shot from Rakovich and Zinoviev's vehicles. One missed, smashing into the buildings beyond. The other exploded against the turret, which stopped, and for a moment Rakovich thought they might have taken the tank out. But instead it retreated, crawling back into shelter.

"I'm going after him," Zinoviev said through the radio. "Get him while he's vulnerable."

"Don't be a fucking idiot," Rakovich snapped.

The whole idea was idiocy. A Chieftain wasn't going to be vulnerable to a lone infantry vehicle, especially not one charging straight towards its main gun.

But Zinoviev still had his transmit switch depressed, blocking Rakovich's transmission. A voice emerged from the speaker, someone in the background urging Zinoviev on.

"Let go of the radio, you cretinous streak of shit," he snarled, but Zinoviev couldn't hear him as the BMP accelerated down the street.

"You want we follow?" Akayev asked as the vehicle approached the corner.

"No!"

At last, the radio went silent.

"Zoryn 219, do you hear me?" Rakovich barked into his headset. "Stop right there!"

"I can see him," Zinoviev replied, as his BMP turned into the corner, its front rising as it crossed a heap of broken bricks. "We're almost—"

There was a boom. The front right hand side of the BMP exploded. The rest of the vehicle, already off-balance on the rubble, was flung back by the low blast. It landed on its side and slid a dozen feet across the street, hitting a lamp post. The lamp post fell and the BMP rolled over the stump, ending on its back. There was another boom, another explosion, and flames burst from half the BMP's firing ports.

Rakovich stared for a moment in horror. His men were in that blazing wreck.

"Akayev, get over to them," he said. "Plakans, get another missile ready in case that fucker comes back."

"Vlad, what do you want us to do?" Even through the radio channel, Zimyatov sounded shocked.

"Give us covering fire," Rakovich said. "I'm going to get them out."

They accelerated out of cover and towards the beleaguered BMP, bumping across rubble and craters torn from the street. The ground shook as an artillery barrage landed to the east. Rakovich didn't care. His eyes were on the ruined BMP. Flames licked the exposed remains of what had been the underside, but they weren't coming out of the troop compartment. That was good.

Wasn't it?

Akayev pulled up between the street corner and the rear doors of the wreck, offering cover as Rakovich and the riflemen rushed out. He couldn't see the Chieftain any more, but that didn't mean it was gone. They had to be fast.

The riflemen raised their guns, pointing out at the surrounding buildings, while Rakovich and Kholodov grabbed hold of the rear doors. One was buckled and refused to budge. After a moment of straining, the other opened, letting out a billow of oily black smoke.

Rakovich took a torch from his belt and shone it inside. There were bodies all over the floor. One man lay with his face pressed against what had been the ceiling, his neck twisted at an angle no-one could survive. His back was blackened and charred, just like the face and chest of the man who lay lifeless next to him. Beyond them, near the jagged hole that been the far corner of the compartment, lay the torn and tangled remains of more men.

Kholodov let out a low, trembling moan.

"Praporshchik?" someone groaned.

"Who is that?" Stifling his nausea at the stink of burnt flesh, Rakovich ducked inside.

To his right, Szolkowski was crouched against the buckled door. His face was red, his jacket singed, and he was clutching his shoulder. But just seeing someone alive was a huge relief.

"Come on," Rakovich said, gesturing to the open door. "Out, quick. We can't stay here."

As if to punctuate the point, a pool of oil in the far corner burst into flames, the fire lapping hungrily at the twisted bodies.

Rakovich sidled past the flames and looked into the front of the vehicle. Shistyev was dead in the driver's seat, run through by several long shards of shrapnel. The gunner was dead too, impaled on his own controls.

Zinoviev lay crumpled in the command space. Buckled panels and broken equipment had closed in on him, crushing his chest. Even in death, he bore a look of youthful excitement, despite the blood dribbling from between pale lips.

"You stupid piece of shit," Rakovich muttered, not sure whether to be sad or angry. "You should never have been a sergeant. This shouldn't have been your choice."

Bullets rang against the hull. Rakovich clambered out through the carnage and into the fresh air. Gunfire rang in his ears.

"Infantry," Kholodov said. "Looks like a counterattack's coming."

"Where's Zinoviev?" Szolkowski asked. He'd folded up the front of his jacket, using it as a sling for his injured arm. With the other hand he clutched an assault rifle. He wore his usual expression of pure, calm confidence.

"Dead," Rakovich replied. "What the fuck was he thinking?"

Szolkowski's face fell.

"And the rest?" he asked, his voice faltering.

"All dead. Guess there was only space for one lucky bastard on this fuck up."

"Shit." Szolkowski went pale beneath the soot. "I never thought... It looked like we could... If I hadn't said..."

Rakovich stared at him.

Of course that was where the idea to ride forward had come from. Szolkowski always wanted to be in the fighting, to get the next win. And Zinoviev was like a puppy, always eager to please whoever was near.

"I ordered you to hold," Rakovich hissed.

More bullets rattled off the side of the BMP.

"Praporshchik, we're running out of ammo," Kholodov said. "What do you want us to do?"

Rakovich stood staring at Szolkowski. All year he had been dealing with this man's arrogance and insubordination. He had felt angry at him, furious even at times, but never had he felt such utter contempt.

"Praporshchik?" Kholodov asked. "Your orders?"

"Into the BMP," Rakovich said, shoving Szolkowski ahead of him. "Pull back."

The men sprang into action. As the last one slammed the doors shut behind him, the rest were at their ports, returning fire against British infantry appearing amid the ruined houses. There was a crunch of tracks across rubble and they rolled back towards the other BMP.

The radio squawked as Rakovich got into his command seat.

"Zoryn 218, this is Zoryn 210," Leontev said. "Where are you?"

"Zoryn 210, this is Zoryn 218," Rakovich replied. "We are at the bottom of the big hill, close to a row of shops. Coordinates unknown because we don't have any fucking map. We've lost Zoryn 219 and are under heavy fire. Request permission to withdraw."

There was a moment of silence, then the airwaves crackled again.

"Zoryn 218, hold your position," Leontev said. "Support is on its way."

Rakovich stared at his instrument panel. Like fuck was support on its way. Leontev was leaving them out to die, probably to earn himself a medal because his company held the British up for three more minutes.

Fuck him and fuck the whole corrupt hierarchy.

"What do we do, Praporshchik?" Kholodov asked quietly.

Rakovich knew the answer he wanted to give. But he knew where his duty lay.

"We have our orders," he said grimly. "We hold."

He went back into the troop compartment and sat at a firing port.

"Who's got spare ammo?" he asked.

No-one replied.

"How are we for missiles?"

"All gone," Plakans said from the turret. "Running low on shells too."

More British infantry appeared, running from cover to cover. Rakovich opened fire and one of them fell.

Then a Chieftain appeared around the corner, and another behind it. They lumbered toward the Soviets like great metal monsters, beasts of fire and steel coming to crush them. Smoke billowed around them, as if they were demons emerging from the jaws of Hell.

"We fought well, boys," Rakovich said as he watched their turrets turn. "You can be proud of that."

Suddenly, a roaring filled the air. There was a flash, an explosion against the side of one of the Chieftains, and flames burst from its turret.

Two more explosions engulfed the second tank. It ground to a halt, its crew leaping out amid billowing smoke.

Then came a low, steady rumble from the hill behind. Rakovich sprang across the cabin and looked out through a different port.

Soviet tanks were rolling down the hill. Not just one or two but a whole column, with infantry running along to the sides.

The British held for a moment, standing firm in the face of the oncoming advance. Shells burst among them, hurling bodies about like rag dolls. Bullets filled the air, sending men reeling in long sprays of blood.

They started to retreat, then to run, men dashing back past the ruins of their tanks, bullets chasing them.

Again, the radio crackled. This time Rakovich grabbed it eagerly, pulling on the headset with trembling hands.

"This is Zoryn 218," he said. "What's happening?"

"Zoryn 218, this is Zoryn 210," Leontev said. "The main Bielefeld garrison just surrendered. You can hold where you are — the armour have it from here."

Rakovich turned. His men were grinning in anticipation. All except Szolkowski, who just stared at the floor.

"This crazy push worked," Rakovich said, almost laughing with relief. "We just took out the main British army in Germany."

The men whooped and cheered, slapped each other on the back. Akayev and Plakans emerged to join them.

Rakovich returned to his seat and sat alone, watching the soldiers streaming past. Without thinking, he pulled the book from his pocket and ran his thumb across it, feeling the familiar pages that had once given him such comfort. That had once given him a cause worth dying for.

27

SECRETS AND LIES

E arly morning sunlight seeped through the thin curtains of the apartment. Anna's own hands appeared like pale phantoms from the shroud of night, still clutching a mug of tea that had long ago gone cold. She heard a garbage truck roll down the street and the clatter of bins against the pavement, the detritus of another week being carried away.

So much for returning to sleep. Two hours would have to do, as it had most nights of late. Soon, she would collapse into a stupor and sleep for days, her body finally succumbing to exhaustion.

Or so she hoped.

She rose. A remnant of pain still throbbed from her feet, a final reminder of running with soles full of broken glass. Of that mad flight through the streets of Leningrad, away from the promise of disaster and the sight of Boris, slumped like a huge, broken doll through the shop door, a soldier standing over him with gun in hand. That moment when it had felt the world was collapsing and she realised that she only had the strength to flee.

What sort of person left her friends behind like that?

She poured the cold tea down the sink and put on a fresh kettle of water. While it boiled, she rummaged through the cupboard, pulling out a stale end of bread and a pat of butter. She sliced the bread and laid it on the grill pan, ready to be toasted. Papa would appreciate some breakfast when he came in.

Would there be breakfast for Tatyana in her prison cell? For Pavel Semenov? For any of the people seized during the march?

"Anna?" Papa's voice was soft, his hand gentle on her shoulder.

She turned, surprised to see him there.

"I didn't hear you come in," she said.

Steam was billowing around her, the kettle's whistle screaming.

"Are you alright, my dear?" Papa turned off the hob. "You've not seemed yourself this past week."

"I'm fine," she said. "No need to worry."

"No need to worry?" he said, spooning tea leaves into the pot. "My little girl is up at dawn, looking pale as an old sheet, and you think I won't worry about that?" He shook his head. "When you have children, you will know what foolishness this is."

"I'm sorry," Anna said. "I'm just stressed."

"Are you ill?" he asked. "Or..."

His gaze slid to her belly.

"God no!" Anna said, almost laughing. "No, nothing like that!"

"Because if it is, I'm happy to—"

"I'm not pregnant, Papa."

"Then what?"

She imagined telling him the truth. Imagined the relief that would come with getting it off her chest. Imagined him holding her and telling her that it would all be alright.

Imagined him arrested for sedition.

"It's university," she said. "The war has disrupted the schedule and I lost track of my studies. Now I have important tests coming up and I'm not prepared."

There was enough of real life twisted through it to sound plausible, though not to assuage her guilt at lying to him. Better the guilt of a lie than the guilt of a father lost.

"Sit down, I'll make you some breakfast." Papa put a string bag down on the counter. "A friend from work sold me eggs and ham. We can have a proper meal for once."

Two months ago, she might have laughed at the thought of her father conducting black market deals. Now she found herself close to tears, relieved to find that he too defied the law, if only for the sake of breakfast.

As she settled at the table, Papa put a newspaper in front of her.

"Here," he said. "This should cheer you up."

On the front cover was a grainy picture of soldiers. One was a general in a fancy hat and a big grin. He was shaking hands with a younger man, his uniform worn and stained. Behind them was a church. The headline read:

"HEROES HONOURED AT WAR AND AT HOME."

"Heroes." She all but spat the word. Heroes like them had attacked their protest. They had beaten and killed people who only wanted to have their voices heard. Those heroes could go die in a ditch for all she cared.

"A proud moment for the family," Papa said, cracking eggs into the pan. "Though I would have been happy just to see that he's alive."

Anna frowned, confused, then peered more closely at the poorly printed photo. Realisation dawned.

The general was shaking hands with Vlad.

Her spirit in turmoil, Anna turned her attention to the accompanying article. Her brother had been given a medal — the Order of Glory, Third Class. Apparently he had single-handedly led an assault against a NATO position, allowing the army to take an important bridge. He had been declared a war hero, a symbol of national courage.

For a moment, she felt the pride written across her father's face. Then she read on, and the article turned to a Colonel Kuznetsov, who had been given the same honour for breaking up a riot in Leningrad. That part made her feel sick. The so-called riot had been her peaceful protest, the traitors just people who wanted a better life. Her brother shared his honour with the man who had attacked her friends.

When she looked at the picture again, all she felt was disgust.

"Here," Papa said, laying a plate in front of her. "Eat. Today we celebrate a hero in the family."

He sat across from her, attacking his breakfast with gusto. She managed a forkful of eggs, but they tasted like dirt in her mouth. Looking for an excuse not to eat, she turned the pages of the newspaper, playing at being distracted by its contents.

Then another headline caught her attention:

"LENINGRAD TRAITORS FACE TRIAL."

The story was every bit as awful as she expected. Leading dissidents, many of them arrested during the recent protest, were to be put on trial as traitors to the nation. The wheels of so-called justice would turn quicker because of the needs of war. Every one of them faced the death penalty if found guilty.

The names were horribly familiar. Pavel Semenov was top of the list, which included twenty men and women. Seeing Boris's name was almost a relief, as it showed that he had been captured rather than killed. But there was no comfort in what was coming for him.

At least Tatyana wasn't on the list. Her pregnancy, it seemed, was keeping her alive.

A fresh chill crept up Anna's spine as she reached the final paragraph, a list of further dissidents being hunted by the authorities. Her hands trembled as she scanned the list, half expecting to see her own name.

Of course she wasn't on there. If she were, the police would have broken down the door of their apartment by now. But Klara Ivanova was listed, along with a dozen more.

"You look awful," Papa said. "You need to sleep."

"I have lectures," she said, still staring at the page.

"Lectures can wait." He drew her out of her seat and led her towards her bedroom door. "You're not going to make your father worry about you any more, are you?"

"No, Papa."

"Good girl." He kissed her on the cheek and closed the door behind her.

Anna sank onto her bed. Her mind as exhausted as her body, she finally sank into a deep sleep.

WHEN ANNA WOKE it was nearly night again. She changed into fresh clothes, ate the stew her father had left out for dinner, and read his note urging her to take a few days off to rest.

Energised by hot food and a strong cup of tea, she slid the note lovingly into her pocket and, ignoring its contents completely, walked out of the flat.

An hour later, she knocked on the door of a store room in the back of a public library. It opened a crack, revealing a sliver of Mikhail's face. His expression turned to relief as he let her in, closing the door firmly behind her.

Half a dozen weary men and women sat on folding chairs, glaring at each other. The remnants of the union committee, every one of them rigid with tension.

It would have been a large room to store mops and buckets in, but for a meeting it was far too cramped. The walls were mottled with black mould, the shelves at the back rusty. The air was cold and damp.

"Sorry I'm late," Anna said, looking around for another chair. "Lack of sleep finally caught up on me."

"You saw the news?" Klara asked, holding up a newspaper.

Anna nodded.

"What do we do next?" she asked.

"That's what we were discussing." Mikhail looked around the room. "Opinion is divided."

"We have to rescue them," said Sergei Semenov, Pavel's brother.

"Madness," said the woman across from him, Olga Ledbodev. "All we'll do is get people killed. We have to stay quiet, wait, preserve the network. Maybe in the future we—"

"What network?" Sergei snarled. "If we let them die then—"

Another man interjected, and suddenly the room was full of angry voices, half a dozen of them at each other's throats.

"Enough!" Mikhail snapped. "Do you want the world to hear you?"

Silence fell, the committee staring at each other with a hate they had previously turned upon the government.

In the corner of the room, Klara Ivanova sat silent, her arms folded across her chest.

"What do you think?" Anna asked, looking at the dark-haired woman. They might not have agreed in the past, but at least she could be relied upon to give them some direction.

"I don't know," Klara said. "I've been talking with friends outside the city, about what we could do together. But I've spent so much time hiding, I couldn't stop and plan."

"That won't do," Anna said, stepping forward so that she loomed over Klara. "You can still plan while you're hiding."

"My last plan got us into this mess. Do you really want another one?"

Anna pulled back her hand, palm open. She trembled, not with the exhaustion under which she had laboured for the past week, but with a blazing anger. For the government. It burned for the police, for the soldiers, for this woman who refused to deal with the trouble she had caused.

Slapping Klara would vent some of that fury, but who else would it help?

"You said that you have friends outside the city," Anna said, lowering her hand. "Tell me about them."

DAWN SUNLIGHT SEEPED ACROSS LENINGRAD, its golden glow brightening the rooftops and making the canals shimmer. It silhouetted a delivery truck as it approached the university's chemistry department, the growl of its engine reverberating down an empty street. Anna peered out of a first floor window, checking that it was the truck she had expected. Sure enough, there were the logos for a fake chemical company, designed by her, printed by Mikhail, and stuck across one of his print shop's vehicles. A strip of blue cloth fluttered from the wing mirror, their sign that fake papers had got them safely through police checkpoints and that they weren't being followed.

Still, she waited at the window for two more long minutes, watching the street for other signs of movement. All she saw was a distant garbage truck. It seemed innocent enough, but what if that was another cover, holding government agents ready to arrest them? What if there were observers in the office across the street?

She took a deep breath and turned away from the window. She could have tied herself in knots all day worrying about things that she couldn't see. Sooner or later, she had to trust in her own eyes and the abilities of her friends. Sooner or later, she had to act.

She unlocked a cupboard at the back of the laboratory, using keys she had borrowed from one of her professors. They came with the keys to the chemistry building and its laboratories, places undergraduate students weren't normally allowed at night. Anna had told the professor a sob story about falling behind on her studies because of a boy, had played on the sympathies of a woman whose marriage she knew was falling apart. She'd felt like shit the whole way through that conversation, but what was a little emotional manipulation next to people's lives? What was one woman's heartbreak beside the fate of a nation?

"It's time," she said, ushering Klara out of the cupboard. She was followed by three other dissidents, all of whose names were on the government list. This room hadn't been used all term, its teaching team called away to a government weapons plant, but the night had still been an agonisingly long one, fearing that someone might come in at any moment and find them.

They hurried out of the lab, along echoing corridors and stairwells, until they reached the delivery doors. Again, Anna's keys got them through, and they emerged into the crisp early morning air.

Mikhail stood at the rear door of the truck. He had already replaced the signs on the sides, revealing the logos of a waste disposal firm out of Veliky Novgorod. The company was real, as were the papers its union-friendly owner had provided, even if the truck wasn't really theirs.

The fugitives climbed into the back. Anna pulled on a set of overalls emblazoned with the waste company's logo and joined Mikhail in the cab. She kept looking all around, watching for anyone who might be watching them. She clenched her fist tight, fingernails pressing into her palm, knuckles white with tension.

The engine growled into life and they headed out through the streets.

The first of the day's workers were emerging from their homes. Waitresses heading to cafés, receptionists to businesses, labourers to the factory floors. They ignored the truck as it passed, roaring across a canal bridge and towards the south side of town.

The roads out of the city were still controlled by the army, as they had been since the protest. They talked about the sacrifices citizens must make so that the army could defend the homeland. But if the army was needed at the front, how could they spare so many soldiers for this?

They approached a roadblock on the main road heading south, towards Veliky Novgorod. Anna wiped away a sneer and pulled her cap low over her face, slouching in her seat to make herself less conspicuous. Even in her uniform, she felt like she must look wrong for this role, like the soldiers would see straight through her disguise.

Mikhail rolled down the window and handed his papers to a soldier with sergeant's epaulettes.

"What's in the back?" the sergeant asked, shifting the rifle that hung from his shoulder.

"Waste from the university chemistry department," Mikhail said. "You know how it goes — a bunch of big brains make a poisonous mess, the likes of you and me have to clear it up."

"You should see officers' latrines," the sergeant said, looking from the papers towards the back of the truck.

In the wing mirror, Anna watched another soldier approaching the rear door. Every muscle in her body tensed, her brain screaming at her to get out and run, to get away from these men and this danger.

Instead, she forced herself to lean out of the window and address the soldiers.

"We can lend you one of these, if you want to look inside," she said, holding up a biohazard suit.

The sergeant's eyes went wide.

"Domashev," he said, waving at the other man. "Get the fuck away from there."

The soldier shrugged and returned to the barrier.

"We're all good." The sergeant handed Mikhail the papers. "Just get that shit out of here."

The soldiers lifted the barrier and the truck drove through, heading out of the city.

They drove for another hour before turning off the main road and down a narrowing series of back lanes. At last they reached an abandoned cottage by a river, where a decorator's van was waiting for them. Anna got out of the truck and approached the driver.

"You've got a big job ahead of you," she said.

"Could be worse," he replied. "Could be working in Volgograd."

That was the code phrase, just like they'd agreed.

Anna nodded to Mikhail, who opened the back of the truck. Klara and the others climbed out.

"Misha," Klara said, shaking the van driver's hand. "It's good to see you."

"You too," he said, turning the handshake into a hug. "We've been worried sick about you."

Klara patted her hands awkwardly against his back.

"No need to worry," she said. "I'm fine."

"Like fuck you are." He held her by the shoulders, looking at her with such intensity that it seemed to melt away her stiffness. She finally smiled. "I'm never letting you out of my sight again."

"Same to you too."

Anna was amazed to see this side of Klara, the melting of her brittle exterior in the face of someone who loved her. There were depths to the woman's life that Anna had never imagined, but that she hoped to see more of some day.

"This is Anna," Klara said. "She organised all this."

"Pleased to meet you," Misha shook Anna's hand. "Let me assure you, we've found hiding places for everyone, fake identities, the works. Your people can continue their good work in our city."

"As long as they're safe," Anna said. "That's all that matters."

As the others climbed into the back of Misha's van, Klara turned to Anna.

"Won't you come with us?" Klara asked. "You were one of the organisers of the protest. If someone gives the police your name, you could be joining our friends in front of a firing squad."

Anna shook her head.

"There's still so much to do," she said. "Getting people to safety. Rebuilding the network. Keeping hope alive."

"I feel better about leaving, knowing that the movement is in good hands." Klara hesitated, then hugged Anna. The hug was all elbows and awkwardness, but it made Anna smile.

They released each other and Klara climbed into the back of the van. The driver shut the doors, nodded to Anna, and took his place at the wheel. Overhead, birds were circling, while their morning song drifted through the trees.

Anna watched the van drive away, down the road towards Veliky Novgorod and safety, and for a moment the world seemed at peace.

Then she got into the truck and headed back to Leningrad.

28

PRISONERS OF WAR

T he quiet was uncanny. Where the day before there had been the crash of shells and the screams of dying men, today there were just broken buildings and brick dust, still and silent in the early morning light. The birds, scared away by the sounds of battle, had not returned. The only song that greeted the day was the distant rumble of trucks and the snoring of exhausted men.

For the third time in an hour, Rakovich pulled the magazine from his rifle, counted the rounds it contained, and then slotted it back into place. He adjusted his belt, straightened his jacket, and checked the contents of his pouches. He tried hard not to look at the command tent across the road.

Zimyatov sat next to him at the table of a bombed-out pavement cafe, arms folded, helmet pulled down over his eyes. Across the table, Kholodov sat sketching the ruins. The scratching of his pencil grew more frantic as a pair of Spatsnaz soldiers swaggered by in their camouflage outfits, not even sparing a glance for the infantrymen.

"How long have we been waiting?" Zimyatov asked.

"Long enough for the sun to come up," Rakovich replied. "Maybe another hour since then."

"You think he's still talking about us?"

"I think he's fucking with me. Making me wait before he punishes me for someone else's fuck up."

"You'll be fine, Vlad," Zimyatov said, pushing back his helmet to look his friend in the eye. "We all told him what happened. You gave the right orders. It's not your fault Zinoviev ignored you."

"He's right, Praporshchik," Kholodov said, looking up from his sketchbook. "It's a shame what happened, but it's not on you."

It might not be on him, but Rakovich had a damn good idea whose fault it was. It gnawed at him that he'd been summoned here before he could deal with Szolkowski, but if Leontev felt a need to prove who was top dog then there was nothing he could do to resist.

"We've made a real difference under your leadership, and you've got the medal to prove it," Zimyatov said. "You always wanted to be a big damn hero, to save the world from the imperialists, and now you're doing it. How many people can say that?"

Rakovich sank back in his chair, hands resting on his belly. Why not relax for a while? He'd earned it.

No sooner had he closed his eyes than a voice called him back to the moment.

"Excuse me, are you from Third Platoon, First Motor Rifle Company?"

A young woman in uniform faced them across the table. A pair of bulging satchels hung either side of her body, their combined weights leaving her stooped but still smiling. Her expression was one of nervous enthusiasm.

"That's us." Rakovich straightened in his seat. He couldn't remember the last time he'd seen a pretty girl.

"And you're Praporshchik Rakovich?" she asked.

"That's right."

"I thought so. I recognised you from the photo in the newspaper. We pinned a copy up in the post sorting tent, to remind us of the heroes we're working for." She blushed as she handed him a letter. "I asked to do this run."

Ignoring the smirks of his companions, Rakovich took the letter.

"Thank you," he said. "I just did what any good Soviet soldier would."

"Maybe if they follow your heroic example." She stood smiling at him for a moment, then pulled another letter from her bag. "Do you know where I could find Sergeant Makar Zimyatov?"

"That's me," Zimyatov said, reaching for the envelope. "Did you know that I've fought alongside Praporshchik Rakovich in many of his most celebrated actions?"

"Did you know that he has a girlfriend back home?" Kholodov chipped in.

Still smiling at the woman, Zimyatov kicked out at Kholodov, missed, and smacked his foot against the table leg.

"I'm sure she's a lucky girl," the young woman said, attention still on Rakovich. "Is there anything else I can help you with?"

"No, thank you," Rakovich said, trying to hide his awkwardness. She was pretty but her eagerness unsettled him, and it was hard to find his words with the others listening. "I look forward to seeing you next time we have mail."

"Of course, Praporshchik." She blushed again and hurried away.

Kholodov shook his head as he watched the young woman go.

"No offence, Praporshchik," he said, "but opportunities like that are wasted on you."

"We can't all be smooth-talking artists," Rakovich replied, turning his attention to his letter.

Beneath the annotations of postal workers, the envelope was addressed in Anna's neat hand. The sight warmed Rakovich. He hadn't heard from home in a while.

The warm feeling faded when he opened the letter. Half of it had been blacked out by the censors. What remained was short and direct, the handwriting angular instead of smooth and flowing. Anna had written to him in anger, and though a censor might miss it, he knew her well enough to sense the criticism between her words. When she wrote of soldiers in the streets, of rationing, of what the government said, all he saw were shadows of the arguments they'd had before.

The paper crumpled beneath his fingers. He glared at it, trying to make out what the censor had hidden.

"Fuck." The word drifted from Zimyatov's lips in a soft, drawn-out whisper.

Rakovich looked up to see him staring at his own letter, his face pale.

"Your father's heart again?" he asked.

"Tatya's pregnant," Zimyatov said.

Rakovich laughed in relief.

"That's it?" he said. "You always said you wanted kids. Sure, the timing's a mess, but it still sounds like cause for congratulations."

"She's in jail." Zimyatov looked up, eyes wide with panic. "What the fuck, Vlad? Why would they do that?"

"I'm sure it's a mistake," Rakovich said. "What did they arrest her for?"

"Treason. It says here that—"

"Praporshchik Rakovich." Leontev's first sergeant stood outside the tent, calling to them. "The Captain will see you and your men now."

Rakovich looked from the first sergeant to Zimyatov, then back again.

"Can we have a few minutes?" he called out.

"You've had hours," the man replied. "Get your arses in here."

Rakovich pushed himself to his feet and shouldered his rifle. When Zimyatov didn't move, he ushered him into action, almost dragging him out of his chair. Together with Kholodov, they trudged across the road and into the command tent.

Daylight did nothing to alleviate the cramped, cluttered state of the tent. Wherever Leontev had got it from, it clearly wasn't designed to act as a command station. With a card table holding comms equipment and another for the captain's desk, there was barely space for the NCOs of Third Platoon to stand.

Rakovich snapped to attention and his sergeants followed suit. Behind the table, Leontev sat staring expressionlessly at them.

"I've considered your reports," he said. "And I've discussed them with the Major.

"I'm not a petty man. While a case could be made for negligence on your part, the Major is right to point out that Sergeant Zinoviev, in disobeying orders, brought disaster upon his own unit. How far the culture of your platoon encouraged that disobedience remains an open question, but for now, I will save you all the burden of formal discipline."

To Rakovich, the Captain's words were so transparent as to be insulting. His superiors hadn't let him press charges. But of course he had to present it as all his own choices.

"Thank you, Captain," Rakovich said out loud.

"Private Szolkowski is to be moved under Sergeant Kholodov's command, consolidating your platoon into two sections," Leontev said.

"So our reinforcements will be a whole fresh section?" The thought of a unit of green soldiers was unsettling to Rakovich. He would have preferred to mix them in with men of experience, in hopes that they would learn fast enough to survive the war.

"There will be no reinforcements," Leontev said. "The army is stretched thin, occupying Austria and most of Germany. It takes a long time for fresh troops to arrive. Those we receive will be channelled into the company's more reliable platoons."

"We took that bridge," Rakovich said, fighting to keep the anger from his voice. "We took out the unit at the bear park. We held our ground in the very heart of the fighting, and now you're saying that we can't be relied upon?"

Leontev stood, glowering at Rakovich from beneath his bushy eyebrows.

"Do you think that I don't know what I am doing, Praporshchik?" he growled. "That you could do this better than the officers who command you?"

Rakovich didn't just think it. He knew it. He'd been thrown into every kind of danger, every kind of difficulty, and emerged triumphant. After weeks of trouble, his men were uniting behind him, while Leontev kept pushing feuds against his own subordinates. It was all he could do not to scream his response at the top of his lungs.

"Praporshchik Rakovich is an excellent leader," Kholodov said. He stood stiffly to attention, enunciating each word as if giving a formal report. "Since we entered the FRG he has—"

"I didn't ask for your opinion, sergeant," Leontev snapped. "And I don't want to hear it. Your insubordination in this matter is one more symptom of the problems with your platoon." He turned his attention back to Rakovich. "Well, Praproshchik? What do you have to say?"

Rakovich wanted to stand up to the old bastard, not just for himself but for Kholodov and for all the rest of their men. After everything they'd been through, to hear them dismissed as trouble was like a knife driven into his gut. His body thrummed with tension and he clenched his fist by his side.

But then he remembered the previous times they'd faced each other. The times when he'd spoken out and been shot down. When only Valeev had been able to save him from the Captain's wrath. He owed Valeev this much — to heed his wisdom even now that he was gone.

Leontev wanted him angry, didn't he? This was all about finding more excuses to get rid of them. Rakovich wouldn't give him the satisfaction.

"Nothing, sir," he said.

Leontev kept staring, a muscle twitching at the corner of his eye. Rakovich kept his silence.

"Excuse me, Captain." The first sergeant stood in the doorway, holding up the tent flap. "They're here."

A stiletto-thin grin split Leontev's face.

"Send them in," he said.

Rakovich and his sergeants were crowded into a corner as three other men entered. First was a young zampolit, a captain from the political corps, sharp faced with pale skin and narrow eyes. Behind him came two burly military policemen, hands resting on the clubs at their sides.

Leontev exchanged nods with the leader of the newcomers.

"Is he here?" the zampolit asked.

"Yes, Captain," Leontev replied. "That one."

For a hideous moment, Rakovich thought that his commander was pointing at him. That in spite of everything, Leontev had found some way to put him in front of a court martial. That all his dreams of an army career were about to disappear like morning mist.

But the finger didn't point at him. It pointed at Zimyatov.

"Sergeant Zimyatov," the zampolit captain said, "do you know a woman named Tatyana Orlova?"

Rakovich's heart sank.

"My girlfriend," Zimyatov said, his voice shaking. "Has something happened? Something more? Is the baby—"

"Did you know that Tatyana Orlova was party to seditious meetings?"

"What? No! She would never—"

"Did you know that she was part of a band of terrorists set on bringing down the government?"

"No!" Zimyatov was shouting now. "She would never do that!"

He pushed forward and the zampolit stepped back, letting the MPs bar Zimyatov's way.

"She was caught red-handed," the zampolit continued. "Running a meeting with treasonous dissidents. We have evidence — photographs, documents, witnesses."

"Lies!" Zimyatov shouted. "She would never do that!"

"That's a very strong denial," the zampolit said. "Maybe you didn't really know her at all. Though that seems unlikely, given that she is currently pregnant with your child. Maybe what you're showing us isn't ignorance. Maybe it's the lies of one dissident covering for another."

"You lying shit!"

Zimyatov raised his fist. Rakovich lunged forward, grabbing hold of his friend, dragging him back from disaster. As Kholodov threw his weight in alongside Rakovich, the MPs drew their batons and stepped forward.

The confines of the tent became a scrum of bodies as they swayed back and forth, Zimyatov frenziedly straining to reach the zampolit, his comrades struggling to hold him back, the MPs trying to manoeuvre so that they could strike at him. They stumbled against Leontev's desk, sending it over in a flutter of papers. Then there was a crash as the comms gear was knocked to the ground. A tent pole wobbled and the whole structure threatened to collapse.

At last, Zimyatov's rage burned out. He sank against Rakovich's shoulder.

"Tatyana," he whispered, "what have you done?"

The MPs stepped forward again. Rakovich held up a hand.

"Please," he said, looking at the zampolit. "He only heard today that Tatyana was pregnant. Give him time for it to sink in."

"I have no time for traitors," the zampolit said. "Or those who shelter them."

He looked at them darkly. Kholodov tensed for action.

In Rakovich's mind, the possibilities played out. None of them ended well for Zimyatov.

If he couldn't save his best friend, then he wanted to go down fighting for him. But there were other's fates at stake. Kholodov, it seemed, would now follow him to any feat of daring, including assaulting a superior. That could mean the firing squad for both of them. Without their leadership and protection, what might happen to the unit Leontev so despised?

"Please." Rakovich turned his attention to Leontev. "Sergeant Zimyatov is a good soldier. He's loyal to his country. The army needs men like that."

"The army does not need traitors," Leontev replied.

So that was it. If he couldn't punish Rakovich, then the Captain would punish his friends instead. They could kick and scream all they wanted, but who would listen to them above the word of a political officer?

Rakovich took Zimyatov by the shoulders and looked straight at him. Tears welled at the corners of his eyes when he thought of what he had to do, but he wouldn't let them out. He was a soldier. He was a praporshchik.

"Makar, I need you to listen to me," he said. "Your best hope is to go with them. Tell the truth, help them understand that you're not a traitor. Soon enough, I'll see you back home. This war will be over and we can... we can celebrate that together. You understand?"

Zimyatov nodded.

"I understand," he said. "Goodbye, Vlad. Good luck."

He straightened, pushed Rakovich aside, and walked up to the MPs. They took his rifle from his shoulder, the bayonet from his sheath, the grenades from the pouch on his belt. Then they cuffed his hands behind his back and led him out of the tent.

With a heavy heart, Rakovich turned to Leontev, hands clasped behind his back so that their trembling wouldn't show.

"I'm sorry for Sergeant Zimyatov's behaviour," he said. Every word felt like a betrayal, but he forced them out, one breath at a time. "I will ensure that discipline is enforced more strictly from now on."

"I should think so," Leontev said. "You are dismissed."

Outside the tent, their way was blocked by a long column of marching men, hundreds of British prisoners being marched east. Their uniforms were dirty, torn, and stained, their expressions grim. Many of them were bandaged and some leaned on each other for support. The only noise they made was the thudding of boots against the road, a pattering chorus of footfalls like the sound of a summer storm.

"I'm going to remember this moment forever," Kholodov said. "They look like I feel."

Rakovich just watched, taking in the faces of the men they had defeated.

So this was what victory looked like.

Once the column had passed, Rakovich and Kholodov crossed the road and headed back through the ruined town, towards where their platoon was parked.

As they walked, the feelings Rakovich had suppressed rose again, a surging tide of bitterness threatening to choke him. He had to do something, feel something, say something that was actually honest about the shit they had seen, or he would drown beneath that great toxic wave.

"My sister was right," he said. "The system is rotten. Communism is meant to make life fair and equal, but have you seen any sign of that? We lock up good men for nothing and reward petty shitbags like Leontev. We're supposed to be better off in Russia, but everywhere we go in Germany, I see how much wealthier and happier they are than us."

Kholodov laughed.

"You're not wrong, Praporshchik," he said. "But let's pretend that you never said it, eh?"

The sergeant was an absurd sight, with his rolled up sleeves, a child's brightly coloured sticker on the side of his helmet, and a sketchbook protruding from his grenade pouch. Yet beneath it all there were signs of real military discipline — clean boots, gleaming rifle, back held straight like a proper soldier. A professionalism that Rakovich had never noticed before.

"For a decadent slacker, you're not so bad," Rakovich said.

"Thank you, Praporshchik," Kholodov replied. "That means more to me than I ever thought it would."

29

A MOMENT IN THE RAIN

The first drops of rain fell heavy on the street, bursting against tarmac and paving slabs, leaving dark stains amid the dust and ash that shrouded the former battlefield of a German town. One hit Rakovich's cheek, a brush of cool relief against his skin. Perhaps it could serve the job of the tears he must not shed, for dead comrades and a friend in the hands of the KGB.

"God's doing a Pollock impression," Kholodov said, pointing at the spatters accumulating on the ground.

"What's a Pollock?" Rakovich asked.

"American artist," Kholodov replied. "Very decadent. You'd hate his work." He tilted his head on one side, looking at the pavement from a different angle. "If I'm honest, I don't like it much either. Abstraction isn't my style."

Past the end of the street, they reached the small park where the remains of their platoon were camped. Trees lined the path to where their BMPs stood sentinel either side of a bandstand. The lawns and flower beds to either side had survived the shelling of the town but were now broken by foxholes and the heaps of earth beside them. One soldier had carefully replanted displaced marigolds along the top of his hole, and this improvised window box made Rakovich smile despite himself.

The rain was falling faster now and most of the men had taken shelter in the bandstand. They smoked, talked, and made tea over portable stoves. A soldier in camouflage gear stood with the riflemen, a visitor from another unit. He seemed as relaxed as Rakovich's men, at home in this idyllic corner of a conquered country.

Quiet descended across the group as Rakovich approached. All eyes fell upon him as he walked up the four wooden steps and stopped at the edge of the bandstand, surveying the remnants of his platoon.

"Where's Sergeant Zimyatov?" asked Rebane, Zimyatov's gunner and assistant squad leader.

"He won't be with us for a while," Rakovich replied. "The zampolits have asked him to help them with an enquiry."

A wave of muttered curses swept through the group. Rakovich was very aware of the presence of an outsider and of how easily reports of sedition could reach the political corps.

"Whatever you're thinking, keep it to yourself," he said. "We need to deal with practicalities. I'll be taking direct command of first section, with Rebane's help. Sergeant Kholodov will continue to lead second section."

"What about third?" Plakans asked.

"There won't be a third section, or any replacements for other men we've lost. This is it, for now at least."

More cursing, quieter this time. The camouflaged man lit a cigarette and watched Rakovich with a predator's calculating gaze.

"Fuel and ammunition?" Akayev asked. "Not much diesel left. Also bullets."

"Sergeant Kholodov will talk with the armourers. I'll deal with the rest. Any other questions?"

The riflemen exchanged looks. Several half-opened their mouths then thought better of it. At last Plakans spoke up.

"What's next?" he asked. "Do we get to rest, or is it straight back to fighting?"

"I don't know," Rakovich said. Of all the things Leontev had talked about with them, that should surely have been top of the list. But whether by design or by distraction, the captain had left them in the dark. "Rest while you can, but be ready for the worst."

He rubbed at his eyes. He needed sleep. He needed food. He needed a month in a proper bed. And instead he had to step up for men as weary as he was.

Something bumped against his leg. A brown and white spaniel with long, floppy ears was sniffing at his laces. It looked up at him with big dark eyes and a dopey smile, its tongue hanging out.

"Sorry, Praporshchik." Plakans tugged at the dog's collar and it followed him eagerly back to the side of the bandstand, where he fed it a strip of dried beef and patted its head. "Helmut here was wandering around on his own looking for friends. His owners must have abandoned him." His tone changed, his attention shifting to the dog. "Yes they did, didn't they? The mean capitalists left you all alone."

Helmut barked and licked Plakans' face, leaving slobber across his nose. Laughter filled the bandstand.

"Not the reinforcements I was looking for," Rakovich said, "but he can't be much more useless than some of you."

More laughter and a few cries of mock outrage.

"Alright, I'm done," Rakovich said. "Dismissed."

With a rattle of tin plates and a click of lighters, the platoon got back to eating, smoking, and chatting. The camouflaged man emerged from the small throng.

"Praporshchik Rakovich." He held out his hand. "I'm Colonel Shulgin, Spetsnaz."

"Colonel." Rakovich returned the handshake and tried to hide his surprise. The colonel wasn't wearing any rank insignia. Even if he had been, it would have been strange to see him here, a special forces commander among a group of ordinary infantrymen. "How can I help?"

This was the first time he had met anyone from Spetsnaz, military intelligence's own special forces units. Of course he'd heard of them, read about them in army newsletters, even taken the opportunity to watch them train if they were on the same base as him. But they seldom deigned to socialise with the infantry.

"I heard about your work yesterday," Shulgin said. "And that bridge on the way to Bielefeld. I thought I should check you out, given that we'll be working together."

"We will?" Rakovich asked.

Shulgin's snort was less amusement, more weary cynicism.

"You'll hear about that soon enough." He nodded towards the park. "Can we talk?"

"Of course."

They stepped out of the bandstand and into the rain. Shulgin donned a rolled up balaclava, using it as a woollen hat. Rakovich let the rain fall on his head, washing away the dirt and sweat.

"I wanted to get a sense of your men," Shulgin said as they strolled down the path. "Are they capable?"

"These are the survivors," Rakovich replied. "They wouldn't be here if they couldn't fight."

"How's morale?"

"As well as can be expected. We lost most of a section yesterday and there's no sign of reinforcements. But you saw how they took the news. They'll bitch about it, but they'll hold their ground."

"Any discipline problems?"

Kholodov and Szolkowski flashed up in Rakovich's mind. One of them seemed to have sorted himself out. The other...

He clenched his fist.

"Nothing I can't deal with," he replied. "Unless you've got a problem with what you see?"

He turned to face Shulgin directly. The colonel looked straight back at him, expression unwavering, watching Rakovich like a scientist might watch a slide beneath a microscope.

"No problem, Praporshchik," he said. "No problem at all."

Rakovich held the man's gaze. Was it really the unit he was interested in or was it Rakovich?

"Anything else?"

"I think we've covered it." Shulgin held his hand out again and

Rakovich shook it. "Good meeting you, Praporshchik. I'll see you soon."

Alone in the rain, Rakovich watched the special forces officer walk away. He felt as though he'd been shown the corner piece of a jigsaw puzzle and then been asked what the whole picture was. But that picture was his future and that of the men under his command.

He yawned and rubbed his eyes again. So much had happened in the past forty-eight hours. A whole section lost thanks to a sergeant's stupidity. His best friend arrested for his girlfriend's treachery. Now military intelligence soldiers sniffing around his command. He hadn't had time to rage against his losses, never mind to mourn them. The world had gone to hell and all he seemed to be able to do was trudge through the ruins.

A helicopter flew past, heading towards the front line. Jets followed, roaring through the sky on their way to attack NATO rallying points. The battle for this town might be over, but the rest of the war still raged. Given what the colonel had said, they would soon be back in action. If that was happening, then Rakovich needed to make sure his men were ready. That meant he had one more problem to deal with.

Back at the bandstand, he took Kholodov aside.

"Where's Szolkowski?" he asked quietly.

Kholodov looked around, his expression cartoonishly puzzled.

"I haven't seen him since we got back," Kholodov said. "Should I ask the others?"

"No." Rakovich's voice was hard as steel. However he dealt with this, he didn't want an audience. "Just keep an eye on them while I find him."

He walked away from the bandstand and around the side of the first BMP. As he went, he clenched and unclenched his fist, feeling the urge to violence within him. Szolkowski had finally pushed things too far. It had been bad enough when he was stirring petty acts of disobedience. But yesterday, he'd urged Zinoviev to disobey a direct order, and he'd got their whole section killed. No leader could let that stand.

Rakovich knew what Valeev would have said. He would have told him to follow procedures, to write Szolkowski up and have him court-martialled. To use the proper paths of discipline. Valeev had been smart like that. He'd understood the importance of using the rules.

But Rakovich understood the importance of pain. His own swelled inside him. A system that favoured Leontev wouldn't give justice where it was due, whereas kicking the shit out of Szolkowski would make the little turd think twice before he acted up again. It would remind the others why they should fear their commander. And it would feel so good.

There was no sign of Szolkowski in the first BMP. Rain running down his face, Rakovich headed for the second.

When he'd set out for war, Rakovich had believed that there was more to life than might makes right. He'd tried to become a better leader, to learn from the likes of Valeev. But over the past month, violence had become the final arbiter. If might didn't make right, then why did they have to fight to spread communism? And if it did, why shouldn't he use it now?

He would teach Szolkowski a lesson from which he would never recover. If the fucker had to live off soup for the rest of his life, wouldn't that still be better than what had happened to Zinoviev? Wouldn't it be the very least he deserved?

Or had Valeev been right — was the system the only way of getting men into line?

A light was on in the back of the second BMP, countering the gloom brought on by the rain clouds.

Szolkowski sat on the floor at one side of the vehicle. In front of him, the parts of a rifle lay spread across the floor, with cloths, a tin of grease, and a bowl of water. Two piles of weapons lay to either side of him — one heap gleaming, the other grimy from weeks of use. Szolkowski was carefully reassembling a rifle, examining each part as he put it in, checking the view down the barrel as he slotted it into place. A blood-stained sheet of paper lay on one of the vehicle's seats.

The rifleman looked up with a start as Rakovich approached. There wasn't space to stand straight inside the transport, but his back stiffened.

"Praporshchik," he said, his expression grim. "I thought you'd come."

He slotted a magazine into the rifle and added it to the pile of clean weapons.

Rakovich took a step inside. The blood pounded in his veins at the sight of Szolkowski, sat here as calm as any man alive. He imagined drawing his foot back, kicking the private in the face, watching teeth and blood spray. It felt right.

"Do it," Szolkowski said. "Whatever it is, I deserve it."

Rakovich took a step closer. Perhaps he should punch him instead. It would feel good to flex his fists, to lay down a layer of bruises before he got to the real business. Sure, it wouldn't be so satisfying if Szolkowski didn't resist. But any satisfaction was better than none, wasn't it?

He unclenched his fist and took a deep breath. He wasn't an animal. He could do this right, like Valeev would have wanted him to. He could use the law instead of instincts.

Another deep breath. Szolkowski looked up at him, all his old arrogance replaced by resignation. He was just a weary young man in a uniform, piles of rifles to either side of him, a sheet of paper behind.

"What's that?" Rakovich asked, pointing at the paper.

"A letter," Szolkowski replied. "Zinoviev was writing to his father. He was so desperate to impress him, it was tragic. Desperate to impress you too. Stupid son of a bitch."

He shook his head.

"I found the letter, when the burial detail came for him. It was full of such stupid bullshit. I thought maybe I could write a new one, one that would actually make his father proud. But the words wouldn't come. I couldn't do even this little thing to make up for killing him.

"So I thought, maybe I could stop the others getting killed instead. If I stop putting bullshit in their heads, and sort their weapons out, and fight as hard as I fucking can when the time comes, then maybe I won't feel like the worst piece of shit for the rest of my life.

"But it's not enough. So whatever you're going to do, please do it, because I can't take any more."

He was leaning forward, his whole body shaking, almost begging Rakovich to hit him.

Rakovich couldn't do it. It would have been like kicking that pathetic dog Plakans had found. Szolkowski had become his own punishment. Maybe if he learned from this, he might even become a good soldier.

Rakovich couldn't afford to waste good soldiers.

"When you're done with that, help Akayev tune up the engines," he said. "And don't forget this moment. Because I won't."

RAKOVICH SAT on a wobbly chair near the back of a school sports hall, alongside Leontev and the lieutenants of his other platoons. The place was full of officers and the occasional NCO, filling in for their dead and injured commanders. The biggest command gathering Rakovich had seen since the war started was enough to make him nervous.

"Comrades," General Chaykovsky said from a podium at the front of the hall. "This is the Ardennes forest." He pointed to a map projected on a screen behind him. The slide changed to reveal a picture of densely packed trees. "During the Great Patriotic War, the Nazis launched an attack through here to seize France and Belgium. Tomorrow, we will follow their lead."

The slide changed again to reveal a different map, this one showing arrows for troop movements.

"Once again, the Ardennes is the West's great weakness," Chaykovsky continued. "Not because of complacency this time, but because of the hole we have torn in the British army. While they scramble to fill that gap, we will punch through it.

"Most of you will be involved in direct assaults along these lines." He used a stick to point out labels on the map, showing which units went where. "But a select few will be involved in another, equally vital mission. Colonel Shulgin?"

The spetsnaz officer took Chaykovsky's place on the stage. The slides moved on again, revealing an aerial reconnaissance image of a clearing in the woods. The clearing was full of vehicles.

"Thanks to our capture of British intelligence staff, we have been able to disrupt their communication lines," Shulgin said. "They have been forced to bring in new equipment, which relies upon transmitters such as this one. If we can take it out, then the British will be unable to coordinate against our southern flank.

"Spetsnaz units are infiltrating enemy lines around this point. During the main attack, my men will break off and close the noose. We will be supported by Captain Leontev's company, but we expect strong resistance, and so may call on others for support..."

As he began outlining backup plans, Lieutenant Chugainov leaned across to Leontev.

"I heard that they pick backup from the soldiers they're considering as recruits," he whispered, just loud enough for Rakovich to hear. "Is there something you want to tell us, Captain?"

Leontev smiled smugly. "Maybe I'm finally getting the recognition I deserve."

Rakovich fought to keep from laughing. The rest of the picture Shulgin had hinted at was finally coming into view, and Leontev wasn't part of it.

30

LIVE LIKE GERMANS

The sun shone down on the park, its light glinting off puddles on the paths and illuminating the brightly painted bandstand. Somehow, the men had got hold of a dozen chickens, which they were roasting over a fire pit made from half an old oil drum. After weeks of surviving on rations, interspersed with the occasional looted luxury, the smell made Rakovich's mouth water like it never had before.

As he crossed the park, a battered tennis ball bounced across the grass in front of him, followed a moment later by Helmut the spaniel. The dog returned, ball in mouth, and dropped it at Rakovich's feet. Then it looked up at him, eyes wide, tongue lolling from the side of its mouth.

"It's alright for you to play around," Rakovich said, patting the dog on the head. "You don't have a war to fight."

Helmut licked his hand and then nudged the ball with one paw.

"Alright, maybe I should play too." Rakovich picked up the ball. "While I have the chance."

He flung the ball across the park and Helmut bounded after it, ears flapping.

"Good throw," Plakans said, approaching with a lead in his hand. "That'll keep him busy for at least half a minute."

"Is good dog," Akayev said, walking up beside Plakans. "Very friends, yes?"

"That he is," Rakovich said.

"Look at this." Plakans held up the lead. "Yuri, my dog growing up, his lead was an old piece of rope my brother stole off a farmer. He mostly ate our leftovers and the pieces of animals even a butcher couldn't sell. But I found a pet shop here, so much food! Big bags of biscuits and cans of meat. Toys too. And the leads!" He shook his head. "Helmut will never have to live like Yuri did. I promised him that."

"And did he say thank you?" Rakovich asked with a chuckle.

Plakans snorted. "Dogs are smarter than we think."

"If you say so," Rakovich said. "It's good that you got something out of this war."

Of course, they still had to find a way to keep Helmut with them, to look after him through the rest of the fighting, and to get him home at the end, all with Captain Leontev watching and judging them. But Rakovich's men had been through so much, they had earned their dreams and their prizes from the West. If this war was to have any meaning, it had to be in making his men's lives better.

"You think we get nice houses now?" Akayev asked, pointing across the park to a stone-clad terrace. "Like those?"

"The capitalists can't hoard their wealth any more," Rakovich said. "The motherland will grow rich. Soon, we'll all be living like Germans."

That made the others grin. Then Helmut came bounding over with his ball and it was time to play catch.

Drawn once more by the smell of roasting chicken, Rakovich headed for the bandstand. He had to share their orders with the men, but that could wait until after they'd eaten.

THE BMP's engine growled as it advanced through the forest. Amid the steep hillsides and towering pines of the Ardennes, the company couldn't make the sort of breakneck charge with which it had started the war. Instead, they progressed through the woods in single file, each vehicle close behind the one in front, crushing undergrowth and tearing up the dirt beneath.

Through a periscope in the roof of his BMP, Rakovich watched the woods roll past. He sat tensed and ready, gripping his rifle tight. These woods would be a proving ground — for him, his men, and perhaps the whole Red Army.

At the top of a ridge they fanned out. Ahead lay one more slope up to the clearing where their target lay. Occasional bursts of small arms fire told them that, as promised, the Spetsnaz forces were already engaged with the enemy.

The back doors of the BMP opened. Rakovich followed his men out into the forest. None of them spoke a word. The air was thick with the scent of pines, a refreshing change if you could ignore the diesel fumes from their vehicles.

He looked to Kholodov, whose section held the end of the line. The sergeant nodded, signalling that he was ready.

Rakovich took a radio from his belt, a top-end device they'd been given by Colonel Shulgin.

"Zoryn 210, this is Zoryn 217," he said quietly. "I am ready for go."

"Affirmative, Zoryn 217," Leontev replied. "We are go in one minute."

Rakovich clipped the radio back onto his belt and looked down the line. The whole company was waiting for action, including Leontev's own command vehicle. The men stood ready, rifles clasped tight in their hands. One man kissed a locket before tucking it inside his jacket. Another made the sign of the cross. Rakovich instinctively reached for the pocket where he had long kept his Communist Manifesto, but it wasn't there any more. It was buried in the bottom of his bag, out of sight and out of mind.

He could still hear shooting somewhere ahead of them.

"This is Zoryn 210," Leontev said through the radio. "All sections go."

The engines of the BMPs roared and they began climbing the hill-side again, accelerating through the trees. Rakovich followed with his squad around him, walking at first, then jogging, then racing up the slope, sweat soaking his shirt in the summer heat.

Machine gun fire burst from the undergrowth ahead. Bullets clanged off the front of the BMPs and hurled clouds of half-rotted pine needles into the air.

The main guns of the BMPs replied. A tree trunk burst apart, filling the air with splinters as it toppled to the ground. Another shell exploded close to the ridge, but not close enough to take out the British gunner. More bullets zipped past Rakovich's head and he put on an extra burst of speed, catching up with the BMP and the cover it provided.

Something glinted in the undergrowth.

"Barbed wire," Rakovich called out. "Where are the cutters?"

As they reached the wire, most of the BMPs stopped. While their gunners gave covering fire, two men from each vehicle crawled forward, wire cutters in hand. Bullets flew around them as they sliced through the metal strands, frantically trying to make enough space for the vehicles to get through.

One of the drivers was either feeling cocky or hadn't noticed the wire. He went straight over it, tangling it around his tracks. As he advanced, the wire came with him, wrenched from the ground by the power of the vehicle's engine. It wrapped around the final drive, snarling the mechanisms. The BMP swerved to the right, almost collided with another vehicle, and ground to a halt.

Away from the BMPs, the barbed wire thrust up through the undergrowth in loops and tangled lumps, catching at the men's legs as they advanced. His attention divided between the ground and the enemy-infested tree line, Rakovich felt on edge, as though disaster must strike at any moment. Either he would miss the wire and fall tangled to the ground, or he would miss a soldier amid the trees and go down in a burst of gunfire. His heart raced as he forced himself to take measured steps, watching for the telltale glint of steel amid the ferns.

A man fell, twisting and cursing in some eastern dialect as he tried to free his legs from the wire. Another went tumbling down the slope, blood spraying as a bullet knocked him off his feet.

Amid the trees to his right, Rakovich saw a sandbag emplacement. The barrel of a machine gun turned towards him.

There was no time to worry about the barbed wire. He flung himself behind a tree just as the gun opened fire. Splinters filled the air and bullets whistled past his head as he stood, back pressed against the tree trunk, waiting for the moment of pain.

It never came. Instead, there was the thud of a grenade. The machine gun fell silent.

Rakovich emerged from behind his tree and ran towards the emplacement. If the gunner had been disabled then this was his chance. If not, then he was fucked anyway.

Szolkowski was ahead of him, rifle raised as he rushed the British. He thrust one foot in among the sandbags and used it to propel him over the top, screaming as he went.

To a backing of thuds and shouts, Rakovich followed Szolkowski over the sandbags. Two British soldiers lay dead. Szolkowski was grappling with a third, the two of them clinging to his rifle as they shoved and kicked. The Briton slammed his head into Szolkowski's face and blood streamed from the rifleman's nose. His grip on the rifle loosened.

Drawing the knife from his belt, Rakovich lunged forward and stabbed the enemy soldier in the guts. Flesh gave with sickening ease and blood streamed out across Rakovich's hand. The man looked at him in surprise, mouth hanging open. Rakovich twisted the blade and dragged it upward, beneath the ribcage and into the chest. With a last gurgling breath, the man slumped to the ground, his guts spilling from the hole the knife had left.

Ignoring the bloody mess of his own face, Szolkowski shifted his grip on the rifle and looked around.

"Where now, Praporshchik?" he asked.

They were at the top of the slope, looking out across the clearing. In the centre, the British had corralled their trucks and APCs, creating an improvised fortress. Machine guns and rifles thrust through the gaps.

On the far side of the corral, there was a sudden, violent explosion. A vehicle covered in antennae and satellite dishes blew apart, its mast falling like a tree amid the ruin of the forest.

Spetsnaz had hit their main target, but that didn't mean the fighting was over. Captives taken here might know more about NATO plans than anyone else near the front. Taking prisoners could save lives.

Soviet forces surged into the clearing. Rakovich was amazed to see the command BMP in the lead, Leontev running along behind. Had the captain finally found some guts, or was he just so determined to impress Spetsnaz that nothing else mattered?

A missile shot from the trees to the left, racing across the clearing with a familiar whoosh.

Flames burst from the command BMP. There was a second explosion, something igniting inside. Leontev flung himself to the ground as a chunk of armour plating flew past.

Renewed gunfire burst from the trees. British reinforcements had arrived.

Crouching behind the sandbags, Rakovich and Szolkowski returned fire. It was hard to make out the camouflaged British, so they just shot at anything that moved. If they could keep the enemies' heads down then they could buy their exposed comrades some time.

First platoon had followed Leontev into the open. Men Rakovich had known for years, who had fought their way unscathed across Germany, dropped like flies. A second BMP was hit by a rocket. Its rear doors burst out in a gout of flames, then the driver's hatch opened and a blackened, flame-licked figure crawled out before collapsing dead on the ground.

The remaining troops pulled back, taking cover in the trees and captured British emplacements.

Out in the clearing, Leontev still lay on the ground, blood oozing from a gash in his leg. Of all the people Rakovich could see die today, this was the only one that would make him happy. The loss of his captain, the man who had brought him so much grief, gave Rakovich a feeling of relief despite the desperate fighting all around.

Then Leontev turned his head. He started crawling for cover behind one of the ruined BMPs, but the moment he moved his injured leg he cried out in pain and slumped motionless once more.

Rakovich stared, the battle around him all but forgotten. This was it. All he had to do was leave Leontev to die and it would be over. No more punishments. No more snide remarks. No-one holding him back from becoming a lieutenant.

His own thoughts sickened him. Had he become so jaded that this was all he could care about? That he would leave a comrade to die?

"Fuck." He slapped his hand against the sandbags. Szolkowski turned to him in alarm, eyes running up and down as he looked for a wound.

"We have to rescue the captain," Rakovich said.

Szolkowski turned his gaze across the open ground, taking in the bodies and ruined vehicles, the gunfight still raging between the corral and the woods.

"Whatever you say, Praporshchik," he said.

"I'll get him," Rakovich said, shouldering his rifle. "I need you to provide me with covering fire."

With a grunt, Szolkowski picked up the British machine gun and brought it around to their side of the position, setting its tripod to face across the clearing. He knocked aside a couple of sandbags and pointed the gun through the gap. Crouching behind it, he squeezed the trigger and nodded in satisfaction at the spray of bullets.

"Ready when you are, Praporshchik," he said.

For a moment, Rakovich hesitated. Could he really trust his life to Szolkowski, after everything the man had done?

Strangely, he felt he could.

Rakovich took a deep breath and forced the memories of who Leontev was out of his mind. He had nothing left to fight for except his people. If he left one of them behind then what did that leave?

He unclenched his fist and took another deep breath.

"Ready," he said.

The world seemed to shrink as he dashed into the open. Bullets still flew. The boom of rockets and grenades still filled the air. Somewhere a soldier was screaming. But as he ran across the clearing, all of his attention was on Leontev and the few square feet around him. All his fear, all his hate, all his bitterness roiled together in his chest, but they would not rule him.

Something exploded to his right. A piece of shrapnel scored a line across his shoulder as it hurtled by.

Then he was at Leontev. He rolled the captain onto his back, ignoring his groan of pain, and picked him up.

Bullets flew fast around them. The safety of the tree line seemed impossibly distant. But only a few meters away was the wreckage of the command BMP.

Rakovich ran to the BMP. In the shelter of its charred steel frame, he set Leontev down. The angle of the vehicle would protect them from British fire, at least for a minute or two.

Leontev's eyes were wide and his skin pale. His chest rose and fell rapidly.

"Rakovich," he whispered. "What are you doing?"

Rakovich pulled a bandage from a pouch on his belt.

"Saving your life," he said, wrapping the bandage rapidly around Leontev's injured leg. A medic could do a proper job of it later. For now, he just needed to slow the bleeding.

"You're saving me?" Leontev laughed, but the sound trailed off into a weak splutter. "That's funny. Why is that funny?"

Rakovich tied off the bandage and looked around. The fighting seemed to have stalled, neither side having moved since the Soviet withdrawal. They couldn't wait for the tide of battle to sweep past and leave them safely behind.

They needed to reach better cover before the British started using grenades. Leontev was going to be no use, so Rakovich would have to do it all himself.

He raised his rifle and peered around the edge of the BMP. Maybe if he could pick off a couple of British soldiers then the rest would think twice about sticking their heads up. That might give him time to get Leontev to safety before he lost too much blood. It wasn't an impressive plan, but what else could he do, out here on his own?

The rumble of an engine made him look around. Second section's BMP was approaching at speed across the clearing, main gun blazing, bullets flying from the ports in the troop compartment. In the treeline, the platoon's other BMP flung suppressing fire at the British.

The first BMP skidded to a halt beside Rakovich. Kholodov leapt out and took hold of Leontev's legs.

Rakovich lifted the captain by his shoulders and together they carried him into the back of the BMP. He slammed the doors shut while Kholodov tapped the driver on the shoulder.

"Off we go!" Akayev shouted.

The engine growled and the vehicle swung around, heading back towards the trees. The riflemen still sat at their firing ports, rifles raised, swaying as they jolted across rough ground. Bullets clanged off the armour.

Gripping hold of the seat next to him, Rakovich found himself mumbling something close to a prayer. If a missile hit them now, he wouldn't have saved a life. He would have put more of them in danger.

"You shouldn't have taken that risk," he said.

"You would have done it," Kholodov replied, grinning. "If our leader is painted in the colours of courage, what else can you expect from us?"

They slowed as they reached the treeline. Akayev turned the BMP so that its front was facing the enemy, then brought them to a halt. Obolensky left his firing position and pulled a first aid kit from beneath the seats.

As Obolensky stuck Leontev with a dose of morphine, Rakovich's radio burst into life.

"Shulgin to Rakovich, do you read me, over?"

"I hear you, colonel," Rakovich replied.

"Is Leontev with you?"

"He is."

"Put him on."

Rakovich looked at the captain, who was staring glassy-eyed at the ceiling.

"Captain Leontev is out of action," he said. "Lieutenant Chugainov should take control of the unit."

"Fine." Shulgin sounded tense, his familiar Spetsnaz confidence gone. Outside, the sound of fighting had almost stopped. "You deal with your own platoon. Disengage and get back down the hill. We'll regroup there."

"Are we giving up on prisoners?"

Shulgin laughed, but there was no humour in the sound.

"We might be giving up on more than that," he said. "Just get your men out of here before any more die. Everything else can wait."

The radio went silent. Rakovich stared at it, his brow crumpling as he tried to make sense of Shulgin's words. What did he mean, giving up on more than that? What had Rakovich missed while he was rescuing Leontev?

When he looked up, every face in the squad was turned towards him.

"What's happening?" Kholodov asked.

"I don't know," Rakovich said, trying to keep his face neutral despite the weight of dread bearing down inside him. "Let's just get out of here."

From the floor of the BMP, Captain Leontev hummed a few bars of an old marching tune.

"Maybe it's time to go home," he sang.

31

A CITY REWRITTEN

P etrol rationing meant that there were few cars on the roads of Leningrad. Truck drivers waited until night to make their deliveries, rather than risk being mobbed by civilians looking for more food. The only vehicles out during the day belonged to the army or to top tier Communist Party officials.

Pedestrians studiously looked away as those vehicles drove past. Everyone had heard of a friend of a friend who challenged a military policeman and was arrested for sedition, or who looked the wrong way at a Party official and vanished that very night. People kept their eyes downcast, both fearful of the authorities and ashamed of that fear. No-one wanted to look into a stranger's eyes and see their own humiliation reflected back at them.

It was an atmosphere that sickened Anna, and yet one that suited her. As long as she avoided the checkpoints, no-one would notice where she went or when. She had grown adept at avoiding those checkpoints, watching out for the junctions where they might spring up, turning aside before her evasion became obvious to the guards.

The summer sun shone down, raising a stench from the bins that lined the alleyway. Mere months ago, Anna would never have dreamed of walking here, too afraid of what might happen to her as a young woman alone, her disgust at the smell only adding to that instinct. Now, it was the safest way to travel, unseen by anyone except stray cats and an occasional kitchen porter.

One such woman sat on an upturned bucket halfway along the alley, smoking a scraggy hand-rolled cigarette. She nodded as Anna approached and gestured through the doorway behind her.

"You're the last one here," she said, the words emerging on a cloud of cheap tobacco smoke.

"Thank you, Olga," Anna said. "How are the kids?"

"Still they give me no sleep." Olga rolled her eyes. "At least while I keep watch here I get some rest from them and from work."

"Just make sure you don't fall asleep," Anna said. "Or we might all be kept up by something worse than children."

Olga laughed darkly and held up a coffee cup. "Don't worry, I've got ways of staying awake."

Anna walked through the door and into the kitchen. As in so many Leningrad restaurants, it lay idle for half the day, its business strangled by rationing and the tension that kept people in their homes.

Instead of the kitchen staff, half a dozen mismatched figures sat around the central table, drinking weak tea and smoking cigarettes. Some wore overalls, others skirts, and one man was wearing a suit. As Anna walked in they leaned back in their chairs and allowed themselves slight smiles.

"We were worried," Mikhail said.

"That I'd been caught?" Anna asked, taking a seat.

"That I might have to run the meeting," Mikhail said. "But now I see that I'm safe."

"For now." Anna leaned forward. "Alright, let's hear your reports."

Few of the union cells had done anything other than watch what was happening around them. But Anna made them go over the details. Every little hint that they were being followed. Every snippet of information about police business. Every rumour leaking out of the

Party machine. She could not afford to neglect the details, not with everything that failure could cost them.

The tea was cold by the time they finished reporting. Anna rubbed her eyes and stifled a yawn. Studying in the day, scheming at night, trying to fit eating and cleaning the flat into the gaps between, there wasn't much time left for rest.

A packet of cigarettes sat on the table in front of Sergei Semenov. Anna reached across the table and took one of them.

"Next business," she said, rolling the cylinder of tobacco back and forth between her fingers, enjoying its scent. "Recruitment. Before we take any other action, we need more people. Not just bodies on the streets but people with real influence. People who can sow the seeds of our ideas in the public consciousness or who can provide the resources we need."

"My printing shop has some contact with publishers," Mikhail said. "I could fish for invitations to meet writers and journalists."

"That's good," Anna said. "I'll try to be more sociable at the university, get to know academics in other departments. There have to be some on the arts side who will be sympathetic."

"My cousin manages bands," said Olga Ledbodev, one of the union's old hands. "He's always happy to make introductions for fans."

And so the ideas started to flow.

After recruitment they talked about organisation, about propaganda, about contact with networks in other cities. They threw ideas around, embracing some, rejecting others, setting a few aside to reconsider later. Then they got down to the practicalities, turning thoughts into plans.

There would be protests some day. There would be riots. Anna didn't just accept that now, she craved it. A chance for them to kick and scream and rage against the system. To bellow the names of those who had been arrested or killed. To make sure that the world never forgot about the people brave enough to start this struggle. Tatyana, Boris, Pavel — they didn't deserve to vanish forever into dark, damp cells, or to be whisked away to a Siberian camp. When the time came, she would fight for them with every ounce of strength she had.

But that day was not now. It could not come until they had the strength to win, and at this moment they were as weak as infants. First they must grow, then they could fight.

"Are you going to smoke that?" Mikhail asked her during a lull in the conversation.

Anna looked down at the cigarette. She had worried at it so much, rolling it back and forth between her fingers, that half the tobacco had fallen out onto the table, a scattering of fragrant brown flakes.

"I suppose not," she said, setting it down. She looked around the table. "Are we done?"

"Do you think we are?" Mikhail asked.

Anna looked around at the expectant faces.

"Alright, we're done," she said. "Go work, rest, whatever you need to do. I'll see you all in two weeks."

One by one, they left the room, each heading off separately and in different directions, making sure that they would not be seen together.

When only the two of them remained, Mikhail swept up the remains of the cigarette and put them in a small dish on the counter.

"Olga will appreciate that," he said. Then he turned to face Anna. "You know that you've saved us here, don't you?"

Anna blinked in confusion.

"Saved you from what?"

"From collapse. The union is gone, but you've salvaged something from the wreckage. Maybe we can do the same for our poor ruined country."

"I'm sure we can." Anna laid a hand on his shoulder. "But it's not just me. It's all of us combined."

"Somebody has to hold us together. Otherwise we're just tobacco flakes, not a smokable cigarette."

Anna laughed.

"That's the least dramatic metaphor I've ever heard."

"Maybe it's best if we're not dramatic."

They said their goodbyes and left by different doors. Anna emerged into the alley, where Olga still sat on her bucket, watching the flies buzz above the bins.

"We're done now," Anna said. "Thank you."

"No, thank you," Olga said.

Anna took a different route home from the one that had brought her here. Always better that way. Break up the patterns. Leave too many tiny pieces for their opponents to put the picture together.

There was more graffiti on the streets than there had been before the war. Many of the men and women in the city's street cleaning teams had been mustered into the army, that ever-growing juggernaut supposedly bringing the glory of communism to the West, and those who remained didn't have time to clean off the paint. Much of it was just scrawls and obscenities, young people venting their frustrations at a world beyond their control. But some of it meant more.

On a wall across from the alley, a string of red letters caught Anna's eye. They raised a melancholy smile to her lips.

"NO CHILD BORN BEHIND BARS," the letters read, and below that, "FREE Tatyana."

~

"GOOD EVENING, PAPA," Anna said as she walked through the door. "I didn't think you would be home."

Papa looked around from the stove. The wrinkles around his eyes bunched up as he smiled at her.

"I asked to start my shift late tonight," he said. "The foreman was kind enough to agree."

"Probably because you've already put in so many extra hours." Anna kissed him on the cheek. "You must be the hardest working man there."

"I just do my job," he said, but his smile widened proudly.

A pan was steaming away on the stove. Anna leaned over and took a deep breath. The smell of beef stew made her mouth water.

"Why did you do that?" she asked.

"Because I was hungry," Papa replied. "And I thought that you deserved a treat."

"I mean why are you going to work late?"

Papa shrugged, not quite managing to feign nonchalance.

"You are so busy at the moment," he said. "I never get to see you for more than a few minutes. I thought it would be nice to share a meal."

"You're right," Anna said, hiding her concern. "That would be nice."

While Papa cooked, she took plates and cutlery out of the cupboard. They didn't normally bother with a tablecloth, but today she spread one across the table, an old favourite of her mother's. Its embroidered roses brought back memories of childhood, being summoned to the table with her brother, greeted by her parents' smiles and her father's cooking. The warm glow of nostalgia battled with a mounting dread at what her father was hiding.

As she laid the table, her eyes darted around the room. If something had happened to Vlad then there would be a telegram, wouldn't there? Some sort of official notice. She couldn't see any sign of an envelope, but maybe Papa had hidden it while he gave her one last moment of happiness. It was his way, always providing comfort no matter how hard the times.

He brought the pan to the table and spooned out stew onto both their plates. Then he brought over another plate, piled with slices of freshly baked bread. Anna sat watching, gripping the side of her seat so tight that her nails dug into the wood.

At last he sat down and dipped a spoon into the stew.

"I don't mean to brag, but I've outdone myself this time," he said after his first taste. "You should be proud of your old father."

"I always am." Anna forced herself to follow his lead and eat a little. It tasted as delicious as it smelled. Soon she was gobbling it down, rushing to fill a stomach left empty by rationing and tension.

But the more she ate, the longer the uncomfortable silence grew between them, each catching the other's eye just for fleeting moments.

"Have you heard from Vlad?" she asked at last.

"Only a brief note last week," Papa replied. "He mostly writes to you."

"No news from the army?"

"Not since his medal." Papa laughed. "And even on that, I heard it from the newspapers first."

"And you?" Anna asked, unable to contain her concern any longer. "Are you well?"

"My appetite's still strong," Papa replied, wiping his plate with a corner of bread. "At least the years haven't taken that from me."

"And the rest of you?" Anna set her spoon down, bracing for the worst.

"I'm fine." Papa pushed his plate aside and finally met her gaze. "But I'm worried about you."

"Me?" Anna stared.

Papa took a deep breath. Reaching out across the rickety kitchen table, he laid his hand on hers.

"I know that I'm not as smart as your mother was," he said. "And that you have grown into an even more insightful and intelligent woman than she was. But did you really think that we could live under the same roof without me realising what was going on?"

Now it was Anna's turn to take a deep breath while she mustered her thoughts. Perhaps he hadn't realised the truth. He might just think that she was partying too much. It would have been more fitting for the person she had been for so many years. And yes, it would be awkward to deal with that, but at least it would keep him safe, cut off from the dangerous truth.

"What do you think you know, Papa?" She kept her voice low and brushed a thumb across the back of his hand, trying to keep things calm, to preserve the bond between them as best she could.

"I know what happened to your friend Tatyana," Papa said. "And you stopped talking about your new friend Boris just after that demonstration."

A chill ran through Anna. She had tried so hard to keep this from him, to protect him from who she had become. Afraid of something she didn't even dare acknowledge.

"There were other things too," Papa said. "When you hurt your feet and were limping. That you don't smile when you tell me you are going to see friends. The tiredness in your eyes. On their own, these could be so many things. But when people disappear from conversation... I remember what that means."

She wanted to deny it. To spin some web of lies, like she had done for her professors, for her friends, for any policeman or soldier who stopped her as she roamed the city, doing what needed to be done.

But this was Papa. She couldn't lie to Papa. Just the thought made her nauseous.

"I wanted to protect you," she said. "This thing, it's dangerous. If you knew about it they might hurt you."

"They might hurt me anyway," he said, withdrawing his hand. "You must realise that."

She looked down at her plate. On some level, she had known. She saw that now. Any suspicion on her could easily fall upon him, regardless of the truth. But as long as she didn't admit it to herself, it didn't seem real.

"I'm sorry," she said, her voice becoming that of the lost little girl she had once been. "I just wanted to do the right thing."

"Your mother..." Papa's voice halted as if something had caught in his throat. He looked away.

And then it hit her. The thing she truly hadn't wanted to consider.

She was fighting against the system her mother had helped to build.

"I didn't mean to..." she began. "I didn't want to..."

Her mother's memory was everything to Papa. Whenever he talked about the Party, it was with pride at what the love of his life had done. And here was his own daughter, leading a rebellion against the party. A traitor in his home.

"Your mother was a proud Communist," Papa said. His tears matched those running down Anna's cheeks. "She worked every day of her life to make our country better, through the Party."

Anna forced herself to her feet.

"I'll go," she said. "I can stay with friends. I didn't mean to... I'm so sorry."

"No." Papa's face was red. He slammed his fist against the table. A plate jumped, teetered on the edge, and fell with a crash to the floor. "You're not listening."

Anna trembled. She had never seen him like this. What deep anger had she unleashed, to break through the kindness and calm that was her father?

"Your mother wanted to make the country better," Papa said, his voice wavering. "But is this a better country? One that sends its sons out as conquerors? One where so-called Communists drive limousines past breadlines?"

He looked up at her. Now he was smiling through the tears.

"Your mother would have been so proud of you," he said.

Joyful tears burst from Anna as she flung her arms around her father. She knelt beside him, the two of them holding each other tight, as sobs turned to laughter. He stroked her hair, just like he had done when she was small.

"I wanted you to be my little girl forever," Papa said, finally disentangling himself and wiping his cheeks. "But you are so much more than that now."

"I love you, Papa."

"I love you too, my little Anna."

Outside, a flash cut through the evening gloom.

"Come, we should clear the table," Papa said. "And then maybe you can tell me what you have been doing, before you go out to save the world some more."

As they carried their plates to the sink, Anna looked out the window.

Between the tower blocks and across the rooftops, the sky was fading from blue to grey. To the south, something new rose above the horizon. Like a distant tower block but taller, it seemed no thicker than her thumb, but must have been enormous up close. A pillar of smoke, stretching from the earth up into the sky.

As she watched open-mouthed, its top spread out, becoming a mushroom cloud.

"My God," Papa whispered, his voice tight with dread. "Is that...?"

Words failed Anna. She knew what lay in that direction. She had driven there only a week before, taking the people in her care to a place of safety. Tears ran down her cheeks as she realised what she was watching.

That mushroom cloud had been Veliky Novgorod.

32

THE SHADOW OF A CLOUD

R akovich finished reading the official announcement. He folded the sheet of paper, typed out the previous night by some anonymous clerk in the regimental support team. Careful to keep his hand steady, he slid it back into his pocket.

At last, he looked up at his men.

At the start of the war there had been thirty of them. Now only fifteen stood beneath the shelter of the bandstand, some of them replacements who had joined along the way. The rest had been left in a trail of field hospitals and graveyards the length of Germany.

Every one of these survivors had been through so much. They had seen death and destruction. Some had been injured. All had struggled through firefights and bombardments, had walked through the ruins of cities and across the smoking wilderness of battlefields.

Every one of them stared at him open mouthed, their faces pale and eyes wide. They looked like he felt.

"Did any of you have family in Veliky Novgorod?" Rakovich asked.

A dark cloud advanced across the sky, casting them into shadow.

Obolensky raised a trembling hand.

"My sister," he said, his voice dull. "Her children."

"I'm sorry," Rakovich said.

He wished that he could offer some crumb of comfort, but what was there to say? Even those who had survived the city's destruction would die soon enough, radiation eating them from the inside. Farms and villages downwind of the blast would be poisoned, their livestock worthless, their inhabitants doomed to a hideous decline as cancer took hold.

To offer any comfort now would be a lie, a betrayal of the bond between a leader and his men.

Obolensky pushed himself away from the edge of the bandstand. He blinked hard.

"I have to check some supplies," he said. "Bandages."

"Of course."

The medic walked away into the trees at the edge of the park, his shoulders slumped, feet dragging across the grass. Rakovich had to force himself to turn away and back to the rest of his men.

"Why did they do it?" Kholodov asked. "Why now?"

"Because we were winning," Rakovich said. "And we were going to keep winning. Fuck it, maybe we should be asking why they didn't do it sooner."

"So why not nuke our armies?"

"The ones that are all over their territory?"

"Oh. Shit. Yes."

Silence fell. No-one moved as raindrops started to fall, pattering against the roof of the bandstand. They almost drowned out the grief-stricken wail that burst from among the trees.

"Why Veliky Novgorod?" Szolkowski asked. "Why not somewhere that matters?"

"General Chaykovsky called it a warning shot," Rakovich said. "By leaving the most important cities alone, they've left the government with everything still to lose. It's a way to avoid a full-blown nuclear war."

"So what now? How do we get back at them for this?"

"We don't."

Rakovich was glad that Obolensky had gone. If his nieces had been the ones to die, he would have beaten the man senseless who told him they would not be avenged. Even at one remove, it made him sick with anger.

His men clearly felt the same way. Almost every voice rose in protest, words tumbling over and around each other in a maelstrom of furious indignation. They waved their arms, stamped their feet, grimaced and growled. Helmut, Plakans' dog, joined in with excited barking.

Rakovich let it wash over him, just as General Chaykovsky had done in the officers' meeting. Like Chaykovsky, he waited until the first wave of noise had subsided, then cut across it with a short, silencing shout.

"Enough!" He looked them over, hands clenched at his sides. "You're soldiers of the motherland, not children. If you're told not to fight then you don't fight."

This time, the silence wasn't one of shock or sorrow. It was one of indignation.

"This is the price we pay to win," Rakovich said.

"To win?" Plakans exclaimed. "But they just—"

"Silence!"

Rakovich lunged forward, fist raised, before he could control himself. As Plakans rocked back, Rakovich froze in place. He took a deep breath, lowered his fist, and shook his head. The rush of adrenaline subsided as quickly as it had come, leaving him slumping against one of the bandstand's pillars.

"NATO know they can't take back what we now control," he said. "So this is the end. If we go any further, they nuke Moscow, we fire back, and the whole world dies. But if they push against us then we'll retaliate for Veliky Novgorod.

"We've captured most of Germany. The Fourth Army holds Austria. That's two whole countries liberated from the capitalist yoke."

Those last words tasted like ashes on his lips, but he kept going.

"What you've done over the past weeks hasn't been in vain. We've won a great victory for the motherland. And if you don't think the price was worth paying then you shouldn't be a soldier.

"I don't know what happens to us now, but I do know that our work's not done. Tonight there are no new orders, but I have to go and see Captain Leontev. Kholodov, you set watches just in case. The rest of you, do whatever it takes to deal with this. Tonight, you're comrades who've suffered a terrible shock. Tomorrow, I need you to be soldiers again."

RAKOVICH HAD SEEN his share of aid stations and surgical tents since they'd entered the Federal Republic of Germany, but this was the first time he'd been to an actual hospital. Local staff mingled with army medics treating the wounded in the over-crowded wards. Many of the casualties were soldiers, but there were civilians too. Men, women, and children crowded the corridors, waiting to have their wounds bound, their infections treated, their dressings changed.

A small boy with tears at the corners of his eyes looked up at Rakovich as he passed. Then the boy's older sister pulled him close, letting him cry into her skirts while she gave the soldier a hostile glare.

There would be more of this. That was the one thing Rakovich was sure about for the days to come. While the politicians worked out what peace would look like, he and his men would sit here, keeping control of a resentful population and watching for forces mustering across the border. There would be spies and saboteurs to deal with, looters and profiteers too. When they started shooting them, maybe there would be less trouble, but the resentment would surely increase. The village they'd occupied early in the war had taught him the bitter truth, that no matter what the ideologues back home said, no-one welcomed them here.

An army clerk stood near the rear of the hospital's foyer, a clipboard in his hands. He had the harassed look of a man facing blame for events beyond his control.

"I'm looking for Captain Leontev," Rakovich said. "He sent orders for me to find him here."

"Officers are on the top floor," the clerk said, flipping through the papers on his clipboard. "Captain Leontev is in ward C."

He pointed Rakovich towards the elevator and gave him instructions for where to go at the top. By the time he was done, a military policeman had arrived with another enquiry.

Rakovich got into the elevator and hit the top button. The thought of facing Leontev filled him with weariness rather than the tension such meetings had once held. He didn't know what to expect. Would Leontev be grateful to him for saving his life, or was the captain's hatred strong enough to survive even that event? It was impossible to know. Given everything that had happened, it felt equally absurd to care.

As Rakovich stepped out of the elevator on the top floor, he caught the acrid smell of bleach. It wasn't a surprise to discover that more care was taken of the officers' wards. Maybe that would change once the initial chaos subsided and the casualties stopped coming in. And maybe he would wake up tomorrow to find that he was Party chairman and hung like an ox.

This floor was less crowded than the rest, so he didn't have to push his way through crowds of staff and patients. The clerk's instructions took him past several small private rooms to a ward holding half a dozen beds. Most of them were empty, the patients having apparently found better things to do than rest. Instead, they sat on folding chairs around a man who had lost both his legs, playing cards on the empty bottom half of his bed.

They turned to look as Rakovich stood saluting in the doorway. With their uniforms replaced by striped pyjamas, he didn't know what these men's ranks were, but he knew that they all outranked him, and he wasn't sure that this counted as being in the field any more.

"Deal me out," Leontev said, throwing down his hand of cards. "I've got business to deal with."

"How convenient," the legless man said with a chuckle. "Would you still have business if the game was going your way?"

"Of course, Colonel," Leontev said with a strained smile. "But duty calls."

With the aid of a walking stick, he hobbled to one of the beds, picked up a small box, and then carried on into the corridor. Rakovich followed him to a pair of cushioned seats beneath a window. The corridor was calm, quiet, almost empty.

"How are your platoon doing, Praporshchik?" Leontev asked as he settled into one of the seats.

"As well as can be expected, Captain," Rakovich replied, standing to attention and staring straight ahead. "Shaken, but tough enough to cope. Obolensky might need some time off. He had family at Veliky Novgorod."

"I meant practicalities. Numbers, supplies, combat readiness."

"Fifteen remaining, including me. I believe that everyone could fight if it came to it. Colonel Shulgin made sure we had plenty of ammunition before the last mission, but we could do with more rations and water treatment tablets."

"You always had an eye for details, didn't you, Rakovich?"

"Thank you, sir," Rakovich replied. He glanced down at the Captain, trying to work out what he meant. How was this going to turn into a criticism?

Late afternoon sunlight streamed in through the window, casting a warm glow across them both.

Leontev frowned, his bushy eyebrows shifting like caterpillars arching their backs. He looked away and then back up at Rakovich.

"You saved my life," Leontev said. "I didn't expect that."

"I was just doing my job," Rakovich replied.

"You have never just done your job," Leontev said. "A point Valeev kept trying to make to me. And now it strikes me that there might be more to gain from using that."

He paused, apparently waiting for Rakovich to say something. But Rakovich had endured enough of his superior's little games and power plays. He was fucked if he would give the man the satisfaction of whatever he was after now.

Leontev opened the box he'd brought from the ward and held it out towards Rakovich. Inside were a lieutenant's epaulettes.

Rakovich's eyes widened. How many times had he dreamed of wearing those?

"You've wanted to be an officer from the moment you joined my company," Leontev said. "And I've been held back as a captain for far too long. Together, I think we can rise to what we deserve."

Rakovich reached out. His fingertips brushed the lieutenant's epaulettes, then withdrew.

Yes, he had wanted to be an officer. But that was when that role had meant something to him. When he had thought that he could lead men in a great war of liberation, bringing freedom and equality to the world. A just war.

But there was no justice in this war or in the system he served. He wasn't being offered his promotion because he had earned it. It was just one more ploy from a corrupt Party man. Leontev saw something to gain from Rakovich and so sought to harness him with rank.

"Thank you, Captain," Rakovich said. "But you should find another lieutenant."

"What?" Leontev scowled. "Do you think you can get something more by pressing me here? Because I'm telling you now Rakovich, this is all there is."

"It's not a negotiation," Rakovich said. "I just don't want it. I've had my taste of command, Captain, and as you always suspected, it's not for me."

IN THE END, Rakovich decided against declaring Obolensky medically unfit for combat. The medic was no use to anyone, not even himself, curled up around a photo of his nieces while he bawled his eyes out. But evacuation because of a breakdown would stain Obolensky's reputation for the rest of his life, not just his army career.

Instead, Rakovich broke into a locked corner shop and took half a dozen bottles of spirits. He left cash behind on the counter, for whatever it was worth in a world turned upside down, and pulled the shutter back into place as he left, hanging the broken padlock through its loop. He didn't want to cause suffering for whoever owned the place, it was just that he needed to take care of his men.

By the light of a fire in an old oil drum, Rakovich opened one of the bottles and handed it to Obolensky. The medic stared at it with bloodshot eyes until Rakovich took hold of his hand, wrapped it around the bottle, and pressed it to his comrade's lips.

Around them, the men of the platoon passed the other drinks around, taking what comfort alcohol had to offer. They talked quietly among themselves. Some played with Helmut, bouncing balls for the dog to catch, patting him on the head and telling him what a good boy he was. Helmut's barking provided more happiness than all the booze they could have found, but it still wasn't much.

Within half an hour, Obolensky was rocking back and forth with a half-empty bottle, tears streaming down his cheeks, singing mournful songs over and over. He talked about his nieces to anyone who could bear the pain of listening, and they all took a turn lending him an ear. Later, having hurled his guts up, he fell unconscious in the corner of the bandstand. Kholodov draped a blanket over him and pried the empty bottle from his fingers.

"You think that'll help?" the sergeant asked quietly.

"Fucked if I know," Rakovich said. "But he needed something to get him through this."

"We all do." Kholodov tipped his head back and let the last liquid dribble from the bottle into his mouth. He wobbled a little, then straightened suddenly. "You said we had to soldier tomorrow. I should have coffee."

He swung around and grabbed a pan of water, but Rakovich stopped him before he could reach the fire.

"Leave it," he said. "You're enough of a soldier to do the job hungover."

"Thanks, Praporshchik." Kholodov flung his arms around Rakovich. "That means a lot, coming from you." He took a step back. "I should go sleep now."

Other men were in a less jovial mood.

"What if they don't stop with Veliky Novgorod?" Plakans asked, stroking Helmut's head and peering into the fire. "Now that one side has dropped the bomb, surely there has to be more? We've opened the floodgates of destruction."

"Maybe," Rakovich said.

"My brother moved to Moscow," Rebane said, his voice hollow. "If they drop another bomb, it's got to be Moscow, hasn't it?"

"Maybe," Rakovich said again, thinking about Papa and Anna. Leningrad would be high on the list of targets too. That thought was like a weight bearing down on his chest. "But all we can do about it is to keep things calm here. The fewer excuses we give anyone to fight again, the more likely it is that our families survive."

Rebane nodded glumly, pulled a blanket up around himself, and drifted off to sleep.

By midnight, almost everyone had slipped into a drunken, exhausted stupor. Rakovich looked across them and felt something like satisfaction. He had done what he could — a sticking plaster on a bullet wound, perhaps, but better than letting their hearts bleed out.

He looked across the fire at Szolkowski. The rifleman hadn't touched a drop of spirits. He stood, one hand on the rifle slung across his shoulder, watching the darkness around them. His only concession to relaxation was a cigarette slowly burning down between his fingers.

"I'll keep watch tonight," Szolkowski said. "Let the rest of you sleep."

He stood stiffly, still bearing the world on his shoulders. Rakovich was fine with that. Szolkowski had earned himself a long stretch of self-inflicted punishment. If he came out of it a better man, that would be for the good, but that didn't mean he had earned any mercy.

"Go check the perimeter," Rakovich said.

"Yes, Praporshchik."

Szolkowski discarded the cigarette and slipped like a shadow out into the park, noiseless despite his heavy boots.

Alone at last, Rakovich rummaged in his pack. He pulled out his battered Communist Manifesto and flipped through it. There was still the same comforting smell of old paper, the same softness to those worn pages. The creases on the cover were so familiar he could have identified this copy by them alone.

Once, these sensations had brought him comfort. Once, the world had been a different place.

His whole life, he had dreamed of serving this book and the cause it represented. He had wanted to go to war, to take up arms against the capitalists and imperialists, to make the world a better place.

It had all been lies. He had seen a better world now, and it was the one his government wanted to tear down. Perhaps the West was every bit as greedy and corrupt as the East, but at least the people had wealth and comfort. Why fight for a system that dressed itself in the rags of equality only to bring poverty, injustice, and destruction?

Maybe this book had meant something good once, back when his mother was young. But not any more.

He tossed it into the flames in the old oil drum. Pages blackened and curled. Thin sheets of ash soared on the hot air, flew to pieces and tumbled away on the wind. That familiar cover flared and then was gone.

From his pocket, Rakovich pulled out his medal. Holding the ribbon between two fingers, he watched the firelight glint off the Order of Glory, Third Class.

Glory could go take a shit in the street for all he cared. Just one more lie, a way of keeping them in service.

As he reached out towards the fire, a hand clamped around his wrist. Szolkowski stood next to him, a red reflection in his eyes.

"Let go," Rakovich hissed, "or I'll beat you until your balls bleed."

"After everything we've lost, you're going to throw that away?" Szolkowski asked, his voice an angry growl.

"Because of everything we've lost," Rakovich replied. "Fuck the party. Fuck communism. And fuck you if you think you get to take the high ground."

"I never fought for communism," Szolkowski said, letting go of Rakovich's hand. "I fought for my country and for my people. They still deserve your courage, and that courage deserves to be recognised."

Caught unawares by the passion in the man's words, Rakovich stood staring at him.

"Who were you, before all of this?" he asked.

"No-one worth knowing. Changing that is my reward. The medal is yours. Don't throw your honour away just because others have."

A renewed sense of conviction washed over Rakovich.

"We fought for our motherland," he said, putting the medal back in his pocket. "Against people who would have destroyed her."

"Yes, we did," Szolkowski agreed. "And I would do it all again. Wouldn't you?"

33

WHAT WE DO NOW

Anna sat in the corner of the café, fingers tight around her teacup. Vadim had saved her a table amid the lunchtime crowd, making a fuss about the special occasion. That made her uncomfortable, but she let him have his way. What else could she do? Expose her soul to the straight-thinking veteran? Explain why she was squirming in her seat? She and Vadim weren't those sorts of friends.

She almost didn't recognise Vlad when he walked in. Wearing closely fitted jeans and a leather jacket, he looked nothing like the brother who had gone off to the army. Only his short-cropped hair marked him out as a soldier.

Her stomach tightened. Here he was at last, in the flesh instead of one of his increasingly brief letters. If they could get through this without arguing then all would be well with the world.

As if their world would ever be well again.

Standing in the doorway, Rakovich looked for any sign of his sister. She might not be here yet — she had always been worse at time-keeping than he was, even before the army had taught him real discipline.

A movement caught his eye, Anna waving to him from a corner

table. He smiled and walked over. Other customers were trying to get out, but they stepped aside to let him through.

He reached the table and sat down across from her. Somewhere inside, he had been looking forward to the warmth of a family reunion. After all this time among soldiers, even ones he respected and admired, the thought of home had gained a rosy glow. But they greeted each other like strangers, their words full of stiffness and uncertainty. He had so much to say to her, but how could he start, here in the open, surrounded by people he didn't know?

"You're not wearing your uniform," Anna said, surprised. Ever since he'd been called up, Vlad had lived in that uniform. Even when he came home to visit her and Papa, he wore it out around the town, chest puffed out. Yet here he was in jeans and a t-shirt.

"It needs washing." He took off his leather jacket, carefully hung it over the back of the seat, and ran a hand over it to make sure it sat smoothly. It made a good excuse not to look Anna in the eyes. She could always tell when he was lying.

Vadim strode over with a crowded tray balanced on one hand.

"Praporshchik Rakovich!" he said, saluting.

"Please, just Vlad," Rakovich said, feeling his cheeks glow. "I've left my rank back in Germany for the week."

"So humble." Vadim started laying things out on the table. There was tea and coffee, sandwiches and cake, pickles and biscuits, everything short of caviar and fine wine. Anna's mouth watered just looking at it. She hadn't eaten this well in weeks.

"This is too much," Rakovich said. "I don't have a lot of spare money, and—"

"Nonsense!" Vadim boomed. "This is on the house. No expense spared for a local hero."

"I can't let you—"

"Oh yes you can. How many of my customers do you think have the Order of Glory, eh?"

More and more people were looking their way, attention drawn by Vadim's excitement and Vlad's flashy western clothes. After months of learning to become inconspicuous, Anna felt their gazes like a gun aimed at her head.

"Thank you, Vadim," Rakovich said, forcing a smile. "This is very kind."

"You must tell me all about Germany," Vadim said, his one eye shining brightly. "The full story of the bridge."

"Of course," Rakovich said. "I'll tell you all about it later. But my sister and I would like a chance to catch up, if you don't mind."

"Of course!" Vadim turned to walk away. As he did so, he caught the gaze of one of the gawpers. "What are you staring at, eh?"

As the other patrons turned back to their own food and drinks, Anna finally let out a breath.

"It really is good to see you," she said, reaching for the teapot. "But couldn't you have come to the flat? Papa would love to see you."

Rakovich shifted uncomfortably in his seat.

"I will," he said. "Just not yet."

How could he explain it to her? She wouldn't understand. Papa had entrusted him with their mother's book, a precious family heirloom, and he had left it as ashes half a continent away. How could he face Papa knowing that, or walk around a flat filled with reminders of his mother's life? Worse still, what if Papa wanted to talk about politics? He couldn't bear to tell the old man the truth, that he had cast aside everything his parents stood for, his faith shattered in the face of the western world.

Anna watched her brother's brow furrow. She'd seen him lost for words before, frustrated as he struggled to express himself. But something was different this time.

"What's the matter?" she asked quietly.

He shook his head.

"You wouldn't understand," he said. "After the things I've seen, I can't go back to life as normal."

She wouldn't understand? That drew a snort from Anna. Here was the old Vlad, the arrogant arsehole, so sure of the system that there was no place for doubt.

"If you're not here for us," she asked sharply, "then why are you back?"

"Now that the treaty's signed, they're giving us all leave," Rakovich said. "Someone I know has an art show in the city. I wanted to see it."

"An art show?" Anna laughed in surprise.

"There's something wrong with that?" Stung by her response, Rakovich clenched his fist on the table top.

"No, no!" Anna shook her head, trying to repress her instinctive response, to avoid causing further offence. "It's just not what I expect from you. Who is this friend of yours?"

Rakovich hesitated. Was friend the right word? Perhaps it was now. And if he said otherwise, she would just laugh at him again, make him feel foolish for being so defensive.

"His name is Kholodov. He served under me in the war."

"Pyotr Kholodov? The artist?" Now Anna was impressed. "Everybody is talking about him! They say he brings the war to life like no-one else."

"They do?" Rakovich was surprised. He liked Kholodov's drawings, but thought that was because they showed moments from his own life. He had been surprised when the army had sent through the special secondment, calling Kholodov home to share his war art, but at least he had been able to make sense of it. The pictures would be presented to self-impressed party officials and school children, used for propaganda and self-congratulation. It never occurred to him that they would draw the attention of students and art aficionados.

"Before he was called up, Kholodov made art about loss and futility," Anna said. "It's said that you can still see those themes in his work, buried amid the triumphalist imagery. That the horror and sorrow are hidden in plain sight, for anyone who doesn't look with the eyes of the Party."

"Huh." Rakovich scratched his head. He didn't understand how you could hide horror in a painting, but then he'd never understood much about art. "He drew a sketch of me once, after we took a bridge. It was pretty good."

"Do you have it?"

"No, but maybe he's still got it somewhere. I'll ask."

He gazed down at the food and drink spread across the table. It was strange to eat like this, instead of in a mess tent or hunched over in the back of a BMP. To have tea made from fresh leaves, not ones that were on their third brew. He'd taken so much for granted before the war — food, drink, family, friends. It all looked different now.

Maybe that was how Kholodov could show things that the Party wouldn't see. Because the war had opened their eyes.

"When are you going to the art show?" Anna asked. "Will you have time to meet again afterwards? I'd love to hear about it."

"I have tickets for the opening tonight," Rakovich said, patting his pocket.

"I'm so jealous!"

"Then come with me." He smiled at her, pleased to have found something they could share.

"Really?"

"Really."

Anna hesitated. She was meant to meet with one of the reconnaissance cells tonight. They had seen trucks moving around the edge of the nuclear zone, a place where no-one was meant to be. If they found out that the government was covering something up, it could give them another angle for recruitment, more fuel for the fire. But maybe Mikhail could deal with that...

"I'd love to come," she said.

VLADISLAV RAKOVICH CLENCHED his fist into a tight ball, took a deep breath, and knocked on the door of his childhood home.

There was a scurrying of footsteps and then the door flew open. Papa stood in the hallway, smiling at him.

"Vlad!" Papa threw his arms wide. "My son the hero!"

"I don't..." Rakovich stood at the threshold. Part of him willed his foot to cross over and step inside. But something else deep inside held him back.

"Oh, Vlad." Papa stepped forward and flung his arms around his son, hugging him tight. "Whatever you have done or seen, it does not matter to me."

Rakovich returned the hug.

"It might," he said. "If you knew."

"You are my son and I love you. Nothing can change that."

Rakovich wished he could believe it.

Anna appeared behind Papa, wearing a simple blue dress and a black jacket. Rakovich had always laughed at his little sister wearing earrings and makeup, but they suited her now. She had truly grown up while he was away, carrying herself with confidence instead of youthful self-assertion.

"I'm ready when you are," she said, looking him up and down. He was back in uniform, though something about it was different. Something other than the medal pinned to his chest. She had preferred the civilian clothes, which carried no reminder of the soldiers who had attacked her friends, but she was used to hiding the tension she felt at the sight of a uniform. She could keep that facade up for his sake.

Together, they walked down the stairwell and out into the street. By the front door of the building, old Mrs Romanova stopped them. Her face crumpled into a smile as she looked up from beneath her grey curls. For a moment Rakovich thought he was going to have to tell the bridge story again, as he had to every acquaintance he had met since his return. It came as a relief when she just told them about her cats.

They took a bus into town. Rakovich reached for his wallet as they got on board, but then the driver noticed his medal and waved them on without charge. At Anna's suggestion, they got off a few stops early and walked along the banks of the River Neva. She was used to the cold of Leningrad nights now, having spent so many of them skulking through the streets. She could accept a little chill for a chance to catch up with her brother.

"Is that a different uniform?" she asked.

"Spetsnaz," Rakovich replied. "Transfer papers came through a month ago. These things move quicker when you're a war hero."

There was an edge to the way he spoke those last words, but Anna decided not to pry. He would only shut down again.

The words "NO CHILD BEHIND BARS" were scrawled in red paint across the front of a riverside house.

"What does that mean?" Rakovich asked. "I keep seeing it."

"I think it's a dissident thing," Anna said, feeling a wall rise inside her. There was so much she wanted to say but couldn't. Not to her sternly Marxist brother. Not to a soldier in government service.

"Dissent is spreading," Rakovich said. "I saw those same words in bus stations on the way to the city, and some reservists were cleaning them off the sides of transport trucks in Poland."

Anna fought back a smile. She couldn't let him know how much this pleased her. He listened better now than he had before the war, even seemed to hear what she said. But she had changed too, and he would never forgive her life of secrets, her rebellion against party and state.

"Have you heard anything about Tatyana?" he asked.

"They transferred her to a hospital, ready for when the baby comes," Anna said. "It's better than being in jail, but they still won't let me see her."

Of course, that hadn't kept her contacts from smuggling letters in and out. Tatyana knew that she was not alone.

"Have you heard anything about Makar?" she asked. Tatyana always asked about the father of her child, but they had no agents in the military, no-one who could find word of him.

Rakovich clenched his fist. Every night, he thought about when the political officer had come for Zimyatov. He saw his friend being marched away and a little part of him died inside. He could have fought for him, like a friend should. Instead, he had let them take the best man he knew, all out of fear of facing the same fate.

"I've heard nothing," he said. "Which means Siberia."

They walked on in silence, each weighing their regrets.

At last, they turned away from the river and up the road to the Suvorov Military Museum. Its normal visitors were patriots, school parties, and parents trying to educate their young. Tonight, it had drawn a more unusual crowd. Artists, writers, and musicians, their dress ranging from the elegant to the eccentric, walked through the doors alongside generals, party leaders, and their wives.

The guards on the door frowned at Rakovich in his praporshchik's uniform. He drew the tickets from his pocket, both stamped with his name, and an identity card that proved who he was. The guards scrutinised them closely, compared his photo to his face, and eventually, grudgingly, let him in.

Inside, the museum was a strange sight. Sheets had been thrown over the usual exhibits, so as not to distract from the art on opening night. It made the place look like it was being redecorated, except that instead of handymen there were smartly dressed waiters carrying trays of champagne.

Most of the pictures were sketches in pencil and charcoal. They had the simplicity of Kholodov's work in the field, but drawn on a larger scale. They showed the trenchlines in the woods that Rakovich's men had dug on the first night of the war; their BMPs in the streets of a German village; men relaxing in the bandstand where they had heard that the war was over. So many familiar faces, many of them lost now — dead, crippled, or taken away.

So many pale images of the past, Rakovich felt as though he was standing among ghosts.

"Vlad?" Anna whispered. "Are you alright?"

He realised that he had been staring at the pictures, ignoring the bustle around him. People were staring at him in turn, some pointing, many smiling.

"Why are they doing that?" he hissed.

Anna pointed to the back of the room. "Because of that."

There hung a vast oil painting in a gilt frame, its bold colours standing out amid the pencil sketches. It showed Soviet soldiers storming heroically up a riverbank, charging straight at an enemy position. NATO troops cowered behind their sandbags, rifles raised in a futile attempt at resistance. Guns blazed everywhere. In the background, planes fought above a bridge. And in the centre of it all stood the image of Rakovich himself, a hero of the motherland.

He stared at it, bewildered.

"It's not finished yet," said a familiar voice beside him.

Rakovich turned to see Kholodov in dress uniform, a sheepish look on his face.

"I worked on it flat out for the past month, but something this big needs longer," the soldier-artist explained. "The higher ups insisted that we show it tonight, so..." He shrugged. "Sorry, I guess."

Rakovich stood, red-faced with embarrassment, as a politician and his wife walked past, raising their glasses to him. Was this painting what people expected of him now? That was absurd.

"Did you really do that?" Anna asked, looking from the painting to her brother and back again. She had read about the fighting at the bridge, of course, but it had never felt so real.

Rakovich snorted. "I would have been shot in an instant if I'd done it like that."

"Artistic licence," Kholodov said, his smile expanding. "And who's your charming friend?"

"This is my sister," Rakovich replied, shooting him a warning look. "Anna, this is Sergeant Kholodov."

"You can call me Pyotr." Kholodov shook her hand. "Would you like to see a picture I'm actually proud of?"

"I'd love to," Anna replied, smiling brightly.

They followed Kholodov out of the main gallery, stopping every few feet so that someone could congratulate him on his work. Those who recognised Rakovich congratulated him too, wittering on about his heroism and shaking his hand until he thought it might drop off.

Eventually, they broke free of the crowd and reached a smaller room, one with no other guests. In the corner, standing on an easel, was a large picture in charcoal on off-white board.

"I saw this the day they took Zimyatov," Kholodov said. "These men's war was going so differently from ours. I wanted to remember how easily it could be us too."

Rakovich remembered that moment too. A column of NATO troops, hundreds of men who had fallen captive, being marched away to a prison camp. Some looked broken, but others held their heads high, proud even in defeat.

Anna gazed at the painting. She could relate to these men in a way she couldn't with the soldiers she had seen around the city. The men behind the uniforms were revealed, lending them a humanity she had forgotten they shared.

"I'm surprised they let you show this," Rakovich said, taking a step closer.

"I insisted," Kholodov replied. "Famous war artists, much like famous war heroes, have some sway around here. The question now is what we do with that influence."

That thought struck Rakovich like a hammer blow. After everything he'd seen, what would he do with the fame he had earned? Was it enough just to find his place in spetsnaz, away from the toxic influence of Captain Leontev? Did he want to keep serving the state? Or did he want more?

"What are you working on now?" Anna asked, moving closer to Kholodov.

"That bridge painting still!" he replied. "I'll be working on that bastard for months."

"Yes, but what are you working on that you're proud of?"

Kholodov grinned.

"You get me already," he said. "It took your brother a lot longer."

He looked around furtively, but there was no-one else in the room. He reached inside his jacket, pulled out a single sheet of paper, and unfolded it.

It was a rough pencil sketch. A row of army trucks parked in a roadside resting place. On the side of one of them were scrawled the words "NO CHILD BEHIND BARS".

"I'm not sure why I drew it yet," Kholodov admitted. "Perhaps because it wasn't about the war. I need to explore what happens next, how we shape the peace, how we live amid the ruins. I want to know what it means to live on when the violence has ended. Don't you?"

"Yes," Anna and Vladislav Rakovich said as one.

They turned, each surprised by the passion in the other's voice. A moment of recognition passed between them as they saw each other anew.

DIGITAL REINFORCEMENTS: FREE EBOOK

To get a free ebook of this title, simply go to www.shilka.uk/dr and enter code TBCS97.

THE FREE EBOOK can be downloaded in several formats: Mobi (for Kindle devices & apps), ePub (for other ereaders & ereader apps), and PDF (for reading on a computer). Ereader apps are available for all computers, tablets and smartphones.

ABOUT THE AUTHORS

If you enjoyed this book, we'd really appreciate a review or a share on social media. It really helps people to discover the book.

Andrew Knighton lives in Yorkshire with his computer, his cat, and far too many unread books. He writes novels and short stories in a wide range of genres, and military adventure stories for Commando Comics. You can find more of his books on his website at www.andrewknighton.com/publications

Russell Phillips writes books and articles about military technology and history. His articles have been published in Miniature Wargames, Wargames Illustrated, and the Society of Twentieth Century Wargamers' Journal. Some of these articles are available on his website. He has been interviewed on BBC Radio Stoke, The WW2 Podcast, Cold War Conversations, and The Voice of Russia. For a full listing of Russell's books, go to www.rpbook.uk/books